ARIZONA AUTHORS
ASSOCIATION

2021 LITERARY CONTEST

THIRD PRIZE IN NOVEL

John Hansen

for *The Mystery of the Unseen Hand*

Toby Heathcotte, President

Jane Ruby, Contest Director

The Mystery of the Unseen Hand won Third Place in the Fiction Novel Category of the 2021 Arizona Authors Association Annual Literary Contest.
This prestigious contest has been open to authors in all states for four decades.
The judges all rated the writing with top marks.

John Hansen
2022

Praise For
THE BLUESUIT CHRONICLES

Praise For
THE BLUESUIT CHRONICLES

"Having grown up in Bellevue in the '60s and '70s, I bought the entire series for my husband for his birthday. He is completely engrossed in them. Thank you, John, for writing them, it's hard to get him to relax, and the books are doing it with laughter and 'do you remember' comments. We are eagerly waiting for the next book to come out."
~ Jeanie Hack, Bellevue, WA

"From the moment I started reading *The War Comes Home*, I couldn't put it down. I was captivated by the balance of action and drama that John Hansen expertly weaves throughout this fast-paced historical fiction. I'm looking forward to reading the next one."
~ S. McDonald, Redmond, WA

"Book 2 of The Bluesuit Chronicles series, *The New Darkness*, continues the story of Vietnam veteran Roger Hitchcock, now a police officer in Bellevue, Washington. The spreading new drug culture is taking a heavy toll on Hitchcock's generation. Some die, some are permanently impaired, everyone is impacted by this wave of evil that even turns traditional values inside out. Like other officer, the times test Hitchcock: will he resign in disgust, become hardened and bitter, corrupt, or will his background in competition boxing and military combat experience enable him to rise to meet the challenge? Romance, intrigue and action are the fabric of *The New Darkness*."
~ Amazon Review

"*Valley of Long Shadows* is the third book in The Bluesuit Chronicles... Returning Vietnam veterans who become police officers find themselves holding the line against societal anarchy. Even traditional roles between cops and robbers in police work have become more deadly...The backdrop is one of government betrayal, societal breakdown, and an angry disillusioned public. The '70s is the decade that brought America where it is now.
Four Stars Rating ~ Red City Reviews

Praise For
THE BLUESUIT CHRONICLES

"By the time I finished reading the series up through Book 4 (*Day Shift*), I concluded most men would like to be Hitchcock, at least in some way. What sets him apart is the dichotomy of his makeup: he grew up with a Boy Scout sense of honor and right and wrong, yet he isn't hardened or jaded by the evil and cruelty he saw when he went to war, though he killed in combat. As a policeman he *chooses* good and right: to do otherwise is unthinkable. He is a skilled fighter, yet so modest that he doesn't know he is a role model for others around him, and women feel safe with him. I know Hitchcock's type—two of my relatives were cops who influenced my life:"
~ Tracy Smith, Newcastle, WA

"Book 5 (*Unfinished Business*) moves to show how difficult it is for Officer Hitchcock to do right. Bad people are out to get him for his good work. He is a threat to their nefarious activities. There is even a very bad high-ranking policeman who puts Hitchcock and his family in extreme peril. Organized foreign crime is moving into his city, he works hard to uncover the clues to solve this evil in his city. I'm still waiting to find out what restaurant owner Juju is up to and who she works for. Great series and story. Another fine book by John Hansen. Yo! ~ T.A. Smith

"I've read all of John's books and rated them all 5 stars, because those stars are earned. I worked the street with John as a police officer for years and what he speaks of in his books is real. John is an excellent author; articulate and clear, always bringing the reader directly into the story. I like John's work to the point that I've asked him to send me any new books he writes, I'll be either the first or almost the first to read all of them. I lived this with John. He's an author not to be missed. You can't go wrong reading his books. I strongly encourage more in the series." ~ Bill Cooper, Chief of Police (ret)

Praise For
THE BLUESUIT CHRONICLES

"John Hansen has written another great read. *Unfinished Business* is filled with conspiracy, corruption and crime, much of which is targeted at Hitchcock. From the beginning of the book, I was hooked. The author has a gift with words that drew me into the story effortlessly— I could not put the book down. I have read all in the series and I look forward to reading more of John Hansen's books." ~ S. McDonald

"A viewpoint from the inside: I worked with and partnered with John both in uniform and in detectives, and like him I came to the Department after military service. This is the fifth (as of this date) of five books in this series. I have read and re-read all five books, and for the first time, recently, over a two-day period, read the entire series in order. All five books were inspired by John's experiences, during many of which I was present. John is an extremely gifted author, and I was transported back to those times and experienced a full gamut of emotions, mostly good, sometimes less so. His use of humor, love, anger, fear, camaraderie, loyalty, respect, disapproval, devotion, and other emotions, rang true throughout the books." ~ Robert Littlejohn

"The whole series of The Bluesuit Chronicles brought back a flood of memories. I started in police work in 1976. This series starts a couple of years earlier. The descriptions of the equipment, the way you had to solve crimes without the assistance of modern items. John made me feel that I was there when it was happening. This whole series is what police work is about. Working with citizens, caring about them, and catching the bad guys. Officers in that time period cared about what they did. It wasn't all about a paycheck... We were the originators of community policing. We knew our beat and the people in it. I am not saying we were perfect; however, we were very committed to our community. I can't wait for the next book. Please read the whole series. Once you start you won't stop."
~ Garry C. Dixon, Ret. LEO-Virginia

Praise For
THE BLUESUIT CHRONICLES

"Received Book 4, *Day Shift*, on a Wednesday. Already done reading it. Couldn't help myself. Was only going to read a couple chapters and save the rest for my upcoming camping trip. LOL. 3 hours later book finished. Love it. 2 Thumbs up!!! ~ Alanda Bailey, Kalispell, MT

"Retired Detective John Hansen is a master writer. He brings to life policing in the Northwestern U.S. during the '70s, a transitional period. One must wonder of how much of his writings are founded in personal experience vs. creative thinking. Either way, his stories are thoroughly enjoyable and well-worth purchasing his original books in this series, his current release, as well as the books yet to come."
~ Debbie M.-Scottsdale, AZ

"I urge you to complete your 'to do' list prior to reading *Unfinished Business*, as once started, I could not put it down. It was always, 'one more page' and soon I was not getting anything else done, but it was well worth it. The author has an amazing way of drawing the reader into each scene, adding to the excitement, sweet romance, raw emotion and revealing of each fascinating character as the plots unfold. I highly recommend this book to anyone who wants a truly good read. Looking forward to the next book from this highly talented author." ~ Cynthia R.

"I received Book 5 in The Bluesuit Chronicles and started reading and per usual, didn't stop until I finished the book. I am a huge fan of John's stories. I grew up in the general area that the stories are set in. Also, in the same timeframe. John's books are always fast paced and entertaining reads. I would recommend them to all."
~ A. Bailey-Kalispell, MT

Also by John Hansen:

The Award-Winning Series: The Bluesuit Chronicles:

The War Comes Home
The New Darkness
Valley of Long Shadows
Day Shift
Unfinished Business
The Mystery of the Unseen Hand

Published & Award-Winning Essays and Short Stories:

"Losing Kristene"
"Riding the Superstitions"
"The Case of the Old Colt"
"Charlie's Story"
"The Mystery of Three"
"The Prospector"

Non-Fiction Book:
Song of the Waterwheel

The Mystery of the Unseen Hand

Book 6 of The Bluesuit Chronicles

JOHN HANSEN

The Mystery of the Unseen Hand
by John Hansen

This book is a work of fiction. Names, characters, locations and events are either a product of the author's imagination, fictitious or used fictitiously. Any resemblance to any event, locale or person, living or dead, is purely coincidental.

Cover Designer: Jessica Bell - Jessica Bell Design
Interior Design and Formatting: Deborah J Ledford - IOF Productions Ltd

Issued in Print and Electronic Formats
Trade Paperback ISBN: 978-1735803050

Manufactured in the United States of America

The Mystery of the Unseen Hand

JOHN HANSEN

To Patricia, the one on earth I love most.

This book is dedicated to the memory of Officer Harold Hill, Badge P-46, a good man and a fine officer. I am proud to have served with you.
Rest in Peace, Brother.

"So do not be afraid of them. There is nothing concealed that will not be disclosed or hidden that will not be made known."

~ Matthew 10:26

PROLOGUE

Winter, 1972

NORMALLY, HORACE MACAULIFFE, one of Seattle's foremost business tycoons, enjoyed his superb view of the Seattle waterfront from the top floor of his office building. It refreshed his mind and impressed his clients to watch the Winslow Ferry make its run between Bainbridge Island and Pier 51 every two hours from twenty floors up. But today MacAuliffe stared unseeing, oblivious of the rain streaking his window, or the ferry crossing the steel gray waters of Puget Sound.

The reason was in his hand.

With long-legged strides he crossed the teal carpeted floor in time to pick up his phone on the second ring. "I have your attorney, Oscar Travis on line one, Mr. MacAuliffe," his secretary said.

"Put him through, Margaret."

After a click, indicating the call had been transferred, he said, "Oscar, I have something important to consult with you about."

"I'm always here for you, Horace. Go ahead," Mr. Travis said.

"I received a letter in the mail yesterday. No return

1

address, only a Bellevue postmark. It's addressed to me, marked personal. I haven't been able to sleep since I read it."

"What does it say?"

"I'll read it to you. 'Dear Mr. MacAuliffe, because of who I am, this letter must be anonymous. I am writing concerning the welfare of your grandson, Trevor. As you already know, Trevor's mother, Allison, married Roger Hitchcock, a Bellevue Police officer, a violent man who has killed people, including babies as a soldier in Vietnam. Last year Hitchcock gunned down a negro and the white woman who was with him. Although the coroner's inquest ruled the shootings as justifiable, there are reasons to believe Hitchcock murdered them.

"'Allison should have stayed away from Hitchcock, but she married him anyway, putting herself and your grandson at grave risk. A few months later, Trevor was present when two men attacked them at their home in Bellevue.

"'Before the men were arrested, Hitchcock savagely beat one of them, and the other man was torn apart by Hitchcock's dog, a vicious animal. Both men needed emergency medical treatment. After their release on bail, one fled the country, and the other was found brutally murdered, for which Hitchcock should have been the primary suspect, but he was never even questioned.

"'Your grandson continues to be in danger because his mother continues to expose him to a man who is a prominent figure in the police subculture of violence.'

2022

JULY	AUGUST
S M T W T F S	S M T W T F S

(calendar months: July, August, September, October, November, December 2022)

er he finished. "That's it, f it?"

hroat. "The specificity of the riter is someone inside the Police Department, who has nd has an axe to grind with nusual that the writer would r's stepchild. The writer must oing out of his or her way to

"Trevor is in danger, Oscar!"

"This is the first you've told me about this, Horace."

"My grandson doesn't belong with his mother. She's trash! He's a MacAuliffe, my only heir. One day he will own this building."

"What about your son Glendon, the boy's father?"

"A child in an adult body," MacAuliffe scoffed. "He got us into this mess by toying with a girl from the lower class he met at the University. That was all right if toying was all he did. But he married her without our knowledge *after* he got her pregnant. She would *never* be acceptable to us, and we made Richard divorce her. Now he wants nothing to do with Trevor because Hitchcock terrified him over his delinquent child support payments."

"If you had called me, we could have sent Hitchcock a cease-and-desist order."

"I want to move on this right away, Oscar."

"All we have at this point is unverified information from an anonymous source."

3

MacAuliffe struck his massive mahogany desk with his fist. "Damn it! Trevor's mother *is* unfit! She's the type our kind keeps on the side as mistresses, *never* as wives. And although his father was a doctor, Hitchcock is a killer, a thug with a badge!"

Mr. Travis waited a few moments before he said, "We fought for custody of Trevor before and lost. It would very damaging if we try and fail again. We'll have to build a more compelling case than last time."

"Explain," MacAuliffe said.

"We must show the court that new circumstances have arisen that override those which led to the ruling in the mother's favor. The burden is on us to present compelling evidence showing *why* Trevor is in danger if he remains in his mother's custody."

"What's involved?"

"Taking a good hard look before we leap. Hitchcock is the wild card in a new picture. We'll focus on him, his background, his lifestyle—is he a drinker, does he gamble, chase women? He's a champion ex-boxer—does he pick fights? What's his credit like? Those are the sort of things we should know first off.

"Then we turn to Allison. What has she been up to since Hitchcock came along, what kind of people does she associate with, that kind of thing. Most everybody's got dirt hidden somewhere, we just need to find it. I'll subpoena Hitchcock's personnel file, order copies of the investigation of the shooting and the coroner's report. I'll order a copy of his military service record. If I see a pattern of violent behavior, we'll file. If not, we'll consider other options."

"Do it, Oscar. I want my grandson. I'll stop at nothing to get him."

MacAuliffe hung up abruptly. He removed his black wingtip shoes and his gold cufflinks, rolled up his monogrammed cuffs, exposing hairless wrists and forearms. Selecting a cigar from the humidor on his desk, he lit it with a wooden match and sucked and puffed his cheeks like a blowfish until a small cloud of blue smoke hovered above him. All this was MacAuliffe's way of kicking back when he knew there would be no more visitors for the day, and he needed to think.

Lounging back in his chair, he assessed his next move. A cop in the picture meant he had to exercise discretion. *Damn it! I have none of the information Oscar said. I can't make a move without it!*

He hit the buzzer for his secretary.

"Yes, sir?"

"Get my private investigator, Toby Olson, on the line."

A few moments later, "I have Mr. Olson on line two, Mr. MacAuliffe."

"It's been a while since I've heard from you, Toby," he snapped. "I want an update regarding my ex-daughter-in-law and her cop husband."

"Well, sir, Allison quit her waitress job just before she had her second baby about six weeks ago, Mr. MacAuliffe. Our surveillance team confirms that she stays at home with Trevor and her newborn son," Olson replied.

"What about Hitchcock?"

"He plays baseball with your grandson and takes him fishing. He teaches boxing to junior high age boys at the local Boys Club. He goes to work in plain clothes and works nine-to-five now."

"What do you know about the two men who attacked her and Hitchcock at their home?"

"Only what was on the news."

"Then what am I paying you for, Toby?"

"We've done what you said you wanted us to do, Mr. MacAuliffe," Olson snapped back. "We're learning a lot about Allison and Hitchcock's activities and their associations through surveillance and undercover work."

"Undercover work?"

"Yes—Allison maintains close ties to people at the Pancake Corral after she quit to have her baby. She goes there every week, sometimes twice. I've placed an agent inside as a waitress. She's got a criminal record, did prison time in Purdy, drugs and robbery. She's on friendly terms with Allison. I expect to develop inside information which we would never know otherwise, but it takes time to build trust."

"That's what I like to hear," MacAuliffe said, his tone congratulatory. "Good man, Toby. I knew I could count on you. Now, I want you to find proof that my grandson's in danger or is being neglected. Create something if you have to."

"Excuse me, sir?"

"You heard me. Like we did before with that radical ex-convict you hired to get close to Allison to set her up. He failed because of that Hitchcock character. Now that she's married to him, we have to create a new crisis or situation to show Trevor's mother and her cop husband are unfit parents."

"What type of crisis do you have in mind?'

"That's your department," MacAuliffe snapped. "I want surveillance of Allison seven days a week, around the clock. For the next thirty days, I want photo documentation of Trevor whenever and wherever possible. You are to report your findings to me by telephone every Friday morning."

"We're on it. Oh, and one more thing, Mr. MacAuliffe."

"Yes?"

"A house right across the street from Hitchcock just became available for rent. We could monitor and document everything around the clock, without detection or alerting anyone."

"Capital idea," MacAuliffe exclaimed, nodding his head. "I'll send you the funds to rent the place for two months to start. Your surveillance stays in effect until I say otherwise."

CHAPTER ONE
Night Moves

JAMIE LAID BELOW his master's side of the bed, reading the message in the air of an enemy lurking outside for a way to enter the sleeping household. In keeping with his wolf heritage, he forsook growling or barking. He listened and waited, still as a stone, for the right moment to attack.

The intruder was outside the master bedroom window now. Jamie's muscles tensed and his coat bristled, but that was all. The hardened ninety pounds of German Shepherd-Siberian Husky mix raised his head only enough to nudge his master's hand.

Hitchcock's eyes popped open. For days, his gut instinct foretold of trouble of the darkest kind. He felt Jamie's chest rumbling. He touched the sleeping bodies of his wife and their newborn son between them. Motionless, he strained to hear what Jamie had alerted to. The luminescent hands of his Timex read 2:12 a.m.

The master bedroom window began a slow upward glide as the intruder pressed his hands against it and up. Jamie's ears flattened as he coiled his muscles.

A sudden flash of lightning lit up the sky, followed

by a clap of thunder. A howling wind shook the house. The intruder ducked behind a bush and peered between rustling leaves as the bedroom light came on. A crying little boy in pajamas ran into the bedroom. Hitchcock scooped him into his arms and into bed. The night sky belched rain, hammering the roof in a deafening clatter, driving the intruder back into the shadows as the light in the bedroom went out.

Another mighty blast of wind shook the house. At the sound of shattering glass Hitchcock bolted out of bed. Allie sat up, looking at him.

"Call the station," he said.

She lifted the receiver.

"The line's dead."

The bedroom felt like a cold storage locker when he slid his feet into his slippers, his body into his robe. He took his .38 snubnose and a flashlight from his nightstand.

"Be careful," Allie cautioned as he left the room.

Expecting an intruder, he crept down the hall, gun aimed, flashlight in his left hand. He followed a cold draft to the kitchen. A branch from the fir tree in the yard poked through the window above the sink. The rest of the house was secure. Cold air and rain gushed into the house when he pushed the limb back outside.

A few feet from the broken window, concealed by shrubs and shadows, the intruder watched Hitchcock set his revolver on the counter and seal the window with cardboard and duct tape.

Jamie stood by the door, growling, hackles up.

"I know someone's out there, but it could be a trap—so we're staying inside," Hitchcock muttered as he finished securing the window.

Hitchcock reheated yesterday's coffee and sat at the kitchen table, lights on, sipping, looking at Jamie, posted at the door, looking at him quizzically. He smiled, stood, and stretched his arms overhead, yawned and turned off the kitchen light. Instead of returning to bed, he hurried through the dark to the spare bedroom down the hall.

In near-total darkness he stood five feet back from the window, motionless, his eyes fixed on the cars parked on the street. It was raining hard, and the streetlight shone on the cars parked along the curb. As far as he could tell, all the cars were empty.

A minute passed, then another, then another.

Hitchcock's pulse quickened when he saw the brake lights come on of the light colored, older pickup he was watching across the street. He heard the engine start. It lurched forward as the driver let out the clutch. The truck plunged into the dark downpour without headlights until it passed by. The driver was male, alone, and not young.

We're being stalked again.

He whirled at the sound of Jamie wagging his tail.

"Is everything all right?" Allie asked softly, standing in the doorway behind him.

"You gave me a start, baby. The wind blew a branch through the window above the sink. I fixed it and cleaned up the glass. How come you're up?"

She ran her hands over his shoulders and down his arms. "The boys are asleep. How come you're in here?"

"Just watching the storm," he fibbed. "Going back to bed now."

"See you between the sheets," she said as she tiptoed up to give him a kiss.

The storm cleared as suddenly as it came, and he fell asleep wondering why Allie often got up at 3:00 a.m.

† † †

IN THE SHADOWS of a hangar at the private airport in Eastgate, two well-armed, well-dressed, special forces-types waited in a new black Mach I Mustang. Both men were in their late twenties. The driver was white, the passenger Asian. Each carried the new subcompact model of the Israeli Uzi submachine gun in a shoulder holster under their matching Italian leather carcoats.

At 3:50 a.m., a '60s vintage Beechcraft M35 Bonanza airplane dropped out of the night sk
y onto the unlighted runway. The driver flashed his headlights twice. The plane stopped. The men in the Mustang approached on foot. The driver carried a small hard-side leather case, the passenger a black briefcase.

The pilot was a sandy-haired white man in his early forties. He wore khaki pants and s leather sheepskin-lined military aviator's jacket, open at the front, revealing a .45 automatic pistol in a shoulder holster.

With him was an Asian man of the same age, carrying an aluminum briefcase. His hairline was receding. He wore a dark suit under a gray wool overcoat. He carried a Walther P-38 9mm pistol in a belt holster. His face was serious as he faced the men from the Mustang.

No one spoke. The passenger from the plane set the briefcase on the wet asphalt, opened it and stepped back. It was packed tight with clear plastic bags containing white powder.

The Mustang driver tested a sample from a bag in the middle. He nodded to his partner when the color inside the glass test tube changed from white to yellow, proving the powder to be pure heroin. The Mustang passenger set the black briefcase on the pavement, opened it and stepped back, revealing bound stacks of one-hundred-dollar bills.

The plane passenger counted the money while the pilot stood guard.

As the plane rose into the night sky, the Mustang sped east on I-90, took the Newport Way exit, went up the steep, winding gravel road for a mile to the crest of Cougar Mountain. It stopped in the driveway of a certain house that had a sweeping view of Lake Sammamish.

The lights were on inside.

† † †

ON THE BELLEVUE side of Clyde Hill, at the same time, widow Florence Abernathy awoke to the sound of her outside faucet being turned on. Her withered hands trembled as she reached for the phone on her nightstand and dialed the police emergency number. She broke down sobbing when the dispatcher answered.

"Police emergency. How can I help you?"

"H-help me! This is Florence. Help me!" she pleaded. "He's-he's back!"

A man wearing a blue hooded sweatshirt snatched the phone from her and hung it up. Holding a knife against her throat, he ripped open her nightgown. The phone sounded. He tore it from the wall and threw it across the room.

When he finished, he realized he had spent too much time with Florence. The surging power of the storm that just ended put him in a daring mood. Snickering at her sobs and screams, he rushed through the kitchen to the backyard. Adrenalin coursed through him as he paused to determine how close the cops were.

His mothlike tendency to flutter around the scenes he created took over. Instead of escaping when the escaping was good, he hid and waited for the cops. He held an adversarial admiration for the police. Watching lawmen arrive at scenes he created was a thrill almost on the level of stalking and raping. But now he worried that he had delayed too long this time, but his vague subliminal urges kept him there.

Police cruisers were fast closing in. On the edge of panic, he dashed across the street, then down one house where he hid in a clump of leafy rhododendrons. From here he watched and listened to policemen in action. It was that moth syndrome again—he couldn't help himself.

The first marked patrol car arrived. When the officer

entered the victim's house, he headed to his car at a brisk walk.

Suddenly he was in the headlights of a vehicle coming around the corner. It stopped. A spotlight from a police cruiser blasted him. He panicked and ran. The cruiser accelerated after him.

"Police! Stop right there!" The voice over a loudspeaker commanded.

He sprinted between two houses, scaled a fence into a backyard, raced across it to the back fence, and vaulted over it into the next backyard. He crouched deep in the shrubs. A small dog with short legs came sniffing around. Unable to penetrate the foliage where he hid, it went into a barking frenzy. Lights came on in the house. He shook the dog off his pant leg as he raced across the lawn and vaulted over a locked gate.

Three houses down the street he saw the headlights of an another approaching police cruiser. He flashed across the street and slipped under thick shrubbery by the curb.

The cruiser headed slowly in his direction. Its spotlight pierced the foliage around him. He laid flat on his stomach under dense bushes and watched, his heart pounding in his ears. When the roof-mounted spotlight turned to the opposite side of the street, he slid deeper under dead leaves and decaying bark, and laid, still as a corpse.

The cruiser stopped, its right side a few feet in front of him. Without moving his head, he looked at the front passenger door. He could hear the radio traffic.

Underneath the cruiser he saw the officer's boots step out of the driver's door. His hand found the hilt of his knife.

The officer crossed the street, shining his flashlight into the shrubs by the driveway, then returned and left. The blue-hooded sweatshirt-clad rapist leaped out of the foliage and dashed across the street, desperate to get to his car.

Rounding the last corner, he saw the taillights of another police cruiser stopped on the street where he left his car. He ducked down under tall rhododendron bushes, watching, growing more anxious by the second. He had stashed his car in the driveway of a vacant home to avoid suspicion in the event something like this happened.

The cruiser remained stopped in the middle of the street, engine running. *Leave, damn you!* as his heart pounded frightfully hard in his chest.

Only partial relief came when the cruiser left. He still had to get to his car. *I'll walk casually the rest of the way, like a neighbor out for a morning walk in case someone in one of the houses sees me and calls the police.*

For even this he was too nervous. Every ounce of him trembled. It was all he could do to not run. He trotted to his car instead, pretending to be a morning jogger. He stuffed his blue-hooded sweatshirt under the front seat and drove west, where the city limits of Bellevue ended, and the limits of the Town of Clyde Hill began, where he knew only one officer was on duty.

It was dawning and the air had turned thick and

turgid after the storm. The sheet metal sky hung low, brooding, even sorrowful as the rapist took the ramp onto Westbound 520 and the Evergreen Floating Bridge. The adrenalin rush of stalking and raping his victim, a narrow escape and outfoxing the police made him feel intensely more alive.

He checked the gold Rolex his parents gave him for his twenty-first birthday. It was the top of the hour. He switched on the radio. Breaking news reported that a man had just been killed by Seattle Police when he opened fire on two officers from his second-floor room at the Bush Hotel downtown.

The news report brought a smirk of smug superiority to his face as he merged into the early morning traffic of the 520 freeway toward the Evergreen Floating Bridge. In Seattle he knew where to find a bar open at that early hour.

As he drove, he pulled out from inside his shirt the hunk of his victim's gray hair he had yanked from her head as he finished with her. He told her last time he would come back, and he did. He decided to come back again. He grinned and fondled the gray strands, blood and roots attached.

Time to celebrate.

CHAPTER TWO
The Taiwan Connection

LATER THAT MORNING, Allie awakened to the tantalizing aromas of bacon and hash browns on the stove, bread in the toaster and coffee chugging in the percolator. Refreshed, she changed Jedidiah's diaper, slipped into her matching light blue terrycloth bathrobe, and slippers, tucked the baby to her chest and followed Mister Rogers' theme song, *Won't you be my neighbor?* to the kitchen.

Jamie was lying down, thumping the kitchen floor with his tail when she appeared. Hitchcock was at the stove, spatula in hand.

He greeted them each with a kiss. "You two slept in late."

She nodded sleepily. "That was some storm last night. What's Trevor been doing?"

"Watching TV now."

"Well, duh. I never figured you for a Mr. Rogers man."

"He just finished a scrambled egg, bacon and a pancake. He set the table perfectly and he'll clear it when we're done."

"With training like that, what do you guys need me for?" she smiled dreamily.

He cupped her face in his hands and kissed her again, longer this time. "Now don't you worry your purty little haid about a thing, ma'am. Like last time, just lay back and do ever-thang the nice policeman tells ya."

She broke out laughing. "Well, yeah! That's how I got into this baby-making business!"

He kissed her on the lips again. "How are you feeling?"

"Hmm. Like two over easy, spuds and bacon."

He watched as she sat down at the table and opened her robe.

"Jed's hungry," she said, casting a knowing look at him as he set two plates at the table.

"Like what you see, Roger?"

Pleasure and satisfaction spread across his face as he broke the yolks of two eggs with his fork and poured on the salt without looking at his plate. "I'm a blessed man," he said, beaming.

"Good," she said, "because I'm pregnant again."

He inhaled as he grinned. "Hallelujah!"

The love in his eyes broke into a lusty smile as his gaze moved from her bosom to her eyes. "That's music to my ears, baby. See, you did what the nice policeman said..."

"Whatever you say, officer—whatever you want, *whenever* you want it..." she said, her voice purring.

Jamie moved to the kitchen door and woofed once. Hitchcock let him out. A minute later he glanced outside as he rinsed the dishes. "Jamie's alerted on something by the garage," he said.

Allie came to window. "He's staring at whatever it is and walking around it. Please check, honey. Something's wrong."

Jamie stepped aside as Hitchcock approached. About a pound of raw hamburger, soggy from last night's rain, laid on the ground. "Good boy," he said, patting Jamie's shoulder. The dog watched him scoop a portion of the meat into a plastic lawn bag with a shovel and put the rest in another bag.

He returned to the house.

"Tom Sherman's poison-proofing paid off. The meat is water-logged from last night's rain but it's fresh. Jamie didn't touch it."

"I thought the two guys who came to kill us were gone," she said.

"So did I."

Allie frowned at the two plastic bags. "One we know is dead. Do you think Zhang came back?"

"If the phone line is up now, call the station, ask for an officer to come out," he said without answering.

Three Hours Later
Detectives' Temporary Office,
Old Main Street

SERGEANT STAN JURGENS and the five detectives under him were either typing reports or on the phone.

Jurgens, a fit, trim, former Marine and Border Patrol agent whose gnarled hands looked out of place in the starched cuffs of the white dress shirts he always wore, looked up at Hitchcock. "I thought you'd be along," he said.

Hitchcock gestured at the barren white walls. "I see familiar faces, but this ain't no bull pen."

"What's that supposed to mean?" Jurgens asked, irritated.

"No wanted bulletins on the walls, no boxes of evidence on the floor next to desks, no noisy, smelly coffee machine, overflowing ashtrays, or whiskey flasks hidden in desk drawers."

"These are temporary digs. Anything else?"

Hitchcock snapped his fingers. "I know—it's got no integrity, no soul."

Jurgens ignored him. He held up the patrol officer's report. "Says here, the raw meat found in your yard has some kind of whitish-gray powder mixed into it."

"That it did."

"I had it taken straight to the state lab. Test results will be back in about two weeks."

"I appreciate your fast response, Stan. But because I knew the lab takes time, I got my own test results—informal, but accurate. There was enough strychnine in the sample to kill a horse."

"How'd you get it done so fast?"

"My former landlord, Doc Henderson, is a vet. He's got testing equipment in his clinic. Now what?"

Jurgens leaned back in his chair, twirling a pen in

one hand. "First off, we'll have the State Department check on the status of Jinjie Zhang in Taiwan."

Hitchcock shook his head. "It wasn't Zhang."

"How do you know?"

"After I defeated him, I tried to browbeat him into telling me who hired him to attack me at home. He seemed genuine when he said he *couldn't* tell me, and that he was sorry. He didn't have to apologize, Stan. Whoever did this is a different player."

"You sound pretty sure of it."

"Martial artists don't poison dogs, in my view, and we were stalked last night by an older guy in an old truck. I think he's the one who left the poisoned meat in our yard for our dog."

He gave Jurgens the details.

"We'll get an update on Zhang anyway. Maybe we'll learn something new. If he was sincerely apologetic, maybe he'll help us," Jurgens said.

"I'm not trying to sound ghoulish, but I'm relieved it couldn't be Zhang's partner, Stanford."

"No doubt Stanford's execution brought you some peace of mind." Jurgens said, looking at Hitchcock. "Changing the subject, why did you transfer to Crime Prevention? You're only twenty-six, on your third year on the Department, yet you were sweeping up crime in Eastgate like a new broom."

"I promised Allie."

"You've been out there by the new college for six months now. Like it?"

"You're not in the station anymore, either. How do

you like it?"

Jurgens shrugged. "I don't like our office being separated from Patrol, but it's temporary. When the remodeling is completed, we go back. *Your* move was voluntary. Answer my question, wise-guy."

Hitchcock folded his arms. "I like the time it gives me to be with my family. It's opened my eyes to what Mike, Al and Bob do. And Ian's a good boss."

"Hmm...a non-answer," Jurgens frowned. "Just what have your eyes been opened to?"

"The goodwill they spread by working with businesses and schools to make them safer. It benefits the department, the public, and discourages crime. I like working with kids and doing mock armed robberies with bank employees, teaching them to be better witnesses. Plus, learning how to analyze crime trends has given me a new perspective."

"Good stuff, Roger, I'll give you that. But how do you like having your office out by the community college, with probation people instead of the station?"

"Disconnected, like I've left the Department."

Jurgens leaned forward in his chair. "The rise in drug-related incidents indicates more dope has come in, which will result in more crime in every category. Yet, arrests in Eastgate, your old beat, have fallen off to practically nil. Strange, isn't it?"

"I admit it is."

"The copycat, blue-hooded rapist beat and raped poor old Mrs. Abernathy a second time last night."

"Damn!" Hitchcock exclaimed, scowling.

"You've made your point, Stan."

"One more—who do you think would try to poison your dog?"

He shrugged. "A random act, is my guess."

"Random act you say!" Jurgens scoffed. "I checked. There are *zero* reports of dog poisonings or attempts anywhere in the city, from lake to lake."

"Okay, not random, then."

"Through your informants you pulled off the biggest drug seizures in the city's history. After Stanford's release from jail, he went to where you used to live and poisoned a dog that looked like yours, not knowing you'd moved."

Hitchcock pursed his lower lip. "True. A reliable source also told me I have a bullseye on my back."

"Well, duh! Stanford and Zhang were hired hitmen. For their failure, Stanford was executed, and Zhang was whisked back to Taiwan, where he's in hiding, *if* he's still alive. A Taiwan connection hired those two to bump you off to stop you. This isn't over, Roger—those people don't just give up and move away. The money is too big."

"A question, Stan?"

"Shoot."

"I'm being targeted—so what's the Department doing about it?"

Jurgens paused. "All I can tell you is that we aren't sitting on our thumbs."

"What's being done to hunt down Mike Smith?"

"I only have five detectives and each one is carrying

the caseload of three."

"Smith's not a burglar or a check forger," Hitchcock countered, "he's a killer, a drug dealer, a Pied Piper. He gets juvenile girls addicted then kills them by overdose so they can't turn him in once he's done with them. Same story with his guy followers—he can't risk letting them go either—they know too much."

"Like I said, give us some leads and we'll get him."

"I would, but I'm not on the streets anymore."

Jurgens pointed his finger at Hitchcock. "Bingo!"

† † †

AT 3:00 A.M. the next morning Hitchcock awakened. He reached across the bed. Allie was up, Jedidiah slept. In the hall, Jamie was lying at the guest bedroom door. His tail thumped the floor as his master approached.

He found her kneeling at the foot of the bed, praying hard, her words indistinct. His nightstand clock read 4:05 a.m. when she slipped back into bed.

He picked up the morning paper outside the front door as he left for work. The headline and composite sketch on the front page stopped him cold.

RAPIST STRIKES AGAIN.

He studied the sketch. It was the same generic white male face enshrouded by a dark hood. The attack on Florence Abernathy happened only four blocks from his home. He took the paper with him to prevent Allie from seeing it and protect the baby she carried from unnecessary stress.

† † †

EARLY THAT AFTERNOON, a series of visitors streamed through the back door of The Great Wall restaurant, wads of cash in hand. Each one left moments later with bindles of black tar heroin, which they would sell in parks, school parking lots, hallways, and certain bars.

It would be a matter of days before police and medical personnel would respond to another cycle of drug overdoses and homicides disguised as overdose deaths, not to mention robberies and homicides.

CHAPTER THREE
The Omen

FOR TWO DAYS, the Hitchcock home hummed with preparation for Easter. Allie made blueberry and blackberry pies from scratch. Hitchcock smoked turkeys and hams in the smoker. Trevor helped Hitchcock mop wood floors, vacuum area rugs, dust furniture. Hitchcock washed the wood and brick exterior with trisodium phosphate and water, cleaned the windows, raked fallen leaves from the lawn, swept the driveway and front walk.

There came a loud thud against the front of the house as they sat down for lunch. Hitchcock dashed outside, thinking it was vandalism. Seeing no one around, he spotted a new dark smudge on the wood siding. He looked down. A dead raven laid on the ground, blood dripping from its beak.

Allie approached as he picked it up. "Stupid bird," he muttered, showing it to her.

Her face was ashen.

"What's wrong?"

"Someone's going to die," she said as she turned and went back in the house.

He followed her into the kitchen. "What's this—more of your North Carolina Tarheel folklore? It's just a dead bird, for Christ's—"

She clapped her hand over his mouth. "Shut up! *Never* say that in our home!"

He fell silent.

"Wash your hands before you touch anything," she ordered as she left the room.

† † †

ALLIE'S SENSE OF impending tragedy grew as she laid down for the night. Trevor slept in his room across the hall. Her infant son Jedidiah slept between her and her husband, who slept soundly. She stared at the ceiling, grasping for the meaning of the dead bird.

After an hour with no letup in her uneasiness. She arose as quietly as possible.

"Why are you up?" he asked before she had crossed the bedroom.

"I'm all right. Go back to sleep."

"You're not all right. What is it?"

"Give me some space."

"Don't be so long this time."

TWO HOURS LATER Hitchcock entered the spare bedroom. "What in God's Name are you doing?" he asked. "It's past three-thirty in the morning."

"Somebody's going to die," she replied.

"You said that. Who?"

She shook her head. "Somebody close to us."

After a long pause he asked, "How do you know?"

"You wouldn't understand."

"Try me."

"No. I'm praying for this person."

"You're praying for someone, you don't who, but the person is about to die?"

"I said you wouldn't understand."

He waved his hand as if he was clearing smoke. "So, you've been getting up in the middle of the night for days to pray an unidentified person? I don't get it."

Still on her knees, Allie turned to face the bed.

Troubled by her mysterious behavior, he waited. She didn't move. "Come back to bed soon, okay?"

She didn't answer.

CHAPTER FOUR
Of Things To Come

Easter Sunday
The Neighborhood Church
Bellevue, Washington

THE MORNING SKY was cloudless. Cold nipped and reddened the noses and cheeks of early churchgoers as they left their cars for the church doors. As if to honor the day, the sun shone in cathedral-like fashion. Joyous organ and piano worship music filled the air as they arrived; men in suits, ties, and wool overcoats; ladies in dresses, scarves, gloves and long coats, many wearing hats.

They packed the sanctuary, the overflow section in the back, and the balcony. Others stood in the side aisles. Rays of sunlight streamed through the stained-glass windows, giving an ethereal effect to the three large wooden crosses behind the pulpit.

Allie stayed in the church's nursery with Jedidiah.

Hitchcock sat on a bench pew close to the front with Trevor on one side, and Randy Fowler and his family on the other. He glanced at Randy, amazed to see him dressed in a dark suit, white shirt, tie, short haircut. His childhood friend's recovery from heroin addiction, and other changes a Christian conversion produced in a little more than a year astounded him. *But will it last?*

THE HITCHCOCK HOME gleamed like a new penny when a stream of relatives and friends began arriving after church. A crackling fire in the fireplace pouring forth warmth and the aromas of food warming in the oven drew them in from the cold. Warm greetings and laughter rose to a gentle crescendo that filled the house. Platters of smoked ham and salmon with wild rice, baked potatoes and green beans from the garden covered the long farm-style table, with place settings of family heirloom china, silver flatware, and a bouquet of red, yellow and purple flowers gracing the center.

Hitchcock savored every moment. Trevor helped him clear the table as guests came and went, and Allie happily made the rounds, making everyone feel welcome while she held Jedidiah.

The Fowlers were among the first arrivals. Connie, the oldest and the only daughter, seemed unusually outgoing. Randy took a seat next to Hitchcock at the table. "We're grateful for all you've done for us, Roger," Randy said. "Without you knowing it, God used you to bring my family to a saving knowledge of Christ."

He looked at Randy. "How so?"

"It was no accident that you saved my life by giving me CPR after I died from overdose, then you took me to the hospital. It was no accident that you were a medic when you were in the army, which gave you the know-how to save me and others. You weren't ashamed to be friends with me when we grew up together, even though my family was from the wrong side of the tracks. Because you were a champion Golden Gloves boxer, no one dared to mess with you, so school bullies left me alone. You lifted me up when I was down, and you never judged me."

Moved by Randy's words, Hitchcock asked, "As a Christian, how do you feel now about the two who tried to kill you with heroin—Tyrone Guyon, then Mike Smith?"

"You killed Guyon shortly after that."

"Yeah, but what are your feelings about what he *tried* to do to you, and your sister?"

"That's something I had to face early in my walk with Christ. It wasn't easy, but I forgave Tyrone."

"That's well and fine, Randy, but Mike Smith is still out there, dealing dope and killing people with it. What would you say to him if he approached you now?"

After a thoughtful pause, Randy looked up. "It'd be hard, but I'd tell him, 'Even though you tried to kill me, I forgive you.' Then I'd walk away...and tell you where he is."

"Even if he doesn't apologize and mocks you instead?" Hitchcock asked, surprised.

"The problem at that point is his, not mine," Randy nodded. "It encourages me to see how much God has blessed you, Roger," he said, changing the subject.

He noticed the change in Randy's eyes, from old to young, from lost to found. "You'd do it for me if our situations were reversed. What's your plan now?"

"I'm going to become a pastor. With my experience and my testimony, I'll have credibility with people on drugs, and those who come from broken homes."

"How'd you come to this decision?"

"For the last six months I've been on a team with four other guys from our church who go down to Skid Row on Monday nights."

"And do what?"

"We don't get on a soapbox and preach, if that's what you're thinking. We share with street people what Christ has done for us on a one-to-one basis. The ones who receive Christ we lead to one of the missions downtown, so they have a Christian environment to go to. And we follow up on them."

"The Seattle waterfront is a rough part of town."

"We've had our scary moments," Randy recalled, nodding. "We intervened one time on a guy being led away by two young chicks from the Scientology den nearby. Another time we stopped a suicide in the nick of time, yet another time we saved a man's life from a deadly assault in a dark alley. Saving lives led to saving souls. From the first time I went, I knew this is what God wants me to do."

"How so?"

"I have compassion for those who are like I was. I can relate to them, even if they're older, 'cuz I was an addict too, once upon a time."

"How will you support yourself?"

Rubbing his hands on his lap, he said, "I'm laying a foundation, like building a house. I've been accepted at Northwest Bible College in Kirkland. I start classes tomorrow. The college gave me a limited scholarship and a part-time job as a custodian."

Hitchcock grinned, shaking his head in admiration of his friend. "You could knock me over with a feather right now. I'm proud of you."

"This means I won't be informing for you anymore. Unless, of course, I can help someone by turning them in."

"Time to move on with your new life, I'd say," Hitchcock affirmed.

Randy got to his feet. "Thanks again for inviting us. One day the Lord will bless me with a wife and kids, like you have, Roger. Happy Easter."

"I think you better stick around a bit longer," Hitchcock said, looking at the dining table. "Looks like Allie's found two new friends in your mom and your sister."

Randy smiled when he looked at the three women laughing in earnest conversation. "Your childhood secrets are gone, Roger."

Hitchcock chuckled. "For sure. We'll have to stay in touch to keep tabs on what they're up to."

AS RANDY AND his family were leaving, Allie's family arrived. The oldest was Billy, a short, beefy, red-faced man in his early thirties the family nicknamed "Stout" because he was built like a fire hydrant. The younger brother, Tommy, a lean and muscular type, heartily shook Hitchcock's hand.

Police cadet Will Hodges arrived with his mother. "I'm signed up with the Marines. I go to boot camp right after high school graduation in June," he proudly told Hitchcock.

"Good on you, Will. Better start getting in shape."

"What do you do to stay in such great shape?"

"Come to the Boys Club next Saturday. I teach boxing to a group of junior high age guys. You'll burn a thousand calories in less than an hour, and what you'll learn you can do at home. We train from ten until eleven-thirty. Until then do one set of pushups, sit-ups and jumping jacks until you can't do another. Then rest for a day. Three days a week. Load up on steak and eggs and green salad, and don't smoke."

Two waitresses he knew from the Pancake Corral and a third woman arrived together. He noticed Allie's odd reaction to the latter.

Hitchcock's mother and his sister Jean came, followed by his sister, Joan and her husband Darren with their three kids. Among the other arrivals was Joel Otis, his boyhood mentor and neighbor, with his wife and two kids.

"OKAY, EVERYBODY, GATHER 'round, because this is

our first family performance," Hitchcock announced. "We've been practicing this song from Allie's part of the country, North Carolina, called *Say Darlin' Say.*

The guests crowded together, some sat on the floor in front of the couch.

Allie stood next to him, fiddle and bow in hand, Trevor held a youth-size banjo on the other side as Hitchcock strummed a few notes on his guitar. Allie counted one-two-three, then her crystal-clear vibrato took the lead, in time with Hitchcock on guitar and Trevor plucking a string on his banjo in time with the beat.

The guests broke into excited cheering and clapping as the three singers took their first bow together.

Otis sat next to Hitchcock on the living room sofa, facing the fire. "In addition to everything else you've got going for you, you have the start of your own family band. You've come a long way since we were kids."

"I'm a blessed man," Hitchcock mused, gazing at the fire.

"I didn't know Allie's from the Carolinas."

"Her family moved here when she was eight or nine, but she's a Tarheel."

"I see the stork'll be making another visit here soon."

Hitchcock grinned and nodded. "Due date's about six weeks away, the doc says."

"Boy or girl?"

"Boy."

"Congrats," Otis said. "I got off work late today, or

we'd have been here earlier."

"A busy shift on Easter morning?"

Otis shook his head. "It was quiet until I got a DOA call during the last hour."

"Oh."

"Someone you used to know."

Hitchcock turned to him. "Who?"

"Bridget Thompson. Your high school sweetie."

He frowned. "I knew a Bridget, but Thompson wasn't her last name…"

"Maiden name was Howley."

"Tell me about it outside," he said after a moment of stunned silence.

They stood face-to-face on the back patio.

"Guests found her body in a car parked in the far parking lot of the El Escondite Inn," Otis said. "She'd been dead for about ten days. Her skin had turned black, and maggots covered her."

Hitchcock held his hand up. "Wait-wait—what, and where is the El Escondite?"

"The Hilltop under new ownership."

Hitchcock folded his arms across his chest. "Go on."

"She was married, fancy new home in upper Somerset. Two kids. Husband said they separated a year ago because of her drug addiction and running with criminals. He hadn't heard from her in six months."

He shook his head. "This is hard to believe. She was a prude in high school. Did she overdose?"

"Garroted from behind by someone in the back seat. The cord was embedded into her neck. She'd been homeless, living in her car, doing sexual favors for drugs, according to the husband."

"What kind of place has a dead body in a car in the parking lot for ten days and no one reports it?"

"She was in the driver seat, laying down, out of view. Unless you were standing right next to the window and looked in, you wouldn't see her," Otis said. "As bad as the old Hilltop Inn was, it was a church compared to the El Escondite. The autopsy is tomorrow."

† † †

AFTER EVERYONE LEFT, and the boys were asleep, he sat next to Allie on the couch, undecided if he should tell her what Otis told him. A sudden realization hit him as they stared at the fire in reflective silence.

"I'm sorry for mocking you yesterday," he finally said.

She took his hand in hers, still looking at the flames. "No big deal."

"You were right, by the way."

She glanced at him. "About what?"

"Someone dying." He told her what Otis said about his dead high school classmate.

"Who was she to you, or should I ask?"

"We dated maybe three times and went to the junior prom together. She dumped me because I was too busy to see her as much as she wanted."

"How did you handle being jilted?"

He grinned at the memory. "Relieved, actually. I

was training every day after school and competing on weekends for a shot at the Olympic boxing team. That, plus keeping my grades up, left little time for girls."

"What happened to her?"

"She became a cheerleader. Wound up marrying the star quarterback of our varsity football team right after graduation."

"Was she—?"

"Knocked up?" He nodded. "Yep. Turns out our class prude had a knack for shocking people. First to get pregnant out of wedlock, first to get married, first to have kids, first to become an addict. Now her final claim to fame is first to become a murder victim."

"Must be hard on her husband and kids."

"Changing the subject, I recognized the two waitresses you work with at the Corral that came today, but who was the rough looking gal with them?"

"She's the new waitress, the ex-con I told you about. Her name is June."

"You seemed upset that she came."

"She came to spy on us. She looked the house all over and asked too many questions."

"Like…?"

"You, your hours, how long you've been a cop, how long we've been married, about Trevor and Jed. I told her nothing."

He sat up suddenly. "She was spying on us *for* someone. What's more, only the worst women serve hard time in this state. We need to know what she did time for."

"You said before you'd check, but you haven't. Please, honey, I need to know."

"I need her last name. Her employment application will have it."

"I don't work there anymore."

"Keep going there for breakfast or lunch when she's working until you have the license plate number of her car. I'll take it from there."

"Something else is bothering you," she said. "What is it?"

He told her about his conversation with Randy.

"That's great, Roger. Sounds like he's doing well and has a plan for his future. Why do you seem down?"

"Because I've heard this before from Randy. The Christian conversion, the changes..."

"But?" she asked.

"A drug dealer named Mike Smith introduced Randy to drugs—from pot to heroin—his sister Connie, too. After Randy became a Christian, Smith got ahold of him and tried to kill him with an overdose. Smith's still on the loose and liable to finish the job with Randy."

"I see." Allie yawned. "I'm confident you'll catch Mike Smith. You can't solve it tonight, though. Come to bed with me."

She fell asleep in seconds, but he laid awake, staring at the ceiling, thinking about the fate of Bridget, the stuck-up, knockout brunette. She was active in the Lamplighters, a group of Christian students that met on the school campus. He couldn't get his head around the thought of "Frigid-Bridget," as she was called, selling her body for drugs, let alone using and dealing.

He awoke at the sounds of Allie tiptoeing out of the bedroom and Jamie's toenails clicking on the wood floor.

The sound of her pleading voice floated down the hall. He peeked around the open door. Allie knelt at the foot of the bed; hands folded. He couldn't understand a word she was saying, so he knocked on the doorframe.

"This time you've got to tell me what's going on, baby," he said softly.

She stood and faced him. "Someone we know is going to die. Someone close to us."

"Maybe it's me."

She touched his arm. "It's not you. I've been taken downward into utter darkness, so dark I can't see my hand in front of my face. The darkness is a veil. Beyond the veil are people who have died and there's no way they will ever escape."

He looked at her, shocked. "Are you sleeping when this happens?"

"Wide awake."

"Can you see or hear them?"

"No. I just know the person I'm praying for will go there."

He took a step back. "I've seen a lot of death, Allie. Dead is dead."

"Seeing a lot of death doesn't mean you have all the answers, honey. It doesn't prove the life we see on a physical plane is all there is. There's a mental plane, like the mathematical theory that split the atom, and there's a spiritual plane too, which is eternal."

He said, "If you've seen what I've seen—"

"I knew you wouldn't understand," she cut in. "You who were raised knowing the truth. It saddens me."

CHAPTER FIVE
The Hideout

COOL, MOIST MORNING air filled Hitchcock's lungs as he took a short run around his neighborhood. After jumping jacks, pushups, pullups and punching the heavy bag in his garage, he showered, dressed in slacks, necktie, and sport coat.

Allie came in the kitchen as he gulped down a shake of milk, protein powder, molasses and two raw eggs. He took her into his arms. "I've got to go in early today."

She took a step back. "I want to tell you something," she said, holding his hands and making eye contact.

"What?"

"The dead woman Joel told you about, the one you dated in high school?"

"Yeah?"

"It isn't her."

"The timing is sure right."

"She was already dead when the bird hit our house. And she wasn't close to us."

"Who is it, then?" he asked, hardly believing he was asking her the question.

A muffled cry came from down the hall. She put her hands on his shoulders and tiptoed up to kiss him. "Jed's hungry. See you tonight, honey." She turned to go.

"Who is it, Allie?

"The visions stopped. *You* will know, not me," she said, without looking back.

† † †

HE DETOURED TO see the El Escondite Inn for himself on his way to work. A strange twinge of alarm hit him when he saw a new black Lincoln Continental with tinted windows and California license plates in the manager's parking space. He copied the number on his pocket notepad.

The Crime Prevention Unit shared office space with the City Probation Department in an old house on the edge of the new Bellevue Community College campus.

"Well, look what the cat dragged in," one of the senior officers said.

"At a quarter after," teased another.

"Sorry I'm late," he apologized as he hung his jacket on the coatrack. "So, who are you old ladies having for breakfast this morning?"

"Your archenemy, the former Loo-tenant Bostwick, recently busted back to buck *sah-jent*. Wanna know what the latest is?" the first officer asked.

Hitchcock flipped through the messages stacked on his desk. "I don't have the Bostwick Watch," he said without looking up.

"You should. He's got the Hitchcock Watch."

"What is this, anyway, the Dear Abby Hour?"

"Bostwick appealed his demotion to the Civil Service Board," the second officer said. "The hearing is next week. We were about to bet on the outcome when the issue of his timing came up, so all bets are off."

"Timing?" Hitchcock repeated.

"The little Nazi waited until Captain Delstra left for the FBI Academy to file his appeal. The Academy is in Virginia and lasts three months."

Hitchcock shrugged. "There are other witnesses. "

"Worried?" the senior officer asked.

"Should I be?"

"Our mouse in the corner says your name comes up a lot with the big-wigs on the third floor," the first officer replied.

"What about the internal investigation?" Hitchcock asked.

"There's an internal going on?"

"If you girls will excuse me, I've got work to do," Hitchcock said as he turned to his desk.

HIS PHONE RANG minutes later. "Roger? It's Eve, City Attorney's Office. Remember me?"

He smiled at the sound of her voice—and the memories. "Of course. How's it going?"

"You tell me. We were just served a subpoena for your personnel file and all records pertaining to the shooting you and Sherman were involved in, as well as the arrest reports of the two guys who were arrested for attacking you at your home."

He felt his chest constrict. "Who is it from?"

"Downtown law firm of Cloward, Dockins and Travis."

"Don't know 'em."

"You wouldn't. They're a big-gun, white-shoe outfit. Strictly corporate clients."

"What is this about?"

"Looks like somebody thinks the best way to get to you is through the civil process."

He paused. "Thanks for the tip." He felt nauseated as he hung up the phone. Allie was pregnant again, so she mustn't know anything about it.

The bald, pot-bellied Probation Department supervisor, a little man with glasses who picked his nose when he thought no one was looking, stepped into the room. "*Mister* Hitchcock, this is the *umpteenth* time I've had to remind you to remove your gun when you're in this office. We don't want to *offend* or *scare* people," he said like a scolding old lady, his voice squeaking.

The three other officers turned their backs to hide their snickering.

Hitchcock stood and slipped into his sport coat. "I'll be in the field," he muttered to his partners, ignoring the little man.

† † †

ON HIS WAY to a meeting with Frederick & Nelson store detectives, he detoured through the El Escondite Inn employee parking lot again. The sight of more new, expensive muscle cars and luxury sedans parked in the back, all with darkly tinted glass and bearing California and Nevada plates made him uneasy.

He received a call from Patty in Records as soon as he returned to his desk.

"Heads up, Roger. The three California license plates come back to a C & E Finance Company, Inc. in Los Angeles."

"Sounds like a three-dollar-bill outfit."

"It's legit," she said.

"Why the heads-up, then?

"As soon as I began checking the company officers nationally for warrants, the local FBI office called."

"The FBI! What did they want?"

"Do we have those guys in custody, are they under investigation, what do we know about the company. I had to give them your name and phone number."

"Did they say what this is about?"

Patty scoffed. "The day the FBI gives us anything, my life will be complete, and I can retire in peace."

"Easy, girl. I'm just a rookie."

"This thing is hot. I'll send you the details in an inter-office envelope before it's pulled. You'd better safeguard it. It includes information on the registered owners of the Washington plates you gave me."

"You're a godsend."

"Save it for the Feds," she said. "They love hearing praise from you lowly bluesuits."

Hitchcock's phone began ringing as soon as he hung up. He ignored it and glanced around the office. "Any of you guys speak Spanish?"

"My wife is Mexican," a probation officer said.

"What does El Escondite mean in English?"

"The hideout," he replied.

"The hideout?"

"As in hiding from the law."

Hitchcock stared like a wolf that had just found his next prey. His phone continued ringing as he put his sport coat on.

The nosy little probation supervisor popped his head out of his office. He peered suspiciously at Hitchcock over the top of his round-rim granny glasses. "Aren't you going to answer your phone?"

"Nope," came the swift reply.

The phone kept ringing.

"Might be important."

"It isn't."

"Who is it?"

The phone kept ringing.

"The FBI."

The little man's jaw fell open. "What? Th-the FBI?!" He almost fell as he scrambled past chairs, desks and waste baskets to get to Hitchcock's phone.

"Hello? Hello?" An expression of disappointment came over his face. "They hung up. Darn! I've never talked to a federal agent before." He turned around. "How *could* you turn down a chance to talk to an—"

But Hitchcock was gone.

† † †

PATTY RADIOED HITCHCOCK to call her as he left a meeting with the Nordstrom Best store detectives. He called from a downtown phone booth.

"Ready to write, Roger?" she said. "There's a lot here."

"I'll come by and pick it up."

"Bad idea. Your favorite lieutenant is back."

"Bostwick? No way. He was demoted and banished to the property room."

"He just left a minute ago."

"What happened?"

"The straight skinny is that by order of the City Manager's Office, as of today, Bostwick's been *temporarily* restored to the rank of lieutenant, but he has no access to or command over Patrol and Traffic officers until his hearing with the Civil Service Board."

He coughed once to clear his mind, then took out his notepad and pen. "Okay, what have you got?"

"The three Vasquez brothers, Carlos, Tomas and Enrique are officers of C and E Finance. Carlos and Tomas have served time in Federal prison for Interstate Transportation of Stolen Property. Enrique, the oldest, has a 1969 conviction in L.A. County for Promoting Prostitution. They're from Yuma, Arizona, I'm told."

"Okay, let me guess—C and E stands for Conspiracy and Embezzlement?"

Patty laughed out loud.

"Any of them wanted?"

"No, but the man running the place fits the company initials."

"You mean The Brothers Three don't run it?"

"They own the company that owns those cars and the motel. City Business License records show the manager is a Simon T. Vollmer, out of San Francisco. If his date of birth is 2/21/1943, there's an unconfirmed warrant for him out of San Francisco for embezzlement. No bail. He hasn't applied for a Washington driver's license, or I'd confirm it that way."

"I'm almost afraid to ask if there's anything else."

"Oh, there is!" Patty said cheerfully. "Outstanding misdemeanor warrants are out on the registered owners of the two cars with Washington plates you gave me. I've confirmed them already. Want to write 'em now?"

"My two new pens combined don't have enough ink for all this."

Patty laughed the hearty belly laugh she was known for. "You crack me up, Roger."

"Best put the printouts in Walker's inbox. Get Simon Vollmer's mugshot, if it's him, see if they'll extradite."

"Confirming the warrant and verifying extradition is a couple phone calls and a teletype, a couple hours at most. An out of state mugshot takes a few days."

"Thanks, Patty."

"I can only help you on the QT from now on while Lieutenant Hitler Jr. is here. Don't come here during business hours, Roger. It's no secret that Bostwick blames you for his troubles."

"Noted."

✝ ✝ ✝

IT WAS LUNCHTIME and curiosity was eating Hitchcock alive. He drove out of his way to cruise past to the El Escondite Inn. As the former Hilltop Inn, the place had been an infamous haven for pimps, pushers and prostitutes. He saw the same type of cars, beaters and pimpmobiles in the front parking lot as before. The restaurant had few customers. He decided to have a look around.

The lobby floor had been redone in large Saltillo tiles; Aztec-style area rugs strategically placed. Murals of hunting scenes of jaguars, Mexican wolves and sombrero-wearing mounted vaqueros spearing and roping a grizzly bear were painted on its walls. Heavy, dark furniture, and a large wooden paddle fan rotated slowly in the ceiling, created a quasi-South of the Border atmosphere.

A gorgeous, well-groomed Latina with a slender figure in her early twenties was at the front desk. Smooth brown complexion, lustrous black tresses, a dark gray pinstripe business jacket over a white blouse and pearl necklace and earrings made for a heart-stopping presence. She ignored him. He guessed she smelled cop. After several seconds, he held his badge under her eyes. Large, luminous dark eyes met his.

"Yes?" she asked. Strong south of the border accent.

"I'd like to see the manager, please."

She didn't crack a smile. "May I tell him what this is about?"

"Police business."

CHAPTER SIX
Subrosa

THE BEAUTIFUL LATINA left the front desk for the manager's office, her high heels clicking on the Mexican tile floor like castanets. Hitchcock figured she didn't call the manager because she wanted to warn him. He glanced around the lobby as he waited.

Two heavily made-up young women, seductively dressed in mostly unbuttoned, tight-fitting blouses showing cleavage, short skirts and red high-heel shoes, lounged in a corner of the lobby, smoking cigarettes, staring hungrily at him as they would a hunk of meat. *I must not smell like cop to them.*

Three cleaning maids came through the lobby. The oldest and by far the most attractive one, long honey-blonde hair, a figure loose-fitting clothing couldn't hide, seemed familiar. She did a double take and gave him a subtle nod of recognition as she wheeled a laundry basket toward a service door.

As he wondered where he had seen her before, a narrow-shouldered man came to the front desk, taller than Hitchcock, late thirties, the edges of crude prison-type tattoos on the sides of his neck poked above his shirt collar, buttoned to the top.

He said nothing as he faced Hitchcock. His large, pale blue eyes were cold blue orbs that could stare you down without one blink. "I'm Simon Vollmer, the manager. Is there a problem, officer?" He spoke with measured words in a voice so quiet Hitchcock had to strain to hear him.

He smiled as he extended his hand. "No problem, Mr. Vollmer. I'm Roger Hitchcock with the Crime Prevention Unit. Since you just opened, I came by to introduce myself and welcome you to the city," he said, purposely omitting the words police department.

The back of Vollmer's hand bore a crude tattoo of a lightning bolt. His shake was cold and limp as a dead fish. "Nice of you, I'm sure," he murmured in the cautious tone of the cell block and the exercise yard.

Vollmer reminded Hitchcock of Colin Wilcox, the ex-con hitman he arrested two years earlier whose executed body was later found in the deep woods. "We do risk assessments and training to help you, your employees and your customers avoid being victimized by fast-change artists, burglars and armed robbers."

"Our company doesn't anticipate having problems like that here. The owners chose Bellevue as a place to do business because of the low crime rate."

"It's a fact that motels along Interstate freeways experience armed robbery, assaults on guests, and theft," Hitchcock countered. "Lawsuits against businesses by customers and employees for alleged negligence are common these days. It wouldn't look good for a manager to have to testify in a civil trial that he turned down free crime prevention training from the police. A demonstrable lack of due diligence could cost your employers big bucks."

"Doesn't your department already know the layout of this building from when it was The Hilltop? All we've changed is the lobby."

"Do your front desk people and cashiers know what to do in the event of an armed robbery, Mr. Vollmer?"

"I guess not," he admitted, his face as deadpan as a dummy on the lap of a ventriloquist.

"Are your managers trained to spot employee theft when it happens? It *will* happen, you know."

Vollmer hesitated, staring blankly at him. "Okay, Mr. Hitchcock, we might as well do the training."

"Good. First, show me around and introduce me to your people, then we'll work out a schedule for a few brief training sessions that won't disrupt their work."

Knowing Vollmer might be wanted in California, Hitchcock avoided casual conversation to avoid putting him on alert. He memorized the names of the daytime bartender, front desk manager, restaurant manager, cooks and waitresses by repeating them as Vollmer made the introductions.

During his guided tour he noticed the older cleaning maid he saw in the lobby. He still couldn't place where he had seen her before. She acknowledged him again with a grin of recognition. He hoped Vollmer didn't notice it.

"Thanks for the tour, Mr. Vollmer. Nature calls.

Which way is the—"

Vollmer pointed. "Down the hall, on the right."

In the privacy of a toilet stall he wrote stall down the employees' names and their positions on his pocket notepad while they were fresh in his mind.

† † †

THE OTHER MEMBERS of his office were drinking coffee and telling war stories when he returned. They stopped when he came in. "Don't let me stop you, girls," he said as he phoned Patty in Records.

"Roger here. Any word yet if California will extradite Simon Vollmer?"

"Not yet, but I found out he got off on a manslaughter charge in Arizona in '65, hung jury. In '67 he served two years in Nevada for felony assault. He was paroled in '69 and was convicted of embezzlement in San Francisco last year. His parole must be over if he wasn't extradited."

"I just left the El Escondite Inn. Met Vollmer. He's hardcore, prison tattoos, got the stare, the attitude. To make sure we're talking about the same guy, find out if California will extradite him, and get me a mugshot of him."

"Done," Patty said.

He admired her efficiency. "While we're on the phone, here's a partial list of El Escondite employees. I have only names and age estimates, no DOB's. Several of them had a big 'C' for 'crook' on their forehead."

"My, my, Roger, aren't you still the busy boy?"

THE OTHER OFFICERS were quiet when he hung up. He turned in his chair to find his supervisor standing behind him. "I thought you wanted to do crime prevention," Sergeant Windham said.

"That's what I'm doing," Hitchcock replied.

Windham folded his arms. "What I heard sounded like detective work."

"I stopped by to introduce myself to the new management. We've got a new gang of criminals in business where the old Hilltop used to be. I'm *preventing* them from becoming established."

"Going undercover isn't within our scope, Roger," Windham said. "When you come across criminal information, pass it on to Patrol or the dicks."

Hitchcock faced his desk and shuffled papers to hide his frustration. "I wasn't undercover. When the information I've requested comes in, I'll forward it to whoever has the Eastgate beat, and-or the detectives."

"And you won't act on the information yourself."

"Understood," he grumbled.

FOR AN HOUR every morning the rest of the week, Hitchcock trained El Escondite employees on handling emergencies, evacuations, alarms, and detection of criminal activity. They were tight-lipped, as if they had been instructed not to answer questions outside the scope of the training.

At the end of the last session, the cleaning maid who smiled at him earlier lingered after the others left.

"I remember you," she said. "You were Gayle's secret boss."

"You worked here then?" he asked, surprised.

She affirmed with a nod. "When it was The Hilltop. I was one of Gayle's sources. I helped her set up Tyrone Guyon and Mae Driscoll for you. A couple other girls did too. We drank a toast after you guys killed them. We helped Gayle set up Davis and his big nephew, too."

"It was great work. Any of those gals still here?"

"Everyone quit but me when the Hilltop sold."

"How come?"

She scoffed. "In case you haven't noticed, these people are Federal–mafia–L.A. and Vegas. Killing to them is like taking the car through the car wash is for us. I'm Dolly, by the way."

"Why did you stay on?"

She shrugged her shoulders in the familiar manner of those who have accepted the cards life dealt them. "Work is tough to find in this economy for a middle-age, uneducated widow with little mouths to feed. The pay is here low, but steady."

He snapped his fingers. "Ah–now I know where I've seen you–Charlie's Place."

She smiled. "I'm a regular there on weekends, to make ends meet."

"You're a barmaid at Charlie's? I saw you sitting with a man on either side of you. You must be a new barmaid," he said, knowing better.

He saw cynicism in the way she shook her head. He tried the only other option. "Uh, Kane's Motel?"

She nodded.

He said nothing. She was east of fifty, but attractive, buxom, trim, shapely, and smooth-skinned. Old-timers would describe her as well-preserved. Younger men would want to be seen with her. She didn't look the hooker type.

After an awkward silence, she straightened her posture. Her smile took on a confrontational aspect as she looked into his eyes. "You look shocked, officer. Don't be. I'm a provider and a survivor. What I make cleaning rooms full-time doesn't support even me, let alone my three grandkids. I limit myself to select clients and Wally's protection. I just hope my health and my looks hold up until my little ones are grown and on their way."

He held his silence, not knowing what to say.

"Your memory is good," she said. "I was at Charlie's the night you arrested that man hiding in the ladies' room. I'll never forget when you came out, your gun under his chin, his hands in the air. He didn't look so tough anymore. Folks around here still talk about it," she said, smiling at the memory of it.

"We paid Gayle well for her information," he said.

"She always split it with us."

"You're on my payroll as of now if you want. It's dangerous, but less so than what you're doing."

"What would my code name be?"

He had to think for a moment. "La Paloma."

"La Paloma," she repeated. "What does it mean?"

"Spanish for 'The Dove.'" He wrote on a slip of

paper and handed it to her. "Use a pay phone when you call with anything you think I should know about. Leave a message for me to call La Paloma, and the phone number. We'd better get back. We can't be seen talking too long."

"'La Paloma' already has information. She will call you after the weekend," she whispered.

He remembered noticing her that night at Charlie's Place, sitting between two men about her age or older. Both had their eyes on her. He thought it remarkable that she hadn't aged.

He returned to his office and found a message on his desk. The note read: CALL YOUR WIFE. URGENT.

CHAPTER SEVEN
Mystery on Highway 18

HITCHCOCK'S MIND RACED, wondering what could be wrong as he dialed his home phone number. He heard panic in Allie's voice when she answered on the second ring.

"It's me, baby. Is everything all right?"

"Roger, go to the Fowler's house right away. They need you."

"Is it Randy?"

"No! Connie's missing!"

"On my way."

An unmarked Bellevue detective's car and a marked King County Sheriff's patrol car were parked in the driveway of the Fowler home. In the kitchen he saw Detective Joe Small, Barbara Fowler sat at the table, pale and shaking, answering questions from a uniformed deputy. Randy and John sat on either side of her, tense and silent. The deputy stopped speaking when he saw Hitchcock.

"It's all right, officer, this is Roger Hitchcock of Bellevue PD," Randy said. "He's a family friend."

Hitchcock lifted his chin, questioning the deputy.

"Miss Fowler's car was found abandoned this morning by the State Patrol on the shoulder of Highway 18 at I-90," the deputy said. "The passenger door was open. The trooper found blood on the front seat and the driver's door. Her purse and wallet were inside."

"Mrs. Fowler, Connie's mom, reported her missing to us yesterday," Detective Small added in a muffled voice.

"Who took the initial report?"

"One of the new guys, McCabe."

"I understand you've known this family a long time, Roger," Small said. "Got any input for us?"

Hitchcock shook his head and shrugged. "We went to church with them Easter Sunday, then they came to brunch at our place. Connie seemed normal but I didn't talk to her much."

"Any drug or alcohol history?"

"Heroin. She's been clean for the past two or three years. Her family can tell you more than I can."

Hitchcock listened to the deputy and Detective Small finish their interviews with Barbara. "I never knew her to go that far east," she told Detective Small.

Small turned to Hitchcock. "Let's you and I run out there to look around while there's still daylight."

† † †

COLD MOUNTAIN WINDS swept the grassy slope of the cloverleaf where Interstate-90 interchanged with State Highway 18 in a wooded, rural area. Little yellow flags on metal wire rods were stuck in the ground in the shape of a full-size car, marking the spot where troopers found Connie Fowler's maroon '66 Oldsmobile 88. The nearest development of any kind was the Echo Glen Reformatory for juvenile offenders, about a mile away.

"This is no place to pull over unless it's an emergency," Small said. "It's so steep a car would roll over if parked wrong."

"For the passenger door to be standing open, the car would've been parked facing east, so the passenger side was facing downhill. It would be difficult for anyone getting out to keep from falling," Hitchcock said.

"It would require above average strength to push open a driver's door against gravity enough to climb out. Someone else brought it here," Small speculated.

"It was left here so it *would* be found."

"Agreed. Instead of leaving it just anywhere, two people put it here, as a taunt," Small said.

"Or a false lead," Hitchcock added. "I see two different sets of tire tracks, one wider than the other, like a pickup or a van."

"Tread impressions aren't definitive in this hard ground, but let's do what we can."

As daylight was fading and an evening wind chilled the air, they hastened to mix plaster and distilled water and made frames make casts of the tire tracks. They scoured the ground for more clues after the mix was poured but found none. Small put samples of the soil and the vegetation in separate jars. Hitchcock took photos.

It was cold when they finished. "I hope you can join

me in looking at Connie's car tomorrow. The County has it in evidence storage," Small said.

"I'll ask permission."

"One more thing: When Connie was on heroin, who was her supplier? Maybe her dealer reconnected with her."

"Tyrone Guyon," Hitchcock replied.

"The guy whose ticket you punched about a year ago?"

"The same."

"Who else could it be?"

"No idea."

"We'll need an updated list of who knew her."

† † †

HE SAID LITTLE and ate about half of Allie's roast chicken dinner. After the boys were in bed, he sat with her in the living room. The silence was heavy.

"Connie's dead, isn't she?"

"I said *you* would know, remember?" she said.

"This is the fulfillment of what you said."

"This *you* must solve, Roger. That family has gone through too much."

"I'm not in Detectives. And I'm not in Patrol anymore either. I'm—"

She interrupted him by shaking her head. "I sense God's hand on this family, and He wants to lead *you* to the truth."

"I don't understand."

"I don't expect you to, but at the Easter brunch I

sensed that Connie was in danger of some kind."

He leaned away from her. "What are you talking about? Are you turning psycho on me?"

She stood up. "Don't insult me or my faith. You'll see."

He said nothing.

"I'm going to bed now. Coming?"

"Be there in a few," he said.

He stayed in his leather easy chair and poured a glass of Jack Daniels. The spiritual side of Allie conflicted with his views of life and death, which were molded by his combat experiences in Vietnam. He saw life as cheap, brief, often brutal and unfair. Death can come at any time–no guarantees. There was nothing beyond the grave. Dead is dead.

But Allie...how well did he really know her? Her confidence that God reveals things to her confounded him, yet he couldn't question her integrity. After all, he had a strange ability of his own to foresee danger, and he didn't understand that either.

He decided to summon Mr. Jack Daniels further. He would settle the issue. He poured another three fingers. *Now then, Mr. Daniels, these differences between my mystic wife, and my irreverent self, are they reconcilable? Maybe– maybe not. Even if not, I can't live without Allie. She is life itself to me. And that...well, that settles that, and that calls for another round of Jack–just to clear the cobwebs, to finalize things, you know. Good old Jack.*

CHAPTER EIGHT
The Dangerous Dunce

AS IN TIMES past, Rowland Bostwick drew attention to himself when he swaggered like a conquering general through the front door of The Great Wall, his pressed dark blue uniform, gleaming gold lieutenant's bars on his collar and badge, dark aviator style Ray Bans hiding his eyes.

A moment after a waitress hurried to the back, Juju emerged, wearing a revealing black dress of filmy fabric. She acted shocked to see him.

"Rowlie-sahn! You back! What happen?" she demanded, faking surprise and indignation.

Bostwick had spent hours in front of a mirror rehearsing what he would say when this moment came and how he would say it. He bowed his head slightly as he removed his sunglasses with the somber *"I can only tell you so much"* look he had seen Steve McQueen use in his latest movie, *Bullitt*.

"I had to disappear for a while," he said in a low, confidential voice, trying to sound as if danger and intrigue were mere routine to him.

Juju, using acting skills honed by years as a bar girl

and prostitute in Taiwan, took him by the arm, led him to her office and shut the door. She confronted him, pouting, with her hands on her hips. "Disappear? You leave me. No say anything. You tell me now!"

"I had to go undercover for several months to save the Department. I can't tell you more. It was, and still is, too dangerous," he said, straight-faced.

His ridiculousness caught Juju off guard. Before she laughed in his face, she grabbed him with both arms, buried her face into his chest to keep him from seeing her smile. She gathered herself and turned on the tears. "Why you no trust me? You no tell me?" she sobbed.

He wrapped his flabby arms around her. "I had to. I couldn't risk your safety. But I'm back now."

Astounded by his brazen folly, Juju turned away to keep from cracking up. Once composed, she turned toward him, wiping fake tears. "For how long you back? Till next time? You make me angry." She hit her sobbing switch again.

"I got rid of Hitchcock for you, didn't I? He's gone and won't come back. He's not in Patrol anymore. Isn't that worth something, Juju?"

She stepped close to him. "Yes, Heetchcock gone. New officer much better. Nice boy. So how much 'worth' you want today, hmm?" she asked as she removed his hat and tie.

BOSTWICK WAS LATE getting back to the station. He realized he might have been premature in approaching

Juju before the question of his restoration to the rank of lieutenant had been decided, but it was necessary to his plan for Juju to see him again with gold bars on his collar.

He had avoided her after his demotion and exile to the new Property Room, miles from the station, by the loathsome Captain Delstra. The Civil Service Board hearing on his appeal was weeks away. He had "Plan B" ready if the Board reinstated his demotion to sergeant.

He had to work fast. Delstra would be back from the FBI Academy in five weeks. If he survived the Civil Service Board hearing before the captain's return, he would implement the next phase of his plot

A sealed envelope from the Civil Service Board was on his desk when he returned from lunch. The date of his hearing had been moved up three weeks to 9:00 a.m. the following day. An evil smirk spread over Bostwick's face. It paid to have connections.

BACK AT THE Great Wall, Juju Kwan sat her desk, laughing hysterically after Bostwick left. She laughed so loudly that her employees came to check on her. She laughed because her other sources in the police told her the truth about Bostwick. She had to admit that he was as creative a liar as she herself. Almost.

CHAPTER NINE
The Rats Roost

SPEED'S CAFÉ WAS EMPTY as Hitchcock met Otis, Sherman and Walker sat in a booth. A swarthy, middle-aged waitress spoke with a foreign accent as she greeted them and poured coffee.

"We gotta act fast," he said, these guys are real heavies," Hitchcock stressed.

"Don't keep us in suspense, Roger," Otis said.

He opened a file folder. "Just got the rap sheets of the El Escondite personnel from Patty."

"The man in the California Department of Corrections mugshot of Simon T. Vollmer is the man I met in the lobby. His rap sheet included extortion, witness tampering, bribery and promoting prostitution. Right now, he's not wanted, not on parole and not around."

"What can he be arrested for?" Walker asked.

"That's the catch—he seems to have disappeared."

"Disappeared?" Otis asked.

"Hasn't been seen by anyone since my first visit there ten days ago. Nobody knows where he is, and interestingly enough, no one has reported him missing."

The resulting silence among them was significant.

"What else you got there?" Walker asked.

"The bar manager, Luis Armijo, is tending bar without a license. He's got warrants out of Clark County, Nevada for aggravated assault, illegal firearms possession, first degree escape, and assaulting an officer, all confirmed. The Clark County Sheriff's Office will extradite."

Sherman smiled as he looked at the unread papers in Hitchcock's hand. "Keep going."

"The assistant manager, Jorge Bordenero," Hitchcock continued, "is wanted by the U.S. District Court of Los Angeles for Unlawful Flight to Avoid Prosecution. The Feds've confirmed they will extradite from anywhere in the lower United States."

"Anything more?" Otis asked.

"There're two young hookers who hang out in the lobby every afternoon and evening. They're part of the organization but neither has a criminal history."

"Is that it?" Walker asked.

"Two local employees, Dirk Mignolet and Van Stuart, have outstanding warrants and rap sheets that include convictions for Possession of Controlled Substances with Intent to Sell, Contributing to the Delinquency of a Minor, DWI, and shoplifting."

Otis looked at the others. "Let's make a plan."

CHAPTER TEN
The Ballad of Dolly Searles

HITCHCOCK STOPPED AT Charley's Place after his meeting with Otis and Walker. Even empty and just cleaned, it smelled like all taverns, musty, smoky, of beer and cheap wine. He found Wally Evans, its mountainous owner, at his desk, a large ledger open before him, shirt sleeves rolled up, exposing his huge hairy forearms. He wasn't smiling.

"Who are you, and what have you done with my friend Officer Roger Hitchcock?"

Hitchcock pulled up a chair. "How goes it?"

"Worse around here since you quit being a cop."

"I've still got a badge."

"You're not here."

"How are things worse?"

Wally pushed his chair back and cleared his throat. "Cocaine's the 'in' thing now, more than pot or heroin, it seems, and there's a lot of it around. I've kicked several customers out and barred them from coming back because of their using or selling it here. Word on the street is there's a big new shipment of heroin just in. All this has been happening since you left, so no, I'm not happy and I don't feel as safe as I did."

"What about the new officer?"

"Gerry McCabe? Don't get me started." Wally scoffed with a dismissive wave of his hand.

Hitchcock leaned forward, earnestness in his eyes. "What about McCabe?"

Evans put his palms flat on his desk. His eyes bore holes into Hitchcock's. He shook his head slowly as he stared, saying not a word.

Accepting Wally's silent message of contempt for the officer, Hitchcock replied, "Okay, Wally—I'll look into it. Next, any appearances by Mike Smith or word of him?"

"He stopped in here one night about a month ago, when I wasn't here. Nothing since."

"Was he with anyone?"

"Barmaid said he was alone."

"Do you know a blonde woman named Dolly?"

Wally raised his eyebrows. "Dolly Searles, a poor neighborhood widow. I knew her husband Tommy. Good man, a long-haul trucker."

"Tell me about *her*."

Wally leaned back in his chair, eyes on Hitchcock. "Tommy was a local stud, movie-star handsome and a success in the trucking business. Women, married or not, were after him. But Tommy had eyes only for Dolly. He was twelve years older. She was a teenage beauty queen, known for her physical perfection. Tommy eloped with her to Idaho on her sixteenth birthday. Her parents were *very* upset, but they liked Tommy too much to object. They were a popular couple around here."

"Funny I never heard about them," Hitchcock mused.

"You were in high school and then the Army at the time," Wally said.

"Anyway, her two kids became dopers. Tommy suddenly had a heart attack. He left Dolly with a paid-off car and a paid-off home in lower Eastgate, a little cash in the bank and a little life insurance but not enough to keep her going when her kids got strung out. She used up her savings helping them. All for nothing. They were so strung-out it was up to Dolly to take in their three little ones to prevent the state from breaking up the family."

"I saw her here a couple times. always with two or more guys," Hitchcock said reflectively.

Wally nodded but kept talking. "Even with a paid-off house and a car, with only an eighth-grade education and no job skills, the only work Dolly could get full time was as a cleaning maid at the Hilltop. To survive in this economy, she stayed on after the Mexicans bought it. So now I gotta ask you, why the interest?"

"I met her the other day, just verifying that she knows you."

Wally's eyes burrowed into Hitchcock's. "Let me tell you a story about me that almost nobody knows. When I was ten, my mom lost our house after my dad died. We had no relatives to take us in, so we moved into a tenement building on the south side of Chicago. Mom got a waitress job at a diner down the street, but she didn't get off until eight, which meant she couldn't be there when I came home from school. Down the hall was a hooker named Glenda, who entertained her 'clients' in her place. She was a hooker, as I said, but a nice lady, Glenda was."

Wally shifted in his chair, eyes gazing into a time long gone as he continued. "To help Mom out, Glenda put her 'business' on hold when I came home from school."

"She fixed me dinner every night at her place and helped me with my homework until mom came home. Never exposed me to any aspect of her trade," Wally said, wagging his forefinger at Hitchcock. "This went on for a year, I think. Treated me like a son, Glenda did. I remember Mom trying to pay her, but she always refused. One morning we woke up to find the cops at Glenda's apartment. Some guy, a customer, I guess, beat her to death the night before. Glenda, who looked out for me, had no one looking out for her."

"That's some story, Wally, " Hitchcock said, visibly moved. "Was her killer ever caught?"

Wally shifted his gaze to Hitchcock; the shake of his head was barely perceptible. "I never forgot poor Glenda, she was good people," he said sadly.

"Oh," Hitchcock said, soaking in the story.

A reflective silence fell between them.

"I told you about Glenda, so you'll understand that

I'm answering your questions about Dolly before you ask them. Dolly's poor but she's still a looker. She supports three young grandchildren the best way she can. Her deadbeat kids can't and probably wouldn't even if they could. They're addicts. Her support from her husband's Social Security ran out on her youngest kid's eighteenth birthday two years ago, so she turned to this on weekends. Her only customers are older truckers who knew her husband. She meets them here, they use her room at Kane's across the way, always away from her grandkids."

"Why don't you give her a job?"

"Did. She quit after a couple months. Said even with the tips, two jobs on her feet took too much time from her grandkids and drained her physically. Cleaning rooms plus bartending makes for a lot of time on her feet for a woman her age." Wally paused, turning a pencil around in his fingers.

As if he read Hitchcock's mind, Wally said, "To answer your next question, I don't know exactly how Dolly got into hooking for a small group of customers, but she found she could make ends meet for herself and her three little ones in less time a one or two nights a week. Hooker or not, Dolly's good people. She can tell you a lot of what goes on around here and she won't sell you out or lie to you.

"In answer to your next question before you ask it, Roger, no I don't take a cut from Dolly's using my place to meet her half-dozen or so customers. No one does. She pays the regular room rate at Kane's, too."

"You're a real clairvoyant, Wally," Hitchcock said, grinning.

"I know you're big on morals, Roger. We all need 'em. It's one of the things I like about you. But if there's a problem with what Dolly does to keep what's left of her family together and make ends meet, mercy gets the cigar. Her kind you don't just use and throw away."

With an appreciative nod, Hitchcock said, "Got it."

"Think hard about coming back, Roger. This place has been going to the dogs since you left."

HE RAN A records check on Dolly Searles as soon as he left. It revealed only a traffic ticket for speeding six years ago. She paid the fine. *Wally is right. Dolly is legit.*

The rest of the afternoon passed with armed robbery training for the personnel at Seattle First National Bank in Eastgate. The receptionist handed Hitchcock a note when he walked into the office. "This just came in, Roger. Call Patty in Records, ASAP."

"Some woman named Palo called for you," Patty said.

"Palo? You mean La Paloma?"

"That's it. She said it's urgent for you to contact at this number in an hour."

CHAPTER ELEVEN
Ducks in a Row

DOLLY ANSWERED ON the second ring. "Roger, teenagers from the high school and a few that look old enough to be in the community college are coming to El Escondite every afternoon. I just overheard two of the younger girls who work with me saying Luis, the bar manager in the cocktail lounge, is selling cocaine."

"Out of the bar?" he asked, alarmed. "Kids come into the bar?"

"One of the girls who works the front desk sells it to the kids for him. I don't know which one. Luis sells it directly to adults in the bar during the afternoon. He has it in his pocket and more under the drawer in the cash register. His main stash is in his office safe."

"He works daytime hours?"

"Ten to six."

"Keep your head down, your eyes and ears open."

AFTER HE RE-CONFIRMED the warrants for Luis Armijo, Hitchcock met with Gary Tremaine, inspector with the State Liquor Control Board, and Otis, Sherman, and Walker at Speed's Café in Lake Hills. He filled them in on Dolly's information, identifying his source as "a concerned citizen whose credibility is known to me personally."

"Doesn't your department have a narcotics unit for this sort of thing?" Tremaine asked.

Otis, Sherman, and Walker exchanged glances as they scoffed. "The city deciders have decreed those drugs and serious crime don't happen in Bellevue. You must have seen the little white picket fence around our lovely little town on your way here. It keeps bad people, bad things and bad thoughts out, so the town paper has nothing to write about except school sports teams and business banquets."

Tremaine chuckled. "Seriously, though, why aren't we discussing this at your station instead of here?"

"There's a leak, maybe two, in our department, which haven't been identified yet," Hitchcock said in a low voice. "We can't take a chance."

"Well, knock me over with a feather."

Hitchcock leaned forward to emphasize his next words. "The El Escondite is a new business. The owners and most of the employees are career criminals from California and Nevada. We need your help in shutting down the bar because of license violations. We'll take it from there. If we don't nip this in the bud when they're getting started, we will not be able to stop it later. So, my question is, "are you in?""

Tremaine grinned as he slammed the tabletop with his hand. "Hell yes, I'm in! I'm starved for action. Let's hear your plan."

CHAPTER TWELVE
One Fell Swoop

IT WAS COLD, cloudy, and not raining as Hitchcock waited in an adjacent parking lot the next morning for Simon Vollmer to arrive at The El Escondite. He watched Luis Armijo, the bar manager, arrive in a shiny new red Camaro with Nevada license plates. But Vollmer continued to be a no-show. After two hours he left for the Crime Prevention office.

At 2:00 p.m. Simon Vollmer's black Lincoln was still not there. Hitchcock went in. The front desk clerk was another tall, slender, Latina in her mid-twenties. Her smooth, tawny skin contrasted with her white silk blouse. Lustrous black hair cascaded over her shoulders. Hitchcock flashed his badge and a friendly grin. "Good afternoon, miss. I have an appointment to see your assistant manager, Mr. Jorge Bordenero."

Without a word she picked up the phone. "There's someone from the police here to see you, sir. Says he has an appointment." Without a word to Hitchcock, she hung up and went about her work.

Bordenero watched as Hitchcock taught the front desk clerk how to spot counterfeit bills and how fast-change artists operate. After he finished, Bordenero introduced him to Luis Armijo and the barmaids.

In the process of teaching a technique to stall quick-change artists, Hitchcock started to lift the drawer out of the cash register as part of his demonstration. In a flash Armijo seized the cash drawer from Hitchcock's hands before he could peek under it. He coolly concluded his training session and asked if he could train their night shift personnel.

"Come back tonight after seven," Bordenero said brusquely.

Otis and Walker waited in a marked car across the street, with Inspector Tremaine next to them in his unmarked car as Hitchcock came out. He gave the two-finger signal to Otis and Walker to switch to Channel 2. "The bird is in the dark nest," he radioed. He moved his car to a different location and watched them move in.

Tremaine parked in front of the double front doors and entered the lobby. After five minutes, Otis and Walker entered the lobby. Tremaine came out, giving the thumb-up signal to Hitchcock. He drove across the street.

Hitchcock drove up next to him.

"Armijo was behind the bar serving a drink to a customer when I walked in," Tremaine said. "He admitted he had no Health Department license, for which I cited him. The other guy working behind the bar didn't have a license either, so I cited him too. The bar's been operating under the old license of the Hilltop, which it formerly was. As I was explaining the law to the manager, and closing the bar, your uniformed officers came in and arrested Armijo. He resisted, but that was over quickly. The whole place is abuzz now."

Hitchcock focused his binoculars on Otis and Walker as they escorted Luis Armijo out in handcuffs. Armijo began emphatically shaking his head when they took him to his red Camaro. Otis radioed for an impound truck. Nervous employees and guests watched from a distance as Otis seated Armijo in his cruiser. They headed for the station as soon as another officer arrived to handle the impound.

"Why are they taking the Camaro?" Tremaine asked Hitchcock.

"It's stolen."

Thirty minutes later, Hitchcock radioed Sherman who was waiting nearby in a marked cruiser: "Suspect Two hasn't left. Car's still here."

Five minutes later Sherman emerged from the lobby with Bordenero in handcuffs.

† † †

HITCHCOCK RETURNED TO The El Escondite at 7:00 p.m. A different front desk clerk, a chunky freckle-faced girl in her twenties with light red hair was on duty. "I'm here to see Mr. Bordenero," he said, displaying his badge and police ID.

"I-uh-I-uh, Mr. Bordenero had to leave suddenly this afternoon. I don't know when he'll be back."

"You seem troubled, miss. Is there anything wrong?"

"Well, yeah! My shift started at seven. When I came in, I learned the liquor inspector closed the bar and the police arrested two of the managers this afternoon."

He feigned surprise by shaking his head. "Wow! Sorry to hear that. Nevertheless, I planned with Mr. Bordenero to put on some training for the night shift employees, especially those who handle cash."

"Mr. Bordenero is one of the managers the officers arrested. He's in jail, and I know nothing about this training."

"Well, how about Mr. Vollmer, then?"

"I'm told he's away on an emergency of some kind. Look, officer, this is not a good time for us. There's no one in charge here but me. Could you come back tomorrow morning?"

"Who should I ask for?"

"Dirk. Dirk Mignolet, I guess."

CHAPTER THIRTEEN
Pay Dirt

HE CALLED DOLLY from the Crime Prevention office. She gasped when she heard his voice on the phone. He could hear a child talking in the background. "You were there when we hit 'em," he said. "What happened after we left?"

"I had no idea this was coming down," she said, her voice shaking. "Everybody was shocked and scared, me included. I heard two officers found cocaine in Luis's pants pocket, under the cash register and that detectives came later with a search warrant and recovered more drugs from his office safe."

"I didn't warn you to protect you, Dolly. They'd suspect you if you weren't as surprised and upset as everyone else."

"Thank you for that. No one suspects me."

"That's the idea," he said. "Tell me the rest of it."

"I was moving a laundry cart down the hall with Jill, one of the maids. We saw Dirk and Van in an open room. She told Dirk the cops were arresting Luis. Dirk and Van were in the room with two young guys who were from the college, I think."

"What were they doing?"

"A dope deal. What type, I don't know. They split up when Jill told them what was going on."

"And then?"

"Word of the arrests spread fast. Everybody was scared. None of us worked for the rest of the day. We gathered in the restaurant and talked. Then, the same two cops came back and took Jorge out of there in handcuffs."

"What happened after that?"

"The girl at the front desk began turning guests away. For most of us, me included, that was it, we didn't finish our work, we were too scared to stay there, so we went home, except Dirk and Van."

"What did they do?"

"I heard one of them say they were going to find the pot and the cocaine that Mr. Vollmer has hidden, probably in the safe."

"Ah. Vollmer too, huh?"

"Simon's the head of the whole thing. He's out of town on a family emergency of some kind, or so I hear."

"Anything else?"

"The two young hookers that hang out in the lobby afternoons and evenings. They work directly for Simon. They weren't there today, for some reason."

"Are you going back tomorrow?"

Dolly snorted as she said, "If I still have a job!"

"Stay in touch."

† † †

HITCHCOCK CAME HOME late. The boys were asleep, Allie was up, waiting. They sat in the living room.

"You've had a long day today, like you had when you were in Patrol. What happened?"

He told her about Dolly, the results of her information, and what Wally said about her.

"Do you know the Bible story about a prostitute named Rahab?" she asked.

"You're kidding, right?"

"Rahab was a prostitute in Jericho to provide for her family. She knew the Israelites were coming in force. She knew they would conquer the city and kill everyone in it, so she helped hide the spies."

"*This* is in the Bible?" he asked, shocked.

Allie nodded as she continued. "By helping the Israelite spies who came in advance of the soldiers, she was grabbing hold of the hope that was held out to her for survival and a better life. She knew she could be executed for treason if she was caught, but she took the chance. Because of what she did, the Israelites spared her and her family when they conquered Jericho. She later married an Israelite man, they had kids, and were part of Jesus's earthly ancestry."

"What! One of Christ's ancestors was a hooker? They didn't teach us *that* in Sunday School!"

"How did working with this Dolly make you feel?"

"I'm not judging her, but I've never been okay with the idea of sex for money. I will say, though, that I understood it when I saw it in countries where it was the best or only means of survival for poor women with no education, especially widows with kids."

"Look at all the good she did you guys on her first job," she said. "Thanks to her, great evil has been nipped in the bud."

"I've told her I can't, and won't, look the other way. I'm done as a cop if I do."

"You're on a tightrope, honey."

"Would you read the story to me?"

Allie laughed as she opened her Bible.

"What's so funny?" he asked.

"Us. Here you are, relaxing with a glass of whiskey while I read you a story about a prostitute in the Bible."

He laughed with her. "Ain't we a pair, now!"

† † †

PATTY IN RECORDS called the next morning. "Because of Lieutenant you-know-who, I'll make it quick: No-bail King County warrants are confirmed as of an hour ago for Dirk Mignolet and Van Stuart. You can pick them up any time."

His phone rang again as soon as he hung up. It was Detective Small.

"Great work, Roger. Otis and Walker found bindles of cocaine in Armijo's pants pocket when they took him into custody. Luis resisted arrest, as you may already know."

"I don't imagine that went well for him."

Small chuckled. "He needed the usual medical attention one needs after tangling with Otis or Walker. Williams and I seized over a pound of cocaine on a search warrant for the safe."

"Is that Armijo's office or Vollmer's office?"

"They share it. Their desks across the room face each other. They share the safe, too."

"How did you get into the safe—locksmith?"

"No honor among thieves," Small said cheerfully. "Armijo gave us the combination to take Vollmer down with him on felony drug charges. We now have Probable Cause to arrest Simon Vollmer when he comes back."

"*If* he does," Hitchcock said.

"Right. We got another search warrant for the red Camaro, which was stolen out of Las Vegas."

"And?"

"Surprise, surprise, we found more cocaine behind the driver's side door upholstery panel."

"Outstanding," Hitchcock exclaimed. "Now what?"

"Felony charges are being filed against Armijo, who is in the slammer awaiting extradition to Nevada," Small replied. "Your turn. What else you got?"

Hitchcock gave him Dolly's information about employees Mignolet and Stuart, without naming her.

"I've got an appointment to meet Dirk Mignolet there this morning, to continue my training of their employees. The night employees were too rattled for training last night."

Small chuckled. "Gotta hand it to ya, Roger, using Crime Prevention to go undercover is as original as anything I've seen. And your new snitch hit a grand slam first time out. Great stuff."

"Thanks, Joe. Should I go back out there this morning?"

"Always keep your appointments. If either of those two are dumb enough to come in when they know they're wanted, it's even more reason they should be locked up. Stupidity is contagious," Small said.

"They won't show up. Nobody's *that* dumb."

CHAPTER FOURTEEN
The Second Swoop

TO HITCHCOCK'S DISMAY, the cars of both Mignolet and Stuart were in the employee parking lot when he arrived at 10:00 a.m. He radioed Dispatch to send a Patrol unit by in ten minutes for at least one, if not two arrests.

A woman he hadn't seen before, a white girl, auburn hair, early twenties, well-groomed, dressed in a navy-blue suit, stood behind the front desk, looking down, fully engaged in a phone call. He walked past her to the manager's office, where he heard male voices laughing. He knocked, then opened the door. Two men appearing to be his age or younger instantly stopped their chatter and stared blankly at him.

"Excuse me, gentlemen. I'm from the Crime Prevention Unit. Mr. Bordenero gave me permission yesterday to continue my training of the night shift employees. He asked me to come back today instead and ask for a Mr. Mignolet. Dirk Mignolet. Would that be either of you?"

The taller and skinnier of the two snickered as he raised his hand and smiled. "That's me. I'm in charge until Vollmer—I mean *Mr.* Vollmer gets back."

"Fine. I've trained the daytime employees already, including you two. Would it be all right if I came back tonight at seven to train the night crew?"

"Sure thing, officer," Mignolet said cockily as he put his feet up on the desk.

Hitchcock turned to leave, then stopped and smiled as he pointed at Van Stuart. "Let me test my memory. Your name is...don't tell me—Van! Van, uh, Stuart?"

The young dunce grinned stupidly. "You got it!"

Hitchcock snickered and shook his head as he left.

Two first-shift patrol cars waited in the far parking lot, out of sight of the lobby. Hitchcock didn't know either of the officers as he approached. "They're both in the manager's office right now, yukking it up. The dummies identified themselves to me, so there's no mistake. I'd be there to point them out, but it's necessary to the investigation that they don't see me with you."

The officers wrote down the suspects' physical and clothing descriptions and went inside. Hitchcock watched from a distance as both Mignolet and Stuart were brought out in handcuffs minutes later. He drove away before they could see him.

† † †

HE COLLECTED $340.00 from the Department's special fund, plus contributions from himself, Otis, Walker, Sherman, and Packard. He met Dolly in the parking lot of Charlie's. Tears filled her eyes when she counted it.

"This is more than I expected, Roger."

"It's from our special fund, plus contributions from

myself and four other officers. One is leaving the Department tomorrow because he passed the bar exam. He'll have an office in Bellevue. You might need him later. His name is Ray Packard."

Dolly sniffed as she wiped her eyes. "Ray what?"

"Packard."

"Ray Packard, okay," she repeated as she printed the name on a notecard in her purse.

"I bet it's also more than you make on any given weekend," Hitchcock said, changing the subject.

"Not always," she said, wiping her tears.

"I have more spy work for you if you want it."

She nodded, sniffling. "Yes."

"A pre-condition is that you stop hooking, period."

She looked at him in surprise. "It's how I've survived these past two years."

"You can rationalize anything."

"Gayle had been a hooker, under the control of a pimp named Rulee."

"She put it behind her when she left Tacoma before I met her. I wouldn't have offered informant work to her otherwise. She's married now and has a baby."

"So I hear," Dolly said.

"Prostitution was legal and acceptable for Rahab back in ancient times. It's illegal now and I'm the law."

"Huh?"

"It's in the Bible."

"What?"

"Think about it," he said kindly.

CHAPTER FIFTEEN
Dark Secrets

AFTER TWO WEEKS of no new leads, Hitchcock believed Connie Fowler's body was rotting somewhere in the deep woods of east King County. If nothing else, he wanted someone, somehow to find her remains so her family could at least have closure.

At the detectives' office on Old Main Street, Joe Small gestured to the chair in front of his desk.

Hitchcock took a seat and folded his hands.

"Anything new on the Connie Fowler case?"

Small handed him a folder. "Lab report says the blood on the driver's seat and steering wheel of her car is Type A Positive. Connie's is O Positive."

"It's a reason to hope she's alive, but awfully slim."

Small continued as Hitchcock read the report: "We lifted identifiable prints from the steering wheel, the driver's door and window. Connie has no arrest history, but with the help of her family we obtained her prints from personal items in her bedroom. The prints the County processed from her car are sufficient for comparison. As of today, she's listed as a missing person in the national and state computer systems."

"Have any of Connie's work associates been contacted?"

"She only worked part time in bars and restaurants around here, according to her mom," Small said.

Hitchcock nodded briefly. "She was unemployed when I saved her brother's life two years ago. Any friends?"

"Few. One of the county dicks told me that a girlfriend described Connie as having low self-esteem, gravitating to low-life characters, men who abuse her. She seemed to think she deserved it."

"Figures. She got hooked on heroin at one point, supplied by Tyrone Guyon."

Small leaned back in his chair and laced his fingers behind his head as he made eye contact with Hitchcock. "I know more about it now than you do."

"No doubt. Tell me."

Small lit a cigarette and exhaled the first drag upward in a long plume. "It's best if the family doesn't know about or see any of this."

Hitchcock gave a curt nod.

"From the pictures I've seen, she was *not* attractive. To compensate for her lack of desirability, Guyon made her pay for her dope by performing degrading sexual acts for his friends' entertainment."

"How do you know this?"

"The Seattle narcs had a snitch inside the group, who saw it all. I've pulled the worst photos. As a family friend, are you sure you want to see them?"

Hitchcock nodded. Small handed him another file.

The first photos shocked Hitchcock. They were of Connie, smiling with Guyon and Mae Driscoll, who was Guyon's madam and his moll at the old Hilltop Inn and the trailer Guyon used as a brothel at Eastgate Mobile Manor. Seeing them stunned Hitchcock. The other photos, the ones Guyon and Mae took of Connie so sickened him he had to set the folder down to keep from throwing up.

"According to a friend," Small explained, "Connie went into heroin withdrawal after you and Sherman killed Guyon and Driscoll. She hid it from her family until she could find another source."

"Who did she get it from?"

"We don't know."

"Did you find anything helpful in her room?"

"The county detective found a needle kit and traces of white powder."

Hitchcock lowered his head, grieving. "Connie was gone a lot two years ago. Her standard explanation to her mother was that she was job hunting."

"With Randy's history, how could he not know this about his sister?" Small asked, speculating.

"People usually don't tell everything, especially if it's shameful. With your permission, I'll find out what he knew."

"Go ahead, but remember, her car was found in the county, so even though she's our missing person, if she's found dead outside the city, the case is theirs."

† † †

HE PICKED RANDY up from work at Lake Hills Chevron and parked across the street at the Samena Club community swimming pool.

"Tell me about Connie and Guyon," he said.

Randy seemed surprised. "She got her smack from Guyon like I did," he answered with a shrug.

"How did she meet him?"

"Don't know—she introduced me to him."

"It appears she wasn't working, so how did she pay for her heroin?"

"I was too wasted to wonder about it. Guyon wanted her to be a hooker for him. We told you about that."

"You and your mother told me Connie didn't go for it. How did you know that?"

"Connie."

He showed Randy the first set of photos, withholding the graphic pictures. "The Seattle narcotics squad took these. They took them in the trailer and the rooms at the Hilltop where Guyon had women addicts turning tricks for him. Is it possible you knew about this and chose not to tell me?"

Randy began shaking his head. His hands trembled as he studied the photos in somber silence. "I didn't know about this. Connie's been lying to us the whole time. Looks like she went to church with us to hide what she was really doing," he said thickly.

"I remember she was gone almost every time I came over to see you. Didn't any of you ask her where she'd been?"

"It was always the same story: She was out working or looking for work."

"What about her friends?"

"The only one I know personally is a half-Indian chick named Monica. She came to church with us a couple times."

"Tell me about Monica."

"She's Indian but looks white. Dresses nice. Works at an office in Eastgate."

"What's her last name?

"Don't know."

"How many times have you seen her?"

Randy shrugged his shoulders again. "A dozen times over the past year, I guess."

"What does she drive?"

"Datsun 240Z. Root beer brown. Looks new but isn't."

"Where does she live?"

"An apartment near here somewhere."

† † †

HE FOLLOWED RANDY into his house. The worry lines on Barbara Fowler's face had deepened since he saw her two weeks ago.

"Any word on what's happened to my daughter, Roger?"

"They've entered Connie as a missing person into the national crime information center, NCIC, it's called, and the state system. We'll need her dental and medical records to add to the file."

She went back to her stove. "I'll get the records tomorrow. Anything else?"

"Randy says you know this friend of Connie's named Monica. What can you tell me about her?"

"Monica's a nice young lady. She took a sisterly interest in Connie."

"Do you know her last name or where she works?"

"Dwyer. She's a secretary at some engineering firm in Bellevue."

"Randy said she lives in an apartment near here."

"The new complex next to Sammamish High School."

Barbara faced him, eyes pleading. "Please find my little girl, Roger." Her voice quavered. "The longer this goes, the more it looks like the worst has happened." Randy put his arms around her as she burst into tears.

HE CRUISED THE parking lots of the two new apartment complexes on the south side of Sammamish High School until he found a metallic brown Datsun 240Z like Randy described at The Pines apartments. He copied the plate number and left.

CHAPTER SIXTEEN
Dead or Hiding

A RECORDS CLERK called Hitchcock at his desk the next morning. "Call La Paloma at this number in ten minutes, Roger," she said.

Dolly answered on the second ring. "I'm not at work today," she said. "Our manager still hasn't returned, and the place is in chaos. No one knows who's in charge or who is authorized to write our paychecks."

"Vollmer hasn't returned?"

"It's been over a week. None of the people you arrested have come back."

"No one's reported Vollmer as a missing person to us."

Dolly scoffed. "Don't hold your breath," she said.

"Why do you say that?"

"Knowing this crowd, he's probably taking the long dirt nap."

"What about the two hookers who hung out in the lobby?"

"Lolita and Raquel? They're back, and busy. They're the only ones able to turn a buck there right now. Afternoons and evenings. Also, the same high school and college kids that bought heroin here are back, so I guess that means a new shipment and new dealers."

"Keep your eyes and ears open. I'm going to stir the pot a little."

He hung up and called Records.

"A felony charge of Drug Possession With Intent to Sell had been filed against Simon T. Vollmer in King County Superior Court," Patty said. "The judge issued a no-bail bench warrant for his arrest when he didn't appear for the pretrial hearing last week."

Dolly is right. Vollmer is missing, but no one has reported it. He's either dead or in hiding. Even if he's alive he won't be back if it means jail time.

HIS WATCH READ 10:30. "Got a meeting with the manager at the Bellevue Ice Plaza about cash handling and security, then a lunch meeting with the Frederick & Nelson manager, assistant manager and their security director," he told Sergeant Windham.

On his way there, he stopped by the El Escondite Inn. The lobby was empty except for the same beautiful cold fish who was working the front desk when he was there last time. He put on his best dumb-cop act. "Howdy, miss. Could I see Mr. Vollmer, please?"

"He's not here," she said, her voice cold, ignoring him as she busied herself with the guest register.

Of course, Hitchcock knew that. Vollmer was taking the long dirt nap somewhere.

CHAPTER SEVENTEEN
Cracking the Great Wall

"MONICA DWYER'S BEEN renting Apartment 131 for the past year," The Pines apartment manager said as he handed Hitchcock her application. "She listed her employer as Cascade Engineers in Bellevue, and the emergency phone number of her mother in Kelso, Washington."

The engineering firm was in a new glass and steel office building across the freeway from The Great Wall. He found her 240Z parked in the back. He set up surveillance on it at 4:30 p.m.

A woman matching Randy's description of Monica came out, headed for the Datsun. Between twenty-five and thirty, plain features and a straight up-and-down boyish build. Her mahogany brown hair, meticulously done in a bouffant style, set off her fair complexion and eyes set in high cheekbones. A silky off-white blouse, pearl necklace, and a rust brown skirt coordinated with her hair color. Only her red high heel shoes didn't fit with the rest of her outfit.

A stocky white male in his twenties, military

haircut, gray tweedy sport coat and khaki pants got out of a car next to hers as she fumbled in her purse for her car keys. *Cop,* Hitchcock figured as he focused his binoculars on the meeting.

The young man flashed a brass sheriff's star. Monica's demeanor was calm as she and the county detective talked for about three minutes. She left in the brown 240Z after he handed her a business card.

Hitchcock followed her across the freeway overpass, expecting her to head to her apartment. Instead, she parked in front of the Great Wall and went inside. He set up surveillance from the bank parking lot a block away.

Monica emerged from The Great Wall forty-five minutes later with another woman of the same age, a friend or co-worker, by all appearances. After he followed Monica to her apartment, he called Dolly.

† † †

AT 5:04 P.M. the next day, Hitchcock tailed Monica Dwyer from work. The same friend followed Monica to the Great Wall in a light blue Ford Falcon that had seen better times. He called Dolly from a pay phone. Minutes later she met him in the bank parking lot. Despite the twenty-plus age difference and her hair in a ponytail, lack of makeup, loose sweater and black polyester pants, Dolly had more man-appeal than Monica and her friend combined.

She smiled. "Reporting for duty with my grandkids, like you said. What's up?"

He handed her a twenty. "Here's for a Chinese dinner at The Great Wall for you and your grandkids, on the Department." He described Monica and her friend. "See if you can connect with them. The dark-haired one is either a possible witness or a suspect in a missing person case."

"I'll try, but why bring my little ones?"

"No one will suspect a woman with children."

Dolly and her grandchildren entered The Great Wall. Twenty minutes later, he saw a Patrol cruiser entered the back lot of The Great Wall from the west end, out of Hitchcock's view. When it left twenty-two minutes later, he noted the time and patrol car number.

Dolly came out of The Great Wall a half-hour later, carrying a sleeping infant. Monica followed, holding hands with Dolly's grandson. Monica's friend carried a sleeping little girl to Dolly's car. Hitchcock chuckled and shook his head when he saw the three women hugging each other before they left.

He waited an hour before he called. "I didn't expect you to do *that* well," he said when she answered.

"I didn't either, to be honest," she laughed. "I was nervous about bringing the kids into it, but your idea worked. They fawned all over them, and the talk flowed from there."

"What talk?"

"Monica is from Kelso and Longview, near Portland. She moved here after a divorce. No kids. Drinks vodka. Says she's three-quarters Indian. She doesn't look it. I didn't ask what tribe."

"Anything else?"

"The owner of that place, a slinky Chinese woman with a strong accent visited her at our table. They seem to be friends. Monica said she goes there after work two or three times a week."

"That's good to know. What else?"

"A few minutes after I got there, a man came in through the back. Young guy, lean, blond hair. He came up to where the owner was talking to us. She led him to the back. She must have an office there. In a few minutes she came back to our table. I didn't see him again."

"What's your impression of this?"

"He's a hard type, has an evil air about him, but the China woman controls and uses him. Whatever the purpose of his visit was, it was quickly done. Her name is Juju, by the way."

"Anything else happen?"

"A young cop came in, a stocky kid. Juju left us and took him to the back too. She was with him for almost a half-hour. They've got a relationship going."

"How do you know?"

Dolly's laugh was spontaneous. "Are you really asking *me* that?"

Hitchcock laughed with her at his dumb question. "Great job, Dolly. I'll give you another twenty this afternoon so you can treat the kids to dinner there again tonight."

"*Treat* is the wrong word."

"It's that bad?"

"The only thing the kids will eat there is what I call

'slop suey.'"

He laughed. "It's for a good cause."

"What if Monica doesn't show up?"

"Even better. By just going there two or three times a week, your cover as a regular will become established."

"I deserve a raise for this," she said, laughter in her voice.

† † †

AFTER THE BOYS were asleep, Hitchcock sat in his leather chair, staring at the fire. He stroked Jamie's head when the dog plopped on the floor next to him.

Allie joined him. "What's troubling you, honey?" she asked when he didn't turn toward her.

He let the silence stretch before he said, "Connie is still missing. This friend of hers, Monica, is a red flag. She's too different from Connie or any of Connie's crowd."

Allie smoothed her skirt on her lap with her hands. "How so?"

"Connie is homely, a high school dropout, overweight, unemployed, bad teeth, dresses poorly. Monica is nice looking but not *good* looking. Trim, well groomed, dresses nice, has a job and apparently an education. Nothing in common with Connie."

"Well," Allie began, "maybe this Monica is a compassionate type who needs to be mothering or saving somebody."

"That doesn't fit with what I learned today. She's

from Kelso and Longview, rough towns across the river from Portland. I've only seen her from my binoculars at a distance. If she's a doper, she hides it well."

"Maybe she came up here to start over. People do that all the time."

"I haven't told you the worst of it," Hitchcock said.

"Tell me."

"She's friends with Juju, the owner of the Great Wall."

"Uh-oh."

† † †

MIKE SMITH'S MUGSHOT arrived the next afternoon. Hitchcock phoned Dolly. "It's best that we aren't seen together," he said. "Phone contact only for now."

"Why?" she asked.

He sensed her nervousness. "Keeping several steps ahead of Juju."

"Is she having me followed?"

"No, and I don't know that she will. But she does have people who will spy for her. I'll understand if you want to quit now, but first tell me what's happened since we spoke last."

"I met Monica at The Great Wall Friday after work. Her friend Suzette wasn't with her. I got a sitter so I could go with her into the lounge."

"And...?"

"She said the police questioned her twice about a friend of hers who disappeared. She told them she didn't know anything."

"What did she tell you about her friend?"

"She said her friend *was* a heroin addict but got off it cold turkey after the police killed the two people who were her source."

"What did you say?"

"I kept it simple. I told her again my whole adult life was being a mom, a widow and a grandma. Pretty drab compared to her and her friends."

"Did Monica tell you when this happened?"

"About a year ago."

"Go to the phone booth outside the Eastgate Denny's. Pretend to be making a call as you look at the mugshot inside an envelope I'll leave there. If you recognize the guy, tell me. If you don't, memorize the face. Leave it there when you go. I'll call you later."

"Ten minutes," Dolly replied.

He waited in the phone booth until Dolly's car appeared at the traffic signal a block away. He moved to the Denny's entrance a few yards away when she arrived. He watched her pick up the phone and look inside the envelope as she pretended to dial. She looked at the mugshot for less than five seconds, then left.

He retrieved the envelope and called her at home.

"Well?" he asked.

"That guy or his twin brother was at The Great Wall Friday night, 'cept his hair is shorter now," she said.

"How sure are you?"

"Like I said, it's either him or his twin. Who is he?"

"It's better if you don't know. He's wanted by us

for several things."

"Felonies?"

"Yes."

"Well, that fits. Like I said, he has a deadly look about him, like a Doberman on alert, the way he walked into the bar. He's got business ties to Juju."

Hitchcock was fuming as he hung up. By a quirk of fate Smith entered The Great Wall from the other side of the building, out of his line of sight, and left the same way, unaware that Hitchcock was right around the corner in an unmarked car. Smith had slipped through his fingers again.

CHAPTER EIGHTEEN
The Stranger

11:45 A.M.

IT WAS RAINING. A middle-aged man sat in a tan early '60s Ford pickup down the street from Hitchcock's home. To avoid being noticed, he didn't turn his wipers on. He patiently peered through the rain on his windshield at Allie loading her sons into a gray Jeep Wagoneer.

He followed her to the Pancake Corral. It puzzled him when she circled around the back, stopped for a moment behind the three employees' cars there, then parked in the front lot.

Only after Allie and her two boys were seated inside by the front window did the stranger enter, walking casually past them, cheerfully greeting the waitress as he seated himself two booths away, facing Allie. He ordered pancakes and coffee. Pretending to read the newspaper, he studied her and the kids. *Too bad the young stud she's married to isn't here, this place would be as good as any to complete my mission.* Still, Allie's trip behind the restaurant hinted there was something he should know about.

He listened as the waitress approached Allie's table. "Nice to see you again, Allie. It was a treat to see your lovely home," the waitress said.

"Good to see you too, June. I hope you liked our singing."

"I loved it! You should take your act on one of those TV talent shows."

The stranger watched Allie race through the front door in time to see June leaving in the oxidized red Chev Impala. He saw her write on a notepad, then return inside to her kids. He held up the newspaper, pretending to read it.

He followed her home, then left.

CHAPTER NINETEEN
The Setup

Tuesday Morning
Crime Prevention Office

HITCHCOCK'S SUPERVISOR CALLED him into his office. "I know you believe in making a positive impact on kids before they become teenagers. With your name in the paper so often you'd be perfect to visit elementary schools in uniform, driving a marked patrol car."

"I'd like that. What would I talk about?"

"We have pre-written scripts to choose from. Topics are general safety, why the law is important, and so forth. Pick one to review before you go. Plus, throw in a couple war stories, like that high-speed chase you were on that ended with catching a murderer, but tone it down by saying he was crazy and was out to hurt people, so you had to catch him."

"When do I start?"

"Day after tomorrow. One o'clock. Somerset Elementary will be your first one, then Enatai and Ashwood on Friday."

"I'll be ready."

† † †

AT NOON, LIEUTENANT Bostwick did his conquering general strut into The Great Wall, the brass on his uniform gleaming, trying to look aloof and powerful in his uniform and dark sunglasses.

Juju took him to her back office. She stopped him in the middle of his advances. "I need favor, Rowlie-sahn."

"Name it, my love."

"This big favor, Rowlie."

"What—marry you? Yes, yes, of course yes!" he chortled.

Juju put her hand on his chest as she shook her head. "You have heroin in evidence room, much heroin. Cocaine and Ecstasy too."

He stepped back in surprise, eyes blinking, mouth gaping. "How do you know?"

"Never mind. I know. It come from Mexicans at El Escondite. Heetch-cock, he do it. You get for me."

He trembled as if a blast of cold air hit him. He couldn't believe her request—yet it wasn't a request, she was *ordering* him. How did she know of the drugs in evidence? Then the realization hit—she could only know if she had other sources inside the Department. The idea of that terrified him. It meant she knew the truth about him, that she knew all about his lies about himself. And Hitchcock again?

After a long pause, he said, "It would get me fired, my love. And put in jail. If you need money, I—"

She stopped him by pushing his chest with both palms of her hands. "You, your parents no have enough money for this. They not rich enough—I find out. *You*

109

have *power*, you *lootenahnt*. You *must*, Rowlie-sahn. Go think about it." Juju led Bostwick to the door instead of feeding and fawning over him. He left, oblivious to the stares of lunch customers, walking the numb shuffle of the doomed.

† † †

Noon, Thursday

HITCHCOCK SUITED UP in his uniform. He checked the ammunition in the cylinder of his revolver and the ammo pouches. His twenty-four-inch black fiberglass baton in its ring on his left side and his eight-point billed hat felt like old friends. He grabbed the keys to the only marked patrol car available.

Lieutenant Bostwick stopped him in the parking lot as he was about to leave. "You can't take the shotgun to the school, Hitchcock."

It surprised him that Bostwick knew he was going to a school. "Why not?"

"It will scare the teachers and the students."

"We've always gone to the schools with the shotgun where it belongs. The kids find it exciting. Nobody is scared. By whose order?"

"Mine. Give me the shotgun."

"You're not connected with Crime Prevention or Patrol."

"I'm a lieutenant. You're just a patrolman. Give me the shotgun."

Hitchcock stepped out of his cruiser. He removed the twelve-gauge Remington 870 from its rack, opened the action and handed it to Bostwick.

Bostwick walked toward the station door when Hitchcock stopped him. "It's against Department regulations to carry it loaded into the station." He pointed to a sand pit next to the building. "You need to unload it there first, and keep the barrel pointed at the sand at all times."

Bostwick scowled as he fumbled with the weapon. When the slide went back accidentally, Bostwick's hands shook as he ran it forward, chambering a round. The safety was off.

Fearing an accidental discharge, Hitchcock took it from Bostwick's hands, jacked the live rounds out until it was empty and handed it back.

Bostwick wouldn't receive it.

"Now unload your revolver in front of me and your spare ammunition, so I know you'll be safe before you go," Bostwick said. "Then carry the shotgun into the station for me."

"Forget it," Hitchcock said as he pushed the shotgun into Bostwick's chest.

"You're on report for this, Hitchcock."

"So are you."

† † †

1:30 P.M.

HE LEFT SOMERSET Elementary school after a talk with the kids, showing them his equipment, his patrol car and keeping them enthralled with a couple war stories. It felt good to be in uniform and driving a marked patrol car again. He decided to visit the Newport Bay Marina on his way to the station. He didn't notice the older blue Dodge pickup with a camper mounted in the back that dropped in behind him as he left the school.

When he saw that the marina manager and his wife weren't in, he took a slow swing through the boatyard before returning to the station. It was a treat to savor the smell of the lake again and see the rustic setting of boats moored to the wooden docks, bobbing with the waves, and others above ground on davits, in various stages of repair.

The blue pickup with camper waited by the marina entrance, facing 118th Ave SE, a two-lane ribbon of asphalt, densely lined on both sides with trees and impenetrable brush. When Hitchcock's patrol car appeared from the marina, the pickup approached the stop sign ahead of Hitchcock, turned left onto the street and began weaving across the centerline.

Hitchcock accelerated.

CHAPTER TWENTY
The Stop

THE CAMPER FORCED an oncoming sedan to swerve onto the narrow dirt shoulder to avoid a head-on collision. Then another car behind the sedan blasted its horn in protest as it passed. Hitchcock activated his overhead light. The pickup kept going, swerving over the centerline twice more.

He grabbed his radio mic:

"This is Officer Hitchcock, I'm following a blue Dodge pickup with camper, erratic driver, possible DWI, northbound 118th Avenue Southeast at 2700 block. The license plate is covered. It is not stopping. Requesting backup."

The camper stopped abruptly in the northbound lane the second Hitchcock hit the siren. He got out of the cruiser and approached.

A dark-haired white male in his early twenties, a construction worker type, was alone in the cab. He stared through the driver's door window at Hitchcock.

"Roll your window down!"

The driver didn't move. Hitchcock knocked on the driver door window. "Roll your window down. I want to talk to you!"

The driver cranked the window down four inches and stared numbly at Hitchcock. "All the way down!" Hitchcock demanded. A strong odor of intoxicants hit when the driver rolled the window down.

"I stopped you for erratic driving. You crossed the centerline several times and almost caused a head-on accident back there."

The driver said nothing.

"Show me your driver's license."

The driver's eyes were half-shut as he shook his head and said nothing.

Hitchcock checked to see the driver's hands were in his lap, empty. He opened the driver's door.

"Step out."

"I ain't," the driver slurred, shaking his head woozily.

He reached inside, turned the ignition off and put the keys on the roof of the cab. "One more time. Step out."

"No way, man."

Hitchcock dragged the driver out by the front of his shirt and marched him to the open space between the back of the camper and the front of the patrol car. The short, stocky driver swayed on his feet.

"Stand with your feet together, arms out to your sides, and when I say left, tough the tip of your nose with your left hand."

"Ain't doin' no shtupid tests," he slurred, swaying slightly on his feet.

"You're under arrest for Driving While Intoxicated."

He fought Hitchcock's efforts to handcuff him. Hitchcock easily put him face down on the asphalt. As he knelt on the suspect's back and handcuffed him, he felt a tug at his belt on the right side. His right hand felt an empty holster. Then he felt cold steel pressing against the back of his head.

"Get the cuffs off or die," a young woman's voice behind him said.

"Okay," he said, "just take it easy." Hitchcock reached under his belt for the .38 derringer he used to carry for this very reason. But there seemed to be no need for it when he left Patrol for a plain clothes job. There was no shotgun in the patrol car—Bostwick had seen to that. He fumbled in his pocket for his keys and removed the handcuffs. He was still on his knees when the driver, no longer seeming intoxicated, got to his feet.

A woman driving a late model station wagon drove by slowly, headed in the other direction. She stopped, put her window down and smiled, "Oh look, kids, they're making a movie!" Two little kids in the back seat pressed their faces against the window, waving as they went by.

"What are you waiting for, Jeanette? Shoot the pig!" The driver urged.

The barrel of his gun was no longer pressed against the back of his head. He heard the hammer cock behind him. His mind saw Allie, holding baby Jedidiah and Trevor standing next to her when he closed his eyes, waiting for the bullet.

I love you, Allie. I love you, Allie, I love you…

The girl behind him began sobbing.

"Shoot! Shoot!" the driver screamed at her.

He felt the barrel of his gun pressing against his head again. *Click.*

No bang, just the click of a dry trigger pull.

A carload of teenagers drove by slowly, jeering. "Yeah, off the pig! Beg, you oinker!"

I love you, Allie. I love you, Allie.

"Shoot again, Jeanette! Kill the rotten bastard!" the driver urged the girl, his voice guttural.

"I'll do it!" The driver didn't sound at all drunk now. He grabbed the gun from the girl and faced Hitchcock, aiming at his face, feet away. "Beg for your life, you son of a bitch."

Still kneeling, Hitchcock put his hands down and spit on the driver. Hate darkened the driver's face. Hitchcock closed his eyes as the driver pulled the trigger.

Click.

The sounds of approaching sirens suddenly filled the air. Another man jumped out of the rear door of the camper. "Give me the gun," he yelled as he snatched the revolver from the driver.

Hitchcock opened his eyes. Pointing his own gun at him now was Mike Smith.

"Bye-bye, Hitchcock. See you in hell," he said as he aimed Hitchcock's gun at him and pulled the trigger twice. *Click-click.* Frustrated, Smith struck Hitchcock on the forehead with the gun, threw it down and drew a revolver from his shoulder holster. He aimed at Hitchcock's head and pulled the trigger several times. Nothing but clicks. Smith looked at his weapon with an expression of disbelief.

Wailing sirens grew closer. "Joey, we've gotta get outta here!" the girl shouted frantically. She hopped into the driver seat of the pickup. "No keys! Where are the keys, Joey?" she squealed.

Joey slammed his foot into Hitchcock's stomach. He hurried to the truck. "I don't have the keys! Where in the—"

Jeanette started slapping Joey's face, rapid-fire with both hands, screaming. "The cops are coming! I don't want to go to jail! Where are the keys?"

Joey punched her, then stopped as he remembered Hitchcock had taken the keys. Hitchcock remained on the ground, holding his stomach when Joey went to him.

"Give me the keys!"

"No," Hitchcock grunted, still holding his stomach with both hands.

Joey aimed another kick at Hitchcock, but Hitchcock caught his foot at the heel and jerked up. Joey fell, the back of his head slammed the asphalt. Hitchcock seized his collar and jerked him to his feet. Joey threw a punch. Hitchcock blocked it and landed a blow to the right side of Joey's head. Joey's knees buckled. Hitchcock held him by his collar with one hand while pummeling Joey's face and head with his fist until he crumpled under the blows as Jeannette collapsed, blubbering incoherently.

Police sirens were closing fast. Mike Smith made a desperate dash straight into the brush. Hitchcock turned to the sounds of breaking branches, loud at first, then fading as he mustered the strength to keep his grip on Joey.

Two patrol units screeched to a halt behind Hitchcock's cruiser. Hitchcock was bent over, bleeding from his forehead, vomiting, still holding Joey, limp and bleeding from his head, mouth and nose, by the collar with one hand. In the driver's seat of the pickup, Jeanette's hands gripped the steering wheel as she sobbed hysterically, snot and tears running down her face.

The first officer to arrive handcuffed Joey, patted him down for weapons and put him in his patrol car. The second officer picked up Hitchcock's revolver lying in the dirt and gravel shoulder.

Jeanette collapsed as the second patrol officer took her into custody. "Please forgive me! I'm sorry I tried to kill you!" she begged Hitchcock as she was led away in handcuffs.

The on-duty patrol sergeant arrived. "I'm taking you to the hospital," he said as he saw blood running from Hitchcock's forehead.

"I want to see something first," Hitchcock said, his heart pounding, lungs winded from fighting. He walked up to the truck cab. "The driver was alone in the cab when I pulled him over. I forced him out and to the back of the truck for field sobriety tests. We fought there, right at the door of the camper. The girl didn't come out of the camper. Mike Smith did, but that was later."

The sergeant peeked inside the truck cab. "Ah–the rear window slides open. The camper is flush against it and is sealed with a rubber boot. The girl crawled from the camper through the window to the cab and out the passenger door to come up behind you."

Hitchcock stared at the sliding rear window of the truck, still not grasping what had happened.

"Where did Mike Smith go?" The sergeant asked.

"He split into those woods when he heard your sirens."

"It would take a K-9 unit to track him in brush like that."

Hitchcock scoffed as he wiped blood from his forehead with his bare hand and looked at it. "Which, of course, the turd-birds on the third floor won't allow us to have either."

† † †

HIS FOREHEAD STUNG from the nine stitches he received at the emergency room. The sergeant brought him to the station. A clerk handed him a note to call his wife when he entered the detective office.

Allie answered on the first ring. "Honey, where are you? Are you all right?"

He was surprised that she knew already. "Did someone at the station call you?"

"No, no one did. But about two hours ago I felt a knowing that your life was in great danger, and I was to pray for you. That's what I did. What happened?"

Hitchcock couldn't speak, he was so stunned.

"Roger?"

Strange emotions welled up within him. He cleared his throat. "I've been in a little trouble today but I'm fine. I'll be home in about two hours. Don't worry."

DETECTIVE SERGEANT JURGENS approached, with Hitchcock's service revolver in his hand. "The female suspect is spilling her guts about everything," he said. "She says it freaked her out when she and Joe Darby, the driver, and Mike Smith all tried to shoot you with your own gun, but it didn't go off. The ammo looks fine. No firing pin marks on the primers in the cartridges."

"Not only that, but Smith also tried to shoot me with *his* gun, and it wouldn't fire either," Hitchcock said, bewildered.

"I'll see to it that you get the rest of the week off. Do you have the energy to test your ammo with me before you go home?

"Sure."

† † †

The Issaquah Sportsmen's Club

JURGENS PULLED THE trigger of Hitchcock's service weapon at a paper target fifteen feet away. He stared at Hitchcock when the first round went off. The second and third rounds also fired.

"How do you explain this?" Jurgens asked.

"Let me," Hitchcock said as he took his gun in hand. He felt a strange sense of awe when the next round also fired.

Sergeant Jurgens shook his head in dismay. "This is going to be a hard sell to the prosecutors."

"How so?"

"Your ammo wouldn't fire when your gun was aimed at your head, but it did when we tested it. Explaining divine intervention is never easy, but this is the most dramatic example of it I've seen."

"What, then, Stan?"

"They'll ask, so I'm asking. Has anybody but you handled your ammo?"

"No. But, Bostwick tried to."

Jurgens's eyes narrowed as he listened to Hitchcock's account of Bostwick removing the Patrol car shotgun and demanding Hitchcock's revolver be unloaded.

"Let's get you home," he said.

"Stop at Bellevue Florist on Main Street on the way."

"That knock on your head must have been something. What for?"

"For flowers, Stan. Don't worry, they're not for you, the knock on my head wasn't *that* bad."

CHAPTER TWENTY-ONE
Unexplained

ALLIE BROKE INTO tears when she saw the bandage on her husband's face and the condition of his uniform when he limped toward her from the detective car holding a bouquet of red roses.

"I'm okay, and I'm home for the rest of the week," he said, as he kissed her. She held him tightly, as if he would slip away and never come back.

"I've got fresh coffee on if you want it."

What he really wanted was whiskey and sleep, but Allie needed to hear what happened. "Cream with honey this time, baby."

She led him by the hand to his deep leather chair when she saw he was weak on his feet. He rubbed his hands on the armrests. The chair felt different somehow, as if it was in another lifetime that he last sat in it.

She set his favorite mug on the side table next to him. "I made it the way you like it. Strong enough to float a badge." She sat on the couch, waiting, her hands folded in her lap while he took a first sip.

"So, baby, you say you began praying for me this afternoon?"

She nodded once, not moving a muscle otherwise.

"About two o'clock, I had an overpowering sense that your life was on the line. I stopped my housework, knelt at our bed and prayed nonstop for about an hour. Even when Jed woke up, I didn't stop until a release came."

He told her what happened, starting with the time he went to the station to pick up a patrol car as part of his presentation to the school, including the reactions of the two carloads of citizens who drove by as he was about to be executed.

Allie remained silent after he finished.

"So, what are your thoughts about the fact that no bullet, even from two different guns, could touch you?"

"I wouldn't be here now if you hadn't been praying for me."

"How do you think I knew to pray for you at that exact time?"

Almost too dismayed to answer, he replied, "Man Above—the only One with that kind of power."

Allie paused to let that sink in for almost a minute. "Have you thought about finding another line of work?" she asked in a quiet voice.

"Today I have."

"Good. I want you to decide if the risks are worth it. Especially consider the responses of the two carloads of citizens that passed by as you were about to be executed. One woman was so stupid and shallow she thought it was a movie being made. The spoiled punks in the next car encouraged them to kill you and were laughing. Ask yourself if those people are worth the risks you take to protect them."

He nodded. "It's a reality check, for sure."

"And it's obvious that Lieutenant Bostwick set you up. Have you thought about that?"

"It looks that way, but how could he know I'd take a detour to the Newport Marina after I left the school, instead of going straight back to the station?"

"Roger! How did Bostwick know you were going to speak at a school?"

After a pause, he said, "Yeah, I forgot about that."

"Are you sure they didn't follow you from the school?"

He paused again. "You know, they could have. I didn't see the truck until I left the marina, but they could have been behind me the whole time. Still, the why of it escapes me."

"Didn't you tell me that Bostwick was demoted and banished to the new property room?"

"He appealed his demotion to the Civil Service Commission after Captain Delstra left for three months to attend the FBI Academy. I'm told the witnesses against him didn't testify because they weren't notified, so he was restored to lieutenant, on a conditional one-year probation."

"Finish your coffee and get some sleep, honey."

"You'll tuck me in, won't you?" he asked with a sly grin.

She shook her head, smiling. "You men!"

CHAPTER TWENTY-TWO
The Fallout

DESIRE TO ROMANCE his wife evaporated the moment he settled in between the sheets. The room and the bed seemed unfamiliar. His mind flashed back again to his own gun, aimed at his face, Mike Smith at the other end of it. *What would I have seen if my gun did fire? What's really on the other side?* In seconds he fell into a deep, dreamless sleep.

He slept thirteen hours. The stitches in his forehead itched when he awoke. The house was empty. As he wolfed down a bowl of hot oatmeal, with milk and maple syrup, he thought about his dad.

At the cemetery an hour later, he passed a group of mourners gathered at nearby gravesite. A soft breeze carried the words of the preacher to him as he knelt in front of his father's headstone and gathered his thoughts.

"Three people tried to kill me with my own gun yesterday, Dad. By a miracle it wouldn't fire, nor would another gun that one of them had. We tested my revolver and the ammunition. Everything worked fine. God moved my wife to pray for me at the very instant they got the drop on me. I can't ignore this, Dad. What am I to make of it? What am I to do? My wife wants me to quit police work. I don't blame her for feeling that way, but I don't know what or if..."

He stopped mid-sentence, out of thoughts and words. Overcome with emotion, he touched the top of the headstone as if it were his father's shoulder, and went home.

† † †

MYRNA CAME BY the next afternoon. She slammed an unmarked manila envelope into his chest as she walked past him when he opened the door. "Hello to you too, Mom. What's this?" he asked, staring at the blank envelope in his hand.

"Your application to return to the University of Washington Medical School," she said flatly as she flung her coat onto the couch.

He looked at Allie, who shrugged, indicating she didn't know what his mother was up to.

Myrna shook her finger at Allie. "*You* don't know the extent to which my son has been playing Russian roulette with his life."

"I knew about Roger and Tom Sherman being ambushed last year, but—"

"You don't know even a fraction of it," his mother interrupted. "He was in Vietnam for more than two of the three years he was in the army. The first tour was risky enough, but the second year with the—"

"Stop, Mom. You don't know everything, and I

don't want you telling Allie or anyone else what you do know. I'm not asking, I'm telling you to stop."

His twin sisters, Jean and Joan, walked through the front door. Allie took over answering the phone and taking messages for him while he fielded his family's questions.

The phone rang nonstop the rest of the day. Among the callers was Steve Miller, reporter with *The Bellevue American*. Hitchcock wouldn't discuss what happened even with him.

NEWSPAPERS ON BOTH sides of the lake reported that the driver, Joseph Alan Darby, 21, was charged with First Degree Assault, Assaulting a Police Officer, Resisting Arrest, and Driving While Intoxicated. Jeanette Innis, 17, would be tried as an adult for First Degree Assault and Interfering with a Police Officer. A no-bail warrant was issued for Michael Smith, charging him with First Degree Assault and Assaulting a Police Officer.

CHAPTER TWENTY-THREE
The Reckoning

Saturday Morning
Neighborhood Church
Bellevue

PASTOR ED SCRATCH liked to keep his office door open when preparing his sermons on quiet Saturday mornings when the building was empty, so anyone could wander in, looking for help.

The sound of subtle knocking interrupted his thoughts. He smiled the second he glanced up at Hitchcock. "Roger, isn't it? The police officer? Allie's husband? You're a friend of the Fowler family too, aren't you?" he asked, his voice a clear, melodic baritone.

Hitchcock nodded.

"Come in, have a seat," he said, gesturing to a chair. "How can I help you?"

Hitchcock fidgeted as he sat in a mahogany chair with padded brown cloth seat, facing the older man. He rubbed his palms on his knees as he described the stop and what happened afterward in detail. "God prevented my gun from firing, even though it was loaded, same story with another gun they had. God saved my life; I need to know what He wants. That's why I'm here," he said.

The pastor's eyes widened as he listened to Hitchcock. "Was this about two in the afternoon, by any chance, two days ago?"

"Yes."

Scratch looked down, rubbing his forehead. "Wow. I was in a meeting when a sudden knowledge that a policeman was in danger of losing his life overwhelmed me. It was so urgent I left the meeting and began praying for the officer's safety. I kept praying until I felt the Lord give me a sense that the crisis was over. So, it was you."

Hitchcock stared disbelievingly at him. "Have you been talking to my wife?"

"No. Tell me if I'm wrong, Roger, but I get the sense that you've had a number of other close calls in which you should have been killed."

"I've always felt a sense of divine protection, but I never mentioned it to anyone. This tops everything else in my past that I somehow slipped through." He stopped, his eyes pleading. "This spiritual stuff, like you and my wife suddenly knowing when I'm in danger, is over my head. I'm out of my league."

"There's a mysterious answer to your question in the Bible."

"How's that?"

"A religious leader named Nicodemus visited Jesus at night. Because of his status, he was afraid to be seen consulting someone as controversial as Jesus was. Jesus told him he needed a second birth to understand things in unseen realms. He asked Jesus how a man could be born a second time. The Lord's answer to him is the answer to your question. He said, 'The wind blows wherever it pleases. You hear its sound, but you cannot tell where it comes from, or where it is going. So it is with everyone born of the Holy Spirit.'"

"That's a fancy non-answer, Pastor."

Scratch chuckled. "I said it would be mysterious. You see, God works in the physical realm *from* the spiritual realm, which mystifies us in the physical realm. We can't see the wind, but we see its effects on the things around us. Through the spirit realm, God has been protecting and guiding you. This time He protected you in a way you can't ignore. Now He demands your attention."

"That's the part I don't get."

"You have young sons, I'm told."

"Two, and another on the way."

"At their current maturity level, they don't comprehend things as adults, do they?"

"Of course not."

"And being their dad, you provide for their needs and do things for them even though you know they won't appreciate it until later, right?"

"Yes."

"As their dad, you know they will eventually understand what you've taught them as they mature."

"Correct."

"God is that way with us. He provides and does things for those He has a special interest in, even though their spiritual lives aren't mature yet."

"Now I get it," he said, leaning back in his chair.

"Everything the Lord does is for a reason. In your case, you want to know why."

"That's right."

"Notice that Jesus told Nicodemus he had to be born a second time, spiritually, to be able to know these things, to operate in the spirit realm. After your second birth, you begin a lifelong growth process. Want in?"

"What does it involve?"

"Repenting of your sins and asking the Son of God into your life."

"I've been a pretty good guy, I think, Pastor."

"Have you ever stolen anything or lied, even once?"

"Who hasn't?"

"Then you're a thief and a liar, like the rest of us."

Hitchcock frowned. "I guess so."

"Before Jesus came to earth, God had John the Baptist telling people to get ready for Him by repenting, which means deliberately turning away from your old self, your old attitudes to God's ways and values as found in the Bible. You're asking the Lord's forgiveness. Want in?"

He nodded without hesitation. "Show me what to do."

After Pastor Scratch led Hitchcock in prayer, he told him, "Now you have God in you. But did you know He is younger than we are?"

Hitchcock scoffed. "How can that be?"

"He doesn't age. God has all the characteristics of young men—always on the move, full of new ideas, creating new things, building His family, dispensing justice, waging war to rescue those who belong to Him. He's full of energy, never ages, never tires."

New realization spread across Hitchcock's face as Pastor Scratch continued. "Like us, God delights in mysteries. He uses them to keep us seeking Him and His ways. He's been watching over you for a long time. Because you have the Holy Spirit in you now, you are part of the Trinity, God's family. Jesus is not only your Lord, but He is also your Friend. When you pray, do it in His name."

Pastor Scratch stood from his chair and extended his hand to Hitchcock. "Welcome to the family, brother. You're one of us, now."

† † †

ALLIE WAS PREPARING lunch when he came home. He gave her and the boys a kiss, then took a coffee mug from the cupboard. He heard Jamie's tail thumping on the kitchen floor.

"Where have you been, honey?"

"Church."

She stopped making ham and cheese sandwiches, staring at him. "Church?"

He pulled up a chair at the kitchen table, grinning like a kid, wanting to toy with her a little bit. "That's what I said—church."

She pulled out a chair from the kitchen table and sat. "Talk to me, no games."

He struggled to keep from grinning. As he told her the details of his meeting with Pastor Scratch. "I went unannounced. What timing—he was alone in his office. I told him what happened. I spent almost two hours with him. He explained about in the Bible God doing supernatural things through and for His people. Told me the principles clearly, then he led me in prayer. I'm a Christian now, baby, like you."

Allie rushed into his arms, crying, pressing her swollen belly into him. "I knew this would happen. I knew it all along. God has a plan for you, or He wouldn't have spared you," she said through her tears. "How are you feeling now?"

He hugged her gently. "I have great peace."

"You should relax for the rest of the day, honey. You've been through a lot."

"I need to digest what happened today. I've been living on the wrong side, yet God protected and spared me all these years. It's all a bit much."

CHAPTER TWENTY-FOUR
Closing In

THE STATION FELT like home to Hitchcock when he walked in. It took him an hour to write his report of Lieutenant Bostwick removing the shotgun from the patrol car he would use to visit the school, the threats Bostwick made when he refused to unload his revolver, and his encounter with the three suspects in the camper truck.

He made a copy before he turned it in to Detective Meyn.

"You doing okay?" Meyn asked. "The Department will set you up to see a shrink if you want."

"Nah. All a shrink is, is some social science dude picking his nose and when you stop talking, he looks up and says 'Huh? What'd you say?'"

Meyn laughed. "Well, anyway, the driver, Joey Darby, was uncooperative and unrepentant. But the girl, Jeanette, talked like a magpie. She told us she and Joey recently began running heroin for Mike Smith. They live together out in the sticks past Issaquah, near I-90."

"Smith might have returned to the shacks at the old Preston Sawmill. Has anyone staked it out or at least checked?" Hitchcock asked.

"Don't know, but I doubt it."

"What else did the girl say?"

"She told me Joey and Smith picked her up after they'd been in Bellevue. She didn't know what they were doing there. They headed to the elementary school. She said Smith told her they were waiting there to ambush you."

"Did they tell her how they knew where I was going to be?"

Meyn shook his head. "She says they didn't tell her any details. She and Joey were in a bad way for a fix. I saw track marks on her arm."

"What else did Jeanette tell you?" Hitchcock asked, boiling, his voice sharp as cut glass.

"Smith's heroin supplier is someone in Eastgate. He keeps who it is a secret."

"It's the one I call the Dragon Lady," Hitchcock said, an angry light in his eyes. "The dope is flown into that little airport by the freeway at night. Pilots use the freeway lights to land after the airfield is closed. I've written this up many times, but nothing is ever done."

"Dragon Lady, eh? And her real name is…?"

"Juju Kwan."

"I've never seen anything about it, and I read all the FIR's and memos."

"Somebody's intercepting them, then. I've written a dozen memos if I've written one."

"Probably the same person who tipped off Andy Stanford that we were coming for him last year," Meyn guessed. "We still don't know who that was."

"Bostwick?"

"We've accounted for where he was and who was with him that day. We don't know who alerted Stanford, but the setup and the attack on you all points to Bostwick. He'll be facing an internal over that."

† † †

THE CRIME PREVENTION office was his next stop. His desk was the same as he left it, yet it seemed to belong to someone else now. Mike and Al, both former Marines, greeted him warmly. Sergeant Windham stepped out of his office. Hitchcock smiled at him. "Thanks, Ian, for giving me time off last week. I needed it."

Windham studied the stitches on Hitchcock's face. "You can have more time off if you want."

"Thanks, but no thanks—any more sitting around the house and Allie'll put me to work."

"Your stitches look like they're ready to come out," Windham said. "One of us can remove 'em for ya. We were Boy Scouts, except for Al, who flunked Cub Scouts. It'd save you a trip to the doctor's and having a pretty nurse work on you."

Mike and Al chuckled, but not Hitchcock. The good treatment he received from working with them and the knowledge he gained made him uncomfortable with what he was about to say. An awkward silence fell as he searched his mind for the right words.

"I love Crime Prevention," he began. "I came here for the decent hours and days off, but my eyes have been opened to all the good you guys do. But now is too early in my career for me to be here. I want to see Jack Breen about rejoining my old squad."

"You must not have heard," Sergeant Windham said.

"Heard what?"

"Jack was promoted to lieutenant yesterday. Otis is acting sergeant in his place. You can come back with us any time," Ian said as he stood. They shook hands.

ON HIS WAY back to the station, he saw a marked supervisor's car turn off the frontage road and enter the back lot of The Great Wall. He pulled over, waited, then idled in. Bostwick was parked at the back door. Hitchcock ditched his Wagoneer among the heavy equipment just in time to photograph Bostwick, in uniform, entering the kitchen's screen door.

Bostwick appeared in the doorway, fifteen minutes later, embracing and fondling the half-dressed Juju, her blouse unbuttoned, kissing and groping him. Hitchcock snapped pictures until his film was used up.

At home, as he put the roll of film in his gun safe, his eyes fell upon his old backup gun, the flat-sided, two-shot .38 derringer on the pistol shelf. *This isn't over— they've got too much at stake.* He reloaded the little two-shooter, shut the heavy steel door, and spun the dial.

CHAPTER TWENTY-FIVE
Return to Patrol

The Station
Wednesday, 7:30 P.M.

"WELCOME BACK," OTIS said without looking up from the papers on the podium as Hitchcock entered the squad room. "I knew you'd come in early to read up on Patrol bulletins, so here they are," he handed him a stack of papers.

"You'll be the roving unit. When I rotate other guys through it to broaden their experience, you'll be in Eastgate. It needs cleaning up."

"Where do I work tonight?"

"Roving."

"What about this new guy in Eastgate, McCabe?"

Otis didn't look at him as he opened another folder. "It needs cleaning up."

The members of his old squad welcomed him back as they filed in. Hitchcock smiled as he shook hands with a human fire hydrant, the short, powerfully built McCabe. "I hear you were first-string linebacker at Washington State. Welcome aboard," Hitchcock said, watching for his reaction.

McCabe barely cracked a cold grin and said nothing. His furtive eyes and dead fish handshake told Hitchcock where he needed to start.

He noticed McCabe watching to see which way he went from the station after shift briefing. He radioed Dispatch he was in service and headed west toward downtown instead of Eastgate.

Traffic was light and calls were few. He killed his headlights and flipped the console switch to shut down his brake lights as he stopped two houses from his home. Turning the radio volume down, he focused his binoculars on the rental house across the street from his own.

The same two cars were in the driveway. He already knew they were registered to a married couple in Seattle. Neither had a record. The drapes in the front window were closed during the day. Now they were wide open, lights out. He hadn't seen anyone there since it became occupied over a month ago, yet the cars in the driveway changed positions daily, indicating the people inside worked nights somewhere.

A flicker of movement in the big front window caught his eye. He saw a car approaching. Its headlights would illuminate the window in the next few seconds. He focused his binoculars on the window just in time to see a camera on a tripod, a video camera on another tripod next to it, and a mustached man wearing horn-rimmed glasses standing behind the tripods as the car passed the house.

He walked up to the front window and shined his

flashlight into it, catching the man inside by surprise. He knocked forcefully on the front door. "Police officer! Open up!" The man avoided eye contact with Hitchcock as he pulled the drapes together. He opened the door a moment later. Late thirties, medium height, slender, white dress shirt, no tie, dark slacks.

He seemed nervous. "Yes, officer? Have we caused alarm to anyone?" he asked brusquely.

"I happen to live nearby, and I want to know what you're photographing at night, and why."

A look of relief came over him. "Oh, of course. I'm sorry. My wife and I are freelance photographers. We're testing out our new night vision and infrared equipment for our story on the D.B. Cooper plane hijacking case. You must know about it."

"Of course, I do, but who are you?"

The man produced his driver license and a business card showing him as a professional photographer.

"How much longer will you be here, Mr. Donnigle?"

"Our lease is up next month."

"All right, thank you for your cooperation. It takes a load off my mind."

That the Donnigles were clear of warrants didn't completely satisfy Hitchcock. He contacted the primary westside unit off the air, asking him to keep an eye on his home and the people in the house across the street. At the station he switched to an unmarked detective car. An hour had passed since shift briefing. He headed to Eastgate.

† † †

DOLLY'S CAR WAS parked in front of The Great Wall. He cut his headlights as he idled around the building to the back where McCabe's patrol car was parked next to Juju's Cadillac. McCabe hadn't called out. Hitchcock nestled his car between a road grader and a bulldozer in the back lot, giving him a perfect view of the closed back door. He took photos of McCabe's cruiser next to Juju's Cadillac with infrared film and a time and date stamp. He glanced at his watch. 9:13 p.m.

At 9:28 p.m. the back door of The Great Wall opened, pouring a shaft of light into the parking lot. Hitchcock crept close enough to photograph McCabe and Juju, her blouse unbuttoned, kissing and passionately embracing McCabe in the doorway. She followed him out to his cruiser, leaning almost half her body into the driver's door window. McCabe left.

The radio crackled as McCabe came on the air: *"Three Zero Six, Radio, I've been away from my vehicle on a citizen assist. Checking for any calls."*

Dispatch replied: *"No calls holding, Three Zero Six."*

Hitchcock watched McCabe head east on the frontage road. Dolly's car was still parked in front.

He watched McCabe turn in at Charlie's Place and park between the tavern and Kane's Motel. *"Three Zero Six out on a bar check at Charlie's, Radio."*

Slipping around the back of Charlie's with his headlights off, Hitchcock watched McCabe walk to the motel manager's office. He photographed McCabe returning to his cruiser ten minutes later.

The radio crackled as the voice of McCabe came on the air: *"Three Zero Six is clear the bar check at Charlie's, Radio."*

He photographed McCabe entering the lobby of the El Escondite without calling out. A young female front desk clerk Hitchcock hadn't seen before seemed to know McCabe. They left the lobby together and returned eight minutes later.

McCabe and Walker were dispatched to a family beef call. Hitchcock called Dolly from a pay phone. She sounded sleepy.

"Anything of interest happen tonight?"

"Glad you called," she said. "Monica and I met for dinner at The Great Wall tonight. Juju joined us in the bar. She had a drink with us. Then this same young cop came in, and she disappeared with him."

"Disappeared?"

"Her office. Door shut."

"About what time was this?"

"Right after nine, I'd say. About a half hour later they came out. Juju's clothes were mussed up. The officer left."

"Then what happened?"

"She sat with us for a few minutes, then she said good-night. As the bar was closing, I left."

"What did Monica say after the cop left?"

"Monica commented that the young cop was good looking, and Juju said, 'he is useful.'"

A HALF-HOUR later, Hitchcock and Otis met car-to-car behind in the empty Valu-Mart parking lot. Otis listened intently as Hitchcock briefed him. "Let's hope your photos turn out okay," Otis said. "If they do, have Kilmer make extra sets for you, me, and our attorneys."

"Can Frank keep his mouth shut?"

"He was an officer here before he took the job as City Photographer."

"I don't have an attorney, Joel."

"We all may need one before this is over."

† † †

ACROSS THE STREET in the parking lot of a closed Chinese restaurant, off-duty Lieutenant Bostwick sat in his private vehicle, his police scanner mounted under the dash, listening to radio traffic, his binoculars focused on Hitchcock and Otis. He touched his service revolver on the seat next to him as he followed Hitchcock westbound, keeping three car lengths behind him. When he saw Hitchcock enter the station parking lot, Bostwick broke off and headed home.

CHAPTER TWENTY-SIX
The New Rahab

THE CASH UNDER Dolly Searles's pillow brought her mixed feelings when she awoke early Sunday morning. She felt good for a change about working on the side of justice. Unlike her earnings from her weekend clients, this income had no guilt attached to it the next morning, and Hitchcock had, so far, been true to his word.

Even so, given what she learned last week, she hoped it wasn't too late to get out. The way the hard-eyed Asian men who came to The Great Wall looked her over made her skin crawl. *They act like they know about my sideline. Certainly, Juju's checked me out. And Monica too,* she reasoned.

Her other worry was the burly young cop who also often came to see Juju. *A human Pit Bull, rabid over Juju. He hasn't paid attention to me so far, but has he seen me at Charlie's?* Her hand trembled as she called the station and left a message for Officer Hitchcock to call La Paloma.

SHE MET HITCHCOCK in the employee parking lot of Boehm's Candies in Issaquah two hours later. He greeted her kids as he got into the passenger seat of her oxidized light green '64 Chevy Nova station wagon, with threadbare tires and a cracked windshield. He looked at her, questioning.

"You've been up front with me, Roger. I'm doing the same with you now," she said as she looked around for anyone watching them. He held his silence.

"The money I get from you is very good."

"But?"

"I'm in a squeeze. You've been so effective at the El Escondite that they've cut my hours to stay in business. They're not renting rooms like they were, and the bar and the restaurant are still closed."

Hitchcock stared out the windshield, palms on his knees. "You mean *we* were so effective. Without you it wouldn't have happened."

"I'm in fear of losing my income, my home...and my life."

He turned toward her. "Explain."

"Although I never ask questions, I think Juju has found out about me."

"How so?"

"The Oriental men who come from Seattle always check me out and ignore Monica, who is quite a bit younger than me. They openly look me up and down with keen interest. They have strong foreign accents. If they know about me as a prostitute, I'm a marked woman. If they ever find out about me as your informant, I'm dead."

"But they don't stare at Monica?"

"Just me," she said in a frightened whisper. "I have

the impression these guys are into white slavery. I've heard stories of white American women who went or were taken to Asian countries who will never be free."

She gripped the steering wheel with both hands. "I'm scared and I want out, Roger," she sobbed. "I brought my grandkids with me into this as my cover. These people will kill them to get me to do what they want."

"I could write up something to get you and your grandkids into a federal witness protection program, but I'm afraid you might not qualify."

"Can't risk it," she scoffed, shaking her head. "My gut instincts tell me there's a trail of dead bodies behind Juju. There are at least two cops who see her, maybe more."

"How do you know this?"

"I see this young officer with Juju almost every time I'm there. They disappear into her office as soon as he arrives. He's just as friendly with the wrong employees at the El Escondite, where I work. Since he also goes to Charlie's Place as part of his job, he must have seen me there, and told Juju about me."

"Ah, makes sense. Do you know the cop's name?"

"I haven't found that out yet. Only the rank. The older one is a lieutenant."

"How do you know about them?"

"Employees talk."

"How many other cops?"

"Two at least. The officer and the lieutenant."

He allowed almost a minute to pass before he spoke

again. "You want out of being an informant for me, so that income will be gone. Your hours as a cleaning maid at the El Escondite, your only real job, have been slashed. You still must support yourself and three children. Where does that leave you?"

"Guess."

"I told you I won't look the other way."

"You won't have to. I'm not 'going public.' I never have. I'm returning only to my relationships as a mistress to a few of my late husband's friends. I've researched it and it's not against the law for them to help me with my bills. There's no set amount agreed upon. I don't solicit. It's a lot safer for me and my little ones than this, Roger. If my looks hold up, I can do that longer and more safely than I can informing on drug dealers."

She stared at him. "Get me out of this safely."

"Okay," he acquiesced, looking at her.

She handed him a manila envelope. "Here's information that should bring Juju down if you act on it. I wrote it instead of making a verbal report in case something happens to me. When you read this, you'll realize how in over my head I am. I included the license plate numbers and car descriptions of the Asian gangsters in case I disappear."

DOLLY'S ENVELOPE CONTAINED a five-page hand-written narrative with names, locations, license plate numbers and car descriptions. He let out a low whistle and phoned Otis as soon as he read everything.

After shift briefing the next night, they met car-to-car in the rear parking lot of the downtown National Bank of Commerce.

"I made you a copy," Hitchcock said as he handed an envelope to Otis, who scanned all five pages in seconds.

"Juju's expanding into cocaine and a new drug called Ecstasy in addition to heroin. It looks like she's out to eliminate her competition at the El Escondite, before they eliminate her."

Otis smiled.

"What?"

"I'm thinking of the look on Juju's face if she knew she's offering your snitch money to be her snitch on her competitors in drug trafficking, while she's been spying on Juju for you."

Hitchcock snickered. "It *is* funny, now that you mention it, but Juju's crowd, aided by McCabe, are closing in on my informant. I've got to get her out."

"What else is there to this?" Otis asked.

"Juju knows about her moonlighting at Charlie's Place. My informant not only senses Juju's capacity for murder, but she also *knows* Juju's reputation for murder."

"Somebody sold her out?"

"The common denominator is our own Gerry McCabe. He probably saw her with men at Charlie's on weekends and told Juju."

Otis bit off the end of a cigar, spit out the wad and lit it. "Juju wants a cut of what your informant makes–

and control of her."

Hitchcock nodded. "I'd say you're probably right."

"Now that you've got my head spinning, is there anything else I should know about, Roger?"

"The dicks told me they've never seen the FIRs and memos I've turned in about drug smuggling through the airport and Juju's role in it."

Otis frowned. "It's gotta be someone who works in the station. Someone with brass on his collar."

He told Otis about the infrared photos he took of McCabe with Juju embracing at the back door of The Great Wall.

"This is getting to be Federal, Joel. We're just frontline grunts on a po-dunk department with security leaks and weak leaders, facing a growing drug problem with no narc squad. If we turn this in through normal channels it'll disappear. If we go around the Department to the DEA, our heads will be on the chopping block."

Otis shook his head. "The Feds'll want your snitch," he said. "they'll say they just want to talk to her, then they'll pressure her to work for them and throw her away when they're done. That's their M.O."

"Not happening. She trusts only me."

"Find a way to protect her, Roger. I'll be thinking about how we handle this information. We'll meet here, same time tomorrow."

Dispatch began calling for the District Six car. No answer. Hitchcock stayed off the air as he put his unmarked cruiser in gear and headed east, looking for Officer Gerry McCabe.

CHAPTER TWENTY-SEVEN
A Lovers Triangle, and More

AGAIN, HITCHCOCK FOUND McCabe's cruiser next to Juju's El Dorado at the back door of The Great Wall. He parked among road graders and dump trucks stored in the dirt lot behind the restaurant. Light and voices poured through the screen door. He exited his vehicle, and crept, camera in hand, through heavy construction equipment until the aroma of rice, mysterious meats and exotic spices met his nostrils.

Another pair of headlights rounded the corner into the back lot. A dark-colored sedan parked near his position. A man wearing a police uniform got out. Lieutenant Bostwick stumbled as he crept through bulldozers and road graders in the moonless night, his shoes crunching gravel. He stopped less than eight feet from Hitchcock with only a bulldozer between them, not ten yards from the kitchen door of The Great Wall.

McCabe appeared in the doorway with Juju, blouse unbuttoned, bosom exposed, embracing, kissing him passionately and holding on to him as he tried to get to his cruiser. Bostwick was too close for Hitchcock to risk taking pictures of McCabe and Juju. The night air carried her laughter and lusty remarks. When McCabe left, Juju went inside, closing only the screen door. Bostwick stepped out from hiding. Hitchcock could see him shaking as he faced the screen door.

Seconds later he went in.

Hitchcock crept to the screen door to listen. He could almost taste the smells of Asian food. His ears filtered out employee chatter in Mandarin in time to hear Juju's voice.

"Rowlie-sahn! What you doing here?"

"Why, Juju?" Bostwick asked, his voice quavering with emotion.

"Why what?"

"You're getting dressed. Were you with another man?"

She hesitated. "Men I have."

"But does it have to be another officer?"

"Why not?"

"But–I–we were going to get–"

"You no deliver heroin from property room. You break promise."

"I-I'm not *there* now! I told you I need *time!*" Bostwick begged.

"No more talk. Deliver or else," her tone vicious.

"Or else what?" Bostwick asked, his tone fearful.

There was the sound of papers shuffling, followed by Bostwick gasping. "Juju, my love–this would ruin me. Let's work this out. *Please!*" He begged, his voice cracking.

"You no deliver all by Friday, everybody, po-leece,

city council, noos-paper, get this in mail," Juju said, her voice dripping with contempt.

A heavy silence followed.

"Okay then, I will," Bostwick said at last, his voice breaking.

"I own you, Rowlie. Remember that. You do as I say."

The scraping sounds of metal being dragged across concrete overrode the last of the conversation between Juju and Bostwick.

Hitchcock hid by squatting behind Juju's Cadillac as a kitchen helper dragged a metal trashcan to the dumpster. Bostwick walked past the worker, passing within feet of Hitchcock as he returned to his vehicle, defeat in his stoop-shouldered walk. He sat in the driver's seat, engine off, for several minutes. Unable to move without revealing himself, Hitchcock remained crouched where he was, hands on his aching knees.

Bostwick drove away.

Hitchcock rushed to his vehicle and followed him five miles to the new police property room at the north end of the city. He shut off his headlights as the property room came into view. He focused his binoculars on Bostwick as he exited his car, in the shadows seventy-five yards away, and walked up to the property room door. He stood, facing it.

Seconds later, Bostwick walked to the nearby dumpster and urinated on it. He returned to the property room door.

After another minute Bostwick walked to his city

car, revved the engine and screeched out of the parking lot. Hitchcock followed him to his parents' lakeside home in the ritzy Bellevue suburb of Hunts Point. *Bostwick knows the property room is alarmed, so his only chance to enter is to con his way in during business hours, or he maybe he just hasn't got the guts to steal the dope.*

In case Bostwick changed his mind and came back, Hitchcock returned to the property room and sealed the only door with evidence tape and photographed it. He radioed Otis for contact.

They met behind Crossroads Mall. "What do you suppose Juju has on Bostwick that he would consider stealing evidence for her with a street value of a million dollars?" Otis asked after he read Hitchcock's report.

"A million dollars?" Hitchcock echoed.

"That's the estimated street value of the dope we seized from the El Escondite," Otis replied.

"I had no idea. From what I heard and saw tonight, Bostwick's hopelessly in love with Juju who is blackmailing him into stealing those drugs from our property room."

"Blackmail for what?"

"Something sexual, knowing Juju."

"You sure the property room is secure?" Otis asked.

"I didn't know if it's alarmed, so I sealed the only door with evidence tape."

"It's alarmed," Otis said. "But Bostwick still has his key, and the alarm code hasn't been changed."

"Should we move the evidence to the station?"

"I don't have a key or know the alarm code, and I

don't think Bostwick has the guts to do what Juju wants," Otis replied.

CAPTAIN HOLLAND AND Sergeant Jurgens were in intense discussion with Otis in the Patrol Sergeant's office when Hitchcock came in at the end of shift. He was surprised to see them there so early. Otis stepped out and took him aside. "I only have a minute," he said. "The Feds weren't helpful when the dicks asked them for help on Juju's past."

"I bet they're hardly interested in this either," Hitchcock said.

"They're not. My cousin in the State Department called me at home last night. He's sending me information about Juju."

† † †

4:45 A.M.

HITCHCOCK KISSED ALLIE awake. "There will be calls for me," he told her, his voice sounding exhausted. "Unplug the phone until noon."

She sat up, looking at him. "What's going on?"

"Bad cop stuff."

"What? In Bellevue?"

He sat on the bed, removing his uniform. "Hard for even me to believe," he said.

"Who is it, honey?"

"Can't say, but the last name of one of them starts with a B."

"There's more than one?"

"Unless it's an emergency, make sure I'm not disturbed until noon. And don't answer the door unless you know who it is," he said as he slipped his service .38 under his pillow and slid between the sheets.

IT WAS ALMOST 2:00 p.m. when he awoke. Allie brought him a fresh cup of strong coffee with honey and creamer. "Any calls?" he asked.

"Haven't plugged the phone in yet. You were sleeping so soundly I didn't want to wake you."

"You—good woman," he grunted, sipping coffee.

"Me—Jane. You—Tarzan," she grunted back as they laughed and kissed.

"Now, honey, if you tell me not to answer the door unless I know who's there, then you sleep with your .38 under your pillow, shouldn't I know what's going on?"

"We're back to the high alert of a year ago, when we thought the two guys who attacked us would be back."

"I'm home all day with Trevor, who is very mobile now, and an infant who is crawling everywhere, and a third one on the way. I need to know what our risks are."

He exhaled sharply. "Of course," he said, "you'd best have a seat."

CHAPTER TWENTY-EIGHT
The Big Picture

The Following Night

AFTER OTIS READ the latest information bulletins and district assignments to the squad, he said, "One more thing before you hit the bricks: Lieutenant Rowland Bostwick resigned from the Department this morning, effective immediately."

A round of high-fives and cheering filled the room.

"That was a shock. What happened?" Hitchcock asked Otis when they met car-to-car behind the National Bank of Commerce downtown.

"Jurgens and Captain Holland told Bostwick he was the focus of an internal investigation. Before they told him what it was about, Bostwick went into the Chief's office with a signed letter of resignation and his uniforms, gun and equipment. He refused when they tried to talk to him. Told them they could talk to his attorney if they need to know anything."

"What do you think will happen next?"

"The dicks smell blood," Otis said, smirking.

"So, it isn't over," Hitchcock mused.

"Far from it. My cousin's information came in."

"And?"

"Juju is a fairly high-ranking member of the Bamboo Union, the largest and deadliest of the Chinese Triads. It's centered in Taiwan, where it was founded in the fifties by former Chinese Nationalist soldiers when Chiang Kai-shek fled the mainland after the commies took over. It's estimated they number between three to four thousand members. A couple years ago they started expanding into other countries, like the Western U.S., Canada, and Australia. Their businesses are fronts for drug trafficking, money laundering, human smuggling, and prostitution. More than the other Triads, Bamboo Union operatives infiltrate police agencies to protect their business interests. They deal ruthlessly with competitors."

"This is bigger than I thought, but it makes sense," Hitchcock said.

"Juju is a rare case because the Triads are a male-dominated outfit," Otis went on. "There's little reliable information about her because she was born in mainland China before the communist takeover, so her birth record, if there ever was one, was lost in the turmoil of revolution as were her parents and family members."

"So, she came to Taiwan as one of thousands of war orphans in the late forties or early fifties. It's starting to make sense now," Hitchcock said. "What else did your cousin tell you?"

"She grew up in a brothel, learned English from

American servicemen she met as a bar girl in Taipei. Government informers who know her say she is strongly anti-communist. In Taipei she was arrested on suspicion of murder twice but never convicted. She's believed to have ordered the deaths of several rivals."

"How was she able to come here?" Hitchcock asked.

"Despite the fact that there is no record of her birth, being married or having children, in '65 she was sponsored to come to the U.S. by a family of Taiwanese immigrants in Seattle after they became citizens. Ready for the odd twist?" Otis asked."

"Shoot."

"For all her rough background, Juju is self-educated. She has read widely in American law and history. She knows a great deal of our culture and politics."

Hitchcock was astounded. "Now that we know more about what we're up against, are you going to pass this on to the dicks?"

"Except for naming my source."

"What's next, then?"

"We wait, watch and plan for a major strike."

"Waiting will be hard for me, Joel."

"Timing is everything, little brother."

CHAPTER TWENTY-NINE
Walls Closing In

DETECTIVES MEYN AND Small knocked on the front door of the Bostwick residence in the upper crust bedroom community of Hunts Point. No one answered. They walked around to the back, impressed by the kidney-shaped swimming pool and the manicured lawn that sloped down to the edge of Lake Washington's ritzy Yarrow Bay and the private dock.

A woman's voice behind them—crisp, East Coast accent, with clipped vowels asked, "Who *are* you?"

They turned to face a tall, aristocratic-looking woman in her early sixties, silver hair, her face reddened and wrinkled like a winter apple. Her purple one-piece swimsuit exposed the puckered flesh of translucent white arms and legs streaked with roadmap-like blue veins.

Small smiled and extended his hand. "We're Bellevue Police detectives, ma'am. I'm Joe Small, and this is my partner, Larry Meyn. I assume you are Mrs. Bostwick."

Her aloof expression hardened. "Mrs. *Eleanor* Bostwick," she said, ignoring Small's hand.

"We'd like to talk to your son for a couple minutes, ma'am."

"I'm surprised you have the gall to come here after what you did to my son."

"With all due respect, Mrs. Bostwick, would you explain what you mean?" Meyn asked.

She scoffed in disgust. "After all the reforms Rowlie made at your pathetic little department, he was betrayed. He would have made a wonderful chief."

Meyn shot a quick, confused look at Small.

"What reforms are you referring to, ma'am?" Small asked.

"What do you want?" a man's voice behind them interrupted.

Meyn and Small were surprised when they turned around.

Bostwick was almost unrecognizable. His stomach bulged like a pregnant woman's against a light-yellow golf shirt. Thin, flabby arms dangled like limp cotton ropes from the sleeves, his white, spindly legs contrasted with blue linen tennis shorts. His eyes looked owl-like under his wire-rimmed granny glasses, and the pack of fat under his chin jiggled with every step as he scowled his way down the steps toward them.

"We're sorry to be meeting you under these circumstances, Rowlie, but we have a few questions to ask you," Meyn said, "privately."

"You're not speaking to *my son* without *me* present," Mother Bostwick said, spitting her words.

Bostwick folded his arms across his chest. He

glanced at his mother, then nodded his assent. But his mother stayed put, defiant.

Meyn shrugged as he gave Bostwick a cordial smile. "We'd like to ask you about your relationship with Juju Kwan, Rowlie."

Right away the color drained out of Bostwick's face and his mouth fell open. "Uh...who?" he asked after a delay of several seconds.

"The owner of The Great Wall restaurant and bar in Eastgate," Small said.

Bostwick cleared his throat and signaled with his eyes for the detectives to hold off until his mother was away. "Never heard of her," he said in a low voice, glancing in his mother's direction.

Meyn, in no mood to go along with taking cues from a traitor, said, "Are you saying you've never met her or been to The Great Wall?"

Bostwick shook his head and re-crossed his arms. "Never," he answered, winking at them as a way of asking them to play along.

"My son would *never* be involved with someone who isn't white, and of good breeding, Detective," Mom Bostwick interjected.

Bostwick looked pleadingly at Meyn, then at Small.

"Maybe these will jog your memory," Meyn said harshly as he handed Bostwick a stack of enlarged photographs that Hitchcock took of him embracing and fondling Juju at the back door of The Great Wall. "That's you—in uniform—and Juju, with little on, and that's what I call a lip-lock, Rowlie. Still say you don't know the woman?"

Bostwick tilted his head back and dropped his hands to his sides as if to say, "you got me."

"Let me see that!" Mother Bostwick snapped, snatching the photos from her son's hand before he could stop her. "Rowlie–that's YOU!" she screamed when she looked at the next one, and the one after that. "How-how *could* you–with that-that yellow trash! Wait until your father gets home!"

Bostwick hung his head like a shamed little boy.

"Our investigation of Juju Kwan reveals that she's a major organized crime figure, based in Taiwan, and we–" Mom Bostwick's sudden moaning interrupted Meyn.

Detective Small caught her before she collapsed and set her on a chaise lounge. "Take your filthy hands off me!" she shrieked.

Small stepped back. Mom Bostwick closed her eyes, extended her arm, palm down, and flipped her hand up and down from the wrist as she said, "Rowlie, get rid of these...whatever they are. I want them gone before I open my eyes."

"You didn't even advise me of my rights. I have an attorney and I don't have to talk to you. You heard my mother. Leave now."

Small discreetly handed Bostwick his business card. Bostwick nodded thanks as he accepted the card.

ELEANOR BOSTWICK TURNED to her son when she heard the detective car leave. "How *could* you get involved with a woman who isn't white, Rowlie?"

"I had to, Mom. I was undercover for the city, investigating corruption on the force. People at the top sold me out to protect themselves, Mom."

Eleanor digested this for a second. "Still, how could you even *touch* her?" She asked, shuddering.

Bostwick turned away so his mother couldn't see his lusty grin. *If you only knew, Mom.*

† † †

SMALL AND MEYN remained in the car after they arrived at the station. They had been silent since leaving Bostwick. "Why do you think Bostwick resigned so suddenly?" Meyn asked before he opened the door of the car.

"My best guess is he finally faced what he's done and jumped ship when he heard footsteps coming down the hall."

"The footsteps are ours" Meyn said, "the FBI lab report came in yesterday. The latent print on the note that had directions to Hitchcock's address on it matches Bostwick's left thumb. There wasn't quite enough to reach the twelve-point threshold for court admissibility, but it was him."

"That's damning as hell," Small said. "And the handwriting analysis?"

Meyn nodded and scowled. "Pretty much the same story. A hair short of an arrest and charges but it's him."

"More icing on the cake."

"For the good of the Department, we gotta take him down," Meyn said.

A contemplative silence fell between the two sleuths.

"Did you catch what he said before we left?" Small finally asked.

"As bad as Bostwick was and is, I couldn't believe it when he said it."

Small pursed his lips, staring out the windshield. "Something bigger than what we know now has happened. He resigned at once and invoked his rights when we came to him."

Meyn bobbed his head. "He wants to get the guilt he's carrying off his chest. I think Rowlie's tired and wants to be caught."

"You're damn good at playing 'bad cop,' Larry."

"Thanks. You make a decent 'good cop' yourself. I know it doesn't come natural for you."

Small chuckled and grinned as he said, "We'll get Rowlie-boy next time."

CHAPTER THIRTY
The Highwaymen

Bellevue Airfield
Wednesday, 3:47 A.M.

THE AIR WAS dry and cold, and the stars were out. Juju's mules, both ex-military special forces men, waited in the shadows of a hangar, lights out, motor off in the black Mustang Mach I Fastback. The cold penetrated their hands and feet. They shivered and rubbed their hands on their thighs to keep warm.

Tiny red and green lights appeared in the blackness above them.

The driver flashed his headlights twice as the lights above came closer. The same V-tail, low-wing Beechcraft M35 Bonanza dropped onto the runway.

The same pilot and passenger as before met the men from the Mustang on the tarmac. A random sample of white powder in the aluminum briefcase passed the chemical test, the money in the briefcase from the Mustang was counted, and the plane returned to the night sky while the Mustang sped east on I-90, headed for the Newport Way exit.

A beat up, older, red, Dodge one-ton Power Wagon pickup waited on the shoulder of the Newport Way off-ramp, lights out, motor rumbling. With split-second timing, it swung into the Mustang as it passed by. Sparks flew and the screech of metal tearing metal sounded as the left corner of the quarter-inch thick steel plate front bumper sideswiped the entire right side of the Mustang.

The impact forced the Mustang into the ditch on the left side of the off-ramp. The driver of the Mustang gunned the engine, accelerating out of the ditch, back onto the ramp pavement. From out of nowhere a white '68 Dodge Charger roared up along the driver's side of the Mustang. The Mustang accelerated through the stop sign at the bottom of the off-ramp. The passenger in the Mustang turned in his seat, aimed a sub-compact Uzi 9mm submachine gun at the Charger.

The Charger dropped back a few feet and veered right, clipping the left rear quarter panel of the Mustang, forcing it to spin to the right, off the Newport Way frontage road. It crashed head-on to a dirt bank at over forty miles per hour.

The Mustang's front end was crushed, the engine dead, the radiator hissing steam the only sound.

The drivers of the pickup and the Charger wore black ski masks as they ran up on either side of the Mustang, revolvers at the ready. The passenger was slumped against the door, unconscious, bleeding from his forehead, nose and mouth, an Uzi submachine gun laid on his lap. The driver sat helpless in his seat, dazed, slowly touching his face with his right hand.

The driver of the pickup took the Uzi and the aluminum briefcase from the passenger in the Mustang. The driver of the Charger patted down the driver of the Mustang, finding another subcompact Uzi in a shoulder holster. He took it.

The masked men scrambled to their vehicles when they saw eastbound headlights in the distance, heading for them. They turned around and sped back to the onramp and went east on the freeway at the posted speed limit, passing the Issaquah exits until their taillights disappeared.

CHAPTER THIRTY-ONE
Panic

The Great Wall
Six Hours Later

JUJU'S FACE WAS drawn and ashen as she faced her employees in the dining area. She hadn't slept all night. The men she sent to search for the two she called "my army boys" found them as they were being lifted from the wrecked Mustang into an ambulance with a state trooper at the scene.

"We will open at the usual time today. I will be busy in my office all morning. I am not to be disturbed for any reason," she told them in Mandarin. Butterflies fluttered in her stomach and her mouth was dry as she shut her office door and dialed the long-distance operator.

It would be one in the morning in Taiwan, but Juju knew the cost of delaying or not reporting the heist would be signing her own death warrant. She also knew Mr. Chen was old school. At a minimum he would want the driver and the passenger tortured until one talked, then both executed, like others who failed an important mission.

A woman's voice answered on the third ring. Juju

identified herself in Mandarin and asked for Mr. Chen Chi-Li. A full minute later a man's soothing g voice she recognized as that of Mr. Chen answered.

"I am sorry to disturb you, but I have urgent, bad news to report." She told Chen everything she knew about last night's heist of a drug shipment having a street value of over a million dollars.

"Do you know who ordered the attack and how they knew about our shipment?" Chen asked.

"It can only be the Mexicans who took over the hotel next to where the plane lands at night," she replied, "because the police arrested many of them, seized their heroin and shut down almost all of their business operation. They are so desperate that they did this to me to make up for their losses."

"Could the two who picked up our shipment from the plane be involved?" Chen asked.

"I do not think so, Mr. Chen. They were almost killed in the wreck and their car was destroyed."

"They are a threat to us, Miss Kwan."

"They are real soldiers. For now, I trust them. It is clear the Mexicans did this. To recover our loss, I ordered one of my police officials to steal the Mexican heroin from police station for me. He refused at first but agreed when I showed him pictures I have of him with a young girl."

She waited in silence. Chen had the next move. "Make sure the police official understands what we have and what will happen if he doesn't deliver," he said. "Give him only so much time to do as you say, then act if he fails to obey you."

"Of course, Mr. Chen."

"What will you do to recover this financial deficit if you don't get the drugs from police station? Someone inside your group is giving information. How will you find out who it is?"

"If the official fails, I will deal with him, of course. Then I have another plan to recover our losses, Mr. Chen. I have the support of our people in Seattle. I have police protection now, and there is an American, a white woman I know who will help me diversify."

"I give you one month. No more."

Juju trembled when the call ended. She knew what was behind Chen's questions and the changed tone in his voice. She had seen what happened to operatives, even high-ranking ones, who failed in their mission or betrayed Mr. Chen. They would take her back to Taiwan by force. The outcome she didn't want to think about.

She picked up her phone and dialed another number.

CHAPTER THIRTY-TWO
The Marked Woman

A MISTING RAIN drizzled its way to the ground as Hitchcock met Dolly in the gravel parking lot behind Boehm's Candies in Issaquah. Her black ski parka, dark glasses, and blonde hair in a ponytail, reminded Hitchcock of movie stars and fashion models who don't want to be recognized by photographers when out in public. The grim set of her jaw told of gnawing fear and sleepless nights as she opened the passenger door of his Wagoneer.

"You rang?" he asked playfully in a deep voice when she sat beside him.

She was in no mood for humor. Her words burst over him like a breaking dam as she slammed the door shut. "I'm targeted! I need you to keep your word and get me out of this before I get killed!"

"What's going on?"

"You haven't heard?"

He shook his head.

Her shrill voice filled the Wagoneer's compartment as she said, "You haven't heard. Great! Three nights ago, two guys pulled a heist on a big load of heroin and some new drug called Ecstasy as it was on its way to Juju's house. Why don't you know about it? You're the police!"

"My crystal ball is in the shop."

"Stop it," she snapped.

"How do you know about this heist?"

"Juju."

He stared at her. She fidgeted; anxiety was tying her into knots.

"Explain."

"I saw her at her restaurant yesterday after work. She wanted to see me privately."

"Wasn't it our understanding you would be staying away from her until I figured out a way to extricate you from all this?" he chastened, visibly irritated.

"Yes, it was," she replied, her voice wistful.

"So how did Juju reach you?"

"Monica."

"Your mutual friend Monica. Monica Dwyer."

"Right. Monica sat next to me when Juju told me about the heist and described what was stolen."

"How did Monica get you to see Juju with her?"

"She came by my house unannounced. Said Juju was in trouble and wanted my help. She said she didn't know what Juju's problem was, only that it was very important."

"Ah, so Monica already knew about the heist," Hitchcock said in a tone of triumph. "That should tell you something about her."

Dolly's hands fumbled in her lap. "You better

believe it does. She's in on it and I'm mad at myself for not seeing it."

"What does Juju want you to do?"

"Juju knows all about the drugs you guys seized at the El Escondite. I don't know how she knows, but she does. She told me it was heroin, and something called Ecstasy. She knew how much was seized, and the street value. Over a million dollars, she says."

The thought of Juju sharing information on this level with Dolly alarmed Hitchcock. It meant they've marked her. "Go on."

"Juju thinks the El Escondite people hijacked her shipment to make up for their losses," Dolly said.

"You didn't say what Juju wants from you."

"You're gonna laugh," Dolly snorted. "Juju asked me again to spy on the people who own and run the El Escondite."

Hitchcock chuckled as he shook his head. "Like a circular firing squad."

Dolly shifted in her seat. She didn't laugh. "Juju offered me money, right then and there. I refused. I told her flat out this kind of thing scares me."

"Then what happened?"

"This is the part that really frightens me, Roger. She told me she knows exactly what I do for extra money at Charlie's on weekends. She even knew the names of two of my customers. I almost freaked out. Then Juju said she would beat what I make from men by being her informant at the El Escondite."

"What did you say?"

"I told her I only clean rooms there. That I never talk with management people, and I'm too old to be involved in the kind of thing she's offering. She said she would contact me again to see if I changed my mind."

"Juju's persistent, I'll give her that. Anything else?"

Dolly hesitated. "They want me, and I'm terrified," she blurted, on the verge of tears.

"What do you mean?"

She cleared her throat as she recovered her composure. "Juju also told me if I wanted more clients, more money, more time off to be with my grandkids, she could set me up, working for her."

"Damn," he said, stunned by Juju's brazen offer.

"She told me to name my price. She's been digging."

"No offense, Dolly, but the word is out about you. So—how did you respond?"

"I didn't."

"Could she know about your informant work?"

Dolly stared out the windshield, rubbing her palms on her knees. "I'd be dead if she knew I'm working with you. She said nothing that indicates she knows, but she's so sly. It depends on how discreet you've been with my name. More than one person in your department is giving her information."

"I've never mentioned your name to anyone."

Hitchcock became silent. His concern for Dolly's safety conflicted with his decision to not tell her about Juju's supposed trail of dead bodies. So far, the rumors were unconfirmed, but Dolly was on the brink of nervous collapse. He had to extricate her—but given her failure to follow his advice, he wasn't sure he could get her out safely.

"If Juju told you what the shipment was that was hijacked, it was to corner you into working for her."

Dolly trembled as she nodded. "Her offer explains why those Oriental men in her lounge look *me* over like I'm a hunk of meat, but not Monica, who's younger."

"Whatever Monica's role is, prostitution it ain't."

Dolly chuckled. "Maybe she wants to be a madam."

"I'll look into her background."

"What do I do now?"

"Withdraw like I told you in the first place."

"What if Juju or Monica calls me?"

"Let your silence be your refusal. It's likely she'll leave you alone if you leave her alone. Refuse to meet Monica when she calls and don't let her into your home if she shows up at your door."

"What should I say?"

"The truth. Tell Monica you're frightened and not to call you anymore. Then we'll see what happens."

He wrote on a piece of note paper and handed it to her. "This is my home phone number in case you have an emergency. Don't give it out."

"You already gave it to me, remember?"

"So I did. Check in with me by phone every other day so I know you're doing all right."

CHAPTER THIRTY-THREE
Protective Measures

BEHIND CLOSED DOORS Hitchcock briefed Sergeant Jurgens about the heist of heroin and Ecstasy without naming Dolly as the source.

"That explains the sudden spike in heroin overdoses popping up all over the county," Jurgens said, twirling a pencil in his hand. "We were called in on a date rape case at the E.R. last night. Someone slipped a drug into the victim's drink. She woke up in one of the bedrooms, minus her clothes. Lab reports are still out. So, Ecstasy is the latest date-rape tool. I need you to write this up."

"I'm not willing to do that."

Jurgens nodded his acceptance. "Still, one of us needs to speak to your informant."

"Off limits. Same reason."

"We have a drug war going on, Roger."

"I hope they kill each other off. Nobody talks to my informant but me."

"Fair enough," Jurgens replied, exasperated. "If I had the men, I'd set up surveillance on Juju or insert one of our guys into her group undercover and eventually catch her in the act. But we don't."

"The Chinese are too insular for a non-Chinese, even another Asian, to infiltrate them," Hitchcock said. "I learned that during my army years."

Sergeant Jurgens nodded, staring at Hitchcock.

"My informant is afraid of being discovered and executed and wants out."

"Rightly so," Jurgens concluded.

† † †

HITCHCOCK WENT HOME. Jamie, his tail wagging, greeted him. He got an old .38 revolver from his safe.

He loaded it and called Dolly. "I don't want you to panic, but I am concerned for your safety," he said.

"Something else has come up since I saw you?"

"I have something you can use in an emergency."

"I'll have to bring my grandkids."

"Fine. Let's meet in twenty-five minutes," he said.

"Where?"

"The State Patrol office above Eastgate."

Stunned, Dolly asked "The wh-hat? Why?"

"Just the parking lot. It's close, nobody will follow you there. I'll be in my private vehicle."

His meeting with Dolly was brief. Sitting in her car, he handed her the .38. "It's loaded," he said. "All you have to do is pull—"

"I know how to shoot," she said as she slipped it into her coat pocket, "and thanks."

CHAPTER THIRTY-FOUR
Outgunned

UPON LEARNING FROM the State Patrol accident report that the two victims of the heist were Scott D. Sorenson and Allan C. Ming, Hitchcock confirmed that both men were still in Overlake Hospital. Though off duty, he was sitting beside Allan Ming when he awoke.

"Who are you?" Ming asked. He turned toward the window when Hitchcock showed his badge.

"Nasty little accident, eh, Ming?"

"Where's Scott?"

"He went home an hour ago. You got banged up worse than him, I guess."

"You're not the State Patrol. Why are you here?" Ming asked without facing him.

"I'm interested in who ran you off the road."

"As I told the troopers, I never saw them."

"Did you see what kind of car it was?"

Ming kept staring out the window.

"Where were you coming from before the accident?"

Ming shrugged.

"Don't remember that either? Gee. Allow me to

help. You and your soldier buddy, Sorenson, had just left the Bellevue airfield where you received a load of heroin and Ecstasy brought in by plane."

Ming turned toward Hitchcock, shocked. "What... How did you—?"

"You two were trusted with the cash to pay for and receive a shipment of heroin worth a million dollars on the street, but you didn't deliver the dope and the pilot and his passenger have the money. You *say* you were hijacked, but the people you work for will suspect that you and Scott staged the accident, that you have the dope, which you'll use to go into business for yourselves. You two are gonna find out those people aren't good listeners, Ming."

No response came from Ming.

Hitchcock shook his head in fake commiseration. "Know what I think? I think you two should show some consideration for your families."

Ming turned and stared at him, waiting.

"What I mean is, you two should pool your money and buy burial spots side by side and pick out your headstones ahead of time to save your families all that expense because you boys are in it deep, as in six feet below ground," Hitchcock said.

Ming looked down at his hands, as if they could tell him what to say.

Using Ming's silence to press in, Hitchcock said, "Do you want to die, Ming? The people you work for won't take this lying down. Even if you weren't in on it, you and Scott are done. They'll bump you off because you know too much." Hitchcock leaned closer to Ming and poked his chest with his index finger. "But I can help you stay alive."

Ming examined the card Hitchcock handed him. "Say you are Charles Lee when you call," Hitchcock said. "That'll be the signal you want help. Give them the number for me to call you. Allow up to an hour for me to get back to you. Use a different pay phone every time."

"But we're innocent," Ming said as Hitchcock headed toward the door.

Hitchcock stopped and turned. "Sure, you are. You're innocent drug runners, innocent *dead men*. Dead is dead, Ming."

† † †

THE RECORDS CHECK Patty handed Hitchcock when he returned to the station revealed Scott Sorenson's one-page rap sheet consisted of misdemeanors for assault and theft. His felony charges related to drug possession and sales were dismissed, indicating he turned snitch to work off the beefs. Only minor traffic offenses were on Allan Ming's record.

Detective Captain Holland sat in with Sergeant Jurgens when Hitchcock briefed them on the latest development at the hospital. "Set up a meeting with the DEA, Stan," Holland said. "And ask the WSP to not release details of the car Ming and Sorenson were in."

"Not to worry, Captain," Hitchcock said. "The WSP clerk told me the car was totaled and they're still processing it for the hit-and-run investigation."

"That's fine, but we want to go through it for criminal evidence. Tell them so the car isn't released to a junkyard yet."

"One more thing, Captain," Hitchcock said.

Holland looked at Hitchcock, nodding to go ahead.

"As I was leaving the hospital the nurse at the admissions desk stopped me. 'You might want to look at what the patients were wearing when they came in here,' she said as she handed me their property list. Ming and Sorenson were wearing empty shoulder holsters when they came into the ER. I looked at Ming's—it's made in Israel to fit an Uzi, the Israeli submachine pistol. Same with Sorenson. Whoever heisted the drugs on its way to Juju's now has fully automatic weapons while we carry six-shot revolvers and shotguns."

CHAPTER THIRTY-FIVE
More Bad News

HOME AT LAST, Hitchcock's smile vanished when he came through the kitchen door. Allie's face was as ashen, and her hands trembled as he noticed papers in her hand. "What's wrong, baby?" he asked.

"A man was just here."

"Man? What man?"

"He gave me these. Said I've been served." She handed him a folded set of papers. The opening line of the subpoena read, A LAWSUIT AGAINST YOU HAS BEEN FILED... He scanned to the bottom of the document. The plaintiff was Horace MacAuliffe, Trevor's paternal grandfather, suing for full custody of Trevor.

"Old man Mac tried this before and failed, and you didn't even have a lawyer," he said. "So what makes him think... Ah, I know. This is the law firm that subpoenaed my personnel file and the reports of the attack on us when we lived at the Henderson place."

Allie started crying. "You didn't tell me."

"Because you're pregnant," he said tenderly.

"Oh, come ON, Roger!" Allie shouted. "I've carried

babies in my body and given birth twice already, and the first time I had to deal with a missing-in action, deadbeat husband and his snooty, evil parents and work for peanuts standing on my feet. Only my mom helped me in the hospital! So don't you dare patronize me!"

He paused, staring at her. "I stand corrected, baby. I know you're strong, but in times like this my protective instincts come out in force, so please be patient with me."

Allie held her head in her hands. "I couldn't finish reading the papers."

He scanned the pages quickly. "As I thought, your ex-in-laws again claim that you are an unfit mother, only this time it's because of me."

"You? Why you?"

He plopped into his leather armchair and began reading the newest copy of *The Bellevue American.* "Roger—*talk* to me!" Allie demanded.

He put the paper down and looked at her. "Didn't you know I'm a crazed killer, or did I forget to tell you?"

"This is serious, Roger! How did Horace know about the attack?"

"It was all over the TV news, and in the papers."

"Still, it must be somebody in your department who gave them details about Jamie's role in fighting one of the attackers, for they allege he's a vicious dog, therefore he's a threat to Trevor, like you. The press never said anything about Jamie, or that you should have been a suspect in the murder of Stanford," she said, shaking her head.

Hitchcock fell silent, thinking. "You're right, baby. The press never mentioned Jamie, yet the lawsuit mentions him by name. The fact that the Department never asked me if I had anything to do with Stanford's execution could only come from someone in the Department. With his money and connections. the old man has probably found the best judge money can buy, so he can take another shot at us."

"If we lose Trevor, does that mean the court could take *our* children, too?"

At four months into her third pregnancy, Allie's emotions were fragile. He worried that too much stress could put the baby at risk. The thought of losing Trevor in a rigged court proceeding would be too much.

He wrapped his arms around her. "I'll find us a good lawyer."

She pressed her face into his chest. "Lie down with me while the boys nap. We can't do anything, just be with me."

"Huh? You mean I can't–we can't? But-but baby..."

She wiped her tears and laughed as she slapped his shoulder. "What am I going to do with you?"

HE ANSWERED A knock at the front door an hour later. Randy Fowler stood there, looking hesitant. "You look troubled. You okay?"

"We still have no word from or about Connie," Randy replied. "Mom is beside herself with worry. I thought I'd drop by on my way home from school to ask if there's anything new you can tell us."

"Nothing at our end either, Randy. I've distributed posters all around. Not one call. Sorry."

"One of the Bellevue detectives called yesterday to say they've submitted Connie's dental and medical records to her listing in the national computer as a missing person. That's what we wanted, but it sent Mom over the edge."

"As you already know, the county detectives say they found traces of blood of a different type than Connie's in her car," Hitchcock said. "No signs of a struggle, so that's some encouragement, at least."

Randy's eyes pleaded with Hitchcock. "I know it's outside your jurisdiction, but on behalf of my family, I'm asking you to personally investigate Connie's disappearance. This isn't at all like her."

"I know. I've checked the scene where her car was found. And I've stayed in touch with the county detectives assigned to the case. There's nothing new to go on, but I'll check again."

"That's not what I'm asking, Roger."

Hitchcock lifted his chin, questioning.

"I'm asking you as a friend to do more than wait for something to happen. I...*we* ask you to *actively* look for Connie. Find out what happened. She can't have just vanished."

Allie entered the room and stood next to Hitchcock. "Yes, of course he will, Randy," she interjected. "Tell your mom and your brother my husband will find her."

Hitchcock glanced at Allie, then turned back to

Randy. "Forgive my wife. I can only promise to do my best to find Connie."

Randy thanked Hitchcock, nodded goodbye to Allie and left.

"Don't get so compassionate that you volunteer my services for me, baby," he said.

Tears welled up in Allie's eyes. "That poor family has been through so much, I just—"

"What Connie was into before she disappeared is much darker than either you or Randy could grasp, even if you saw the proof. What I saw shocked me, and I wasn't shown the worst of it. None of you know what Connie really was about," he said. "I do. And I'm not saying."

"She was into drugs, right?" she sniffled, wiping her nose with a tissue.

"Worse," he replied, arms folded.

"Then what *can* you do, honey?"

He shook his head slowly. "I'm not the passive type, but waiting for a break in the case is all we have now. We'll have to hope that either someone comes forward with a tip or a lead, or hikers in the woods will stumble into her remains before scavenger animals and the elements erase every trace."

CHAPTER THIRTY-SIX
Rivals

JUJU CLOSED HER office door to shut out the sounds of her employees working in the kitchen as she assessed her situation.

She had been warned that Mexican gangs are fierce, primitive and quick to kill. But after she learned that the El Escondite people had no clue that the devastating arrests and raids by the police were Hitchcock's doing, not hers, she concluded they relied on brute force to compensate for their lack of sophistication, which meant their ability to infiltrate rivals was minimal.

How Hitchcock pulled off the raids and seizures at the El Escondite after Bostwick banished him from Patrol puzzled her. Learning Hitchcock's methods would have to wait. What mattered now was finding the betrayer in her organization who handled the heist.

Her suspicions fell on the Mexican cartel. After all, they met the criteria better than anyone else: motive, ability and opportunity. The El Escondite was situated close enough to the airport to see the night deliveries, they had the people to hijack the shipment, and most of all, they had motive—they had suffered staggering losses from police raids. Plundering her, their rival was the shortest route to recovery and survival. Raiding the Mexican cartel, seizing their drugs and money, had been her intention, but the police beat her to it.

What Juju knew about the El Escondite was but a fraction of the facts. Their revenues were drying up fast. The few remaining people there were paranoid about selling drugs. They didn't know that a certain white male with long blond hair had stolen the last leg of their drug business by selling heroin, cocaine and Ecstasy to teenagers and students in the parking lots of Robinswood Park and Bellevue Community College, thus leaving the El Escondite to swing in the wind.

MEANWHILE HITCHCOCK WAS delighted by the note in his inbox. "Charles Lee" had called. It meant Ming would give him the information needed to take Juju's operation down.

As he went to a phone to call the number, he noticed the message was more than twenty-four hours old. The call had come in on his day off. The fact that Ming called meant he was ready and willing to talk. Angry and frustrated, Hitchcock suspected someone in Records deliberately dropped the ball by not telling him about the call.

He called the number. No answer. Of course.

CHAPTER THIRTY-SEVEN
Without a Trace

UNDER CONTINUED PRESSURE from his wife and the Fowler family, Hitchcock took a stack of posters of Connie's photograph her family made up and drove the country roads in the vicinity of where Connie's car had been found.

He reasoned that the dumping of Connie's car, and the blood inside it, were false leads meant to send the police in the wrong direction.

On his way back through North Bend he saw a Sheriff's patrol car parked on the shoulder of the highway. He displayed his badge as he pulled up alongside the deputy and rolled down his window. They shook hands. Hitchcock handed him a poster.

"I'm looking for this woman, a family friend who disappeared a couple weeks ago. Her car was found abandoned at the junction with Highway Eighteen."

"Haven't seen her," the deputy said as he studied the poster. "I remember her car was found there. Weird place to leave it. She into drugs?"

"Heroin a couple years ago, but she got clean," Hitchcock replied.

"How? Rehab somewhere?"

"Cold turkey."

"Nobody does it cold turkey and stays clean," the deputy said.

"Well, she did."

"If you can spare any more of these, I'll post them in our squad room, the post office and the library, maybe a couple restaurants."

Hitchcock handed him six more posters. "My phone numbers are there in case anyone sees her."

HE STOPPPED BY the temporary detective office on Old Main Street on his way home. He studied again the men with Connie in the photos recovered from Tyrone Guyon's trailer. There were different men in each photograph, and Connie appeared at least two years younger.

He had known Connie and her family since childhood. It grieved him to see photos of her engaged in such depravity she would never do were it not for drugs. He burned with anger again as he memorized each man's face. He handed them back to Detective Meyn. "I don't' recognize any of those men, Larry. Got anything else?"

"Not a call, not a scrap of new information," Meyn said. "Maybe someone will see your posters and call."

RANDY AND HIS younger brother John were there when Hitchcock went to the Fowler residence. Stress had taken its pound of flesh from their mother. She had aged noticeably in the last couple weeks.

"We've heard nothing from the sheriff's office. Left messages with the detective assigned, no reply."

"Not good," Hitchcock said, shaking his head. "I have no news. I distributed your posters in North Bend and Eastgate, so maybe we'll get a call. Thought I'd ask if I could look through Connie's room for clues."

He came out holding a checkbook, a stack of unopened mail, and an address book. "Didn't you tell me Connie didn't have a job?" he said, holding up a checkbook. "Where does the money in this account come from?"

"Connie's always worked part-time, waitressing at restaurants and bars. Never had a full-time job."

"I'll go through all this on my own time. Might find the key to what happened."

† † †

THE NEXT DAY he showed Connie's missing person poster to the Bank of the West manager where she had her checking account. "She disappeared April sixth," Hitchcock told him. "I have your mailed statements, but I wonder if there have been any attempts to withdraw funds or add a name to the account since the date of her disappearance."

The manager left and returned with a file folder, which he handed to Hitchcock. "As you can see, although there is an available balance of one thousand, thirty-two dollars, there've been no changes and no activity since the third week of February."

The February statement revealed a series of small deposits, probably tip money from waitressing. Cancelled checks included local gas stations and restaurants in amounts under thirty dollars.

He copied the names and phone numbers in her address book and returned everything to the family.

At this point he concluded that the death Allie foresaw before Easter had to be Connie's. Connie met Allie's description of who she believed it would be — she was someone close to them, and the timing fit.

He reflected on the forty-eight-hour principle of investigation, that the likelihood of solving a murder or a missing person case diminished exponentially after the first forty-eight hours. Connie had disappeared two months ago. Without telling anyone, he believed she was dead — murdered. He believed it had to do with Mike Smith.

CHAPTER THIRTY-EIGHT
Turf War

AFTER A SLOW night of fighting boredom, struggling against fatigue, no calls, and no arrests, sleep came quickly when Hitchcock tumbled into bed at 4:30 a.m. He was in the middle of a dream when Allie nudged him awake.

"Honey, there's a phone call for you," she said. "The woman says it's urgent."

He opened his eyes. The clock on his nightstand read 7:47. Allie handed him the phone.

"You're not getting me out of this fast enough," the woman said when he said hello.

He sat up, rubbing his eyes. "Dolly? What's going on?"

"Turn on the news, Roger. Channel Seven," she snapped, then hung up.

He had missed the opening lines, but what he saw was enough. A male reporter stood alongside a tree-lined country road, pointing to the trees across the street that were cordoned off with yellow barricade tape. "This is the third dead body to be found in this exact location in two years," the reporter announced into his microphone. "Police aren't commenting at this time, but the previous two victims found here were bound and shot in the head, execution style…"

The phone rang again. "Roger, meet me at the station," Otis said. "No uniform, just come."

"What's up?"

"Not on the phone. Get here quick."

Otis waited for him at the station in a marked supervisor's car, engine running, dressed in jeans, tan wool shirt, black windbreaker. "I assume you saw or heard the news?" Otis asked as Hitchcock slid into the passenger seat.

"I did. That's where we're headed?"

"Looks like the Bamboo Union's work."

"Aren't the dicks going out too?"

"They're tied up on an armored car robbery."

THREE MILES PAST the town of Issaquah on the Issaquah-Hobart Road, television news vans, marked and unmarked police cars, plus a station wagon from the Medical Examiner's office lined both sides of the road.

They showed their badges to the deputy assigned to keep the public and the press out and hiked forty yards uphill through dense forest, following barricade tape to where two detectives stood by a body covered by a dark green tarp. The detective pulled the tarp away. The victim was an adult Hispanic male, appearing to be in his early thirties.

"Know who he is?" a county detective asked.

"No. Should we?" Otis asked as he studied the victim.

"Name's Francisco Garcia. Lives in an apartment in Burien, near the airport."

"We thought you might know this guy," the Medical Examiner's investigator offered. "He had a paycheck stub in his wallet only two days old, from the El Escondite Inn."

"Don't know him," Hitchcock said after looking at him closely.

Otis pointed at the soil disturbance around the trunk of an elm tree where they were. "Is this where he was?"

"Same as last time. Bullet to the back of the head, hands tied, same exact spot," came the county detective's grim reply. "Anything you can tell us?"

"My partner knows more than I do," Otis said.

Hitchcock briefed him on the history of arrests and drug seizures at the El Escondite Inn.

OTIS SPOKE FIRST on their way back to the station. "Unless the victim was killed in our city after he got off work, none of this is our case. The victim didn't live in Bellevue. He walked to his execution scene under his own power like in the earlier two cases. What does that tell you?"

"I don't know. Tell me."

"Animals go elsewhere to relieve themselves, never

in their own nest or den unless they have no other choice. Organized crime people don't prey on their own neighborhoods, at least typically."

"Ah. So, it's someone in Bellevue." Hitchcock placed his hand on his forehead and hummed, looking upward. "Ohhmmm...," he buzzed, imitating a trance. "The name Juju keeps coming to mind... Ohhmmm."

Otis didn't laugh. "The El Escondite people will conclude Juju was behind it. They'll be itching for the county boys to go away so they can retaliate. We can monitor them through your mouse in the corner."

"My mouse in the corner is desperate to get out of Dodge–upright and breathing, not in a body bag."

Ignoring Hitchcock's remarks about his informant, Otis said, "There's a double message in the location and the staging of the bodies. You know that too, right?"

"They want their enemies to be afraid. That's all I'm getting from it."

"The previous executions were to announce their presence to competitors by killing a couple rival gang members," Otis said. "This time they killed an innocent employee as retaliation for the heist that they blame the Mexicans for."

† † †

FROM THE PRIVACY of his home Hitchcock called Dolly Searles. "I went to the scene after you called. Who was Francisco Garcia?"

"Him! Oh no!" she gasped. "He's the new manager of the bar after Luis was arrested. They brought him up from California. How did he die?"

"When did you last see him?" he asked, avoiding her question.

"Yesterday."

"Was he dealing drugs out of the bar like Armijo was?"

"Not that I know of. He had an eye for women. Young or old, didn't matter. Maybe he flirted with the wrong one. Tell me...how did he die?" she asked, voice shaking.

Hitchcock skipped the details of the bullet to the back of Garcias's head or the cord that bound his hands behind his back, tied with a special knot he recognized from his years in Vietnam and Southeast Asia. "Well yeah, could be a jealous husband or boyfriend, maybe," he fibbed to ease her fears. "Anyway, the autopsy will be tomorrow morning. Won't get the report for days. Oh, and one more thing—detectives from the Sheriff's Office will be interviewing everybody at the El Escondite about Garcia. Santa wants an eye on what goes on and to be kept informed."

His humor calmed her enough that she chuckled. A little.

CHAPTER THIRTY-NINE
Message at the Old Preston Mill

ALLIE AWAKENED HIM again the next morning, phone in hand. "It's for you. The station." He glanced at his nightstand clock: a few minutes past ten.

"Roger, this is Patty. I have a King County deputy on the line for you. Says it's important. Okay?"

He motioned to Allie to bring him coffee as he okayed the call. A familiar voice came on the line.

"Roger? This is Dale Hastings, King County S.O. Remember me?"

"Sure do. How's it going?"

"Still plugging along out here in North Bend, which is why I called."

"Oh?" he asked as Allie handed him a steaming mug of coffee.

"Remember when I assisted you and Walker on arresting a Bellevue runaway girl who was with two adult men?"

"Of course."

"Remember the blue Mustang that Mike Smith drove when we were at the Preston Mill, and you almost got a shot at him as he was escaping?"

He took a sip of the strong brew, then set the mug on the nightstand. "Yes?"

"We responded this morning to a car fire. It was Smith's blue Mustang. Gasoline. Burnt to a crisp."

"Damn!" Hitchcock exclaimed. He scooted up in bed to lean against the headboard. "Where was it?"

"Same place. The old Preston Mill."

"Is the Mustang still there?"

"It's too hot to be towed away."

"I'm on my way."

† † †

SMITH'S BLUE MUSTANG was a blackened, burned-out hulk. The heat had burst all four tires, melted the vinyl and plastic interior, and charred the windshield. Hitchcock and Walker greeted Deputy Hastings.

"The pot must really be boiling in your town for something like this to happen, along with that missing woman," Hastings said.

Hitchcock filled him in about Smith trying to kill him.

"I bet the runaway girl you guys arrested here last year told Smith you tried to shoot him but couldn't get a clear shot. You couldn't shoot him, then he couldn't shoot you–like a duel. The destroyed car, parked in the same place where you tried to shoot him, is a message," Hastings speculated.

"You mean a taunt?" Walker asked.

"More like a challenge would be my guess," Hastings replied, thumbs hooked in his leather Sam

Brown gun belt. "Like throwing down the gauntlet. At least now we can be sure Smith hasn't left the area and has a different car."

Hitchcock and Walker inspected the ground around the smoking wreckage. It had rained the day before, making the clay soil soft. Walker pointed out three different boot prints near the Mustang. "These could belong to the firemen who responded, but would you mind taking a plaster lift of these, just in case they belong to Smith and others?" Walker asked.

Returning to the station, he found another note from Records in his inbox. The four-word message came an hour ago: CALL LA PALOMA – IMPORTANT.

CHAPTER FORTY
La Paloma, Spy

THE INTENDED MESSAGE in Smith's burned-up Mustang dogged Hitchcock. He gave Patty a short list of inquiries to run on Smith as soon as he returned from Preston, namely who his cellmates were when he was in the King County Jail, and the juvenile lockup known as Green Hill. Finding these people would take time.

He called Dolly, hoping he hadn't lost an opportunity by delaying.

She got right to the point. "New management people arrived two days ago at the El Escondite. Also, it wasn't planned, but I went with Monica to dinner and drinks night before last at The Great Wall."

What could you be thinking? You broke our agreement again, he thought angrily. *There's no point scolding her.* "Okay. Tell me about the new management team first," he told her.

"They're two Mexican men, big guys in their thirties. One has teardrops tattooed on his face," she said.

Hitchcock went on alert. "*Where* on his face?"

"Um, under his left eye. Why?"

"It's important. Tell me more."

"They're staying in the executive suites. So far, all I've seen them do is hang out a lot in the bar."

"Names?"

"Haven't heard yet. They're too scary to risk asking. I keep a low profile, so I go home every day."

"What else?"

"They got another new bartender, too. Young guy. Name's Emilio."

"Any talk about the former bartender among the employees?"

"I've heard speculation that he probably made a pass at the wrong woman. Nobody knows anything."

"Why did you go to The Great Wall again?" he snapped. "I thought you agreed to lay low, as in stay away from them as a key part of your exit plan."

Dolly hesitated. "You're angry with me. Don't be. Please. It wasn't planned, at least by me. I just happened to see Monica after work. She invited me to The Great Wall for dinner and drinks. Juju joined us. About eight-thirty that young patrolman came through the back door. He showed Juju a sheet of paper. She seemed alarmed when she looked at it. She took him into her office like the other times. He left about twenty minutes later. He never went into the bar."

Hitchcock figured McCabe showed Juju the new Mike Smith wanted poster out of ignorance, not knowing about her connection to Smith. "What else happened?"

"Juju was pleasant, but as I expected, she offered me

more money to spy for her on the operation at the El Escondite. I said I might be able to find someone there who was willing to do that, but I didn't want to get involved."

"What was her response?"

"Strangely, she didn't seem interested in anyone besides me. Maybe she thinks I'm spying on her for the people I work for."

"I doubt it. You have no knowledge of Juju's operation," Hitchcock said. "Did she bring up your weekend sideline again?"

"Yes. She asked what I made on a good night. I told her it's not open for discussion."

"Anything else?"

"We moved from the restaurant to the lounge because of two noisy families. I noticed the same Chinese men there that I mentioned before. They were in serious conversation but stopped when they saw me. They didn't hide the fact that they were checking me out. I hid my discomfort by ignoring them. I was sitting close enough to hear them. I assumed their comments were about me, but they were speaking Chinese."

"What's your assessment of this?"

"Juju's got a plan up her sleeve and wants me in on it."

"I don't like the sound of this, Dolly. You're at risk. Again, *stay out of there*."

He hung up, then dialed Sergeant Jurgens in the detective office. " I understand you were in the Border Patrol before you hired on here," Hitchcock said.

"Eight years," Jurgens replied. "All of it on the border of Arizona and Mexico."

"What does a tattoo of a teardrop on the left eye mean?"

"Each one means a kill under orders. The victim could be a rival gang member, in or out of prison."

CHAPTER FORTY-ONE
"This is Big"

HITCHCOCK ATTENDED THE meeting in Captain Holland's office when Sergeant Jurgens presented two FBI Lab reports in clear plastic sleeves to Captains Holland and Delstra, and King County Senior Deputy Prosecutor Simon Clancy.

"The results of the examination of the handwriting samples and comparison of the writing of the note to Bostwick's writing prove Bostwick wrote the directions to Hitchcock's home. The downside is that because of the small amount of writing on the note, the criminalist could not conclude that the writer was Bostwick and no one else. "

Clancy the prosecutor stared at Jurgens through his thick horn-rimmed glasses. "So far, it's Bostwick but we're a tad short of what we need to charge him. What else you got?'

Jurgens laid another report on the conference table. "A latent print on the note matches the tip of Bostwick's left thumb. But again, the latent isn't defined enough to meet the court standard of twelve matching points."

"How many matching points do we have?" Clancy

asked.

Jurgens hesitated. "Eleven."

The silent frustration in the room was deafening.

The deputy prosecutor shifted his head side-to-side, weighing the evidence in his mind. "it's not a perfect world, but what you got is pretty damn good," he said, nodding "These two finding together may be enough to charge Bostwick. Everything so far excludes over ninety percent of the population. This isn't a bad check case, this note led to an attack on an off-duty officer at his home by one man armed with a knife and the other an accomplished martial artist. This is serious as hell. Is there more?"

Clancy's eyes widened when Jurgens showed him the photographs of Bostwick in uniform, embracing Juju at back door of The Great Wall. "Whoa! Who is *she*?" he exclaimed.

"Juju Kwan," Hitchcock replied. "An immigrant from Nationalist China–or Taiwan. A suspected drug dealer. She owns a restaurant in my beat. I took the photos."

Clancy looked at Hitchcock. "What's her connection to Bostwick?"

"She's got a red-hot thing going with Bostwick. Neither is married, yet they keep the whole thing hush-hush. He doesn't know it, but she's got also affairs going on with other men."

"No doubt about that!" Clancy exclaimed. "So, she imports drugs, but she obviously doesn't touch them herself," Clancy summarized. "At this point you have strong suspicions, incriminating circumstances, but no hard evidence, and she's got her hooks into your lieutenant?" He paused, studying the photos. "This is big."

"We don't yet know who is backing Juju, or all that she's up to, who she sells to when she receives a shipment," Captain Holland said. "We don't doubt she's the supply link for heroin coming in from Southeast Asia, but we have no proof. She has a mansion on Cougar Mountain overlooking Lake Sammamish; it's paid for."

Clancy frowned as he received another file from Captain Delstra. "Here's what we demoted Bostwick for. Read the first two pages."

Clancy read quickly, his eyes moving rapidly as he flipped through the pages. "I've got one question," he said when he finished reading. "Why the hell didn't you fire this bastard, this putz?"

"Two reasons," Delstra replied. "One, Bostwick is the most visible, and clumsiest member of a group of turncoats in the Department and in city management. At first, we thought they were politically motivated to undermine us, but it looks more and more like a criminal conspiracy. By keeping an eye on Bostwick and limiting his activities, we expect to learn what else is going on and who is involved."

"And the second reason?" Clancy asked, looking at Captain Delstra.

"Bostwick came here from the East Coast, a stranger with clear ties to certain city officials who also come from the East. He only applied here and was hired at once. Due to his deep political connections, he rose to the rank of lieutenant in record time without ever making an arrest on his own. Efforts to discipline him are overruled by those above us."

"He resigned immediately when he was told he was under investigation," Holland added.

Clancy scowled as he set down the photographs of Bostwick with Juju. A seasoned prosecutor, he placed his hands flat on the conference table and remained silent for almost a full minute before he said, "What else has happened that leads you to think there are other bad characters involved?"

Delstra related the details of officers' disappearing memos and FIRs that pertain to drug trafficking, and a suspect being alerted that detectives were coming for him minutes after they were assigned.

"You guys realize that this is becoming Federal," Clancy said.

"We've called the DEA, but haven't met with them yet," Captain Holland said.

Clancy sighed, his palms still flat on the table. He looked at the two captains. "What would you like to see happen?"

"Bostwick is weak," Delstra said. "If we could make an investigative arrest, even an Interview and Release, it could break the case wide open."

"I'll get back to you on it, Captain," Clancy said as he turned to Hitchcock. "You've been through a lot in a short time, Officer. What would you like to see happen?"

Hitchcock snorted as he made eye contact with Clancy. "You ask what *I'd* like to see happen? I want to see leaders with guts *besides* the men in this room take bold action—protect the public—go after the predators with a vengeance—jail and execute these unfit-to-live bastards instead of this wimpy hand-wringing."

A look of shock came over Clancy. "I take issue with your terminology, Officer. Let me assure you, I am here to see what we can do for you."

Hitchcock gave him a hard level stare, judgment in his eyes. "Talk is cheap," he said. "When I came back from two tours in the Army in Vietnam, people I grew up with had become addicts. Some died while drug dealers and the greedy businessmen who financed them became rich. I managed to make a dent in the local drug trade. The people I arrested were executed as soon as they were released from jail, then two hit men were sent to attack me at home. My wife and I live looking over our shoulders now, and we aren't alone. All I hear from our leaders and officials is talk. Is this the kind of country we want for our kids?"

At that, Hitchcock walked out of the meeting.

CHAPTER FORTY-TWO
Justice is a Dish...

AT THE END of a busy but uneventful week, Allie, Jamie and the boys greeted Hitchcock when he walked through the door. "Let's go fishing, Dad! The sockeye are biting in the lake and the bass too!" Trevor exclaimed.

"I'll make sandwiches while you change clothes, honey," Allie said, her face aglow with excitement. "I'm going too." The home phone rang as they headed for the back door. Allie's smiled faded when she answered. "It's Joel," she said, handing him the receiver.

"Don't ask why on the phone, just meet me at the station right now," Otis said.

He had a hard time explaining to Allie and the kids that he had to go back. Allie couldn't hide her disappointment but said nothing. He held Trevor as he cried and promised to make it up to him when he got back.

† † †

THE COUNTY DETECTIVE grinned when he saw Hitchcock and Otis hiking up the wooded trail from the Issaquah-Hobart Road, keeping close to the yellow barrier tape that stretched from tree to tree. "Here come the Bellevue boys," he said to the deputies and the Medical Examiner's investigator.

A green sheet covered the body lying on the ground next to where they stood. Skipping formalities except for a brief nod, Hitchcock squatted down and looked under the sheet. Blindfolded, hands tied at the wrists behind the man's back, a bloody bullet wound in the back of the head, ants crawling all over his face and eyes, was none other than his nemesis, Mike Smith.

"Thanks for calling us," Otis told the county detective. "Let me guess…mushroom hunters found the body again?"

"Nope. Someone anonymously called it in to our dispatch center."

"Ah. Well, at least they did this when it wasn't raining," Otis said. Turning to Hitchcock, he asked "That him, Roger?"

"Yep," Hitchcock nodded. "He taunted me into another round with him by setting fire to his car at a spot significant to him and me, but it looks like someone had other plans for Mike." He pointed at the knot in the cord binding Smith's wrists. Otis acknowledged with a nod.

"Is there something significant I should know about?" the detective asked when he saw Hitchcock and Otis exchange looks.

"We've seen this same knot on the other three bodies found here," Otis replied. "We were both medics in 'Nam. The VC used this same knot when they captured our guys and executed anyone who helped us."

"I'll be damned. This is international, then," the detective stated.

"What about the caller?" Hitchcock asked.

"Dispatcher said the caller was female. Said we'd find the body of Mike Smith here, executed."

"The caller used the word, 'executed'?" Otis asked.

"Yep."

"Are your emergency calls recorded?"

"We save all calls to dispatch for ninety days."

"I'd like to listen to the call as soon as possible," Hitchcock said.

A UNIFORMED DEPUTY helped the Medical Examiner's investigator lug a gurney up the muddy trail to the body, wheels up. Smith's body was photographed as it was laid onto the gurney, then strapped down with a sheet covering him.

"Find any evidence?" Hitchcock asked as he examined the ground where the body had been.

"Footprints indicating two subjects walked in with the victim, like the other times. Barely distinct in this mossy ground. We got photographs but I don't think the plaster casts we took will be helpful," a county detective replied.

Hitchcock examined them. "They're indistinct as to tread style, but size-wise I'd say one suspect wore size ten and the other size nine shoes."

"The victim's sneakers are size eleven."

"Anything else?" Otis asked.

"I'll get our dispatcher on a tactical frequency so your partner can talk to her, then we can get out of here before the newshounds arrive."

HITCHCOCK SAT IN an unmarked county car. The detective switched to a restricted frequency and handed him the mic. "Go ahead, her name's Nicole."

"Yes, sir, I took the call," Nicole said. "Her words were 'You can find the executed body of Mike Smith, in the same place off the Issaquah-Hobart Road as the others.' Then she hung up."

"Was it recorded?"

"No, sir. She called on a non-emergency line."

"Did she speak with an accent?"

"Not that I could tell."

"From the voice, what mental image do you have of the caller?"

"Caucasian, twenties to early thirties."

"Would you recognize the voice if you heard it again?"

"Hmm, not sure. She sounded pretty generic."

"NO ACCENT RULES out Juju as the caller," Hitchcock said as he rode back to town with Otis. "Then again, Juju wouldn't call the police to report a dead body."

"Or have someone else do it," Otis said. "The shoe prints appear to be size ten and nine," Otis continued, "meaning men of average height. And no shell casing means they either picked it up or used a revolver."

213

"Or they shot Smith somewhere else."

"Two guys lugging a dead body uphill into the woods? Nope, Smith was drugged and then marched there to his death, like the others," Otis said.

HIS PHONE RANG as soon as he arrived home again. "Sergeant Jurgens, Roger. How was your trip to the dead body location?"

"Informative. Same method as the others."

"Meet me at the station at seven tomorrow."

"What for?"

"The cutting starts at eight," Jurgens said.

"Cutting?"

"Autopsy. "You'll ride there with us."

He hesitated in surprise. "Okay."

"Bring a camera."

† † †

THE STENCH OF decaying flesh and strong antiseptic pierced the nostrils and smote the eyes of Hitchcock, Otis, and Detective Sergeant Jurgens entered the autopsy room at Harborview Hospital the next morning. The cold sterile vastness of the room, its blank white walls and blazing fluorescent lights impressed Hitchcock but he didn't know why.

A dozen cadavers of various races, ages, and condition were lying supine on stainless steel rolling tables. The name and case number were written on a tag attached to the big toe of each body. Their weight and height were inscribed on their abdomens in large numbers with black felt markers. Under each body a red rubber block extended the arch of the back to supply better access to the abdomen and chest organs.

Hitchcock crossed the room to Mike Smith's body. A pert young female autopsy assistant with a crisp air about her finished cutting hair samples from different parts of his scalp and placing them in marked envelopes. She swabbed his hands with cotton swabs soaked with solution and put the samples in separate glass jars.

"This guy one of your cases?" she asked as she took scrapings from under the fingernails of each hand and swapped Smith's hands with an alcohol solution.

"His death is the county's case, but he was wanted by us on several felonies," Sergeant Jurgens replied.

"That's interesting, because X-rays reveal a bullet in his brain," she said bluntly as she used a scalpel to cut a large Y on the chest, then peeled the flap of skin up and laid it over Smith's face. "Want to know something else?"

"Sure, what?" Jurgens asked.

"He's fired a gun recently. The swabs I took reacted positive for gunshot residue on his right hand." She pointed her latex-gloved finger at Smith's right wrist. "And look at the deep indentations around his wrists. This guy was bound before he was killed."

"That's not all. Look at the tracks on his left arm — old and new," Hitchcock pointed out.

As they watched Smith's sternum being snipped open by the autopsy assistant with rib shears, a middle-aged man in a green smock entered and extended his hand to each of them.

"I'm Dr. Gilson. I'm doing the autopsies this morning. Got something to show you." He clipped two X-ray sheets to a translucent light on the wall and pointed to the dark spot in the back of the head. "This is Smith, and that's the bullet I will remove. But first, the body and the vital organs."

Starting at the head, Dr. Gilson described Smith's body, physical condition, signs of injury, organs and abnormalities into a tape recorder. His assistant then removed, examined, and weighed the heart, lungs and connective tissues. The same procedures were followed for the abdominal organs.

Two male assistants rolled the body to one side to examine the gunshot wound to the base of the skull. The rubber block was shifted from the back to Smith's neck, elevating the head. An incision was made from side to side, along the back, and peeled the scalp forward over the face, exposing the bare cranium, bright red blood over white skull bone. A small power saw cut through the skull plate, spraying bone dust in the air, then the top of the skull was lifted off like a cap.

The brain was lifted out, weighed, examined, and dissected. Dr. Gilson removed the bullet with tweezers. Holding it up for others to see, he said, "Twenty-two, the professional assassin's choice. Just enough energy to bounce around in the cranium, breaking things with a minimum of outer destruction or noise," he said in a whimsical tone of voice. "Hollow-point. See how it mushroomed."

"If Smith was thrashing around after he was shot in the head, and he was bound, that would explain the abrasions to his wrists," Otis added.

"Certainly would," Dr. Gilson agreed.

"What do you make of the bruises?" Otis asked. "He's got blunt force injuries to the abdomen, back, arms and chest, and defensive wounds on his forearms. Whoever he fought with either had a blunt instrument, or really could pack a punch.

"Wound discoloration is consistent, showing the decedent received them at the same time. Lab results, when we get them, will be more definitive. Given the condition of the body and weather conditions, I estimate the time of death to be within forty-eight to seventy-two hours ago."

"How long will it take for the lab results?" Otis asked.

"Two to three weeks."

Otis turned to Hitchcock. "How does it feel to see the guy who tried to kill your friend, and then you, being opened up like a frog in biology class?"

Hitchcock gazed at the eyes that radiated hate when they last met, now staring lifelessly at the ceiling. "Justice is a dish best served cold," he said.

CHAPTER FORTY-THREE
Collateral Damage

THE KITCHEN PHONE rang as Hitchcock came through the door. "A Charles Lee just called, asking for a call from Hitchcock. Here's the number," Patty in Records told him. The call meant Ming was alive and was willing to talk. Thanks to Patty, this time Records informed him of the call within minutes. Hitchcock used the bedroom phone to call the number. No one answered. He again ten minutes later. No answer. He waited thirty more minutes and dialed the number again. A woman answered. Her voice sounded young.

"Is Charles Lee there?"

"No one here by that name," she said.

"How about an Allan Ming?"

"No."

"Do you expect him back soon?"

"How should I know? This is a pay phone."

WORRIED FOR MING'S safety, Hitchcock requested Patty to run all vehicles registered to Allan Ming. A '68 Chevy Impala four-door with a different address than on Ming's driver's license came up. Both addresses were in Seattle. Hitchcock was off duty when he went to the address on the car registration first. It was an older home in the International District. Ming's Chevy was not there. The people in the house were Asian. No one spoke English. Same story for the address from Ming's driver's license. Ming's address on the State Patrol accident report was the same as on his driver's license.

† † †

THE LAST KNOWN address of the driver of the Mustang, Scott Sorenson, was in Woodinville, a rural community 25 miles northeast of Bellevue. Hitchcock and Walker went there off duty in an unmarked detective car the following day. A somber, gray-haired woman in her sixties answered the door. They identified themselves and asked if Scott was home.

"Scott was my son," she said.

"Did you say, 'was' your son, ma'am?" Hitchcock asked.

"You say you're cops, and you don't know?"

Hitchcock and Walker exchanged glances. "I apologize for not knowing when perhaps I should, Mrs. Sorenson, but—"

"Scott died."

"May I ask what happened?"

"He was killed by a hit-and-run driver a week ago. Why did you want to talk to him?"

Hitchcock hesitated. "It has to do with the black Mustang he owned."

"That's ironic. Scott told me someone ran him off the

219

road—totaled his car, then drove away. He was in the hospital but came home in a few days. The State Patrol is investigating it. Last week he was killed by a hit-and-run driver when he went out to our mailbox."

"He only told you half the story," Hitchcock said.

She didn't take the bait. "I don't want to know about it—Scott's been in trouble since he was a kid. Work and him never saw eye-to-eye. He always had a lot of cash on him after he got out of the army. I gave up caring or asking how he got it."

"Did Scott ever mention someone named Allan?" Hitchcock asked.

She shook her head and started to close the door when Walker said, "Before we go, could you tell us which agency is investigating your son's accident?"

"State Patrol."

"Again, ma'am, did your son mention any of his friends or business associates, maybe a guy named Allan?"

"Don't you guys get it? My son was a criminal."

"We are sorry for your loss, Mrs. Sorenson," Hitchcock said. "If you change your mind about talking to me, please call this number and leave a message." He handed her a business card and left.

THAT WEEKEND, TWO fishermen found the body of an Asian adult male washed up on the muddy bank of the Duwamish River, where it flows through the industrial area of Seattle and empties into Puget Sound.

No identification was on the body. The autopsy determined the cause of death to be drowning, the time of death was within twenty-four hours of the time of discovery. Blood test results confirmed a high concentration of heroin. A check of the victim's fingerprints through state and federal crime databases did not identify the man.

Two weeks passed. A Seattle Police detective assigned to the Missing Persons Unit noticed the John Doe found in the river matched the description of missing person Allan Ming. A female relative identified him. The case was closed as an accidental drowning.

Otis found out through his connections across the lake. He called Hitchcock.

"Ming was trying to hand Juju and her operation to us, Joel," Hitchcock said. "He was serious enough to try to reach me twice. He must have been scared, and Special Forces guys don't scare easily."

"What does this tell you?" Otis asked.

"We've got a leak. A big one."

CHAPTER FORTY-FOUR
Politics Be Damned!

SERGEANT JURGENS BRIEFED Captain Holland on the death and autopsy of Mike Smith when he returned to the station. "I sent Hitchcock a memo regarding the state lab's findings regarding the blood types on the cigarette butts. Now he knows it was Stanford and someone other than Zhang who surveilled his home."

"Cold comfort," Holland muttered. "What else?"

"Case progress is at a standstill. It's critical that Hitchcock knows we're still investigating to identify all who were involved in the attack on him and his family," Jurgens said. "What we haven't told him yet is that the state lab blood type results tend to *eliminate* Bostwick as being at his cabana with Stanford."

Holland leaned back in his chair, pondering the neat piles of case folders on his desk. "Roger was at our meeting with the prosecutor, so he knows the FBI lab examinations of the writing and the latent prints on the note Zhang had on him eliminate everyone *except* Bostwick, who quit but is still around."

"Yeah, Bostwick's still around, Captain," Jurgens

said, leaning forward. "He still has an irrational hatred for Hitchcock, who has a wife, two kids and a third one on the way."

"What's next?"

Jurgens shrugged. "Bostwick resigned. The internal investigation you assigned me is over. I had planned to interview him the very week he quit."

Captain Holland stared at his sergeant. "Bostwick set a chain of events in motion that is still leaving a trail of dead bodies. One of the hit men paid for the failed attempt with his life. The other assailant may be dead too. Bostwick's not getting off the hook by quitting or because he has rich parents. We're not letting go until we get him."

"Interviewing Bostwick was my next step, but we were kicked off the property. I'm stuck."

"The hell you are. Have Larry Meyn go with you."

Jurgens stared at Holland. "Go with me where?"

"To arrest the bastard. Investigation of Aiding and Abetting First Degree Burglary, Second Degree Assault Upon a Police Officer. See if Meyn can crack him. If he does, book him. If not, interview and release."

Jurgens had the deer-in-the headlights look. "You know if we do it without the support of the prosecutor's office, this will explode politically."

"This isn't a game, Stan! Shake the tree. Shake it hard," Holland shouted, pointing at the door. "Go! Go now!"

CHAPTER FORTY-FIVE
Tightening the Noose

JURGENS AND MEYN returned to the palatial Bostwick residence. They hesitated to get out of their humble black Ford Fairlane with black-sidewall tires and cheap tan plastic seat covers when they parked next to a black Bentley sedan and a new silver Rolls-Royce.

"Maybe we should take a couple days to move our assets offshore before we knock on that door," Meyn quipped, half-joking.

"Why hell, boy! Being here makes me feel like a star on *The Beverly Hillbillies*," Jurgens joked.

Meyn's laughed nervously. "The show was pulled off the air last year."

"Aw, come *on Je-throw*, let's git our toothpicks out, hitch 'ar belts up, an' weel put the grabs on ole *Rowlah*," Jurgens said with a sly grin.

Meyn ignored the doorbell and knocked twice.

The door opened.

A tall, aristocratic-looking male version of Mom Bostwick, holding a copy of *The Wall Street Journal*, scowled down at them over the top of his glasses as if they came to pull weeds in the yard at an inconvenient time. Dad Bostwick said nothing. His face darkened when they flashed their badges.

Jurgens introduced himself and Meyn. "We came to see Rowlie."

"Didn't my wife tell you not to come here again?"

"Yep. She sure did, 'bout a week ago," Meyn said.

"So you're disobeying her orders. I'm ordering you to get off my property. Now. You're trespassing. Leave or I'll call the Clyde Hill Police."

"We're here on police business," Jurgens said.

"This couldn't be handled by phone?"

"No. Now, is Rowland here?"

"He left a week ago."

"Where to?"

Dad Bostwick's face contorted with disgust. "After what your Department did to him, do you *really* think I'm going to tell you anything?"

"We're here on official business, Mr. Bostwick," Jurgens said. "It pertains to your son. This is his address. Make it easy on all of us. Tell me where he is or else we come back, search warrant in hand."

Mom Bostwick appeared and stood behind her husband. "Search warrant!" she exclaimed. "What's going on, George? I studied law. You have to have a crime to apply for a search warrant."

"We have a number of crimes, all felonies, and we're here to arrest Rowlie for them," Jurgens said flatly.

Both parents' mouths dropped open. "Arrest Rowland? For what?" Pop Bostwick demanded.

"Several felony charges relating to an attack on a fellow officer at his home," Jurgens said boldly.

"Ah! Go away. Go away! We'll sue you for this!" Mom Bostwick shrieked, her face turning purple. Dad slammed the door. They began yelling at each other.

Meyn and Jurgens leaned close, listening. In a moment, they grinned at each other and nodded.

Captain Holland called them into his office when they returned. "Well? Where's your prisoner?"

Jurgens described their encounter with the parents. "We can get a search warrant, Captain, but I stood by the door and overheard them talking—yelling at each other. I overheard the dad say Rowlie's in New York."

"Get a search warrant anyway," Holland said, his face darkening, "and serve it. Do it now. If Rowland's there, arrest him. If not, track him down."

† † †

TWO HOURS LATER, Sergeant Jurgens and Detective Meyn returned to the Bostwick residence with a search warrant, accompanied by a uniformed Clyde Hill Police officer. They searched the Bostwick home for Rowland, ignoring the furious objections and threats of his parents.

They found Rowland's room was empty of personal effects. Upon his return to the station, Detective Meyn began tracking Bostwick in New York City.

CHAPTER FORTY-SIX
Butting Heads

CAPTAIN HOLLAND WAS meeting with Captain Delstra in his office when he was ordered to report to Chief Sean Carter's office at once.

The chief sat placidly in his chair, silent, hands folded on his desk. The City Manager, Cabot Taft, a slim, reddish-blond man in his early forties with an acne-scarred, sunlamp-tanned face, was standing when Holland came in. His voice was ice cold.

"What the hell do you think you're doing, Holland, harassing Lieutenant Bostwick and trying to arrest him?" Taft squawked in his nasal East Coast accent, beady snake eyes spewing blue fire.

"Oh, nothing much. Just protecting an innocent officer and his family from the schemes of someone who never should have a badge, or anyone's trust, let alone a gun," Holland fired back sarcastically.

"I just received a call from Lieutenant Bostwick's family attorney," Taft said, his face and neck reddening. "They are furious at the behavior of your detectives and intend to sue us for damages. What's your proof, where are your charges? Why aren't they filed?"

"First off, Bostwick's not a cop anymore, so drop the lieutenant title, which he never deserved," Holland said. "He quit rather than cooperate with the internal investigation I ordered. After further investigation, I directed my detectives to make an investigative arrest of him for aiding and abetting a felony attack on a patrolman at his home by two hired men."

Taft whirled toward Chief Carter, his mouth open. "Hitmen!" he scoffed. "How absurd! This is Bellevue. That kind of thing doesn't happen here."

Carter swiveled side to side in his chair, a noncomital look on his face, saying nothing.

"I would direct your attention to the record amounts of heroin, cocaine, the new drug Ecstasy and marijuana our officers are pulling off the streets," Holland said. "Add to that the increasing number of drug overdose cases, some of which have been fatal."

Taft bristled when Captain Delstra entered the chief's office, uninvited. "What is *he* doing here?" Taft demanded of Chief Carter, as if Delstra was a stray dog who wandered in. The Chief shrugged and said nothing.

"This is my business as much as anyone here," Delstra said.

"This talk about big-time crime is hogwash," Taft sneered. "Where are the stats to prove these allegations? Any serious crime happens outside the city limits. This is a bedroom town, yours a bedroom police department—only necessary for traffic and PR stuff, that's it. This new batch of cops, veterans—are a bunch of violent rednecks who belong elsewhere, and this Department is…is a wannabe agency."

"Hogwash?" Delstra challenged. "One of my officers, who has recently made record arrests and recoveries of drugs, was attacked at his home by two hired thugs, one of whom had written directions in his pocket. The two were arrested. Charges were filed. One was executed after his release on bail, and the other was whisked out of the country. You call that hogwash?"

Taft glared at Delstra, but said not a word.

"A lot happens here away from the eyes of the public, Cabot," was Chief Carter's only interjection.

Silence held the room.

"You say there's no big-city crime here," Delstra broke in, ending the standoff. "What about the shooting almost two years ago when a wanted felon and his female partner ambushed two of my officers? Is that hogwash too?"

"The officers involved should have retreated and called for help. Instead, they killed those two people unnecessarily" he said, still glaring at Captain Delstra, then at Chief Carter.

"Who should they have called for help? The U.S. Army? Wait for troops from Fort Lewis?" Delstra scoffed, mocking Taft.

"They're war veterans, killers who shouldn't be here," Taft countered, ignoring Delstra's questions. "If I had my way they would've been fired, prosecuted and hopefully jailed, but I didn't—"

"Because of me," Delstra interrupted, finishing Taft's sentence.

Taft shut up and averted his eyes.

Holland set a file folder on the Chief's desk and opened it. "Have a look at the kind of cop your boy Bostwick has been," he told Taft, revealing photographs of Bostwick in uniform, embracing Juju Kwan. "The woman is the owner of a Chinese restaurant here and a strong suspect in the trafficking of heroin and cocaine."

Taft's was quiet as he stared at the photos.

Holland continued. "One of the hitmen had a piece of paper with directions to Officer Hitchcock's home written on it. We have strong evidence from the FBI Lab that the writing and a thumbprint on the note are Rowland Bostwick's. We don't have all the pieces yet, but when we do, we'll file felony charges against him and bring him back from wherever he is to stand trial."

Delstra handed Taft another file. "Here are memos Bostwick wrote concerning his intentions to get Hitchcock fired, the same officer who was attacked at his home."

Taft stiffened his back after reading only two memos. "I'm not convinced this isn't a setup. Rowland is a fine man. He comes from a very respectable family."

Holland replied. "With all due respect for your office, you are in denial. It doesn't matter if you're convinced of Bostwick's involvement or not. This is a fraction of what we have on him, but you're so close-minded there's no point in showing you more."

"The attorneys for the family will come after us," Taft said, ignoring Holland's remarks. "Through subpoenas and depositions, *they* will get to the truth. Lawsuits and bad publicity are what I'm trying to avoid, Holland. A lawsuit will be costly. Can't you forego filing charges?"

Holland jabbed his finger in Taft's face. "If it was *your* family that was attacked in the safety of *your* home, is that what *you* would want?"

The question stopped Taft cold. He stormed out of the Chief's office, slamming the door after him. Captains Holland and Delstra gathered their files and started to leave.

"You two stay," Chief Carter ordered in his strong Brooklyn accent. They turned to face him.

"I don't know what's going on downstairs," he said, placing his palms flat on his desk. "After what I just heard, I don't want to know. I'm almost out of here. I'll bust the two of you back to school patrol if either of you interfere with my retirement."

Delstra and Holland exchanged quizzical glances.

Carter aimed his forefinger at Delstra, then at Holland. "Neither of you will file charges against Rowland Bostwick as long as I'm Chief. Understand?"

Holland walked out first. Neither answered.

CHAPTER FORTY-SEVEN
Dead Men Tell No Tales?

A CHILLY MIST floated from the sky as Hitchcock and Walker met off-duty at Brenner Brothers Bakery, a Jewish bakery and delicatessen located a block above Lake Bellevue. Taking coffee with them in paper cups, they went in Hitchcock's Jeep Wagoneer to the address of the '66 Firebird registered to Allan Ming.

The house was a neat white clapboard, of 1920s vintage in the heart of Seattle's International District. Ming's orange Firebird was parked in the driveway.

A plain, stoic Chinese woman in her early thirties answered the door.

They identified themselves. Hitchcock explained their mission.

"Please come in, officers," she said. The inside was clean and neatly furnished. The smell of cooked rice reminded Hitchcock of the kitchen at The Great Wall. She gestured to the couch.

"My name is Fen. The Seattle Police told me my brother Allan drowned," she said in clear, monotone American English, her face void of expression.

Hitchcock and Walker glanced at each other. "We are sorry for your loss, Miss. This is the first we heard of it. We came to ask a few questions about Allan."

"I was three years older than Allan," Fen explained. "Our parents came here from Taiwan before we were born. I am a widow. My two kids are in high school. Allan never married. He joined the Army, not drafted. He was in special forces, Rangers. After the Army he went to live with relatives in Taiwan."

"What did he do there?" Hitchcock asked.

"My auntie kicked him out when he fell in with criminals. He was there three years." He bought that car in my driveway for cash. He made frequent trips to Taipei. He was very good about helping me with my bills. Never asked to be repaid. The perfect uncle to my kids. Helped them with sports, homework, took them grocery shopping, that sort of thing. I never had to ask for the rent for his room."

"How did he pay you?"

"Cash."

"How did your husband die?" Walker asked softly.

"Throat cancer. He was a smoker all his life."

"Did Allan know a woman named Juju?" Hitchcock asked.

Fen paused. "I do not think I ever heard that name. He did not talk about his friends much and never said what he did. He knew I would disapprove."

"How about a place called The Great Wall?" Hitchcock asked.

"Yes. I recall something he said…"

Hitchcock felt he was taking a chance when he said, "We believe Allan was involved in drug smuggling with Juju, the owner of The Great Wall."

"Is it in Bellevue, by the freeway?" she asked.

Hitchcock nodded.

"Yes, he mentioned going there several times."

"Can you be more specific?"

"I'm sure it will come to mind later," she said. "Allan gave me the impression he went there for business, not social reasons. Since he did not have a job, it must have been something illegal."

"What about a guy named Scott?"

"Scott?"

"White guy."

"Yes." She said with a brief nod. "Allan's close friend."

Hitchcock showed her Scott Sorenson's mugshot.

She nodded. "Yes. That is Scott. Allan's buddy in the Rangers. Allan saved his life in Vietnam. I do not know the details. He came here often to pick up Allan and be gone all night. Allan told me Scott raced cars professionally before the Army. He had a fancy new black Mustang. They would be out all night."

"What else do you remember about Scott?"

"He dressed nice. Single, same age as Allan. A hard type. Always wore a long leather carcoat just like Allan's. Always had a lot of cash…"

"Like Allan," Walker finished the sentence. Fen nodded.

"What did Allan and Scott do when they were

together?" Hitchcock asked.

"All I ever heard them talk about was chasing women at bars. They were careful not to talk about it when my kids were up."

"Was Allan into drugs, marijuana or cocaine?" Walker asked.

"He liked marijuana, used cocaine sometimes, but being American, mainly he liked whiskey."

"What do you know about his friends," Walker asked.

"Other than Scott, they were all Chinese" Fen said. "Criminal types. They did not come around here because I would not allow it. I met a few of them when I was in town with Allan a few times. They are bad men."

"Do you remember any of their names?"

"I might be able to later," she said, dabbing tears from her eyes with a tissue.

Hitchcock signaled to Walker with his hand to let him ask the next question.

"Did Allan have any guns?" Hitchcock inquired.

Fen nodded. "My brother was a soldier. He loved guns."

"What kind of guns did he have?"

"A couple pistols that I know of."

"He drowned in the Duwamish River?"

"It was not an accident. Allan could swim well."

"Who do you think killed him?"

"The criminals he was involved with."

"Do you know what The Bamboo Union is?"

Hitchcock asked.

The question startled Fen. "Of course," she said, dropping her gaze, nervously biting her lip.

"And?"

She shook her head slightly. "I won't discuss it." Again, Hitchcock and Walker exchanged glances.

"Even though the medical examiner's report found no indication of foul play, we too believe your brother was murdered," Hitchcock said. "He had a high level of heroin in his blood, but drowning is the official cause of death. We suspect certain people in Bellevue set it up."

Fen impressed Hitchcock as a cultural introvert who only gave information when asked specific questions. "Are you working now?" he asked.

"I am between jobs."

"Will you help us in an undercover capacity?"

She dabbed her eyes again. "He was my brother."

"Juju Kwan is always looking for good help. Your code name when you call and leave messages will be 'Lotus'," Hitchcock said as they exchanged phone numbers. "One more thing before we go, could you show us the guns your brother had?"

She led them to Allan's bedroom and walked away. Walker opened the closet. He removed an Army dress green uniform with the Ranger shoulder patch and showed it to Hitchcock.

The two hard-side pistol cases Hitchcock found under the bed contained an old .22 caliber Harrington & Richardson revolver with four-inch barrel and a 9mm Walther P38 semi-automatic pistol. He sniffed both barrels. The .22 had been fired recently. A box of ammunition for each weapon was in each case. More boxes were in the closet. He wrote Fen a receipt for the weapons and the ammunition and took them for lab testing.

Walker copied the names and phone numbers in an address book he found in the nightstand drawer.

Hitchcock looked under the bed again. He reached for an object that caught his eye. It was a thirty-two-round magazine, filled with 9mm ammunition, stamped UZI.

He held up the magazine and asked Fen, "Do you know anything about this?"

"I have never seen it before."

† † †

FEN'S STREET GLISTENED in the wet from passing headlights in the early evening darkness. "You know you did the impossible just now," Walker said.

"What would that be?" Hitchcock asked, keeping his eyes on the street as he threaded through parked cars on both sides of the narrow street.

"The Chinese are so insular that their gangs can be infiltrated only by other Chinese, yet you landed a Chinese woman as a willing informant. Big things are gonna happen now, Roger. I can feel it."

"Bet my next paycheck the .22 is the murder weapon," Hitchcock said as he headed out of the neighborhood and entered the I-90 Eastbound onramp.

"Nothing doing."

"Mike Smith, Scott Sorenson and Allan Ming, even Colin Wilcox last year…all connected to Juju. All dead. She's eliminating every witness between her and the drug shipments including the murder of Andy Stanford and untold others," Hitchcock recalled.

"Dead men tell no tales, they say."

"Maybe one of them will this time."

"Allan Ming?"

"Uh-huh."

CHAPTER FORTY-EIGHT
The Captain's Gambit

DETECTIVE MEYN EAGERLY knocked on Captain Holland's office door. Holland beckoned him in. "What's up, Larry?"

"NYPD just informed me by phone that they found Bostwick in an apartment in New York, not his family's place. Apparently, he's hiding there."

Holland's eyebrows shot up. "Have you confirmed it?"

Meyn handed Holland a file folder. "The detective I've been working with sent me a copy of the apartment rental agreement Bostwick signed, and surveillance photos."

An amused smile crossed Holland's face as he looked through the photographs. "So Rowlie thinks by shaving off his mustache he's disguised himself?" He snorted, shaking his head.

"Why would he hide out in an apartment rather than one of his family's properties?" Meyn asked.

Holland exhaled sharply and leaned back in his chair. "I hadn't thought of that. You met his parents— what do you think?"

"Mom Bostwick's a snooty old East Coast broad—a plain, wrinkly Mrs. Gotrocks. Started screaming when she saw our photos of sonny-boy embracing a China doll with her blouse open in the back door of Juju's restaurant. Rowland told her he was working undercover but I don't think she bought it. Pop Bostwick is Mom in men's' clothes."

"The dad's femmie?" Holland asked, eyebrows arched.

"Overly refined, let's say."

"I'll get a certified letter off to Rowlie."

"No charges, Captain?"

"The senior prosecutor on the case pulled a Benedict Arnold on us," Holland said. "He's too scared to file charges or even back us on an investigative arrest. So, I'm pulling Rowlie's chain by sending him a nice letter so he knows he can't hide from us, and force his family lawyers to make a move that'll be fatal to their case."

"Aha," Meyn exclaimed. "Brilliant move, Captain. By sending Bostwick a certified letter at his hideout, he'll be forced to come clean and stand trial or leave the country."

Holland peered at Meyn. "Ever been to New York?"

CHAPTER FORTY-NINE
What Goes Around, Comes Around

IN HER OFFICE at The Great Wall, Juju Kwan read and re-read a letter she received from a big gun law firm in Seattle. An attorney for the Bostwick family requested a meeting at their office regarding her relationship with Rowland Bostwick, former lieutenant at the Bellevue Police Department.

How they knew about her and Bostwick didn't matter. She smirked at the thought that Bostwick's parents probably think of her as being on their side. What mattered was her relationship with Bostwick coming to light. If the legal process continued, it would expose far too much.

She knew Bostwick wouldn't talk; he'd go to prison if he did. Still, being subpoenaed as a witness in a lawsuit would ruin her. The date for the meeting with the attorney was next week. The envelope was stamped and posted regular mail. *I will say I never got it. It will buy me at least two weeks to make the necessary adjustments.*

The restaurant side of her business had been doing well until yesterday. One waitress quit to have her baby, and she had to fire another for stealing tips from other waitresses. She sorted through the list of applicants, looking for any with a Chinese name. There was only one, a Seattle address, and the application was recent. Juju dialed the number.

"This is Fen Huang," the woman on the other line answered.

† † †

"BINGO," OTIS SAID as he handed Hitchcock a copy of the toxicology report on Mike Smith just before shift briefing.

"He got a dose of his own medicine in the end," Hitchcock said smugly as he read it.

"It was just enough to sedate him. He probably fought being injected, which would explain the blows to the body and the defensive wounds."

"He went up the trail on his own two feet, bound, to his execution," Hitchcock mused.

"The plaster casts of shoe impressions around his body indicate two men led him to his execution."

"Then a woman who sounded like a white American in her twenties or thirties called in the body location to county dispatch," Hitchcock added. "That doesn't sound like anyone in Juju's circle I know of."

"We know almost nothing about Juju's associates," Otis said. "Last week, Smith's car was torched in the very spot where you tried to take a shot at him a couple months ago."

"Setting his car on fire was Smith's message to me

that it isn't over—he's still around," Hitchcock said.

"Think about it, Roger," Otis said, "the autopsy report estimates the time of death was within twenty-four hours before the anonymous call."

Hitchcock compressed his lips as he nodded solemnly. "Knowing who Smith was with twenty-four hours before he died would lead us to the executioners. Calling in the location of Smith's body so it would be found right away was for a tactical purpose."

"What else do you make of it?"

"That not everything points to the Dragon Lady," Hitchcock concluded. "My snitch named Smith as one of Juju's regular visitors. He comes in the back door, she takes him into her private office, he leaves minutes later, which indicates a business relationship. Juju was his supplier. I think she had Ming and Sorenson bump him off when she knew we were after Smith, then she had Ming and Sorenson executed."

Hitchcock paused and looked at Otis. "Do you think Ming and Sorenson killed Stanford too?"

"Don't go in too many directions at once," Otis advised. "You'll burn out. Focus on the death of Mike Smith. Wait for the lab results on Ming's .22 revolver."

"At least now we know that Juju's got someone at her beck and call who is good enough to take out two former Special Forces soldiers."

CHAPTER FIFTY
New York City

DETECTIVE LARRY MEYN sat wide-eyed as the cab he took from La Guardia airport to the NYPD's 5th Precinct on Elizabeth Street cruised through the city's SoHo District. Even Seattle's International District didn't compare with this eclectic collage of artists' lofts, art galleries, Bohemian and boutique restaurants, sidewalk vendors, and expensive brownstone neighborhoods. He hoped he wouldn't come across as a hick as the cab let him off at the precinct.

Detectives Angel Vargas and Bruno Schmidt warmly introduced themselves. Vargas, a powerfully built Hispanic in his early thirties, contrasted sharply with Schmidt, a tall, pale, lanky sort with a shock of corn-stalk yellow hair, a brusque manner and X-ray blue eyes.

They put Meyn's luggage in the trunk of an unmarked car and piled in. "Your guy Bostwick is a loner," Vargas said, talking over his shoulder at Meyn in the back seat. "Rarely leaves his apartment except to have dinner at the same Italian restaurant most every night, same waitress, old enough to be his mother."

"Does he have a car?"

"An older Jaguar sedan, green. Doesn't drive it

much. Takes a cab to dinner and back every night."

"I noticed from your photographs that he's shaved off his mustache," Meyn said. "Everybody used to remark that he looked like Heinrich Himmler."

"Who?" Vargas asked.

Schmidt nudged him. "Hitler's death squad henchman, the leader of Nazi SS troops, Einstein. Didn't you go to school?"

"We've got a couple other interviews to do, Larry, but since you just got off the plane after a four-hour flight, you're first up," Vargas said. "Lunch is on us, then we take you to your hotel, unless you'd like to go with us."

"Thanks, I appreciate it, and lunch is on my city."

"Nope," Schmidt said. "You're our guest. Relax"

Meyn smiled, looking up at rows of well-maintained elegant nineteenth-century mansions and colorful mom-and-pop shops as they weaved through the heavy traffic consisting of primarily yellow cabs. "Thanks. This is my first time here."

"So what's the deal with this Bostwick character, Larry? They tell us he was a lieutenant on your department out there. He resigned when he came under investigation for something, right?" Vargas asked as he drove through the streets of Manhattan.

"Basically, two hitmen paid a visit to the home of one of our top officers," Meyn said. "The officer had been making record drug arrests and seizures through his informants. He lived with his wife and kid in a secluded location. When the suspects were arrested, one of them had directions to the officer's home in his pocket. The writing and a fingerprint on the note matched Bostwick's."

Schmidt let out a low whistle as he and Vargas glanced at each other.

"Long story short," Meyn continued, "Bostwick quit rather than cooperate with the internal on him before it began. He's fleeing from criminal charges now. He's from here originally, so he came back to hide."

Vargas's jaw dropped. He looked at Meyn. "Damn! What happened to the officer?"

Meyn grinned. "The officer was a champion Golden Gloves boxer, a heavyweight. He was a member of the '64 Olympics boxing team. He destroyed the martial arts guy in seconds. Put him in the hospital. Had to have his jaw wired shut."

Vargas chuckled. "Cool! You said there were two perps?"

"The officer's dog tore up the other guy as he tried to escape. He had a knife on him. Needed a lot of stitches on his head, neck, hands, legs too."

Vargas and Schmidt laughed. "Sounds like the wild west out there," they exclaimed in their thick accents.

"What kinda dog did he have?" Schmidt asked.

"German Shepherd mix. A former junkyard dog."

"By the way, Larry, I ran a check on Rowland Bostwick since he's from here," Schmidt said. "I was surprised to learn he was the focus of our Department ten years ago."

Meyn was startled. "For what?"

"Weird stuff. Peeping, asking showgirls and strippers for pictures, calling them, following them."

"Was he ever interviewed or charged?"

"His family is wealthy. You know how that goes," Vargas said.

"I gotta ask," Detective Schmidt said. "How did this guy get hired by your Department? We had a lot of negative information on him that would have been available before he was hired."

"His family is wealthy...you know how that goes," Meyn echoed, shaking his head.

A weak autumn sun poked through the clouds as they pulled up to a neat, turn of the century four-story brownstone apartment building on Wooster Street.

Bruno Schmidt turned around in his seat to face Meyn. "Unless you tell us otherwise, we'll just knock on the door. If Bostwick opens, we'll invite ourselves in. Then we'll introduce you and we'll witness the interview."

"He knows me."

"So, just stand around the corner, out of sight at first, then surprise him," Vargas said with a shrug.

Meyn nodded. "Sounds like a plan. Apartment 402."

The manager buzzed them into the entry. The elevator was a rickety museum piece that struggled to every floor like an old man on crutches. It settled grumpily on the fourth. Meyn stood to one side, out of sight by the peephole of Apartment 402. Schmidt rang the buzzer.

No answer.

They knocked several times.

No answer.

Schmidt checked his watch. "It's eleven-twenty. Let's grab a bite at the deli two blocks down, then come back."

† † †

THE AROMA OF fresh onions, garlic, pastrami and rye bread greeted them at the door of the local Jewish deli, featuring a long, white Formica counter with round red stools. Small, round white tables and chrome chairs with green padded seats were all occupied but one. Meyn felt like he was an extra in a mob movie when he walked in with two detectives wearing trench-coats. He couldn't finish the pastrami on rye, the meat was piled so high.

Vargas and Schmidt asked Meyn more about how Bostwick became a police lieutenant. They shared details of the NYPD's investigations of him, which were stopped by his parents' attorneys. In the last case, the victim, an off-Broadway actress who specialized in playing seductive roles, disappeared during the investigation. "We checked on her status yesterday," Vargas said. "Still missing after ten years."

Shocked, Meyn took notes and case numbers for later follow-up.

An hour later, they returned to the apartment building. Still no answer at Bostwick's apartment.

Inside, they could hear the phone ring eight times before it stopped. Vargas left and returned with the manager, who let them in. The place reflected

Bostwick's inner man. The living room and kitchen were richly furnished and orderly, but cold and sterile. On closer inspection, everything was dirty, thick with dust and otherwise poorly kept.

In the bedroom they found Bostwick hanging by the neck from the ceiling, his feet dangling two feet above the floor. A dining room chair was overturned on the right side of the body.

"There goes the rest of our day, Angel," Schmidt muttered.

Vargas stared at the body a moment longer, then turned to Meyn. "That him, Larry?"

"*Was*," Meyn replied, staring at the distorted facial features. Meyn, a veteran death investigator, stared at the body of a man he knew enough to dislike, hanging from the ceiling. *Is this Bostwick's response to Captain Holland's letter? No, something's not right—what is it?* he asked himself.

On the unmade bed was Captain Holland's certified letter on Department letterhead. The text was brief and terse—it advised Bostwick that he was facing certain criminal charges and that unless he voluntarily returned and surrendered himself, he would be hunted down and extradited back to stand trial.

"Looks like Bostwick had more to hide than anyone thought, Larry!" Vargas exclaimed when he read Captain Holland's letter.

"What does this do to your case?" Schmidt asked.

"It isn't kaput," Meyn said. "He was in cahoots with certain others in the drug business. It means we gotta go deeper."

Vargas lifted Bostwick's left hand and felt the armpit. "Almost room temperature. No rigor. Most likely been hanging for eight to ten hours."

Schmidt left and returned with a camera. "Medical examiner's on the way," he said as he began snapping pictures of the body, and the rope tied to an exposed ceiling beam.

"Something wrong, Larry?" Vargas asked.

"His tongue isn't sticking out as it should, for one, and his skin tone is wrong for having died from lack of oxygen because of hanging," Meyn said. "If possible, I'd like to attend the autopsy."

"I'll see if that can be arranged," Schmidt said.

While Vargas and Schmidt worked with the medical examiner, Meyn looked around. He found only packed clothes and personal care items when he opened the two suitcases on the floor outside the walk-in closet.

"Who can tell me the name of the waitress Bostwick talked to, and the restaurant she works at?" Meyn asked.

"Luigi's on Canal Street," Angel replied. "The waitress is a tall, older white broad named Norma. Works five till closing at midnight. Tell you what, I'll pick you up at your hotel at seven and introduce you to make it easier."

THE SKY WAS dark by seven o'clock, but blazing lights lit up the city that never sleeps like daylight. Luigi's was a traditional family-owned neighborhood Italian restaurant, red-and-white checkerboard tablecloths, mouthwatering aromas of tomato sauce and pasta. They ordered coffee and small dishes of spumoni.

Norma, a gray-haired woman in her mid-fifties with the type of face people trusted their secrets to smiled as she introduced herself. She cried when Angel told her Rowland was dead.

"I'd only known him for a couple months. Waz he in some kinda trouble?"

"He was, but I'm not at liberty to say," Meyn said. "Did he tell you he was a police officer in the Seattle area?"

"Not exactly. When I first met him, he said he'd been involved in some kinda government work. Had to quit. Getting ready to go to another country where they couldn't find him. He told me yesterday that he received a tip from someone he knew back there that he was about to be paid a surprise visit by the police out there."

Meyn did his best to hide his shock when he heard that. "Did he say if the person who tipped him off was connected to the police department?"

"No, but somehow I had that impression," Norma replied, her voice husky with grief.

"What country was he going to, did he say?"

"Chile, I think he said, or one of those countries down there."

They thanked her for the information and left.

"How do you guys read the waitress?" Meyn asked.

"A lonely soul. We found an airline ticket in his luggage," Vargas said. "He was headed for Santiago, Chile in two days. It's a one-way ticket."

CHAPTER FIFTY-ONE
Damage Control

FEARING AUDITS BY the state or the Feds, Juju pored over her two ledgers in the silence of her office. The first showed income from drug importing and direct sales to street level dealers that she disguised using fake sales records and receipts, creating a false record of profitability for her restaurant and bar. The other ledger showed the true expenses and profits from drug sales.

She responded to a light knocking on her office door. "A white lady name Monica is here asking for you," the waitress said in English, bowing her head.

"Thank you, Fen. Ask her to meet me in the lounge."

Juju closed her books and went out to meet Monica Dwyer.

They forced smiles at each other when Juju joined her at a dark corner table. She ordered Taiwan whiskey, Monica a martini.

"Thought I'd stop by on my lunch break. How are things?" Monica asked.

Juju took a sip. The fiery liquid relaxed her. "Rebuilding. Want in?"

Monica looked surprised. "Seriously? What would I

have to offer?"

"You get me your friend, the part-time hooker, then you my partner."

"You can't be serious," Monica scoffed. "Dolly's old."

Juju shook her head. "She got great figure, she good looking, experienced. I know men. They like her."

"I thought you were only into the import business."

"Bad *joss* lately. I branch out now, rebuild," she said with a broad wave of her hand.

"What is *joss*?" Monica asked.

"You in America call it luck, or fortune."

"Have you considered after-hours gambling?"

"That next. Back to your friend..."

"She turned you down before," Monica reminded.

"You want in, you get her for me. Tell her she name her price. You, me get a cut. I guarantee her customers and protection."

"What kind of protection?"

"You've seen him."

"The young cop? What if she asks me how this works? What will I say?"

"If she asks, it mean yes, Monica. Tell her I set up private, separate room next to my office, furnish nice. Only a few hours, a few nights a week."

"What do I get if she accepts?"

"I make you manager and madam. Like before."

Flustered, Monica asked "What do you mean by *before*?"

Juju leered at Monica as she sipped her whiskey.

"We know. You madam before, in Vancouver."

Monica gasped. "How… Who…?"

"Get me your friend," Juju said in a low voice.

"If she still refuses?"

"Find another like her, then you in."

Monica glanced at her watch and stood up. "I'll get back to you."

† † †

THE NEXT MORNING, the Great Wall's lead food prepper, a dark brown, squat Asian woman in her late forties, a white towel wrapped around her head, appeared in the doorframe, of Juju's office. She was very agitated. She spoke only the Khalkha dialect of the Mongolian tongue, and a smattering of pidgin English. "Bingwen! No here! Bingwen! No here!" she exclaimed.

The news alarmed Juju. Bingwen was her cook. "Maybe he sick," she suggested in English to calm the food prepper. "I call. You wait."

The food prepper grunted and nodded assent as she waited, shifting her considerable amplitude from side to side in a nervous rocking motion.

Juju spoke Mandarin on the phone. An expression of deep concern came over her face. She asked more questions, her brow furrowing as she listened. When the call ended, she turned to the food prepper.

"Wife say Bingwen gone. Know not where. She worried. You get Shu here. She cook today."

The first customer through the front door two hours later gave Juju a small brown paper sack. "Found this taped to your front door," he said. "Looks like a wallet inside. Must be for your lost and found."

Juju's blood ran cold when she recognized Bingwen's wallet in the sack. Identification and cash were present. It was a message, not robbery or an honest person turning in lost property, the equivalent of sending a kidnapped victim's body part to a relative. *Bingwen's wife is a widow now. If I give his wallet to her or the police, it'll start an investigation against me.*

Bingwen's wife called Juju the next day, frantic for some news. On the third day she called Juju, sobbing, saying the police found Bingwen's bullet-riddled body in his car in the rough, low-income South Seattle neighborhood of White Center, locally known as "Rat City." He lived miles north in the International District.

To avoid drawing suspicion to herself, Juju closed her restaurant for two days and required her employees to attend Bingwen's funeral in Chinatown with her to show respect for his family.

Bingwen was murdered well away from home or work, yet his wallet was deposited at his workplace. It was a message for Juju—the Escondite people killed Bingwen to avenge her murder of their bartender, Francisco Garcia.

Alone in her office, she stared at the paper sack on her desk that held Bingwen's wallet. *There will be war,* she decided as she put the wallet in her safe.

Juju reckoned Hitchcock's seizures of drugs and arrests of people connected to her, and the recent heist of the drug shipment headed for her indicated a traitor in her close-knit organization. At great cost she had launched a scorched earth policy to root out whoever it was, with no results. At least there were no witnesses left who could connect her to the drug influx, or the attack on Hitchcock. But rivals were popping up everywhere and new people were needed if she was to survive and rebuild.

Money, new people, and another shipment were needed to rebuild. The heroin the cops seized from the Mexican operation would have replaced her loss perfectly, but Bostwick failed to steal it from the evidence room as she ordered him, as he promised he would, just as he didn't get rid of Hitchcock as he claimed he had.

Personal and business security, plus intelligence on the other side needed immediate attention. For her back door, which she always kept open for fresh air and male visitors, she had a locksmith install a deadbolt lock and a peephole with a brass lid on the inside.

Her sources informed her where Bostwick was in New York, pending a permanent move to Chile, and that the police would send a detective to interview him about the attack on Hitchcock. She picked up the phone and dialed a familiar number.

CHAPTER FIFTY-TWO
Cougar Mountain Drive

TRUCK HEADLIGHTS SHONE in Juju's rearview mirror as she headed east on the frontage road after closing the next night. They followed her east on I-90 and made the same lane changes she did, even took the Newport Way exit and turned right onto Cougar Mountain Drive, a steep, winding, unlighted hard-dirt road covered by a thin layer of gravel with no guard rails. There was no traffic at 2:00 a.m. The pickup stayed less than a car-length behind her, headlights on high-beam, glaring into her rearview mirror, making it difficult for her to focus on the road.

A half mile up, when the road turned sharply to the right, Juju felt a hard jolt to the rear. In her rearview she saw two men in the pickup truck, its engine roaring, tires whining, pushing her toward the road's edge. She panicked as she braked, but her Cadillac El Dorado slid on loose gravel on hardpan, slick as a sheet of ice.

Heart thumping, gasping, Juju screamed as she accelerated and turned the steering wheel to the right in a desperate attempt to avoid going down the mountainside. In so doing she exposed the right side of her car to the pickup, which accelerated, ramming the passenger door. She screamed and covered her face as her car rolled over the edge, flipped side over side down the mountain, crashing into Douglas Fir trees, until it disappeared.

† † †

EL ESCONDITE INN owners Carlos and Tomas Vasquez arrived from California. Repeated police raids, arrests, sloppy management, failure to follow business regulations, compounded with the loss of over a million dollars in drugs placed them on the edge of a financial cliff.

They intended to pull out and return to Nevada until the abduction and murder of their bartender, Francisco Garcia. The previous owners of their hotel warned them that their most formidable competition would be the Chinese woman who owned The Great Wall restaurant and lounge.

At first the Vasquez brothers tried to live in peace with their rival. They had their own supply line. But the abduction and murders of their employees demanded a response. They took revenge by abducting and killing her cook. They knew too much about her to believe the rumor that she had gone into hiding. It was more likely that Juju was laying low to mount a counterattack. The Vasquez brothers held to the belief that best defense is a powerful offense.

CHAPTER FIFTY-THREE
The Rahab Proposition

MONICA DWYER STOPPED by Dolly Searles's home after work, unannounced. She smiled when Dolly opened the door. "Thought I'd drop by to see how you're doing," she said.

Dolly hesitated. "Come in but speak softly. I just put the kids down for a nap. Coffee?"

"Sure," Monica said, impressed to see how neat and clean Dolly's home was, even with so many kids' toys.

"This is a surprise. Haven't seen or heard from you in a while. What brings you here?"

"Oh, life," Monica said as she removed her coat.

"Life?" Dolly echoed as she set a mug of coffee in front of Monica.

"Yes. Is life treating you well lately?"

"Not really. My hours have been cut in half because the cops have all but shut down the El Escondite, and you know what the job market is like. I've got applications in everywhere."

"What about your weekend sideline?"

Dolly took a sip of her coffee. "Still have it, but..."

"But?"

"One of my men is getting married for the third time, and another is getting back with his ex-wife for the kids' sake."

"So, you're down on your luck there too." She said as she put her hand on Dolly's forearm. "I came as a friend, Dolly, so I'll get right to the point. I've been asked to forward you an offer of a part-time job across the freeway that has your name on it, and the money is beyond what you've ever made before."

Dolly studied Monica. "Tell me about this offer."

"Less hours, much more money. I'm jealous that it's you the job is being offered to and not me."

"You haven't said what it is."

"Juju wants you to work for her exclusively, evenings only. Name your price. She says she'll pay it and provide you with everything you need."

"You've *got* to be kidding. I'm in my mid-forties."

"I mentioned that to her."

"What did she say?"

"You have a great figure. You're pretty. She sees how men look at you, and I have to admit, she's right."

Dolly shook her head, dismayed. "Really. I'm flattered. Stunned, in fact. I thought she was doing well with her restaurant and her import business. No?"

"Juju's fallen on hard times and needs to diversify."

"Hmm. So where would I work for her, may I ask?"

"She'd set up and furnish a separate room inside her restaurant, in the back."

"What else would she provide?"

"Nicer clothes, and customers. She gets a cut."

"What's in this for you?"

Monica looked sheepish as she said, "I get a cut too, Dolly. I hope you're not offended. The company I work for has been sold. I'll be out of a job soon. I'll be joining Juju in her business. I *need* you to say yes. I will take care of your interests. I'll be a good manager. *Your* manager."

"Why don't you do it yourself, then? You're what, in your late twenties, early thirties at most?"

"Thirty-two. I would, but the job is offered to you, not me. Men always check *you* out when we're together, not me." Monica said, smiling. "You're my friend, Dolly. It hurts me to see you struggling as a cleaning maid, making what, a buck-and-half an hour, and –"

"A buck sixty and they keep my hours below forty a week, so they don't have to pay benefits."

"How demeaning," Monica said, staring at Dolly. "Working for Juju you'll make much more in less time."

"With so many adventurous young women out there who can't find work, why me, Monica?"

"No offense, but I asked Juju that. She sees you as a trustworthy, stable professional who isn't hardened."

Dolly smiled. "Well, I'm not offended, Monica, and we're still friends."

"Is your answer yes, then?"

"My answer is I'll think about it."

"I see the power company shutoff notice on the table. You can't pay it, can you?"

Dolly's cheeks bloomed red. "I will seriously think about it, Monica," she said, "I'll let you know. Soon."

CHAPTER FIFTY-FOUR
Juju Is Missing

9:00 A.M.
The Great Wall

EMPLOYEES WERE NERVOUS when Juju didn't show up. Her office door was locked. The new head cook used his master key to let the kitchen crew in. The food preppers and cooks scrambled to make up for lost time. Waitresses asked where Juju was when they came in at eleven o'clock. The newest waitress peered out the back door. Juju's El Dorado wasn't there.

Tension mounted when customers began coming in at 11:30 and no one could get the cash register tills because Juju's office was locked. Monica Dwyer stopped by on her lunch break. She called a locksmith.

PERCHED ON THE rugged, heavily forested northeast slope of Cougar Mountain, the sound of rain pelting the windshield and passenger side windows of her Cadillac El Dorado awakened Juju. Now that it was light out, she could see her car had rolled until it came to rest on the driver's side, saved from rolling farther down the mountain by heavy foliage and evergreen saplings.

Searing pain filled her head. Still in the driver seat, pressed against the door, her hair felt caked with something stiff, like dried soap. Her left arm was squished against the driver's door. She touched her scalp with her right hand and looked at it. Dried blood. Her feet were numb and cold. She was trapped in her seat by her seat belt. Her right hand lacked the strength to press the buckle enough to release it.

She struggled against the seat belt to reach the passenger door. Her car slid downward. Brush crackled under its weight. Heart pounding, she stopped moving. She knew she was many yards down the steep mountainside where she couldn't be seen.

Daylight came. The rain stopped. It was deathly quiet. She heard a school bus rumble on the road above. She hit the horn—it worked. She honked repeatedly. No one came. Dizziness overcame her as she listened all her might for sounds of passing traffic on the road above. *Must I die here? Now? Like this?* She couldn't move her left hand, she couldn't feel her legs or her feet, then her mind went blank.

Hours later Juju awoke. It was completely dark outside and the stale air in the car was cold. She stopped shivering long enough to hear the rushing wind in the trees above and below her. *What if a tree falls on me?*

Again, she screamed for help until she passed out, this time from despair and exhaustion. Her body felt weaker when she awoke. She had no idea how much time had passed, for it was still utter darkness outside. *Maybe I am already dead! The men in that truck—who are they? Why did they target me? Who sent them?* She began honking her horn again when she thought she heard a car passing on the road above. Nothing.

She awoke again. It was daylight now. There were more sounds of passing cars on the road above her. She honked her horn frantically. The sound of the horn was much weaker now. *The battery is dying! It is my only hope!* She called on her long-dead ancestors for help. Nothing. Her body felt dehydrated. She relieved itself into her clothes, there being no other choice. She passed out.

At the sounds of more traffic above her, (she didn't know how much time had passed) she honked the horn furiously until it became a faint beep, then gave out, and the noise of traffic above her faded away. As Juju wept, her car shifted and slid very slightly farther downhill, sideways.

She took a deep breath.

Then she smelled gasoline…

CHAPTER FIFTY-FIVE
The Fly in the Ointment

IN HIS OFFICE on the top of his twentieth-floor building in downtown Seattle, Horace MacAuliffe pressed the phone against his ear as he stared out the window at the Winslow Ferry approaching the pier. After the third ring, private investigator Tobias Olson answered.

"Horace MacAuliffe, here, Toby. It's been two months since we reviewed our Hitchcock investigation. I'm calling for a progress report."

"My undercover agent, a woman ex-con named June, became friends with Allison Malloy through her employment at the Pancake Corral, Mr. MacAuliffe," Olson replied matter-of-factly.

"Isn't this a little like closing the barn door after the cows left? Allison quit working there weeks ago, or did you know that, Toby?" MacAuliffe asked pointedly.

"Allison isn't working anywhere because she has another baby on the way. Our surveillance team confirms that she still goes to the Pancake Corral twice a week or more for lunch and social reasons."

"And?" MacAuliffe demanded.

"You'll be pleased to know that June, who was recently paroled from the women's prison in Purdy, has become friends with Allison. She's even been in the Hitchcock's home socially."

"I'm impressed, Toby. Anything else?"

"She's seen your grandson with his mother every one of those times."

"And Trevor's health and living conditions?"

"So far June has nothing negative to report. Trevor appears well cared for and is involved in family activities with his mother and stepdad. Allison already had a baby boy when we started our operation and is pregnant again. She doesn't work outside the home."

"Come on, how can do they do that on a cop's salary?" MacAuliffe grumbled.

"I checked on that. He kept their first house and rents it out at a profit."

So, Hitchcock's got business-sense too, MacAuliffe commented mentally with grudging admiration. "What else did the surveillance team turn up from the house I rented across the street?"

"They have dozens of photographs of comings and goings at their house, plus of Allison when they follow her from home. They've produced written logs of everything. I'll have it couriered to your office this afternoon. They say Hitchcock is going to work in uniform again."

"Probably got kicked out of whatever he was doing."

"Possibly."

"What's your take on this, Toby?"

"As individuals and a married couple, they're as squeaky-clean as it gets."

MacAuliffe drummed his fingers on his desk as he digested Olson's report. "What do you advise, then?"

"Ordinarily I'd advise closing the books on the investigation and the surveillance."

"But?"

"Several times our surveillance team has observed a suspicious man sitting on the street in an old tan Ford pickup, watching the house."

"Could be a maintenance man."

"That's what we thought at first. Sometimes we'd see a lawn mower in the back of his pickup. I was suspicious so I had my people tail him as he tailed Hitchcock to work and Allison to the Pancake Corral which he has done several times. One time my team saw him go into the Pancake Corral when Allison went there with Trevor and her baby. He ate when she did and left soon after she did."

"I don't like the sound of this, Toby."

"Me either, Mr. MacAuliffe. The man is middle-aged, nothing outstanding about his appearance. What's alarming is that he sometimes wears disguises."

"Disguises! What do you mean?"

"Different styles of hats, clothing and eyewear, even a wig. You'll see that in the photographs you're getting. We have no idea who he is, but since your grandson is in the middle of all this, I say let's not pull the plug yet."

"I agree. See if you can identify this man. My

concern is my grandson. I couldn't care less about Allison, her thug husband or their other kids. Let's keep both the waitress and the surveillance team operations going another month, then we'll assess."

"Yes, sir, Mr. MacAuliffe."

MacAuliffe buzzed his secretary. "Get Oscar Travis on the line for me." He returned his gaze to the gray-blue waters of Puget Sound, musing, until his phone rang.

"Your attorney's secretary advises that Mr. Travis is out of town until early next week. If you need immediate assistance, Mr. Travis's associate is available."

"That won't be necessary. Leave a message that I would like to hear from Oscar as soon as possible."

MacAuliffe hung up, his mind swimming with speculations about who the mystery stalker is and who could be behind him. He bit off and spit out the end of a cigar and puffed his cheeks like a blowfish as he sucked and blew smoke until the end glowed orange. He sat back in his chair, puffing smoke, the fingers of his right hand drumming the top of his desk, mulling his next move.

CHAPTER FIFTY-SIX
Postmortem

DETECTIVE MEYN WALKED into Captain Holland's office, where Sergeant Jurgens and Captain Delstra were waiting for him. He gave them the full details of being with NYPD detectives when they discovered Bostwick's suicide, his conversation with the waitress who had befriended Bostwick, and his past as the subject of prior police investigations, all squelched by his parents.

"Was there a note anywhere?" Sergeant Jurgens asked.

"No note. We found your letter on the bed. There were other papers, phone bills, travel reservations and letters," Meyn said, "but I couldn't take any of it with me. They allowed me to take pictures of everything and I have a copy of their report."

"No note," Holland mused. "How sure are the detectives that it was suicide?"

"Bostwick was dressed when we found him. Long sleeve shirt, cuffs buttoned. His apartment was on the fourth floor, door locked. No sign of forced entry, or a struggle. I had a hunch something was wrong, so I extended my stay so I could attend the autopsy. Good thing I did. When his shirt was removed, I saw defense wounds, abrasions on the front of both forearms, and a contusion to his solar plexus. Whoever hit him can really pack a punch."

Holland, Delstra and Jurgens exchanged glances.

"What was the ruling on the cause of death?" Delstra asked.

"It wasn't official by the time I left, but I checked before our meeting. They're holding off on ruling it as a homicide. For now, they're going with 'hanging'."

"Why is that?" Sergeant Jurgens asked.

"Neither of the detectives I was with attended the autopsy," Meyn said. "They generally don't do that there, I guess. I was told a homicide dick would review the file and call me. That could take weeks, from what I saw."

"This stays in this room," Holland said. "I don't want any publicity. Bostwick's parents are in the early stages of a lawsuit against the City and the Department. Since our traitorous city manager is behind the scenes, fanning the flames, we'll keep this back as our ace in the hole."

Holland dismissed Sergeant Jurgens and Detective Meyn. He faced Delstra when they left.

"Something more than an internal investigation forced Bostwick to take such drastic steps as quit, then hide out in New York until he could relocate in another country," Delstra said.

"Have a look," Holland said as he handed Delstra a folder. "Jurgens and Meyn haven't seen these, and they won't. One each was mailed to me and members of the city council."

"Damn!" Delstra exclaimed as he examined the five-by-seven color photographs of Bostwick, naked except for his uniform shirt, in bed with an obviously underage Asian girl, also naked.

"Who would have guessed Bostwick was being blackmailed," Holland said.

"Take a closer look, Dennis. He looks drunk or passed out. I bet they gave him a Mickey Finn."

"Meyn and Small believe he signaled his willingness to talk with them the last time they saw him at his parents' house," Holland said. "Maybe he knew he was coming to the end and wanted to come clean— we'll never know. I doubt he ever knew he'd been set up by organized crime."

"He certainly knew that he set up Hitchcock, a fellow officer, to be attacked at his home by two hitmen," Delstra scoffed.

Holland shook his head. "Whether or not Bostwick was passed out when the photo was taken is immaterial, Erik. Moot. The damage is done."

"How so?"

"Copies of the photos I showed you were mailed to members of the city council and the city manager."

Delstra let out a low whistle. "I almost feel sorry for the bastard."

"Don't. He's a victim of his own schemes."

"I said *almost*. Does the Chief know about the photos?"

"I showed them to him."

Delstra looked askance at Holland. "Had to, Erik. He's the Chief. Besides, others already had the photos. Better for the Chief to learn about it from us than them."

"You're going to be asked this, so I'll go first--how do you feel about your letter sending Bostwick over the edge, Dennis?"

Holland shrugged. "The inner rooms of hell are reserved for the world's Judases."

† † †

THE MORNING AFTER the meeting, Detective Meyn found an envelope on his desk from the King County Sheriff's Office. Inside was a copy of the Washington State Patrol Crime Lab report. He knocked on Sergeant Jurgens's office door as soon as he read it.

"I'm glad King County thought to share this with us," Jurgens said. "Dennis needs to know. Come with me."

Jurgens knocked on Captain Holland's door.

"Captain," Meyn said, "the lab report is in. It says the .22 revolver belonging to Allan Ming is *not* the weapon that fired the bullet that was removed from the head of Colin Wilcox two years ago, or Andrew Stanford, or Mike Smith."

Holland looked at Meyn. "Wasn't Wilcox the felon Hitchcock arrested in Eastgate's Charlie's Tavern, some time back?"

"He was," Meyn replied.

"That eliminates Ming as the killer, but there's

more," Jurgens said, looking at Meyn.

"Ming is dead. Drowned a few weeks ago. He also had a loaded thirty-two-round magazine for an Israeli submachine gun in his room at his sister's home in Seattle," Meyn said.

"Hmm," Holland said. "There's more...what is it?"

"Ming's sister believes her brother Allan was murdered. Says he was a strong swimmer—drowning was unlikely. He had no job, always had cash, nice clothes, a muscle car. He and his friend, Scott Sorenson, hung out at The Great Wall, Juju Kwan' place. Sorenson was killed by a hit-and-run driver the day after Ming's body was fished out of the Duwamish River."

A pensive silence permeated the room.

"Once again our dilemma is jurisdiction," Captain Holland said. "The drugs are imported and sold here, but the murders happen in the county, or Seattle."

"They're exploiting the lack of unity between agencies, Captain," said Meyn.

"We've got three executions by the same gun which says same shooter. All we know now is that it wasn't Ming."

CHAPTER FIFTY-SEVEN
Lotus Checks In

PATTY IN RECORDS called Hitchcock at home. "A woman by the name of Lotus just called. She wants you to call her at this number right away."

Fen Hoang answered on the first ring. "Officer Hitchcock?"

"Yes, Fen. How are you?"

"I have been hired as a waitress at The Great Wall."

"Great work! I am very pleased."

"Juju interviewed me in person three days ago and told me then that I had the job. I started that day. But Juju was not there yesterday or today. Some of the employees went to her house today but she is not there and her car is gone. I thought you would want to know."

"Juju's missing! What's going on in the restaurant?"

"A white woman named Monica, apparently a friend of Juju's, came in yesterday to help. She has her own job so she cannot be there all the time. Everybody is worried."

"I want to know everything that goes on there. Keep me posted. You will be paid for your information."

"I do not want money for this. She had my brother

killed," Fen said, a knife-edge in her voice. "Blood for blood. My pay will be her destruction."

Hitchcock felt a sudden jolt of apprehension as he hung up. *First Connie Fowler disappears, then Smith, who is dead, Juju's drug mules get themselves bumped off, now Juju has vanished. A third man is involved, but who?*

CHAPTER FIFTY-EIGHT
The Plight of Dragon Lady

JUJU KWAN GASPED when she awoke, finding herself in a hospital bed. The sterile room smelled of antiseptics. A large window next to her bed overlooked the 405 freeway. Intravenous tubes infused fluids into her arm. Oxygen from a white plastic cannula flowed into her nostrils. Bewildered, she asked the rosy-cheeked, chubby young nurse checking her vital signs, "Where am I?"

"Overlake Hospital, Miss Kwan," the nurse said softly. "You're lucky to be alive. That was quite a concussion you had. How are you feeling?"

Juju groaned as she touched her head with her free hand. She felt a lump on top, and stitches." I...I hurt. How long I here?"

The nurse handed her a cup of water and two white tablets. "For the pain."

"How long I here?" Juju asked again as she washed the pills down her throat with water.

"Three days. Do you remember what happened? You were trapped in your car for two days before you were found."

It hurt to swallow. Her head ached as she talked. "I drive up road to my house, then I roll down mountain."

"You've got contusions and abrasions on your chest and shoulders from the seatbelt when your car rolled. Your injuries will take time to heal. Luckily you didn't puncture a lung, or worse. You wouldn't have survived a day with a punctured lung."

Juju looked down in shock at the cuts scabbing on her hands and arms. None of them had stitches. She touched her fingers to her cheeks. "My face?"

"Superficial scratches. Doctor said no stitches needed."

"I own restaurant. I must leave."

"You'll need to stay longer, I'm afraid. The swelling in your brain hasn't gone down enough to release you and not all your test results are back. You may need further treatments for your injuries."

Juju winced as she tried to sit up in bed. "Please hand me phone and purse."

She dialed the Great Wall and gave instructions for the restaurant and bar over the phone. She told the bartender to tell Monica Dwyer to come in person.

AT ALMOST SIX in the evening, a worried looking Monica Dwyer appeared in the doorway of Juju's room, holding a bouquet of flowers. Juju managed a strained smile and motioned her in.

"Juju, I am so sorry! We were all worried about you. What happened?"

"I black out. I almost home, then my car rolling down the mountain, then I here. Hurt everyplace."

"You don't remember? What would cause you to black out while you're driving?"

Juju sighed deeply. "Road to my place steep, gravel, no lights, no rail. I alone, black out."

"That's scary, Juju," Monica said, frowning with concern. "Have you ever passed out before?"

"One time. Maybe two time. Not sure. Two, three year ago. Not driving then."

"Did you see a doctor?"

"Yes but he not know why."

Monica pulled up a chair next to Juju's bed. "How can I help you while you're here?"

"Keep eye on my business. Need cash quick. We bring gambling back when I up."

"Poker?"

Juju shook her head. "Mahjong. You talk Dolly? She say yes to my offer?"

"She said she's interested, Juju. She asked questions. Wants to talk to you."

Juju grinned despite the pain it caused her. "Ah, that mean yes. I sleep now. You tell Dolly come see me here."

JUJU WAITED TEN minutes after Monica left, then placed an international collect call to Taipei. After a series of transfers and silent periods interspersed by Juju's requests in Mandarin, Mr. Chen came on the line.

"I will give only a few facts over the phone," she said. Chen listened patiently.

"Two men in truck followed me from work and ran me off the road," she continued. "They thought they had killed me because they didn't return. My car rolled over and over down the mountain. I was trapped inside for two days. A school bus driver was able to see down the mountain saw my car."

When she finished, Mr. Chen cleared his throat, then paused longer before speaking. "In three days, two of our men will contact you. The code word will be 'Fulong.' You will give them the details in person. Expect no further shipments at this time."

Distraught that even after years of making Chen a rich man, he still did not trust her. She wondered, but dared not ask, what the two men he was sending were supposed to do—interrogate her? Go through her books? Abduct and execute her rivals? Take her back to Taiwan?

That last possibility—a forced return to Taiwan, had happened to others she knew. Everyone recalled or forced back at Chen's direction was executed or disappeared. That she could face the same fate angered her. Her brows furrowed. *I will wait to see what Mr. Chen's men will do. If taking me back to Taiwan is what they intend, I have surprise for them,* she resolved.

CHAPTER FIFTY-NINE
Ala David vs Goliath

HITCHCOCK AND ALLIE waited in the lobby of a law firm on the seventh floor of the Smith Tower in downtown Seattle. A dapper, well-dressed attorney in his early thirties introduced himself as Mark Solomon and showed them to his office.

"In case you're wondering, I've been an attorney for six years. I specialize in family law."

"What's your track record?" Hitchcock asked.

"My track record? You mean in court?"

Hitchcock nodded.

"We try to keep our clients' costs and risks as low as possible by settling out of court if we can. The hours involved in preparing a case for trial are beyond the resources of most clients. In the last three years, I've gone to trial on child custody matters eight times and won a favorable verdict six times. The other two trials were a wash. Neither side prevailed."

"Okay then," Hitchcock said. "We're defendants, the plaintiff is the grandfather of my wife's son, her ex-father-in-law. This is his second attempt to get custody of Trevor. My wife won last time, even though she didn't have an attorney." Hitchcock handed him a file folder holding the recent summons, complaint, and documents.

Solomon's eyebrows went up when he opened the file. "*Horace MacAuliffe* is the plaintiff?"

Hitchcock explained the basis of MacAuliffe's previous attempt to obtain custody. "He's basing this effort on the premise that the violence directed at me as a police officer makes our home an unsafe environment for his grandson."

"Is he relying on records subpoenaed from your department?" Solomon asked.

"So, I'm told."

"Is there a particular incident he's focusing on?"

"More than one, I think." He told Solomon about the gunfight on the Eastgate frontage road.

Solomon nodded and smiled. "I remember it in the news. Saw the TV coverage and read about it in the paper. A clean shooting. A big deal in any town. But that was when Roger was on duty. It had nothing to do with his family environment. Unless they present something more compelling, they don't have sufficient cause to remove your child from his home."

"Is there anything else MacAuliffe would base his action on?" Solomon asked, looking at Allie, then Hitchcock.

A profound silence happened. Allie and Hitchcock gazed pointedly at each other. Then Allie described the attack at their earlier home in which Trevor was frightened, and what ultimately happened to the two invaders.

"Ah. *That's* the biggie," Solomon said. "Any judge, jury member, parent or grandparent will wonder if a child in Trevor's position is in a perpetual state of risk." He turned to Allie. "As my client, I'd like to know your thoughts on this, Mrs. Hitchcock."

"Call me Allie," she said. "Both Roger and I lost our fathers prematurely. Roger has enemies for doing his job, and I do for marrying and having a baby with the wrong man. Roger loved me and married me knowing my situation. I'm with him for life. We're here to fight back. Will you help us is what I want to know?"

Hitchcock took hold of her hand as he looked at Solomon.

"I'll take the case. This is David versus Goliath. MacAuliffe, as Goliath is loaded. From what I've heard, he breaks opponents financially with legal costs, subpoenas, depositions and expert witnesses. We'll obtain the same records from your department they did. It will be helpful if we have an expert witness, preferably a child psychologist, interview Trevor and testify to his mental and emotional stability."

Allie breathed a sigh of relief. "Thank you," she whispered.

Solomon handed them a contract and retainer agreement. "My hourly rate is two hundred dollars. I will require a retainer of seven hundred dollars to begin the work. That covers two hours of my time to file a response to the plaintiff's attorney, read the case after our staff has obtained police records."

"How much after that?" Hitchcock asked.

"Your retainer won't cover the interrogatories, a step that is required of both sides. These are written questions the parties answer to in writing, and under oath under penalty of perjury to each other as part of the pre-trial discovery process. The questions must be answered within thirty days."

"And then?"

"After that, both sides may demand depositions of the other side, including witnesses being called. Depositions are held in person, under oath, recorded by a court reporter who records the proceedings. There's a strong likelihood we'll need an expert witness, a child psychologist, the best we can find. There's a fee for the court reporter too."

Allie's voice trembled as she put her hand on Hitchcock's arm. "We can't afford this, Roger."

He shook his head. "We have no choice, baby."

"Your husband is right, Mrs. Hitchcock," Solomon said. "You'll lose your son by default if you don't fight."

"How long do cases like this take to be resolved?" she asked.

"Given the depths of the plaintiff's resources, this could drag on for a year."

Hitchcock lowered his head and muttered, "That would break us."

"MacAuliffe's counting on that," Solomon said. "Along the way, usually mid-point in the proceedings, one side offers settlement terms to the other. MacAuliffe will drag you through the costs to bleed you dry with attorney fees and other costs until you're broke."

THEY RODE HOME in stony silence. "We've got equity
in our home and the rental house," he said at last. "We
also have prime property in North Bend that's paid for."

"Those are our college funds for our kids, and our
retirement. Letting Horace suck us dry us of all we have
out of sheer meanness isn't right."

"Let's offer Horace a chance to see for himself that
Trevor is happy and well-adjusted."

"Trevor's happiness isn't where Horace is coming
from," Allie said. "He and his wife are snobs. It's a stain
on their reputation that their grandson is being raised by
working-class people. Maybe not you because your
father was a doctor."

"A peace offering is worth a try. If he accepts, it'll
work in our favor. If he refuses, it'll be in our favor too.
We win either way."

"Okay, then," she said. "I'm in."

They picked up Trevor and Jeremiah at his
mother's. "What happened, kids?" Myrna asked.
Hitchcock explained the details.

"Trevor's my grandson, too. I'll share the cost of
this, son."

"No, Mom. We won't let you," Allie said. "This is
our fight."

Myrna shot a glance at her son. His eyes met hers.
"No one in this family is left to twist in the wind,"
Myrna said. "We back each other up."

CHAPTER SIXTY
Changing Tactics

HITCHCOCK'S HOME PHONE rang. "The woman named Lotus called for you again just now," Patty in Records said. "Here's the number."

Fen Hoang answered on the first ring. "Juju is in the Bellevue hospital, Officer Hitchcock. She had a bad car wreck and was trapped in it for two days. She has too many injuries to be released yet."

"Do you know where this happened, Fen?"

"The bartender says it was on the road to Juju's house. He says it is very steep. Her car rolled over many times."

"Anything else?"

"Juju cannot be released from the hospital for several more days."

"What do you think, Fen—was this an accident?"

"Nothing with these people is ever an accident."

"Yes, that's true," Hitchcock said after a pause. "What's been happening at the restaurant while Juju is gone?"

"A Bellevue officer comes in every night. I don't know what he does there. He hangs around in the bar and goes into Juju's office with Monica, Juju's friend, a lot. They are in there for about twenty minutes every time."

"What does he look like?"

"Young, white, short blond hair. Stocky build, like football player. Not tall."

"Anything else catch your eye?"

"Monica, Juju's friend, comes in during lunch hour, and again at night. She has been cashiering for the restaurant. She has key to Juju's office."

"Describe her."

"About thirty, well-dressed," Fen said. "Poofed-up, sixties-style hair. She disappears into Juju's office whenever the young cop shows up."

"What do you make of all this change?" he asked.

"Monica told me something happened that made Juju in debt and very short on cash. She plans to start having after-hours gambling when she gets back. Whatever happened, it was big," Fen said. "Any instructions?"

Hitchcock paused, thinking. "Work your way up to a managerial position if you can. You'll probably have to become friends with Monica to get there. She was friends with a woman named Connie who disappeared almost three months ago. Don't ask questions, just listen for any mention of a Connie."

"Of course. I will let you know anything I hear. I am a good Jiàndié."

"A what?"

"It's the Mandarin word for spy."

† † †

ACROSS THE FREEWAY from The Great Wall at that time, Carlos Vasquez watched for Juju in his silver '70 Plymouth Satellite Sebring. He hadn't seen a trace of her since they killed her cook for revenge. Other than surveillance, Carlos and his brother had no way to know her movements. Infiltrating The Great Wall was out of the question, the Chinese were notoriously insular. *If Juju is out of the picture for some reason, perhaps now it is safe to bring in a large shipment of heroin.*

He left his post to phone Enrique, the eldest brother, in California, from his office at the hotel. Speaking Spanish, Carlos said, "Tomas agrees with me that the coast is clear to bring in more stuff, Enrique."

"I will arrange it, then," Enrique replied. "But you must keep the surveillance of the Chinese place going, watch for any changes."

"I'm uneasy not knowing where Dragon Lady is, Enrique," Carlos said.

"Very well. We will go ahead with our shipment, but we need to know what she is doing. Stay with the watching."

† † †

HITCHCOCK RADIOED IN service at the stroke of 8:00 p.m. and headed east. He found Monica Dwyer's brown Datsun 240Z in the parking lot of The Pines Apartments. She opened the door on the third ring of the bell.

"Yes, officer?"

"Good evening. I'm Officer Hitchcock. Are you

Monica Dwyer?"

She smiled. "I am. Can I help you?"

"I hope so. Do you know a Connie Fowler?"

Monica looked to be still dressed for work, chestnut hair coiffed '60s-style, brown skirt, silk blouse, pearl necklace, heels. Not a women's libber. She seemed surprised by Hitchcock's inquiry. "Why, yes. She's a good friend of mine. Connie's been missing for over a month. Is that why you're here?"

"Yes. I got your name from Connie's mom, Barbara. I hope you don't mind my stopping by unexpectedly like this."

She opened the door. "Not at all. Please come in." She gestured toward the couch." Have a seat."

She sat across from him. Her body language was relaxed, hands clasped over one knee, leaning forward. "Do you have any news of Connie?"

"I'm afraid not. Her car was found weeks ago, abandoned. Not a trace of her since then."

She frowned. "Oh, I didn't know that. How strange."

"How often did you see Connie?"

"We went to lunch on Saturdays sometimes, and for dinner occasionally on weeknights. She worked part-time jobs all around, so her schedule was never the same."

"What places did you and she go to?"

"In Eastgate, The Wagon Wheel for dinner and drinks, and the bar at what used to be The Hilltop. And a tavern called Charlie's sometimes."

"Anyplace else?"

She tucked her feet under her into a somewhat curled position and her eyes glanced left before she said, "No."

"Did Connie ever say anything about wanting to go away?"

"Not to me. I always thought she was happy at home with her family.

"Did you and Connie ever go driving around in the countryside, like around North Bend or east of there?"

Monica became silent, staring at the floor. "No. Why do you ask that?" she said, not looking up.

"Her car was found out there. Her family says she never went that far east, so I wondered—"

"Nope. Never," she said, her voice dropping an octave.

"Where were you the last time you saw Connie?"

She paused, thinking. "I don't remember now. Maybe it will come to me later."

"The places you said you two went to, did you go there by yourselves or with others?"

She continued to avoid eye contact and fidgeted with her hands. "Rarely with others, if ever."

"Did you and Connie have any mutual friends?"

Her nervous tension mounted as she toyed with the hem of her skirt. Hitchcock waited but she didn't answer.

"Monica, do you think Connie is dead?"

She stood up. "I sure hope not, Officer. Now if you'll excuse me, I've had a long day and I'm still in my work clothes."

HE MET OTIS car-to-car right after he left Monica. "You don't look like it went well," Otis observed.

"Bad."

"What happened?"

Hitchcock described the interview. "I wish I had the interrogation abilities of Larry Meyn. She lied and withheld information the whole time. I'm convinced she either had something to do with Connie's death or knows who did."

"Did you confront her inconsistencies?"

Hitchcock shook his head. "I don't have the skills for that. I backed off. Better to save that for someone with the right training and experience."

"What lies did she tell?"

"I asked which bars and restaurants she went to in Eastgate with Connie. She didn't mention The Great Wall."

"What does that tell you?"

"She's involved in it somehow."

"Did you ask her how she met Connie?"

Hitchcock sighed. "Forgot."

"What people don't say in an interview often tells you what you need to know."

"I see that now—Damn!"

Otis lit a cigar. "Nothing's lost, little brother. The dust will settle. If she's involved, you'll get her, or the dicks will."

CHAPTER SIXTY-ONE
Connecting Hidden Dots

THE LIGHT WAS on inside the Fowler residence when Hitchcock arrived in his cruiser.

Barbara sat across the scarred wooden kitchen table from Hitchcock, silent, hands clasped. Her deep worry lines and heavy jowls suggested a long run of hard luck.

"Randy and John are asleep," she muttered. "Anything new about Connie?"

"No news yet," Hitchcock replied. "I guess Connie worked a lot of jobs as an on-call waitress, bar maid, and bartender."

"She worked at different restaurants—all that had bars, she sure did," Barbara nodded, her eyes staring into the past.

"Did she ever work at The Great Wall?"

"The Chinese joint in Eastgate?"

Hitchcock nodded. She nodded back, her hands still clasped, elbows on the table. "Tell me about it."

"Connie worked there part time as a food waitress and bartender for several years. She had licenses from the Health Department for both. That's where she met Monica."

Now it gets interesting, Hitchcock thought as he leaned forward. "So, Connie met Monica when she was working at The Great Wall," Hitchcock summarized. "Did she ever mention other people she knew there — like maybe the owner?"

"She didn't talk much about work or her work friends. If she did, I didn't keep track. Connie likes to know a lot of people."

"Where else did she work?"

"The Hilltop before it became a Mexican place. She tended bar there. Made lots of money on tips."

"Did she work there after it became a Mexican place?"

Barbara thought before she replied, "Not that I know of."

"Do you know where she was working when she disappeared?"

She shook her head. "Randy might."

Remembering the degrading photographs of Connie detectives found among Guyon's things, he asked, "How did Tyrone Guyon come into the picture?"

Barbara grimaced at the mention of Guyon's name. "I asked her that, me being as prejudiced as I am. She said she met him at The Hilltop when she was tending bar. How he got her on heroin I'll never know. She was always such a clean-living girl. Next thing you know, she's hooked, then Randy's hooked. But Randy got an early start on drugs through that Mike Smith character. Marijuana. Guyon ran Smith off when he came to Bellevue, according to Randy, but Smith came back after you killed Guyon. Then Smith overdosed Randy and left him for dead."

"How well I remember," Hitchcock reminisced, gazing at the table as if it was an aquarium.

"Smith is dead," he murmured.

Barbara pulled her hands into her lap, staring at Hitchcock. "I hadn't heard," she said, shaking her head. "How did he die?"

"He was executed the same way as two others before him. Same place."

She fell into a stony silence, looking into space. "Do you know who killed them?"

"Not yet, but it has to do with the drug trade."

"Doesn't everything these days?"

"Any changes in Connie's bank account?"

"I call the bank almost every day, hoping for a withdrawal or some sign that Connie is alive."

"And?"

Her eyes watered up. "Nothing. Don't ask me about her anymore, Roger. Please. Hope is all I have left."

"Asking questions is helping me find out what happened. Did Monica come around much after Connie disappeared?" He asked, ignoring her plea.

"She was here a lot. A real comfort to me and my sons."

"Did she know about Connie's car being found?"

"Of course—I told her. She's Connie's best friend."

"You're sure that Monica is Connie's best friend."

"Absolutely—Connie said so."

"Okay, one more thing. Do you have a recent photo

of Connie I can borrow?"

He returned to the station and wrote a detailed memo of his interview with Barbara Fowler before he went home. A call from Patty in Records awakened him an hour later. "La Paloma is asking for a call from you. Says it's urgent. Here's the number."

CHAPTER SIXTY-TWO
Dolly's Way Out

HITCHCOCK IDLED INTO the gravel lot behind Boehm's Candies in his Jeep Wagoneer. He parked where he could see into vehicle interiors from a safe distance. Every car within view was empty.

Dolly arrived on schedule. Her loose-fitting man's long-sleeve denim shirt and baggy jeans enhanced rather than diminished her man-appeal. She stared out the windshield, hands on her knees. "You can tell I'm nervous, right?" she said after a pause, eyes still on the windshield.

He nodded, waiting.

She told him about Juju's offer through Monica.

"What do you think this is all about?" he asked.

"I can't accept that she wants someone as old as me when there are so many willing, young women out there who need work. I told Monica that."

"And Monica said..."

"Oh—I forgot that part—Monica said Juju wants me for my experience and stability, something like that."

"And your response was..."

"I said I would have to think about it and get back

to her soon."

"Then what happened?"

"That was yesterday. Today, Monica told me about Juju's car accident. She told me to visit Juju in the hospital to talk terms. She really thinks I'm willing to do this sort of thing if the money's good enough. What should I tell her?"

"As an informant you're in an ideal position, Dolly, but nothing you could do for us is worth the risk to you and your little ones. For your sake and your grandkids, it's time to nip this in the bud. We don't have a witness protection program. The Feds do, but then you'd have to put yourself at further risk by working for them to be able to qualify for the program, and there's no guarantee you'd qualify."

Tears filled her eyes.

"You said you wanted a safe way out, and to not have to move away," he said. 'Here's what I've set up: I'll introduce you to Ray Packard, the attorney I told you about who used to be an officer with our Department. You visit Juju at the hospital, wearing a wire so the conversation is recorded. Washington is a one-party consent state for recording conversations, so we can use the tape in court if necessary. Use her name when you ask her questions. Let her do the talking. Don't commit to anything. Tell her you are interested in the job and will give her your terms in twenty-four hours."

"Then what?"

"We preserve the recording and have it transcribed. As your attorney, Ray will send a notarized letter to Juju through a licensed process server. The letter will state that her disclosures to you were recorded and transcribed. They will be held by his law firm indefinitely and released to law enforcement authorities if anything happens to you or your family members by anybody at any time in the future."

Dolly nodded vigorously. "Oh, yeah," she said, sniffling. "I like the sound of this. It ought to work. How much of the plan do you have set up?"

"The attorney is on board and has the equipment. We need your answer."

She smiled for the first time. "I'm in. Now, what did you want to show me?"

He handed her a photograph of Connie Fowler.

"Oh, I know her," she said right away. "Name's Connie, right?"

"Where do you know her from?"

"She's a part-time bartender at The Great Wall. She worked part time at the old Hilltop Inn too. Haven't seen her lately, though. What's wrong?"

"She's missing."

"Oh, no."

"What does that mean?"

"It means Connie's dead."

"Talk to me."

"Connie was the main source for Gayle's information on Guyon and Mae, his female enforcer, who you also killed."

"I didn't kill Mae. My partner did."

"Okay, whatever," Dolly said with a wave of her

hand. "She knew everything about Guyon's operation. She fed this information to Gayle, who gave it to you."

"*Connie* set Guyon up?" Hitchcock asked, almost too stunned to speak. "How involved was she in his operation?"

"She was on heroin, but she was more involved than being just a junkie. The details, I don't know, but she spent a lot of time at the little house Tyrone and Mae had in lower Eastgate, near the gas station."

Hitchcock listened, staring at the dashboard, hands on the steering wheel, shaking his head, shocked.

"You didn't know any of this, did you?" Dolly asked.

"Keep talking. How close in time was this to the shooting?"

She paused. "I'd say really close. Why?"

"Because the missing girl from Everett, Claudia Masconi, was being held prisoner there at that time. I forget for how long, but like a week. She was abducted. We found her in the house Hatch was renting, dead, right after the shooting."

"Yeah," Dolly said, nodding. "It was on the news."

"Would Connie have been in the house where the missing girl was being kept?"

"She had to be, Roger. Gayle and I kept a distance from Guyon. Connie was our source of information about him because she was in his inner circle."

"I get it now," he mused, nodding. "The pieces fit."

"Gayle never went near the Hilltop," Dolly went on. "She worked only at The Wagon Wheel, where I met her. When she told me she was dating a cop, I gave her information about Guyon I got from Connie. Connie knew it was going to you, personally."

Hitchcock stared out his windshield, silent, listening, processing, too stunned to speak.

"Guyon liked to brag," Dolly said. "The day of the shooting he was in the bar. A colored maid, a new girl, noticed his gun in his waistband. It made her and me nervous, so to play it cool, I asked him about it. He showed it to us and said he was going to use it to kill the first white cop he saw. That's when I called Gayle."

"You saved lives, mine included. Connie knew Guyon's intentions?"

"She was standing next to Guyon when he said it to me."

"And what about Linda, the other passenger in the car who died later?"

"I only saw her at the Hilltop bar once or twice. She was always with Guyon, pretty but frail, obviously an addict. After the shooting we learned about Guyon's trailer where he kept her, barely alive, turning tricks."

He looked squarely at her. "Are you still up for this?"

She paused, staring back at him. "If it'll get me out of this and keep me and my grandkids safe, hell yes. Let's do it."

CHAPTER SIXTY-THREE
Checkmate

Law Office of Ray Packard
Renton, WA

AFTER BRIEF INSTRUCTIONS from Hitchcock and Ray Packard, such as not asking leading questions and addressing Juju by name, Hitchcock and former officer Ray Packard fitted Dolly with a body wire and recorder. Once the device proved operational, Hitchcock drove her to Overlake Hospital.

Juju was being wheeled into her room by a nurse as Dolly arrived. Overcome at the sight of Juju's head swathed in bandages, she began crying. "Juju! Juju Kwan, is that you? Oh, I didn't know you were hurt so bad!"

Juju said nothing as the nurse hoisted her out of the wheelchair onto her bed. "She just took a pill for pain, so she might become a little groggy in the next half-hour," the nurse explained.

As soon as the nurse left, Juju extended her arm and hand, crusted with inflamed abrasion scabs. "So glad you came to me at last, Dolly," she said, stiffness in her voice.

"How did it happen, Juju?"

Juju gazed placidly at Dolly, resting her head on her pillow. "I black out on my way home."

"How much longer will they keep you here?"

"Not sure. Seatbelt injure my liver when car roll down mountain. I take spess'al medications before they release me. Lose much blood."

"Who is running The Great Wall?"

"Wang Wei, bartender. Monica, friend, help manage."

"Oh. You're protected, that's good, Juju."

Juju turned on the tears. "Dolly, I about to lose everything!"

"You'll bounce back, Juju. You're strong."

"No, Dolly. Before accident, big shipment stolen from me by two men."

"Two men robbed you?"

"Not me. Rob my men. Shipment worth one million dollars. I no can pay back without help."

"What kind of help?"

"You join me and Monica. Partners. I bring back Mahjong in back room."

"I know nothing about running a bar or a restaurant, or gambling."

"We talk this before. You do for me what you do at Charlie's. You say yes, we talk prices. I pay you well. You no work for anyone but me anymore."

"Where would I do this?"

"I make nice room in back for you."

"Hmm. I want to know what the stolen shipment was, so I can decide."

"You know."

"No, I don't."

Juju leaned toward Dolly and whispered, "Heroin."

"Heroin? I've never done drugs, Juju. Men, yes. I only do business with men I know–never strangers. So why do you want me when there are so many younger women."

"Men like you. Men want you. Age not matter. You look good, experienced, like me."

"You look better than me, Juju. You're much younger and have more experience dealing with strange men. Why don't you service them yourself?"

Juju started to laugh but grimaced with pain. "Long ago I backroom girl in Taiwan. Opportunity for me then–I did good, came to America, own business. I front-room lady now. I own men. Men pay me in other ways now. I give same opportunity for you. I show you what to do to make much money, become front room lady like me."

Dolly saw that Juju was starting to fade, so she took a chance to ask another question. "Are you sure your own men didn't steal the heroin and the money?"

"They not take it. I make sure of that."

"Get some sleep, Juju. I'll give this some serious thought and get back to you in twenty-four hours."

EXCITEMENT WAS WRITTEN all over Dolly as she climbed into Hitchcock's Wagoneer. "Juju opened up more than I expected. She said a big shipment of heroin was stolen by force by two men before it reached her and she's in serious financial trouble as a result."

Hitchcock's jaw dropped. "She told you all that?"

"And a lot more."

"She's either really desperate or sedated," he said.

"They'd just given her a sedative when I got there. She was clear-headed when we talked. I ended it as she became drowsy."

"Did she offer you hooker work?"

Dolly smiled. "Wait until we play the tape."

On their way to Ray Packard's office, Dolly asked, "Why are we doing this when with this tape you've got her dead to rights for promoting prostitution?"

"We're protecting your future. Juju won't order anyone to harm you or your family if she knows it would cause her downfall. If we charged her with promoting prostitution now, she'd go to trial and have her attorney bring up your history at Charlie's Place to discredit you."

"Smart thinking, Roger. I'm starting to feel safe again."

HITCHCOCK AND PACKARD gloated as they listened to the tape. "Great work, Dolly. I'll have it transcribed and copies made of the tape. I'll prepare a Cease-and-Desist Letter to Juju. You can read it before it goes out," Packard said when the tape finished.

"What do I do about Monica?" Dolly asked.

"Tell her to leave you alone, say you're applying for

other jobs. They were trying to set you up for a reason. I think Juju is worried that she told you too much. Once this is done, her fears about you will be calmed, and yours about her. You can go about your life safely. In the meantime, you're still on my payroll."

As he dropped Dolly off at her car, she asked him, "How do you feel about letting Juju off the hook for my sake when you've got her on a criminal charge?"

Hitchcock smirked. "Who said she's getting off the hook?"

† † †

TWO DAYS LATER, Monica visited Juju at the hospital. She handed her three opened envelopes.

"What are these?" Juju asked.

"Government love letters. One from the state Department of Revenue, they say they will be conducting an audit. Another is from the state Liquor Board, requesting the names and license numbers of bartenders and servers. The third is from the City of Bellevue Business Licensing Unit. They're requesting contact regarding you not having a city business license. They're threatening to close The Great Wall in thirty days if you don't comply."

Juju stared openmouthed as she reviewed each letter.

"What's the plan?" Monica asked.

"Leave letters with me. I call them, explain what happen, ask for more time."

Monica folded her arms as she leaned against the

large window frame across the room. "Okay, but we still have to respond."

"Yes," Juju said weakly.

"Did Dolly come to see you?"

Juju smiled. "She did. I make better offer. I think now she will accept."

A postman appeared in the doorway. "Excuse me, I have a certified letter for a Juju Kwan in this room."

"Who is it from?" Monica asked.

Juju read the envelope. "Attorney Ray Packard."

"Never heard of him."

The postman left. Juju tore open the envelope. She dropped the one-page letter in her lap. Monica picked it up and began cursing as she read it. "At least we know Dolly won't talk, Juju."

"How do you know that?"

"If Dolly could be swayed by offers of money, she'd have agreed to your offer. She didn't. She turned down a lot of money. Through an attorney she's calling a truce and protecting herself and her grandchildren. Let her go. I'll find you another back-room girl, someone younger, and we can move forward."

Weak as she was, Juju Kwan's face darkened. "You want in, you get me girl, young, pretty, and white!" Juju snapped. "I get her hooked, so she does what we say."

Monica leered at Juju for a moment. "What if I can't get you what you want?"

Juju pointed her finger at Monica. "You in already! You do as we say, or you die!"

CHAPTER SIXTY-FOUR
Mystery Woman

THE REGISTRATION CHECK in Hitchcock's inbox showed Monica's Datsun 240Z was registered to her at a rental house in Carnation. Hitchcock and Sherman were off duty when they contacted the owners, Richard and Sonya Reynolds, who lived across the street.

"Yes, we remember Monica," Sonya Reynolds, a silver-haired woman in her fifties with smiling eyes said. "We rented the house to her two years ago. She'd just moved here from Longview, got a job in Bellevue, I think it was. She was very nice with a neat appearance. Paid her rent on time and kept to herself."

"Did she have any roommates or friends over?"

"Never any roommates. There was a man...Mike, I believe his name was. And a woman friend we noticed visiting from time to time. Both young."

Hitchcock showed them a mugshot of Mike Smith.

"Is this the man you saw?"

"Yes! I saw him there several times," her husband Richard said with a look of concern at seeing it was a police photo.

Hitchcock held up a photo of Connie Fowler. "How about this woman?"

"Yep. Don't remember her name, but she was here quite a lot to see Monica. Rough-looking girl, but pleasant," Sonya recalled, now appearing nervous. "May I ask what this is all about?"

"The woman in the picture I showed you has been missing for weeks now," Hitchcock explained, "I can't comment any further at this time." He took written statements from Sonya and Richard before he left.

HE KEPT CHIPPING away at Monica Dwyer's background. She lived in Longview, the largest town in Cowlitz County, before and after her marriage. The reports he requested revealed Monica's juvenile arrest records included possession and consuming alcohol on school grounds, assaulting and intimidating other girls over boyfriends. Despite her aggressive, criminal tendencies, Monica was a straight-A student.

The Longview PD file revealed multiple arrests for Driving While Intoxicated, witness intimidation plus three arrests for Promoting Prostitution, which occurred in bars connected to the city's high-end motels.

It dismayed Hitchcock that while involved in heavy criminal behavior, Monica graduated *magna cum laude* with a bachelor's degree in accounting.

Hitchcock's mind swirled as he summarized on a legal notepad what he knew about Monica, adding to that what he had learned of Connie's dark secrets. *Not all trails lead to Juju,* he concluded. *Who are the two strange men who hijacked Juju's heroin, And who killed Juju's mules?*

CHAPTER SIXTY-FIVE
Probings

THE BULGING ENVELOPE from Hitchcock's attorney contained interrogatories, plus a copy of the letter from Horace MacAuliffe's attorney, Oscar Travis. "I'm not in the right frame of mind to answer these now," he grumbled as he flipped through the pages. "I'm half tempted to throw them into the fire!"

"Shh!" Allie said. He looked up at her for shushing him. "I just put the boys down. They're not asleep yet," she cautioned in a low voice. "At least read the letter from Horace's attorney, honey."

It consisted of a single paragraph. "You were right, Allie. Horace isn't interested if Trevor is happy and well-adjusted. As you predicted, he refused our offer for him to see for himself how Trevor is doing. It isn't Trevor he cares about, it's his wounded pride at losing the first custody fight to you in court."

"He'll ruin Trevor by making him a spoiled brat like Glendon if he wins," Allie said solemnly.

Hitchcock nodded silent agreement.

"He can destroy us by running the clock," she said. "At two hundred dollars an hour for our attorney, that's sixteen hundred dollars a day before we even get to the courtroom. That's more than you bring home in a month after taxes. If we liquidated our two houses and the land in North Bend, we still wouldn't be able to complete a full trial. Look at our attorney's invoice. It's three times the amount of the retainer we paid."

His silence was long and brooding after he saw the invoice.

"What are you saying we should do? Just give Trevor to him?" he finally asked.

She placed a gentle hand on his shoulder. "Weeks ago, you told me you had a conversion experience. What have you done with your Christianity since then?"

"What am I supposed to do? I thought that was it. No?"

"No. It's an inner journey that ends only when you pass into heaven. You have the highest power there is available to you now. The power of answered prayer, done the right way. God expects us to use it, not just sit on our butts."

"Guess I didn't listen to Pastor Scratch as well as I thought."

She smiled. "Guess not."

"What should I do?"

"Present our situation to God in prayer. Ask Him to intervene for us, right away."

"I don't know how.

She squeezed his hand. "Just talk to Him like you would to me. Do it!"

He lowered his head, cleared his throat, holding

hands with Allie. "God," he began. "Right now, Allie and I are in a hell of a jam. Trevor's grandfather is trying to take him from us. You know we can't afford this. And what MacAuliffe is doing is wrong. We need Your help. In Jesus's Name, please take care of it. Thanks. Amen."

† † †

HORACE MACAULIFFE'S desk phone sounded the next morning. "Yes, Margaret?"

"There's a Detective Larry Meyn from the Bellevue Police Department here to see you, sir."

"Ask him what his business is."

"He says the matter is highly confidential."

MacAuliffe paused. "All right, show him in."

Meyn showed MacAuliffe his badge and offered his hand. "Detective Meyn, thank you for seeing me, Mr. MacAuliffe. This will only take a couple minutes."

His eyes ranged over Meyn's drab Sears suit and tie. He didn't take his hand. "What's your business here?"

"I'm investigating the death of one of our former officers."

MacAuliffe lounged in his chair, lit a fresh cigar and blew a puff of smoke to the side. "What does that have to do with me?"

"In going through the former officer's trash, I found drafts of letters he wrote to you on his typewriter. They would have been anonymous."

Leaning forward, he asked. "May I see them?"

Meyn handed him copies of two crumpled drafts on plain paper. "Did you receive an anonymous letter like this regarding an officer named Hitchcock and your grandson, named Trevor?"

MacAuliffe read the drafts. He looked up at Meyn. "What if I did?"

"The writer was a lieutenant named Rowland Bostwick" Meyn continued. "An expert has verified that the drafts I showed you were typed on his typewriter. He resigned rather cooperate with an internal investigation. He fled to New York when he learned we were pursuing the case. I was with New York Police detectives when we found him dead in his apartment. His death was ruled a suicide at first, but new evidence is likely to change it to murder."

MacAuliffe fidgeted with his cigar and looked at Meyn. He puffed on his cigar and looked at the smoke to him, avowing eye contact with Meyn. But Meyn's eyes locked onto his and held him. The showdown ended when MacAuliffe dropped his gaze to the floor.

"For Bostwick to go to such extremes as to engineer an attack on a fellow another officer at his home and write anonymous letters against him indicates there were other individuals involved. Again, did you receive such a letter?"

MacAuliffe's expression softened. He gestured to the chair in front of his desk.

Meyn ignored the invitation. His stare continued.

"I did," MacAuliffe replied in a humbler tone of voice. "If I show it to you, would you be willing to enlighten me more about this?"

"As much as I can, yes."

Meyn read the letter and handed it back to MacAuliffe.

"For reasons we still don't know, Lieutenant Bostwick had a fixation for keeping a certain type of officer off the Department. Hitchcock was one of those. He tried to fail Hitchcock at the end of his probationary year, but he was outvoted. After that he went to extraordinary lengths to plot against him. When we confronted him with solid evidence that he set up the attack at Hitchcock's home, without denying it, he resigned and went into hiding in New York. Now Bostwick and at least one of the two men who attacked Hitchcock at home are dead. Maybe the other hitman is dead too—we only know he fled the country."

MacAuliffe's mouth was dry. He licked his lips and flicked ashes off his cigar. "And what's this Hitchcock all about?" he asked, clearing his throat.

Meyn paused, his unblinking stare continued. "He's the most decorated officer in our Police Department's history. He leads in terms of service commendations and letters from thankful citizens. He's a former combat medic, he's saved dying people in the field. The only complaints against him were from Lieutenant Bostwick. What motivated the Lieutenant's behavior is my job to find out."

"That's the kind of officer this Bostwick was against?" MacAuliffe asked incredulously.

Meyn nodded.

"How would Bostwick know about me in order to write to me?" MacAuliffe asked.

"Public records would be my guess. He could have known a great deal from your son's divorce from Allie."

"I see you've done your research before you came, Detective. Thank you for coming, it has been enlightening. If you ever need anything from me, please contact me. I would be glad to help."

MacAuliffe phoned his private investigator the second Detective Meyn left. "Toby, I want a written report from your agent. She was a guest in their home last Easter. I want to know what she saw that day and what her impressions of Hitchcock and Trevor's mother are. The same goes for your surveillance team."

"Yes, sir, Mr. MacAuliffe. You'll have June's report day after tomorrow."

MacAuliffe ended the call. The deadly details the detective divulged changed everything. Hitmen. A corrupt cop. He had used a hitman before, but this was big, a tangled mess. He didn't know what to do. The wrong move on his part could endanger his grandson and ruin his other plan.

He crossed the floor to the window and stared at the ferry chugging out of pier 51. The sight always soothed and cleared his mind. Not this time. The detective seemed to not know about his child custody lawsuit against Hitchcock. He dared not use the detective's information in his lawsuit against Hitchcock. By filing a lawsuit, he had, in a sense, stuck a knife in Hitchcock's back. What about Trevor's safety? And what about his real goal? The situation had changed so drastically he had to change course, fast.

CHAPTER SIXTY-SIX
New York Calling

DETECTIVE MEYN WAS bone tired from working all night on a rape case when he received a call at 8:00 a.m. "G'morning, Larry, Bruno Schmidt, NYPD here. How aw ya?"

Meyn smiled, rubbed his eyes and took a sip of coffee. It was cold but it perked him up. "Nice to hear from you, Bruno," he said, clearing his throat. "How are things in nuu-yawk? Been to toity-toid and toid street lately?"

Schmidt laughed. "You sound drowsy. You'd better be awake and sitting down for what I got for ya."

"Yeah?" Meyn said, revived by the detective's two energy foods—caffeine and new leads.

"The medical examiner found evidence that your guy Bostwick was murdered. We've re-opened the case," Schmidt said.

Meyn shot out of his chair. "What? How?"

"First off, Bostwick had defensive wounds on his forearms. Bruises and abrasions, like he was struck with something and tried to fend off the blows. The cuffs of his shirt sleeves were buttoned, which is why we didn't

315

see the injuries. The inside of the sleeves had tiny specks of dried blood and skin from those wounds, so they were fresh. Bostwick fought for his life with somebody.

"Secondly, the pathologist noted a tiny red pinprick under his left armpit, at heart level. Barely noticeable. When they opened the chest cavity, they saw that the heart had been stabbed with an ice pick, or maybe a stiff wire, then twisted around and around, stopping the heart."

In shock, Meyn sat down. "Damn!" he exclaimed. "Where does that leave us?"

"The pathologist was an Army surgeon in Vietnam. He says it appears a wire was inserted between the ribs into the heart muscle, then wiggled, or stirred. Instant death, no mess. A professional hit."

"So Bostwick didn't die from hanging?"

"The hanging was meant to make it *look* like suicide. Two neighbors told us they saw an unfamiliar man in the building about the time of death. One lady saw the stranger coming in the lobby. The other witness is a man on Bostwick's floor. He's sure he saw the man just as he came out of Bostwick's apartment on the same day as the first witness, best we can place it."

"What's the description?"

"Average looking white male, forties, friendly face, like a shoe salesman, carrying a battered briefcase."

Meyn scoffed. "It ain't much but it's something."

"We'll see if we can get a composite sketch from the witness, Schmidt said.

"That would be a help. Whoever the killer is, he had

THE MYSTERY OF THE UNSEEN HAND

to have come from here. As if this isn't enough, what else can I tell my supervisor?"

"The apartment has been kept secure. Our crime scene investigators will go through it today. As you said, the perp probably came from your area. I'll keep you informed by phone and send you copies of our reports."

The call ended.

Meyn stared at the wall, numb. *A professional hit, Schmidt said. Of course, it was. It revealed a depth of criminality in Bostwick's world that Bostwick, with his sheltered upbringing, could never conceive of.*

For the first time in his career, Meyn was too stunned to articulate the details to Sergeant Jurgens. *Writing it out would be better.* He fed a sheet of paper into his typewriter.

CHAPTER SIXTY-SEVEN
The Good Jiàndié

HITCHCOCK AND OTIS met car-to-car in a downtown bank parking lot after shift briefing. It was dark, raining lightly and the evening traffic had thinned out. He told Otis what he learned about Monica Dwyer.

"She fits the profile of women who become madams," Otis said. "Clever and crafty, usually not attractive, but smart and manipulative. She'll be more than a match for Juju."

Hitchcock shook his head as he scoffed. "Don't bet on it."

"What's your plan now?"

"I'm stuck. I contacted Monica at her apartment unannounced, hoping to catch her off-guard. She lied to me on several points. I didn't pursue it because I don't have the training or the experience to break her. I was afraid I'd botch the case if I tried and failed. Maybe after the dust settles, I'll ask Larry Meyn to interview her about what happened to Connie."

"What do you think happened to her?"

Hitchcock took a deep breath before he said, "Given what she's been into and the people she ran with, she's dead. Even if we never catch who bumped her off, I gotta find the body for the family's sake."

Otis lit a cigar. "What's going on with Juju?"

"Still in the hospital, all banged up while others are running The Great Wall into the ground. What happens when she returns will be interesting."

"How will you know?" Otis asked.

"I have a mouse in the corner."

† † †

ALLIE AWAKENED HIM at noon, holding the phone. "Call from the station." She left the room as he sat up in bed.

"Roger? Call La Paloma right away," Patty from Records said.

Dolly answered on the first ring. "What's going on, Dolly? Are you okay?"

"I'm fine, thanks to you. No more calls or visits from Juju or Monica. I'm still working at The El Escondite until one of the places where I've applied hires me."

"That's good to hear. What else is going on?"

"Two of the three brothers that own this place came from California after all those arrests of their employees. Word is they're arranging for a shipment of heroin to come by car from L.A. Should arrive any day."

"That's good to know. Anything else?"

"I'm not seeing teenagers there in the afternoons like I was, which tells me supply is drying up."

"What about the heist from Juju?"

"This place would be busy if anyone here seized

dope in that amount. Instead, it's almost a ghost town."

"There's word about a lot of heroin and cocaine on the streets, here and in Seattle," he said.

"It isn't here, Roger. I'm expecting to be sent home with a pink slip any day."

"Okay then. Stay in touch."

† † †

HE AND ALLIE talked while she ate lunch and he had breakfast. "I'm worried about Dolly," he said. "I need to get her out of her job at the El Escondite, fast. The place is going under, and I get the feeling she's at risk."

"If she's okay with waitressing, maybe I can get her a temporary job at the Pancake Corral."

He smiled. "Now why didn't I think of that? Ask Bill. It would get her out of Eastgate."

"I want to meet her before I recommend her to Bill or Louise."

"I'll set it up for tomorrow."

The phone rang a second time. "It's Records for you again," Allie said.

"Call Lotus this time," Patty said. "Here's the number."

Fen answered. "Hello. Officer Hitchcock, this is Fen," she said in her usual formal manner of speaking.

"How are you, Fen?"

"Fine, thank you. I have information for you."

"I'm ready."

"Juju has been in the hospital for several days. She was injured in a car accident. A friend, a woman named

Monica, has been running the place for Juju. Men from Taiwan arrived today. They kicked Monica out and took over running The Great Wall. Monica was very upset, and frightened. We were glad to see her go. She is not Juju's friend. The men from Taiwan will bring Juju back this afternoon."

He reached for a notepad and pencil. "Tell me about these men. How many are there, how old are they, what are their names."

"Three men. Two are young, in their twenties, maybe. The leader is in his thirties or early forties. I do not know their names. They are deadly."

"Do you know where they're staying?"

"In Juju's house, I am guessing."

"What are they driving?"

"I do not know."

"This is good information. Do you speak Mandarin?

"Of course."

"Good. Pretend that you only speak English, which they should believe because you were born here. Keep me informed on everything, no matter what day or time... Don't be afraid to call me every day if you have to."

"Yes."

"One more thing. Have you seen an attractive blonde, a white woman in her thirties or forties there, a customer? She's a friend of Monica and Juju."

He was relieved when Fen replied, "I have not seen anyone like that."

CHAPTER SIXTY-EIGHT
The Mystery Gang

THE PAY PHONE in Charlie's rang. "JUJU WILL BE released from the hospital in about an hour, Roger, my cousin says there are three Chinese men there to take her home," Patty in Records said.

Hitchcock switched to an unmarked detective car and positioned himself behind the Great Wall among the road graders and oil tankers. Sherman set up in an office parking lot across the four-lane freeway, facing the front entrance.

At 2:46 p.m. Sherman radioed: *"A white Lincoln Town Car arrived. It's going around to the back. Can't see into it."*

"Received," Hitchcock replied as he hastened to fit a 500mm telephoto lens to his camera. The Lincoln rounded the corner and stopped. Chen's young bodyguard hopped out of the front passenger seat. "Welcome back to America, boys," Hitchcock said to himself, grinning.

He began snapping pictures as Bodyguard opened the right rear door for Juju. She wore a Robin's-egg blue scarf over her head and dark glasses, like famous actresses or models do in public. Abrasions on her forehead and right cheek stood out against her pale skin. Bodyguard took her by the arm to help her out. Her movements were stiff as she approached the back door, with Bodyguard at her elbow.

Hitchcock recognized the other two men from his earlier encounter with Mr. Chen. He photographed frontal and side views of each one, then radioed Sherman: "Dragon Lady and company are in the cave."

"Ten-four. What now?"

He paused to consider his next move. Fen Hoang's car was parked in the back. She would be his eyes and ears for anything that happened here, but Juju would likely want to go home. If the visitors were staying with her, they would conduct business there. No chance to spy if they did.

He replied to Sherman: "Let's wait."

Juju and her entourage came out several minutes later. The men scanned in all directions for anyone watching them. One of the men carried an armload of bank ledgers and large envelopes. They headed east on I-90.

Hitchcock tailed the Lincoln to the gravel road that wound its way up Cougar Mountain. When he crested the top, he saw the white Lincoln was parked in Juju's driveway.

† † †

SHERMAN REMAINED IN position across the freeway after Juju left. He watched a van from Security Safe & Lock arrive and the locksmith re-key the front door of

The Great Wall, then disappear inside, presumably to re-key other locks.

MINUTES AFTER THE locksmith left, Monica Dwyer drove around to the back in her brown Datsun 240Z. In a minute she walked around to the front door in an angry huff.

The restaurant was still open. She went inside.

A Hispanic male in his twenties in a black Camaro parked two cars over from Sherman, facing the freeway. Apparently unaware of Sherman, he began watching The Great Wall with binoculars.

Monica walked out of the front door in angry strides. She went around the corner and came back in her car and headed east on the frontage road.

Sherman wrote down the California license number of the black Camaro as he left.

† † †

8:00 P.M.

ACROSS THE FREEWAY from The Great Wall, Tomas Vasquez relieved his brother Carlos from surveillance duty. Tomas parked his silver Dodge Charger where his brother's Camaro had been.

It was a warm evening, and traffic to and around the restaurant was light. He set his paper cup of hot coffee on the front passenger floor, then opened a small bag of pretzels. As he leaned across his front seat to lower the passenger door window, two men wearing black masks ripped open each door. The man on the passenger side struck Tomas on the head with a hard object. His vision blurred and his hands and arms went numb. Tomas was vaguely aware of a pair of strong hands seizing him by the back of his belt and dragging him off the driver's seat to the pavement. He collapsed under a rain of merciless kicks and punches. He felt his revolver being removed from his waistband as consciousness faded.

His last thought before he went under was that his assailants never said a word.

It was 8:35 p.m.

† † †

IT WAS STILL warm at 10:15 p.m. when Carlos waited in the shadows of the A&W Root Beer stand a few yards from Albertsons on the south side of the I-90 freeway. It worried him that his brother Tomas was late. Tomas was *never* late. He tried to ease his fears by rationalizing that there's always a first time. But fear soon overcame his made-up excuses for his brother. *Something* was wrong — very wrong.

Manuel and Lucio, the delivery team, were also late. When it came to shipments they were *always* on time. It didn't look good — none of it did. There was nothing he could do but wait.

At 10:21 p.m. Lucio's black vinyl-over-white 1970 Buick Gran Sport appeared and stopped twenty yards away, facing Carlos.

Fearing a heist, Carlos focused his binoculars on the car. Lucio was driving. Manuel was in the passenger seat. But where was Tomas? The two mules, Lucio and

Manuel would become suspicious and withdraw if everything wasn't exactly as planned. And Tomas was part of the plan.

Carlos saw the headlights of Lucio's Buick flash briefly. Carlos flashed back and eased out of the shadows slowly, lights off.

They met car-to-car.

"*Que pasa?*" Lucio asked in Spanish, meaning: "What's happening?"

"*Nada,*" Carlos replied.

"*Donde esta,* Tomas?" Lucio said, asking where Tomas was, suspicion written on his face.

"*No se,*" Carlos replied. He didn't know.

Manuel's face darkened as he pulled a nickel-plated Government Model Colt .45 Automatic from his shoulder holster and aimed it past Lucio at Carlos. "Pablo said not to deliver unless both of you are here," he warned in English.

Carlos feared for his life, but he didn't flinch. He knew he would be shot if he tried to drive away.

"I am telling you the truth, Lucio. I last saw my brother at eight o'clock. I don't know why he isn't here."

Lucio leaned back in his seat, his head turned toward Carlos, as far from Manuel's line of fire as possible. Manuel had a clear shot at Carlos, less than six feet away.

Carlos knew he was facing two men of questionable loyalties. He feared for his life, for Lucio and Manuel knew he had a fortune in cash on him. He kept his eyes on Manuel as he lifted his hands, palms up from the steering wheel to show he held no weapon.

"Tomas my brother was to meet me here at ten. He is always on time. I don't know what has happened. I agree it must be as my brother Enrique said. No deal unless all of us are here. I am going to leave to find Tomas. Don't you shoot me, Manuel."

Carlos put his car in drive, wondering if this would be the last thing he would ever do. He drove away at idle speed, his heart pounding in his ears, his shirt wringing wet with sweat so much he shivered from the cold.

He found Tomas in the office parking lot where he left him, lying next to his silver Dodge Charger, unconscious on the asphalt, beaten almost beyond recognition. His wallet and his gun were gone.

Relieved that Tomas had a pulse, Carlos struggled to load his brother into his own car, asking himself *who did this to Tomas? A new gang? How did they know where Tomas would be? It wasn't Lucio's people, and regular robbers would have taken the Camaro.*

CHAPTER SIXTY-NINE
Deadly Skirmishes

Bellevue Airfield,
Six Hours Later - 3:50 A.M.

THE TWO TAIWAN visitors waited in the rented white Lincoln Town Car in the shadows next to a hangar watching the runway. Outside it was cold and mild gusts of wind buffeted the Lincoln. The driver, Long Hay, a tall, shambles of a man in his forties, seemed content to stare out the windshield at the empty, unlighted runway, not saying a word.

"Why is this the safest day of the week for us to do this?" the slender one with glasses in the passenger seat of the Town Car asked in Mandarin, breaking the silence.

Long Hay shifted a little in his loose-fitting rumpled black suit. "Because it is the police officer Hitchcock's day off. Madam Juju's officer told her so," he replied, in English, never taking his eyes off the runway. "I smell fear on you."

"I am only an accountant, Long Hay. I know nothing of guns or violence, only women and money."

The accountant could not see the scorn on Long Hay's face. "We are in America, little man. We speak English here. You know Madam Juju hates cowardly men. You also know the penalty for cowards."

Sitting In a blue Pontiac Firebird Formula 400 behind the Town Car, the one Hitchcock called Bodyguard, sat, watching and waiting. On the seat next to him was the new subcompact model of the Uzi 9mm submachine gun.

Finally Long Hay leaned forward and peered up through the windshield. "I hear a plane."

THE RED-AND-WHITE V-tail, low-wing Beechcraft M35 Bonanza appeared out of the darkness and landed smoothly on the runway. The pilot got out first, a tall fortyish white man with a shock of sandy blond hair, wearing a fleece-lined, deep brown lambskin leather WWII Army Air Corps aviator jacket, worn unzipped to show his .45 Government Automatic in a shoulder holster.

The pilot's passenger, a Chinese man in his early forties, waited almost a minute before he got out of the plane. The pilot warily studied the two men he had not met before. He knew better than to ask what had happened to the other two men.

The third man in the Pontiac Firebird remained in the shadows, watching the exchange with binoculars.

The passenger in the plane carried an aircraft-grade aluminum briefcase. The two men from Taiwan bowed to him. He bowed in return, set the briefcase on the runway, opened it, and stepped back. The driver of the Town Car tested a sample, then nodded to Long Hay, who set a black briefcase on the tarmac, opened it, and stepped back. The plane passenger counted the bundles of cash and nodded to the pilot.

When the plane had risen into the night sky, the Town Car left in the direction of the freeway, followed by the blue Firebird, six car-lengths behind.

† † †

FROM THEIR POSITION in the parking lot of The El Escondite Inn, two men, armed with stolen Uzi submachine guns, waited in an oxidized red 1967 one-ton Dodge Power Wagon, watching the transaction at the airfield.

The truck was a wrecking ball on wheels. It had a custom front bumper of half-inch thick steel plate that extended a foot and a half from the grille with a power-takeoff winch in the middle, and a rear bumper of the same material with a trailer hitch and ball extending a foot past the rear bumper. It swooped in behind the Town Car as it entered the eastbound freeway. As it pulled up alongside the driver side of the Town Car to run it off the road, a pair of high-beam headlights appeared in their rearview mirror.

The driver of the Power Wagon shouted curses as he slammed on his brakes, trying to force the car behind him to crash into his trailer hitch.

With lightning-fast reflexes the Firebird's driver swerved left, barely escaping collision. He accelerated alongside the Power Wagon, lowered his passenger window, and held an Uzi submachine gun up and aimed it at the other driver.

The Power Wagon braked hard. The Firebird stayed behind the Power Wagon, harassing and forcing it to forego the Newport Way exit while the Town Car escaped up Cougar Mountain Drive unscathed. On the flats before the Issaquah exit now, the Firebird driver charged up alongside the driver's side of the Power Wagon and again aimed his Uzi at the men in the truck.

The driver of the Power Wagon swerved too much to the right. The truck left the pavement, bouncing over a soggy green meadow to an eventual stop. The Firebird slowed, crossed the grass median and headed west on the freeway.

THE LINCOLN WAS at Juju's home when the driver of the blue Firebird arrived. The aluminum briefcase was on the living room coffee table. "Tell us what happened on our way back," Long Hay said.

Bodyguard gave a detailed verbal report. "They came from that Mexican hotel," he concluded. "They must be from there."

"They killed my cook," Juju said.

"How do you think they knew about your shipment?" The eldest one asked Juju.

"It can only be one person now," she replied. "The others have been eliminated."

† † †

BY EARLY AFTERNOON a stream of drug dealers of every description came through the front door of The Great Wall. One-by-one they asked the hostess for Juju and were shown to her office. Each one left after no more than two minutes.

When the street dealers stopped coming, Fen Hoang knocked on Juju's office door. She handed Juju a black leather, man's wallet. "I was the first one here this morning. I found this propped up against the front door."

Juju looked at Fen, then opened the wallet. She stopped cold when she saw the California driver's license belonging to Tomas Vasquez. "Do you speak Mandarin, Fen?" Juju asked in Mandarin.

Fen stared at Juju, saying nothing.

"Do you speak Mandarin?" Juju asked in English.

Fen shook her head. "I am born and raised American, here in Seattle,"

Juju nodded. "Thank you, Fen. I will see to it that this is returned to its owner."

As soon as Fen left, Juju called her home phone number. A man answered. "Miss Kwan's residence," he announced pleasantly.

Speaking in Mandarin, Juju told him about the wallet. "What do you think? This man is one of the owners. He must be dead now and they think we did it," she said, her voice sharp.

"Sending us a dead man's wallet is a strange way to send a message."

"What do you advise?" she asked.

"With your permission, I will ask Mr. Chen."

"Ask him," Juju ordered.

† † †

CARLOS VASQUEZ HID his brother Tomas in one of the executive suites at the El Escondite Inn. With the extent of his injuries and no ID, the hospital would call the police. Carlos paid the cleaning maids extra cash to bring him food, change his blood-soaked bandages and sheets and keep their mouths shut. He kept a close watch on Tomas's recovery and had his silver Dodge Chargers moved to the hotel. He called his brother Enrique in Los Angeles.

"This is the work of the Chinese mob," Carlos said in Spanish at the end of his report.

"We cannot let this go unanswered, *mi hermano*." d.

"Now you know why Tomas was not there for the exchange," Carlos said.

"It is understandable now," Enrique said solemnly. "We are at war with the Chinese. I will contact the other side to set up another exchange. You will have to pick someone else to go with you if Tomas won't be well enough."

"How long before we can complete the exchange, Enrique? We are in bad shape here."

"A week. Is there a problem?"

"There's no one here I can trust, Enrique. Those China people and the Gringos are everywhere. I don't know anybody. Can't you send me one of our cousins or nephews?"

Enrique paused. "I must think. Call you back in one day."

† † †

IT WAS EARLY afternoon. Hitchcock and Allie had planned to go to the lake after Trevor got out of pre-school but a steady downpour nixed that. A call came in from Patty in Records as Allie handed him his first cup of coffee.

"Someone named Lotus just called for you."

"Did she sound like it was urgent?"

"Miss Mon-o-tone? Sure-ly-you-jest."

"Haha, Patty," Hitchcock chortled.

He sighed as he watched Allie waddle around the house behind a belly so big that a clerk in the Nordstrom store in the Square asked her to leave, fearing the baby could come out any minute. He had asked her why she wasn't angry about it.

"Why would I be? The look on their faces was a hoot," she answered.

He refilled his cup and dialed the number for Lotus.

"Officer Hitchcock? I have news," Fen said.

"Go ahead, please."

"A drug shipment must have come in yesterday, or last night. All day, people—mostly men—have been coming to see Juju. They meet in her office for about three minutes, then leave. There have been over a dozen such visitors today, people I don't recognize."

"Did you see what kind of cars they drove?"

Fen's voice faltered. "N-no. I was busy in the kitchen

and setting up the dining area for lunch customers. I would be in trouble if I stepped outside to write down license plate numbers."

"Where is Juju now?"

"Still at work. I left early to pick up my son at school. He's sick. "I was the first one there this morning. A locksmith came last night and changed all the locks. Juju gave me my own key," Fen said. "There's one more thing."

"What?"

"I found a black leather men's wallet propped up at the front door when I arrived. I opened it. It belongs to a Tomas Vasquez of Los Angeles, California. There were several hundred-dollar bills in it. I gave it to Juju. She seemed very alarmed when she saw the name on the driver's license."

"Anything else?"

"Three men from Taipei arrived yesterday, or maybe the day before. They were dressed like upper class criminal types. One in his forties, the other two are younger and not as big as the older one."

"Who's the boss?

"Juju when she's there. Otherwise, the oldest one. They don't talk to anyone but her. That's all for now."

THE HOUSE PHONE rang again. "It's La Paloma looking for you this time," Patty said. Hitchcock dialed the number right away.

"Hey, Roger. My new job as a waitress at the Pancake Corral starts in ten days. I've put in my notice here and I'm feeling better already."

"That's good to hear, Dolly," he said, expecting to hear more than news about her new job.

"I could have waited to tell you this, right?" she said. "The real reason I called is because one of the owners, Tomas, has been beaten up real, real bad. They're afraid to take him to the hospital which either means he's wanted by the law or was up to something he could get busted for. Anyway, he's recuperating in one of the rooms. Carlos is paying us extra cash to bring him meals, change his bandages, give him sponge baths."

Hitchcock leaned forward in his chair. "Have you heard Tomas say anything?"

"Not a word so far. I overheard that his wallet and his gun are gone."

"What are his injuries?"

"Broken ribs, both sides, broken nose, bruises everywhere on head and body—like he was kicked after he went down. He will probably lose an eye."

"What's being done for his pain?"

"Guess."

"Okay. Great work. Keep me posted. Whatever you do, stay with the job change. Leave when the time comes and don't look back."

He hung up, staring at the phone. "What was that all about, honey?" Allie asked.

He glanced at her and shook his head. "Work stuff."

CHAPTER SEVENTY
Dark Schemes

THE FIRST STATEMENT in Horace MacAuliffe's packet from private investigator Tobias Olson was that of his informant, June, the paroled convict who had been gathering information on Hitchcock and Allie through her job at the Pancake Corral.

He read the details to his wife.

"She's too favorable to them, Horace."

"I told Toby to get from her an unbiased, objective report, so we can see what we do and don't have. If she testifies to all the positive things she saw in their home, especially that they're teaching Trevor to play a banjo and sing Hillbilly crap, the judge and certainly the jury will melt, and we'll lose again."

"So, what's your plan?"

He lit a cigar. His cheeks billowed in and out like a blowfish. Puffs of bluish smoke rose until a thin blue cloud hung in the room. "The surest, time-tested way to get Trevor away from them is to break them financially with attorney fees," he said.

"That could take a year and we could lose again."

"Exactly. We're not looking good now. So do you have a better idea, my dear?" he asked.

"It's risky."

"What is it?"

"Arrange for an all-day or afternoon visit with Trevor and not take him back on the basis that the police reports of the attack on the family and Trevor's own fears make it imperative that he stay with us pending a court hearing."

"They'll call the police on us for custodial interference. We'll get arrested."

"The point is, Horace, the authorities won't return Trevor to his mother when we show them the police reports our attorney obtained and the court papers, and Trevor tells them what we'll coach him to say."

"Hmm."

"It's a strong point in our favor that there's never been a professional evaluation of the emotional impact the attack had on Trevor. Their attorney fees will devastate them, and it will break Allie, which is what you want. And we avoid a year or more of litigation."

"You mean play them along. Make them think we're having a change of heart. Set them up so we can snatch Trevor, we fall on the mercies of the court, begging for sanctuary," he mused.

"Exactly. Well put," she said.

"I still want to break Hitchcock financially. Teach him a lesson about being a traitor to his class."

"We can do both, my dear."

MacAuliffe chuckled. "Milly, my dear, if you'd gone to law school, I'd make myself your only client."

Mildred gave him a sly look as she chuckled back.

"You already are."

† † †

FROM HIS OFFICE at The El Escondite, Carlos Vasquez called his brother Enrique in Los Angeles. They spoke in Spanish. "Everything okay, *hermano*? I have been waiting for your call."

"Tell me what's going on at the hotel."

"We have nothing. Especially after the China woman robbed us. As soon as we can make the exchange, I will rebuild our distribution."

"Sounds good, Carlos. Now, what have you done to find out who attacked our brother Tomas?"

"It can only be the China woman's people. There's no one else who would dare do that. Rebuilding both sides of this business and finding out who attacked Tomas and getting revenge takes time and money."

"We will deal with that after you receive the shipment," Enrique said.

"You need to know, brother, that the China woman just got another shipment in by plane a couple nights ago. It must have been big, because the stuff is everywhere on the streets, and we are being avoided. From here I can see if a plane comes in, but I never know what night it will be."

"We need someone on their inside to know that. Do you have anyone in mind?"

"The woman hires only people of her own race, Enrique."

"We must take risks if we are to survive, Carlos."

† † †

MONEY FROM DRUG sales in King County started pouring in. After two weeks, Juju repaid the loan from her bosses in Taiwan in full.

In keeping with Bamboo Union practices, Juju had a lock on Officer Gerry McCabe. Like Bostwick, McCabe didn't know Juju was recording with hidden cameras his affairs with her and Monica while on duty, his asking for and receiving money, and his giving her information about patrol shifts and district assignments.

Juju told no one else about her failed efforts to recruit Dolly Searles. The standoff protected them both. But Monica Dwyer knows too much. She must either pass certain tests to prove she is not an agent for the police, or suffer the same fate as the others.

Juju wanted her visitors from Taiwan to find out who robbed the shipment from Ming and Sorenson and tried to kill her. She was convinced they were El Escondite men, but there was no evidence. With so many people turning up dead or missing, the stakes were too high to wait for real proof.

† † †

TWO DAYS LATER, Carlos Vasquez met his cousins Alonzo and Cesar at the Seattle airport. They were fit, in their twenties, street tough. Both had done time in the Los Angeles County Jail for misdemeanors involving assault, theft, and possession of stolen property. Carlos drove them to the hotel and showed them to their room.

"Here are the rules," he said in Spanish. "You are here as soldiers; you are not on vacation. You can have what you want at the restaurant but limit your drinking to two drinks per day. No drugs or you will be sent home. I don't know when I will need you, so I need to know where you are always. Be sober and ready to act at all times. Be polite to our customers but don't visit with them. Any one of them could be a cop or the DEA. Tomorrow I will get you a rental car. Any questions?"

IT WAS LATE when Carlos received a call from his brother Enrique.

"In five days, the same delivery team will arrive. Where do you want them to meet you?"

"There's an A and W Root Beer drive-in on the south side of the freeway overpass, across from Denny's. It will be closed, but no one will notice if a couple cars are there. They close at nine. We can meet at eleven. I will be driving the same car as before," Carlos said.

"Anything else?"

"I have all the money from last time in a safe. But how much are they bringing this time? We should know that."

CHAPTER SEVENTY-ONE
Allie's Dreams

TWO DAYS PASSED. It was almost one in the afternoon when Hitchcock woke up. He smelled coffee and the fresh scent of his very pregnant wife, when she waddled into the bedroom. "Coffee with honey, creamer, and something else," she said.

He propped his pillow against the headboard and sat up. He smiled as she handed him the steaming mug. "What's the 'something else?'"

"A letter from our attorney," she said.

"You haven't opened it?"

"Nope."

He tore open the envelope and read quickly. "Wow, baby. If this is what prayer can do, I'm in."

"What are you talking about?"

"The MacAuliffe's attorney says that because his clients want the best for Trevor, they are reconsidering their position. If our offer for them to visit Trevor is still open, they would like to arrange a visit at our convenience."

"Sounds like another miracle, honey."

"I'll call our attorney to tell him that we agree."

"Tonight, and tomorrow are your nights off," she said. "What would you like to do?"

"I'm not tired enough yet to go to sleep when you do. I'll read until I'm drowsy."

An hour after Allie went to bed that night, while Hitchcock was reading in the living room, he heard her cry out, "Stop! Oh no you don't!"

He rushed into the bedroom and flipped on the light. Allie was sitting up, hand on her chest, her breathing was rapid. "What's the matter? Is it hospital time?" he asked, rushing to her side.

"No. I had the same dream twice. I saw Horace taking Trevor by the hand and leading him away to where his wife was waiting. I woke up each time, realized it was just a dream and fell asleep again. Then I had the dream a third time, but it was different. This time Horace's wife was with him, and they each had Trevor by the hand, running away. The dreams were from God. Roger, my ex-father-in-law and his wife are planning to take Trevor from us against our will. This change of mind of theirs is a trick."

He was too surprised to move or speak. She looked at him. "What's the matter, don't you believe me?"

"I'll call our attorney in the morning and tell him we decline."

"Don't tell him about my dreams."

CHAPTER SEVENTY-TWO
Setting Up, Times Three

THE NEXT DAY, Hitchcock answered his home phone. Dolly sounded bubbly and excited. "I'm calling to thank you and Allie for getting me this job. I just finished my second day at the Pancake Corral. I love it. Everybody is great to work with, and the customers leave good tips. I'm glad we met, and your wife is so thoughtful and considerate. You're a lucky man. Thanks to the two of you, I have a new start."

"I'm glad you're out of Eastgate, Dolly. You're safe now."

"I have to go back to the El Escondite tomorrow to pick up my last paycheck. Then I'm gone."

"We'll be seeing you at the Corral, then."

† † †

MONICA DWYER SAT in her Datsun 240Z in the parking lot of the El Escondite Inn, sketching the layout of the hotel's entrances and exits. Then she mapped the closest freeway ramps and the frontage road on both sides of I-90 in conjunction with the A&W Root Beer drive-in.

† † †

ACROSS THE I-90 freeway, Lucio drove his black vinyl-over white 1970 Buick Skylark Gran Sport slowly past the A&W drive-in. He turned to his passenger as he stopped in the parking lot. "What do you think, Manuel? Is this a good place to meet after dark? It has quick access to either direction on the freeway. It'll be closed, so no people will be around."

Manuel looked all around him and sighed. "Looks good to me, Lucio. There will be enough light from the streetlights, and from here we can see them coming from the hotel before they cross the freeway."

"I will call Enrique and tell him we agree to the plan for tomorrow night."

CHAPTER SEVENTY-THREE
The Eve of Destruction

The Next Evening - 7:45 P.M.
Shift Briefing

BECAUSE OF SECURITY leaks within the Department, Otis said nothing about drug shipments at shift briefing. "Crime Analysis hasn't released their reports yet," he said, "but I've noticed another spike in drug overdose cases in the past week. It's worse in Seattle. Not just marijuana, but LSD, Ecstasy and heroin. Be extra careful when you do a pat-down search of a suspect that you don't get punctured by a needle or cut by safety razor used to cut cocaine. Watch for small gatherings outside all-night stores and restaurants. Hit the bricks, boys."

Knowing Gerry McCabe would be watching which way he went when he left the station, Hitchcock left, headed toward the downtown. By prior arrangement, he met Otis behind the National Bank of Commerce just a block above Old Main Street.

"The heroin that's hitting our streets now came from The Great Wall," Hitchcock said. "The El Escondite is about to go under. Two of the three brothers who own it are here to salvage what's left. The one who was attacked is named Tomas. He was on surveillance across the freeway from The Great Wall, sitting almost right next to Sherman. Someone brutally attacked him seconds after Tom left."

"So, the Mexican mafia comes into town, buys the old Hill Top Inn, takes on The Great Wall as competition in the drug trade and Juju sends her boys in to teach them a lesson," Otis concluded.

"Right, but there's a fly in the ointment," Hitchcock said.

"Which is…?"

"Whoever attacked Tomas took his wallet and left it at the front door of The Great Wall where the employees would find it and give it to Juju, which they did."

Otis nodded. "So, an unidentified third party *is* behind the scenes, stirring the two sides against each other."

Records came on the air, asking Hitchcock to call. He went to a phone booth.

A new clerk answered. "Officer Hitchcock, someone named La Paloma just left a message for you to call her. She says it's urgent." He called the number.

"Roger, it's Dolly. I came to the El Escondite after dinner to pick up my last paycheck. A big shipment of heroin is coming in tonight."

"Where?"

"At the A and W Root Beer drive-in across 150th, near the Denny's."

"How do you know this?"

"Two of the cleaning maids who've been taking care of Tomas told me they overheard the young cousins telling him their plan when they went there to change his bandages."

"Young cousins?"

"They came here three days ago, just before I quit. They're from L.A. Their names are Alonzo and Cesar. Gang types."

"What time is this supposed to happen?"

"I heard them say eleven."

"Who is involved?"

"Carlos and these young guys, I guess."

"What about the new officer?"

"I don't see him because he works nights. Rumor is he's in and out of the El Escondite a lot. He sees the girl at the front desk"

"Thanks, Dolly. You're done now as La Paloma. Go home."

He immediately briefed Otis.

† † †

AT 10:00 P.M. Otis sidelined McCabe from the coming action by posting him on guard duty at the Property Room five miles north of Eastgate.

Hitchcock positioned himself in an unmarked car partially hidden behind the Albertsons store, facing the A&W drive-in.

Sherman hid across the street in a marked patrol car around the corner of Denny's.

Otis watched the El Escondite across the freeway, in

the Albertson's parking lot in an unmarked car. watching the El Escondite across the freeway.

At 10:10 p.m. Otis radioed Hitchcock. *"Four men in a black-over-white Buick Skylark left the El Escondite parking lot, headed your way. Duck down."*

Hitchcock laid flat on the front seat. Seconds later he heard the high-performance engine rumble by him at idle speed.

"They're parking at the A and W now, facing the freeway," Otis reported.

The minutes seemed like hours. The radio remained quiet. Hitchcock's hands were clammy from the cold and nervous tension. At 10:38 p.m. the radio crackled as Otis came on the air again. *"A red Dodge Power Wagon pulled into the Albertson's front parking lot, facing the A and W. Two men on board. They're at the far edge of the parking lot."*

"Copied," Hitchcock acknowledged.

Otis came on the air again. *"A red Dodge Charger just showed up in the Albertsons front parking lot. One male occupant. Stopped close to the store front. White male in bib overalls getting out, walking to store. The store's closed...he's returning to his car now."*

Sherman came on the air. *"Two more cars are leaving the Escondite, passing the airport. They're on the frontage road headed to the overpass at a pretty good clip...crossing the overpass, headed here."*

Hitchcock focused his binoculars on the black-over-white Buick Skylark. The two men inside were watching the cars approaching on the overpass. The passenger fidgeted in his seat. *Probably checking his gun,* Hitchcock thought.

"Get ready," Otis radioed.

CARLOS VASQUEZ AND his cousin Alonzo arrived at the A&W in his black Camaro with enough cash in his briefcase to buy the drive-in. In a rental car behind him and off to one side was his other cousin, Cesar.

Not knowing who attacked his brother Tomas, and knowing the size of the transaction about to take place, Carlos carried two pistols under his jacket. He parked about ten feet away, got out, and greeted Lucio and Manuel by name. The two men with Lucio stayed in the car.

"My brother Tomas was not here last time because he was attacked by some very bad men," Carlos explained, smiling tensely. "He may lose one eye."

Lucio and Manuel nodded their acceptance of his explanation, never taking their eyes off Carlos. They noticed Alonzo, standing back, holding an oversized briefcase. "My cousin is with me," Carlos explained. "Show me what you have, my friends."

Manuel set the case on the trunk lid of Lucio's car, opened it and stepped back. "None of it has been cut even once, Carlos. Go ahead—test it."

Carlos nodded approval after the sample he tested indicated purity. He motioned to Alonzo to bring the briefcase for payment.

The men didn't notice the red Dodge Power Wagon until it was too late, nor did they have time to escape when it rammed both cars in one mighty crash. The red Dodge Charger swooped in. The stocky man in bib overalls bailed out, grabbed both briefcases, and fishtailed across the parking lot onto eastbound I-90.

"Roger, Tom, go after the Charger!" Otis shouted into his mic. Sherman gave chase, red overhead light flashing, Hitchcock following in a Dodge Aspen detective car. At a hundred-fifteen and climbing the Charger was gaining distance over Sherman's Plymouth Fury cruiser until Sherman reached the open eastbound lanes of I-90. The distance between Sherman and Hitchcock increased as the chase went past the two Issaquah exits and headed uphill, along a winding curve toward the left, then to the right. Hitchcock saw a pair of taillights go airborne trying to take the offramp at the Preston exit.

Sherman spotted red lights on the shoulder beyond the Preston exit. Hitchcock caught up with him as he pulled over behind the red Charger, upside down on the gravel shoulder.

They ran up to the Charger. Sherman shone his flashlight into the interior. An adult white male in bib overalls and a red ball cap was passed out, crumpled in the driver seat, held in place by the seatbelt.

"No passengers," he said.

"I smell gasoline," Hitchcock said. "No flares."

Sherman busted out the driver's door glass with his eight-cell Kel-Lite. The odor of gasoline grew stronger. Sherman cut the seatbelt with his knife. Hitchcock tilted the body head-first out the window. He and Sherman dragged the unconscious driver by the armpits onto the pavement. Gasoline streamed onto the gravel shoulder and the pavement toward the engine.

Hitchcock broke out the passenger door window and retrieved both briefcases.

A state trooper pulled up and started to light a highway flare. Sherman stopped him. "Gas on the ground—this thing could explode any second."

Gallons of gasoline burst into flames, bathing the scene in hellish orange firelight and billowing black smoke as Hitchcock and Sherman dragged the driver by the armpits to a safe distance from the heat and the roaring flames. As they laid the driver down, the ball cap and a black wig slipped off. Hitchcock's heart almost stopped. The 'man' was Connie Fowler.

CHAPTER SEVENTY-FOUR
The Unmasking

COLD MOUNTAIN WINDS made a loud rushing sound as the gusts blew through thick stands of Douglas Fir on the mountain slopes, whipping the flames higher into the black night sky. Hitchcock stood speechless, staring at Connie, still unconscious. Sherman touched his arm, inquiring. Hitchcock couldn't speak.

"You know her?" the state trooper asked.

Numb, Hitchcock stared at the heavyset, manly woman in bib overalls, passed out on the gravel shoulder. In a voice thick with bafflement and grief, he replied, "Connie Fowler, missing person. Family friend."

An ambulance arrived. Two white-clad attendants rushed to Connie. "Her blood pressure is low," one of them said to no one in particular as he placed a surgical collar on her neck and his partner helped him strap Connie onto a gurney.

"I'm arresting her, Tom," Hitchcock said. "I'll follow her to the hospital."

"Better look inside those briefcases first."

They set the cases on the trunk of Hitchcock's car.

Sherman held his flashlight as Hitchcock opened the first, finding it full of stacked one-hundred-dollar bills.

The acrid smoke burning his nostrils, Hitchcock motioned for the ambulance to leave. "No going to the hospital for me," he said as the ambulance lit up its red emergency lights, its siren whined, and the state trooper halted traffic so it could U-turn and head for the hospital. "We've got to take this to the station together to count it and record the serial numbers."

"Let's see what's in the other one, as if we didn't know," Sherman said as he flipped the clasps. Plastic bags of white powder filled every inch of the briefcase.

Hitchcock and Sherman reacted with disbelieving silence. Neither of them moved. Then Sherman, his eyes still on what he knew was a fortune in drugs, ended the silence. "What do you think the street value is?"

"Half a million would be my guess," Hitchcock replied, shrugging. "Pay attention to everything I do as I pack this up and follow me to the station."

DETECTIVE SERGEANT JURGENS met Hitchcock and Sherman at the station. They counted the cash—one hundred twenty thousand in fifties and hundreds. The bills were photographed, showing the serial numbers. They photographed and sealed the heroin in the briefcase in plastic. Jurgens secured both briefcases in the detective office safe.

A FEW MINUTES past 3:00 a.m., Hitchcock went to the Overlake ER to check Connie Fowler's status. The nurse said Connie was unconscious, on oxygen and IV's. He explained that Connie was under arrest, not to be released should she wake up.

"No chance of that, officer," the nurse replied. "She's got extensive internal injuries."

Barbara, Randy and John Fowler, looking distraught, arrived and waited outside the Intensive Care Unit. Room. Hitchcock explained everything that happened as he knew it. Barbara broke down sobbing. Randy and John caught her before she collapsed.

"I'm as shocked as any of you are. I'll get to the bottom of it," Hitchcock assured them as a nurse and an orderly sat Barbara in a chair and checked her vital signs.

Two other ambulances brought in the four injured men from the scene of the attack. Only Carlos Vargas was conscious. Detective Sergeant Jurgens and Detective Small relieved Hitchcock at the ER. He returned to Eastgate.

IT WAS ALMOST 5:00 a.m. when he tumbled into bed, numb from exhaustion and adrenalin. The shock of finding Connie alive in such circumstances made sleep almost impossible. He did what he learned to do in Vietnam; laid supine, perfectly still, palms on his stomach, emptying his mind of all thoughts. The next thing he knew, Allie set a mug of coffee on his nightstand and awakened him—at noon.

"The phone has been ringing off the wall, honey," she said. "Big night last night?" She gasped when he told her about Connie. "I can't believe it! That poor, poor family! How much more can they endure?"

† † †

THE FIRST CALL he returned was to Otis. "You need to get your report written asap, Roger. This Carlos guy confessed to Larry Meyn at the hospital about their drug smuggling. He also admitted his involvement in the murder of the cook at The Great Wall. He's been booked into the county slammer. The dicks are interrogating the other three at the hospital right now."

Hitchcock shook his head. "This is big-time, Joel. Anything else?"

Otis chuckled. "Believe it or not, the DEA contacted Captain Holland, saying they're interested. They'll *try* to come to the station this afternoon, they say."

"Tell them I'll *try* to be there." Hitchcock said.

"Be here. A captain of the Seattle PD narcs called and offered their help. There'll be a meeting with them here at three this afternoon," Otis said.

"Huge difference in attitude, eh? I'll be there. What do you know about Connie and her redneck boys?"

"Still unconscious with multiple internal injuries is all I know. The truck attacked so fast I didn't get the plate number. They disappeared into Upper Eastgate. The dicks'll get 'em later. See you this afternoon."

His energy drained when he hung up the phone. He

made his way into the kitchen. His heart warmed when Trevor gave him a hug, and Jed looked up from his toys on the floor. Jamie approached, wagging his tail as Allie set his breakfast of four eggs over medium, bacon and buttered pumpernickel toast on the table. *If Allie's ex-father-in-law has his way this could be the last time we're together,* was his first thought.

"My clairvoyant wife," he said, smiling at his favorite breakfast. "Who else called?"

"Barbara Fowler, Steve Miller from *The Bellevue American*, Sergeant Jurgens, and somebody who said they were on the City Council. Our moms and our siblings called to check on you."

HE STOPPED BY Overlake Hospital on his way to the station. Connie Fowler had been moved to the Intensive Care Unit. Randy and John had gone home. Connie's mother never left her daughter's side. She greeted him with a hug.

"Connie came to for a few minutes this morning. She was so embarrassed to see us. She cried when a doctor came in and told her she has liver and spleen damage. She's sleeping again now."

"Talk later. I've got work to do at the station," he said.

HIS SEVEN-PAGE report made no mention of Dolly as his source. He handed it to Sergeant Jurgens. "Aren't you going to stick around for the meeting at three?"

"Nope. I trust you to tell me what I need to know."

"The DEA will be here, they'll want to talk to you," Jurgens said.

"That's why I'm not going," he said, thinking of Dolly.

CHAPTER SEVENTY-FIVE
Truth Be Told

CONNIE FOWLER'S EXPRESSION consisted of embarrassment and surrender to the inevitable when Hitchcock entered her hospital room. She stared out the window for almost a minute, tubes in her arms, an oxygen cannula in her nostrils, bruises were everywhere a patch of skin showed. "How did you know?" she asked at last.

"A little birdie told me."

She shook her head. "The doc says I'm dying, Roger. Liver damage. Spleen and kidneys too."

"I see track marks on your left arm, Connie. I thought you were off the stuff. You fooled us all, saying you went cold turkey. Why this charade?"

"I need my brother Randy to hear this. He's supposed to be here any minute, then I'll tell you everything. You deserve to know, Roger."

When Randy arrived, Connie began crying and lifted her hands to him. "Randy, I am so sorry for everything I've done, to you and to our family."

Randy pulled up a chair and sat next to her, waiting.

"Thank God Mom's not here," she said, "or I wouldn't be able to say this. I'm the one who got you on drugs, Randy. Growing up, there was never a boy who liked me. I hungered for male attention, but I never got it. Dad, when he was home, made a lot of cutting remarks about my looks, to my face and behind my back. He often called me a dog or a skank. When he was drinking, he told me in front of his drinking pals that he wouldn't take me to a dogfight if I promised to win. They all thought that was funny. I hated him so much I was glad when he died."

Randy took her hand in his. "I'm so sorry, Sis. I remember Dad saying a lot of bad things to you."

"How did the drug thing start, Connie?" Hitchcock asked.

"I had a job tending bar at the Hilltop. I met Tyrone there. I was attracted to him the first time I laid eyes on him. He paid attention to me when no one else did. For that I worshiped him and let him exploit and degrade me all he wanted. Once he got me onto heroin, there was no turning back. He ran Mike Smith out of town, and I became Tyrone's helper." Connie turned her eyes to Randy. "You'd been getting smack from Mike. To help Tyrone, I made sure you had no choice but Tyrone for your supply."

Hitchcock glanced at Randy, sitting with his hands between his knees, eyes watering.

"Mike came back after Roger and his partner killed Tyrone and Mae," Connie continued. "I started getting heroin from Mike. I told Mike about you being friends with Roger, that you were informing for him. I told him what days you were working at the gas station. Mike told me he had to kill you, Randy, and I said nothing because I was partners with him in the drug business! And my habit was getting worse. I'm so ashamed!" Connie said as she burst into tears. Randy hesitated to comfort her, the look on his face was one of grim shock.

Hitchcock was too numb to ask the questions he had prepared.

Connie wiped her eyes as she continued. "I told Mike the days and times you were scheduled to work at the gas station, knowing he was going to kill you. By a miracle you didn't die when he overdosed you and left you for dead like he did to others. I was stunned and didn't know what to do. At that time, Mike, a guy named Bill, and a girl named Julie were shooting up together all the time, and we were scared when you didn't die."

"Where did you get heroin from, Connie?" Hitchcock asked.

"Mike had been getting it all along from Juju, the Oriental who owns a restaurant in Eastgate."

"I still don't understand why you faked your disappearance, Connie—why?" Randy asked.

"It got to where I needed a fix every day. I couldn't hide it from you and Mom anymore," she said. "When the guy Bill got out of jail, he told Mike that Roger tried to shoot him when they were being arrested at the old mill in Preston. That's when Mike decided he had to kill Roger or be killed. Mike and Bill left my car on the freeway. It was part of the setup. Mike bought the Camaro and set fire to his Mustang at the mill to throw the cops off and send a message to Roger."

"What happened next?" asked Hitchcock, almost overwhelmed by the facts he was hearing.

Connie paused to clear her throat. She spit green sputum with bits of blood in it into a tissue, before she continued: "A couple junkies living out of a camper fell in with us. Somehow Mike set it up to use them to attack Roger. He came back without them, saying their guns wouldn't work when they tried to shoot you, Roger. After that, Mike disappeared."

"How did he disappear?" Hitchcock asked.

Connie kept wiping her tears. The effects of heroin withdrawal were beginning to show. She fidgeted. She shook her head. Drops of sweat beaded on her forehead. "He left one day to buy more smack from the woman, Juju, and never came back."

"Then what happened?"

Connie's fidgeting intensified. "My friend, Monica, approached me about going into business for ourselves. She became my link to getting more heroin."

"How did you meet Monica?"

"Tending bar part time at Juju's place, like I met Tyrone at the Hilltop."

"Who are the two guys who hijacked Juju's dope?"

"They're brothers. Their names are—"Connie began spasming. Her features became distorted. Her eyes rolled up as she pressed the button for the nurse. "Go," she gasped, her entire body tremoring.

Randy shot to his feet. "Connie!" he shouted as he grabbed her hand. What color there was in Connie's face drained away, replaced by a sickly gray pallor, glazed over with sweat that soaked her hair, only the whites of her eyes could be seen through the narrow slits of her eyelids, her lips became bluish. Randy broke into tears, holding Connie's hands in his. "Don't die, sister!" he sobbed. "Whatever you've done, I love you and forgive you."

A nurse bustled into the room. Hitchcock pulled Randy aside to make room for her. "She began convulsing seconds ago," Hitchcock told the nurse as she felt Connie's forehead and hit the call button again. In seconds another nurse and a doctor rushed in, and Hitchcock pulled Randy out of the room. "You've done all you can here, Randy. Your mom and your brother will need you now."

† † †

HITCHCOCK LEFT THE hospital for the station, bewildered by Connie's revelations. He used an interview room to write up a detailed report on what she said and gave it to Detective Meyn.

"This certainly fills in a lot of blanks," Meyn said as he read. "Connie could tell us who the guys in the truck are and where to find them."

"I think you should see her while you can," Hitchcock replied. "The nurse and the doc told us she may not survive her injuries much longer."

Meyn grabbed the office tape recorder and left with

Joe Small.

Hitchcock went home, troubled and depressed by the realization that the sister of a childhood friend had set up her own brother and him to be killed—all for drugs.

† † †

AT 5:40 P.M. Hitchcock was sitting in the family room, holding baby Jedidiah on his lap, watching Trevor play fetch with Jamie, when Allie brought him the phone. "It's Larry Meyn," she said.

"Joe and I went to interview Connie Fowler after you left," Meyn said. "A medical team was trying to save her from another round of the seizures. After over two hours, a doctor told us Connie died. Her family was there."

"Thanks for letting me know, Larry."

"I'm sorry, Roger."

Hitchcock said nothing as he ended the call.

CHAPTER SEVENTY-SIX
The Pair From Hell

AFTER THE DEATH of Connie Fowler, Hitchcock went about his duties numbly, as if on autopilot. "How are you doing with the Connie Fowler deal?" Allie asked.

He looked at her and the boys eating peanut butter sandwiches at the kitchen table, Jamie, laying on the floor next to them. "I've had to bury my feelings because they're a jumble. I don't know how her family will handle seeing me again. Connie was running from me and Sherman when she crashed."

Allie put her hand on his arm. "They won't blame you, honey. You didn't know who you were chasing, and it wouldn't have made any difference if you did. What happened to Connie was due to the choices she made."

He grunted his agreement. "In the end, you were right, Allie. It *was* Connie who would die. It fits, she was someone we knew who was close to us. We just didn't know who or when."

"That was one time I wish I'd been wrong."

† † †

AFTER A QUIET shift, Dispatch radioed him at 3:00 a.m. to go to a pay phone. He radioed in the number. "Your wife says she needs you to take her to the hospital, now," the dispatcher said.

He called his mother to meet him at the house. By the time Myrna arrived, he had changed out of his uniform and had seated Allie in his Wagoneer.

Four and a half hours later, a pink, squalling, healthy Benjamin Ian Hitchcock entered the world, weighing in at eight pounds, twelve ounces, demanding food. Allie nursed him until he fell asleep, then she rested. Hitchcock called his mother and Trevor with the news, then his sisters before he fell asleep in the overstuffed chair next to Allie's bed.

† † †

AT 8:10 A.M. Horace MacAuliffe received the call from Tobias Olson he had been waiting for. "My surveillance team across the street from Hitchcock's house says their camera recorded him coming home early, at 3:17 a.m., Mr. MacAuliffe. A lady we believe is his mother came to the house, then Hitchcock and the wife left in a hurry."

"All right, Toby. Is that all?"

"We called the hospital. They confirmed Allison checked into the maternity ward at 4:35 this morning."

"Fine work, Toby. You will be well rewarded. I'll take it from here. Goodbye now."

MacAuliffe tore up two one-page letters from his attorney at the envelope they came in. "We never got these," he told his wife. "We're acting on the original visitation arrangement."

Mildred smiled at him. "Our bags are packed, Horace. Trevor is waiting for his rescue, and I feel adventure in the air."

"Adventure?"

Mildred lifted her head with a dramatic air and a happy grin. "Yes, dear, adventure—derring-do—like we're in a movie. We're, undercover, dressed down like unimportant people. You, in those stained, faded khakis and flannel shirt your father wore when he gardened, and me, without my diamonds, in my grandmother's old gingham dress and ratty overcoat!"

"Hmm!" MacAuliffe grunted, with a grin.

"And to further blend in and evade the police if anyone reports us, we have the perfect undercover car, that old, oxidized green Oldsmobile station wagon you so brilliantly bought for cash!" Mildred exclaimed, her hands in the air.

They knocked on the front door of the Hitchcock residence at 9:45 a.m. A woman about their age answered. They put on their best smiles. "Hello, we're Trevor's grandparents. I'm Horace MacAuliffe, and this is my wife, Mildred. And you are—?"

"I'm Myrna, Roger's mom," she replied, blushing with surprise.

Jamie stood beside Myrna. Sensing evil, he growled lowly, ears laid back. "Well, I'm taken by surprise, I admit! Roger didn't say anything to me about your coming."

Horace smiled cordially. "Now *I'm* taken by

surprise. We have a scheduled visit to see Trevor," he said. "It was worked out between our attorneys. In fact, here's our attorney's letter to us."

Jamie continued his low growl, never taking his eyes off Horace as Myrna read the letter. "Oh, well, with all that's happened this morning Roger surely forgot," she said excitedly.

"What do you mean? Is everything all right?" Horace lied.

Myrna gushed with laughter." Oh yes! Yes! Yes! Everything is just grand. Allie gave birth to her third baby boy this morning. Roger's with her at the hospital now. I apologize for my manners, making you stand here in the doorway. Please come in."

"Oh, that's wonderful. Congratulations!" Mildred said gushingly. "Would it be too much to ask you to put your dog outside? He makes us nervous."

"Of course," Myrna replied.

"Could we at least see Trevor for a moment? It's been a long time."

"Why certainly, Mrs. MacAuliffe. Wait right here, please." Myrna led Jamie by the collar and shut the door to one of the bedrooms. Her face beaming, she returned to them. "This is Trevor's and his brother Jed's regular nap time, so he might be asleep. Wait here and I'll be right back."

Horace lowered his voice. "If she comes out with him, we grab the boy and run."

"What'll we do if she won't wake him up?" Mildred whispered.

"Play it by ear, I guess," he replied softly.

Myrna returned after a moment. "Trevor is sleeping but Allie limits his naps so that he sleeps through the night. He isn't due to be awakened for another forty minutes. You are welcome to wait here, if you like," she said with a sweeping hand gesture.

Horace smiled as he checked his watch. "Forty minutes? We don't want to impose. I think we'll leave and come back then. I'd like to look your little town over. It seems to have grown some since I was here last. We'll come back for our scheduled visit."

IN THE MATERNITY wing of the hospital, Hitchcock slept in a recliner chair next to Allie's bed. He awoke when she tapped him on the arm. "Ben is sleeping now, honey, and the nurse won't be back for half an hour," she said. He looked curiously at her when she threw the bedsheet back. "I want more babies, Roger. Let's make another – right now!"

"What? You just had–"

"I know my body better than you do. Come on – ride 'em cowboy!"

The nurse came in as they were finishing. "*Mister* Hitchcock!" She gasped. "Your wife gave birth hours ago! She – you can't–"

Allie broke out laughing as Hitchcock dressed hurriedly. "It's all right. I told him to make another baby!"

"WHAT'S YOUR PLAN, Horace?" Mildred asked as he headed toward Bellevue's downtown.

"I don't want us to be there when Hitchcock comes home. We'll snatch him when we come back and let the attorneys sort it out."

"What about Myrna?"

"She won't be able to stop us."

They looked at each other when they saw Kingen's, a drive-in on the corner of NE 8th Street and 104th Avenue. The parking lot was full.

"We haven't split a chocolate shake at a drive-in since we were dating, Milly," he said. "You go inside and get us one while I find a spot to park this old heap. We'll enjoy it in the car, then go back for Trevor."

Ten minutes later, Mildred stepped outside with a chocolate milkshake. She heard approaching sirens wailing as she looked for Horace. She heard screaming and yelling. She ran around the building and dropped the milkshake when she saw a crowd gathered around the station wagon they came in. Trembling with alarm, Mildred pushed her way through the onlookers.

The front bumper and grille had smashed into the driver's side of a '57 Chevy, crushing its door shut, its young male driver being helped out of the passenger door by a heavy-set adult man. Horace was in the driver seat, slumped as if asleep, eyes shut, mouth open. A police officer held one of his hands, asking questions in almost a shout, but getting no response.

Mildred shook his arm. "Horace? Horace?"

An ambulance arrived and two men got out. The officer told them "This man is having a stroke! The ER is two minutes away. Seconds count!"

"Where are you taking him?" Mildred asked.

"Overlake," the ambulance driver replied as he helped load Horace onto a gurney. "Who are you to this man?"

"I'm his wife."

"How old is he and what is his health like?" the other ambulance attendant asked.

Mildred shook her head as if she was shaking out unimportant thoughts. "Uh, he's fifty-eight, he has high blood pressure and takes medicine for that."

"Follow us to the hospital, lady."

† † †

HITCHCOCK KISSED ALLIE and his newborn son. She opened her eyes. "I'm going home to shower and check on Mom and the boys," he said. "Be right back after that." Allie nodded drowsily. Without knowing it, he walked past his adversary as he was being rolled into the Intensive Care Unit.

The ambulance driver approached Mildred as she parked the station wagon. "Sorry about your husband, ma'am. I'd like some information, if you don't mind."

She looked him up and down, scorning his unpressed uniform and scuffed shoes. "Can't this wait?"

"Not really. There's a bill for our service, and we don't know your address and—"

"Oh!" Mildred scoffed, waving a hand. "Don't

worry a bit, little man. We live in Broadmoor, in Seattle. We're millionaires."

The ambulance driver snickered as he glanced over her shoulder at the oxidized green Oldsmobile she drove, then at her worn clothes and lack of jewelry. "Sure, you are, lady," his voice dripping sarcasm, "but my boss wants payment right now, if you don't mind."

Mildred opened her purse. "Oh, all right, I understand how it is with you little people." She got out her checkbook and a pen. "How much is it?"

The ambulance driver held out his hand. "Cash, please, since you're so loaded. Eighty bucks."

"This is insulting!" Mildred shouted, clutching her chest. "Oh! *Now* I get it! You're seeing that old car over there," she said, laughing. "That's not our regular car. We just bought it to rescue our grandson from his mother. Our son got a working-class girl pregnant, you see. She would *never* fit in with *our* class of people, poor thing, so we had our son divorce her. But her son is our blood. We don't want him raised with their kind. We bought this old heap as part of our disguise and left our regular car at home. It's a Bentley—red, in fact."

"And of course, you left it at your home in Broadmoor, with your chauffeur," he scoffed.

"Why, yes. You are more astute than you look. In fact, we own an entire office building downtown."

The driver shook his head as he held out his hand. "And I'm the King of Siam. Cash, or I call the cops, Queenie."

CHAPTER SEVENTY-SEVEN
Stalking Hitchcock

TWO DAYS LATER, at 1:00 p.m. the man in a tan early '60s Ford F-100 pickup with a lawnmower in the bed was parked mid-block from Hitchcock's house. It had been raining with blustery winds and cool temperatures all day, keeping most people inside. He knew Hitchcock's mother had been staying with the other two boys while their mother was in the hospital.

The stranger circled the block to the back property line to view again the rear of Hitchcock's house. He drove the mid-block dirt alleyway for service truck access. A single door at the back. Windows on either side. He noted the top of another door below ground level which he knew led to a root cellar.

The mature apple and pear trees that dotted the back and side yard were too tall and far apart to offer concealment. The bushes at each side window afforded no concealment from alert neighbors or responding police. An approach from the rear wouldn't work. He returned to the street in front of the house. The kitchen door at the side was the best for gaining quick access to the occupants and escape when his mission was accomplished. He would approach from the alley. It would have to be before Hitchcock returned to work. The only sensible time would be right at shift change, when it was still dark.

A gun metal gray Jeep Wagoneer arrived at the house. Hitchcock got out of the driver seat. The stranger focused his Zeiss binoculars on Hitchcock, Allie, and their new baby as they were greeted by Hitchcock's mother, the dog, and the couples' two boys. *One more surveillance, just to be sure...*

CHAPTER SEVENTY-EIGHT
Ruthless

JUJU KWAN RETURNED to her office late to allow for the twelve-hour time difference with Taiwan. Mr. Chen answered on the third ring. "I have been waiting for your call," he said, enunciating his words, softly spoken as usual. "You have repaid your loan earlier than we expected. You are in good standing. We want to know what has happened since you were attacked."

"Good news, Longtou. Two of the three owners of the Mexican hotel and bar have been caught in a drug transaction by the police. I don't know how the police knew," Juju reported in Mandarin. "They must have informers. If the owners are freed quickly, it means they agreed to inform. The government closed the El Escondite Inn, it is empty now."

"How did the men who attacked you know where to find you?"

"I do not know, Longtou. Someone informed on me. Maybe they are the same as the two who stole the shipment from my two runners, Ming and Scott. I must find out who they are. I am afraid there will be an attack on our next plane that comes in."

"Whom do you suspect?"

"I have eliminated everyone who could testify against me, sparing no one, good or bad. Americans call what I did a scorched earth policy. Except one, a woman. I am not sure of her yet. If she can prove her loyalty to me, I will bring her in."

"Why not just eliminate her like the others if you are unsure?"

"Maybe I will. But not yet. If she is loyal, she would be very useful to us. This is very dangerous work now, because of enemies other than the police. I am thinking two more shipments, maybe three, then we can shift into real estate and loans."

"How much longer will you need my soldiers?"

"They are helping me get new help and keeping the shipments safe. I need them as I rebuild, Longtou."

"You may keep them only for another month."

After the call, Juju sat, alone. The past few weeks had been a nightmarish whirlwind of events. A large shipment of heroin headed from the small airfield to her home was hijacked by two armed men almost killed her runners. Figuring the Mexican gang in the former Hilltop Inn was responsible, she had ordered the death of one of their employees.

She barely survived the attempt to kill her by two men who rammed her car, sending it rolling down the mountain, then the Mexicans murdered her cook, escalating the turf war. Repaying her boss, Mr. Chen, drained her financially. All she had left with which to rebuild were her employees, her young patrolman, and another up in the ranks who hadn't paid his dues yet.

A fact she hid from Mr. Chen and everyone else was that through a proxy, a corporate shell, she bought the little strip of businesses where her restaurant was. After all that had happened recently, the safety of commercial real estate appealed to her even more. It would take more money to get in the game and drug sales were the fastest way to raise the necessary capital. She needed a new network to distribute heroin. Her health wasn't what it had been after being run off the road. Frequent intestinal pains needed pain medications from her doctor.

Enemies were out there, known and unknown. The unidentified enemies were probably planning to hijack the next shipment by plane, but with her need for cash to rebuild, she had to take the chance.

There was Hitchcock, who had done almost all the damage. His joss was good, like something was protecting him. Every attack on him ended in disaster. Even Bostwick, a high-ranking police official with powerful connections couldn't prevail against him. Her own efforts to have him taken out failed. At least he wasn't in Eastgate anymore.

She had to know for certain if Monica was friend or foe. Monica knows too much to be allowed to live if she failed the tests Juju had in mind.

CHAPTER SEVENTY-NINE
The Initiation

MONICA DWYER'S HEART was in her throat when she came to The Great Wall after work. Juju had asked her to come. The eldest of three men from Taiwan met her in the bar and led her to Juju's office. She was surprised to see Juju sitting at her desk, dressed seductively in a filmy purple one-piece dress, her facial scars almost completely healed. It made Monica nervous that Juju wasn't smiling. "I'm glad to see you recovering so nicely from your injuries, Juju," she said.

"Have a sit," Juju said bluntly as she gestured to the couch. "We talked partnership when I in hospital. I rebuild business now. You still want in?"

"Of course."

"What can you do? Why bring you in?"

"I'm a good manager of people." Monica fidgeted in her chair, hoping her answer would suffice.

A sly knowing grin spread over Juju's face. "Yes, true. We check what you do in Longview. You a madam, a *mama-sahn*. But smalltime—you have only two, three girls working for you. If you want in with us, you prove that you loyal, that you not spy for police."

"What do I have to do?"

Juju gestured to the big man from Taiwan. "First test, go with Long Hay and his men. He give you cocaine, they watch you sell it. Three times."

"How much is my cut?"

Juju's smile was cold. "Very good, Monica. Let's see how you do."

"And the second test?" Monica asked.

"Pass first test first. Pass second test, we partners."

Monica froze on the couch when two more Chinese men, younger than Long Hay, dressed in suits, appeared at the office door. Juju stared at Monica expectantly. Like a calf entering the iron chute to be branded, she obediently went with the men.

"Where are we going?" Monica asked, fear in her voice as she got in the back seat of the white Lincoln Town Car between the young men.

"Seattle." Came Long Hay's curt reply.

† † †

THE FIRST STOP was the Louisa Hotel, a three-story building from the 1920s in Chinatown. Long Hay reached over the front seat and handed Monica a plastic baggie having a white powder, wrapped in a tube and bound with a rubber band. He led Monica by the hand, followed by the two young men, through a seedy lobby, down a dark stairwell to the basement where the lighting was dim, and the smoke of tobacco and hashish was thick. The place still had the feel of the speakeasy it had been during the Prohibition years of the 1920s and

'30s. Life-size murals of men and women were on the walls. Chinese men sitting at tables, gambling at Mahjong, smoking and drinking. They stopped to look her over.

At a table in the corner a Chinese man sat alone, smoking a cigarette, wearing a white dress shirt, black necktie, black vest, his back against the corner, wary eyes staring at Monica. She trembled as Long Hay led her to him.

The man at the table spoke sharply in Mandarin to Long Hay, pointing at Monica in defiant gestures. She cast a nervous glance at the man when Long Hay answered the man in Mandarin, using a gruff tone. "He thinks you are police agent," he told her.

"What did you tell him?"

"You are here to prove you are one of us. Sell him cocaine. Now."

The man kept staring at Monica as she handed him the container from her jacket pocket. He brought out a hand mirror, straw and razor from his inside vest pocket. He opened the tube and shook out a plastic bag filled with white power, then tapped out a small amount of the drug on the mirror, made a thin line, using the razor, and grunted as he handed her the straw. Monica glanced at Long Hay, panic and pleading in her eyes. "You want in, you show him," he said.

Heart pounding, Monica bent down and snorted half the line, then stood, staring hard at the man as she outstretched her hand, gesturing for money. The man's lips curled upward into a cruel smile as he reached under his vest and handed Monica a handful of bills. She counted it and slipped the bills into her silk blouse.

Long Hay took her by the arm as she headed for the staircase. They reached the Lincoln. One of the young men got into the back seat. Monica started to get in, but Long Hay stopped her. He held out his other hand. She reached into her blouse and handed him a few bills, not all. He slapped and shook her. "You not keep anything. This your test!" He held out his hand again. She gave him the rest of the bills, numb with fear and cocaine.

The next place was an underground den of iniquity on Skid Row. Long Hay led her in, but she had to do her own talking and selling. Long Hay kept the cash.

The third stop was in the manager's office at the Bavarian Gardens, just outside the Bellevue city limits. Again, Monica sold a bindle of cocaine that Long Hay provided, and snorted a slight amount in front of the men and a dancer.

Back in the car, sitting between the two young men, Monica was swooning, dazed, yet feeling excited and daring when she asked, "That's three sales I did for you. What's the next test?"

The driver stopped the Lincoln, looking at Monica in his rearview mirror. Long Hay, in the front seat looked over his shoulder at her. She looked at the two men on either side of her, they were looking at her too.

"We show you now," Long Hay said. He gave an order to the driver, who put the car in gear. They took her to a house in Chinatown.

CHAPTER EIGHTY
An Odd Prelude

MILDRED MACAULIFFE PICKED up her phone on the second ring. "I have Mr. Olson, your husband's private investigator, on the line, asking to speak with you," her husband's secretary said.

Mildred waited for the call to transfer, then said, "This is Mildred, Mr. Olson, what can I do for you?"

"Thank you for taking my call, Mrs. MacAuliffe. Before I get to business, how is Mr. MacAuliffe doing?"

"That's very nice of you to ask, Toby. Sadly, Horace is still in a coma. The doctors say there's nothing they can do for him. He's been declining since I had him moved from that place they call a hospital in Bellevue to Swedish in Seattle."

"Sorry to hear that, ma'am. I'm calling about our surveillance team across the street from the Hitchcock residence. They're still on the job. Nothing relevant to report has happened. Your husband kept the surveillance going because the team had seen and photographed a suspicious character stalking them. The man sometimes appears in disguises. Mr. MacAuliffe felt this could be a threat to Trevor. Do you want to close our investigation down, or keep it going?"

"Didn't Horace want you to warn them anonymously?"

"I suggested that, but he refused."

"What? Well, I'm telling you to tell your team to call the police on this guy if they see him prowling around their house again."

"Yes ma'am. How much longer should I keep them on the job?"

Mildred thought for a moment. "I'm concerned. Let it run for a while longer. Keep me posted."

A half-hour later, Mildred's phone rang again. "Oscar Travis, here, Mildred. My call is both personal and professional. How are you holding up?"

"Marginally."

"I can hardly imagine. How is Horace doing?"

"His pulse is weakening. They have him on life supports. Doesn't open his eyes anymore."

"Terrible. What do his doctors say?"

"He could go on for months on life supports, it is unlikely he'll ever recover or regain consciousness. That's what three different doctors have told me."

"I hate to burden you with this, but as your husband's attorney, and as Horace is incapable of making decisions, I must turn to you, his wife, as you have power of attorney."

"Tell me what it is, Oscar."

"It's regarding your child custody suit against Allie and Roger Hitchcock over your grandson, Trevor. I've just received notice from the court that their attorney has filed a motion for summary judgment."

"Explain, please."

"A summary judgment is a court order, a ruling that no factual issues remain to be tried and therefore a cause of action or all causes of action in a complaint can be decided upon certain facts without trial. It is based upon a motion by one of the parties that contends that all necessary factual issues are settled or so one-sided they need not be tried."

"What do they contend are the settled factual issues?"

"The usual," Travis said. "That Trevor is happy in a loving home, and part of a growing family, he is healthy, well-nourished, well-cared-for in every way, is in kindergarten, involved in team sports, and so on. If the judge agrees, your case over."

Mildred's silence was long. She sighed as she said, "I'm not in the frame of mind to decide right now, Oscar. I only learned an hour ago what I told you the doctors said about Horace's condition."

CHAPTER EIGHTY-ONE
A Fitting End

THAT AFTERNOON A message from the station told Hitchcock to call Lotus at a certain number. She answered on the first ring.

"Hello, Fen. What's going on?"

"The first thing I have to tell you is quite a surprise, Officer Hitchcock. Juju has made this white woman named Monica a minor partner. We Chinese rarely trust outsiders. I think she is trouble."

"She's trouble and she isn't working for us. What does she do there?"

"She lost her other job. I do not know why. She handles the cash registers in the restaurant and the bar and greets customers. She is supervising the construction of a small apartment Juju is having built in the empty office space next door. It will be connected to the bar so men customers can go there."

"What for?"

"In case you did not know it, Juju owns the building where her restaurant is. The other businesses pay her rent."

Surprised, Hitchcock replied, "I didn't know."

"Chinese gambling places often have women

available to keep men spending their money. Did you know that, Officer Hitchcock?"

"I served two years in Southeast Asia."

"Then you will not be surprised when I tell you Juju is bringing in late-night gambling and the customers are all Chinese."

"I'm not surprised. How do you know this?"

"Employees talk. Especially the bartender."

"Anything else?"

"Yes. I have heard that a shipment of heroin and cocaine will be coming in through the Bellevue airport in a few days at a late hour."

"Picking the shipment up and bringing it to Juju is what my brother Allan and his friend used to do. Who will she use to do that now?"

"Don't know. I'll see what I can find out."

Hitchcock reported Fen's details to Otis after shift briefing. "Come to the closed-door meeting with the DEA tomorrow afternoon in the second-floor conference room," Otis said. "This is the kind of information they need."

"Who's gonna be there?"

"Just show up at two p.m."

† † †

THE TWO DEA field agents who showed up looked like old hippies: thinning, graying shoulder-length hair, unkempt salt-and-pepper beards, baggy corduroy pants, threadbare flannel shirts. Their supervisor surprised him. He was dressed dapper in slacks, loafers, windbreaker jacket, short, standard haircut.

Besides them, Andy Redford of the U.S. Attorney's Office, Captain Holland and Sergeant Jurgens from the Detective Division and Otis were present.

Redford began by addressing Hitchcock. "We've reviewed your reports and we apologize for underestimating and not responding to the scope of the problem your department has been facing. What we want to do is intercept the next shipment that comes in and follow the trail to its source."

† † †

THE FOLLOWING MORNING Records told Hitchcock to go to a pay phone. "Call Lotus right away at this number," Patty said when he answered.

Fen picked up on the first ring. She sounded nervous. "A big shipment of heroin and cocaine is coming in tonight at the airport at twelve-thirty, Officer Hitchcock. You must be ready."

"How do you know this, Fen?"

"I was working in the back this morning, unpacking supplies for the restaurant. Juju's office door was open. She was speaking in Mandarin on the phone. I heard her say she had the cash ready and would have two Taiwanese men in a white Lincoln Town Car meeting them on the runway. She said the one in charge is named Long Hay. He will have the cash. I heard her ask if it was heroin only or if there was cocaine, as her gambling customers like cocaine."

"She said all this with you right there?"

"Juju thinks I only understand English because I was born and raised here. I did not tell her I am fluent in Mandarin."

"Is that everything?"

"She also told them the time she wanted the plane to arrive. I heard her mention your name, but regarding what, I don't know."

"I'm not her favorite person."

† † †

THE DEA STAKEOUT team was in place at the airport at 11:00 p.m. Hitchcock and Otis were in position across the freeway, east of the empty Albertsons store front parking lot, in Hitchcock's Wagoneer, listening on a portable radio.

At 12:10 a.m. Otis keyed his radio mic. "White Lincoln Town Car exited the westbound freeway, signaling to turn to your location." The supervisor acknowledged.

Hitchcock and Otis watched as the Lincoln parked in the runway shadows, facing south toward the freeway, and shut off its lights. Hitchcock focused his binoculars on the vehicle. In the dim light he could see two people in the front seat.

12:16 a.m. headlights entered the Albertsons parking lot from the west end, near the overpass. It was a new, dark Cadillac sedan. It stopped at the north edge of the parking lot, facing the runway and shut off its headlights. Hitchcock looked with his binoculars. "It's Juju, and we're less than fifty yards from her. If she sees us, we're done."

"She's got no way to warn her guys without going there herself and getting arrested. Her only choice is to flee," Otis said. He radioed the stakeout team that Dragon Lady had arrived.

The minutes seemed like hours.

12:38 a.m. A small plane dropped out of the night sky onto the runway. The white Lincoln rolled forward and the two men in it approached the plane on foot. The passenger carried a briefcase. Two men exited the plane. One, an Asian, carried a metal briefcase which he set on the tarmac and opened. When the large man from the Lincoln knelt to test the contents, four unmarked cars swooped in, blocking the plane and the Lincoln. Gun wielding Federal agents bailed out of their vehicles and charged the suspects.

"Juju's leaving! Go! Go! Go!" Otis shouted.

Hitchcock raced across the parking lot and onto the overpass after Juju's new Cadillac while Otis called in their pursuit, requesting backup. A car stopped at the red light at the last signal blocked Hitchcock's pursuit. The signal changed to green. He floored the pedal, racing down the frontage road to The Great Wall. The front doors of Juju's Cadillac was open, engine running. The rear door of the restaurant was ajar.

"Arrest her!" Otis shouted as he and Hitchcock ran inside, shoulder-to-shoulder, guns drawn. To their surprise, they saw no one when they entered the kitchen with its attendant smells of food and cleaning fluids.

His heart pumping, images of Juju's trail of victims

flashed through his mind as he led Otis into the lounge—it was dark—lights out—empty. *She's the hunted one now, and knows it. Is this her last trap?*

"Where'd she go, Roger?" Otis asked, his eyes flashing right and left, looking for even the slightest hint of movement as they quickly searched for anyone hiding.

"Her office. She's got a safe there."

"Lead the way," Otis said, the stealth of the hunter in his voice.

They pushed the door to Juju's office so hard it slammed the wall on the other side. Without a word Long Hay put his hands on his head and dropped to his knees. Juju didn't look when they burst in. She stood, hands hanging at her sides, mouth open, in front of her safe, its door standing wide open, shelves empty.

"My safe! Who steal from my safe?" She shouted to no one in particular.

"You're both under arrest for Investigation of Violation of the Uniform Controlled Substances Act," Hitchcock said. Otis handcuffed Long Hay as Juju ran past Hitchcock to her desk, opened the center drawer and grabbed a small, blued revolver. "Drop the gun!" Otis commanded. She raised it, her eyes on Hitchcock.

The gun went off as Hitchcock wrenched it from her hand. The bullet whizzed past Otis's head missing him and Long Hay by a foot.

"In case you didn't hear me the first time, you're under arrest for Investigation Violation of the Uniform Controlled Substances Act, and First-Degree Assault

Upon a Police Officer," Hitchcock said as he handcuffed her.

A marked patrol car arrived. Otis handed Juju and Long Hay to the officer. "Book them both her for VUCSA and her for Attempted Assault First," he said. As the officer led Juju and Long Hay outside, she spit in Hitchcock's face.

Otis chuckled. "Hey, Roger, I thought you said she had the hots for you!" The laughter served as a release valve for the night's tension.

When Hitchcock and Otis arrived at the airport, four handcuffed men, the pilot and his passenger, and the accountant and Chen's young bodyguard were being taken to the station. A tow truck impounded the Town Car. The plane had been searched by DEA agents and pushed to the side of the runway.

† † †

HAVING RAIDED JUJU'S safe minutes before Juju arrived with Long Hay, Monica Dwyer was in her apartment, hastily packing her things before the cops arrived. The money from Juju's safe came to fifty thousand in fifties and hundreds. She had Juju's cocaine, her list of clients and their phone numbers. With what she had learned and stolen, her two-man hit squad, and Connie dead, she had all she needed to build her own criminal organization. She grinned when she saw the confluence of red flashing lights atop police cruisers as she drove past the Bellevue Airfield.

CHAPTER EIGHTY-TWO
The Equalizer

TWO DAYS LATER, Hitchcock was relaxing at home with Allie, the three boys, and Jamie. The exhaustion he felt after the arrest of Juju, his old nemesis, coupled with the large seizures of drugs and drug money differed from anything in his experience. He slept as if in a coma the first day, then stayed up until eleven to practice music with Allie.

He stood up, yawning as he unplugged the phone. "Why did you do that, honey?" Allie asked.

"We're all behind on our sleep. Especially yours truly. No disturbances allowed till morning."

"Fine, but keep your gun on your nightstand so I'll sleep better," she said.

"Yes, ma'am," he said, stifling a yawn.

They went to bed, Jedidiah sleeping in his own crib next to their bed, and baby Benjamin snuggled between them. Trevor had a bed set up in the master bedroom so he wouldn't be alone. Jamie stretched out on the floor beside Hitchcock, who drifted quickly into a deep and dreamless slumber.

† † †

TWO BLOCKS AWAY, at almost 4:00 a.m., a young man wearing a gold Rolex his parents had given him for his birthday and a blue-hooded sweatshirt, prowled outside a house in Vue Crest, a late '40s vintage neighborhood of high-end homes located within easy walking distance of Hitchcock's home and downtown Bellevue.

Since his narrow escape from the police last time, his predator's heart pounded whenever he heard a knock on the door of his parents' home, expecting it to be the one that heralded his arrest.

But the police never came, and his urges kept gnawing at him until he was numb to his fears of discovery. He returned to prowling and quickly found his next target, a widow, in her late forties or early fifties, no children, a bit matronly but good to look at, smooth complexion, very buxom, with a chunky but pleasing figure. He surveilled her night and day until he was satisfied that she lived alone and did not date.

Reading the newspaper about the Bellevue cops hunting for him and his older counterpart, the dramatic police raids, high-speed chases and arrests of drug dealers filled him with violent energy like never before.

He had entered her home twice via the basement when he knew she was away, to learn about her by reading her opened mail and browsing through the items in her bedroom nightstand. The intrusions enhanced his desire to conquer her, subdue her, own her. He took items of her lingerie he thought she wouldn't miss. As he fondled these for days, his urges could no longer be denied. She would be his. Tonight.

Clutching his black felt cloth bag containing his knife, flat-tip screwdriver, rope, gag, and blindfold material tied to his belt, he crept to the dining room French doors, slipped the lock with the tip of his knife, and entered.

It was past 3:30 a.m. when he left her, bound and sobbing. Again, his cursed moth-like tendency to hover around the fiery scene he created instead of fleeing, took over. He hid nearby, barely off the victim's property, watching the police arrive. It was the same thrill he experienced before, watching the cops fumble around, trying to find him. To hear the sirens piercing the early morning air, knowing they would be looking for him, thrilled him, and he lusted for more.

† † †

THE SIRENS AWAKENED the surveillance man inside the house across from Hitchcock's home. He had fallen asleep next to his camera, mounted on a tripod, aimed at the Hitchcock home with an infrared 500mm telephoto zoom lens attached.

The sirens sounded like they were maybe two blocks away—or less. *What could be going on?* he wondered. He detected movement across the street. Through his lens he saw a medium-size man in khaki clothing creeping around the front of Hitchcock's house. He zoomed the lens in closer. The man was trying to wiggle open a side window.

"Helen! Get up quick!" he yelled. He snapped

pictures as a thirtyish woman came from one of the bedrooms, rubbing the sleep from her eyes. "What's going on, Jared?"

"I'm seeing a strange man trying to enter the Hitchcock residence by jimmying a window open. They're home and asleep – all the lights are off. Call the police, quick!"

† † †

At The Station

OTIS AND HIS first shift squad skipped briefing to join the night shift units hunt for the blue-hooded sweatshirt rapist. As he neared the entrance to the neighborhood, Dispatch told Otis to switch to Channel 2.

"A neighbor across the street from Hitchcock's residence says he's watching a white male in tan clothing trying to break into their house. Says he knows Hitchcock is a cop," the dispatcher said.

"Call Hitchcock at home. I'm there now, and out of the car," Otis replied as he shut down his cruiser, and ran into Hitchcock's front yard.

He noticed a light-colored older pickup parked in the dirt alley behind the house. His eyes adjusted to the dark as he moved swiftly across the front yard and rounded the corner toward the kitchen. He came upon a white male wearing matching khaki shirt and pants with bulging front pockets, wiggling the kitchen window open.

"You're under arrest," Otis declared as he closed in.

The intruder spun around, swinging his left forearm

at Otis's head, followed by a kick to Otis's left thigh. Otis blocked the blow with his arm, absorbed the pain of the kick and knocked the man to the ground with a palm strike to the jaw.

On the ground, the suspect swiftly caught Otis between his legs in a scissors movement that brought Otis down. Otis rolled away and sprang to his feet. The prowler advanced in a half-crouch, delivering series of rapid open hand chopping blows. Otis seized the man's extended left arm and stepped into his body, turned and twisted while holding it. The bone made a cracking sound, the man cried "uh!" as he struck the nape of Otis's neck with his free hand, forcing Otis to release his arm-hold. Otis turned, rapid-firing punches, elbow and knee-strikes until the man fell again. He rolled away and came up drawing a small-frame Smith & Wesson .38 revolver with a silencer on the end of the barrel.

Faster than the eye could follow, Otis swatted a nerve in the man's wrist. The gun fell to the ground. The suspect reached into his pocket with his right hand and came out with a short fixed-blade knife, holding it in a fist grip, close to his side. Otis, knowing he was too close to his opponent to have time to draw his gun and fire without being stabbed, assumed a boxer's stance, half-crouch, knees bent, feet shoulder width apart, body at angle. The intruder flung his left hand at Otis's eyes as he closed in, lunging at Otis with a straight-in stabbing motion. Otis struck his wrist hard, stopping the opponent's forward attack for a second, then flung his fingers into the opponent's eyes, causing the intruder to pause again. Otis seized his knife hand by the wrist. The man struggled to drive his knife into Otis. They locked, grappling, grunting, each looking for an opening to make the fatal blow. Otis slammed him backward against the side of the house, gripping the hand holding the knife.

The suspect's many knee-strikes to Otis's groin had no effect. He tried to wrest his hand from Otis's grip, but couldn't break free. Keeping a death-hold on the suspect's hand that held the knife, Otis body-slammed the stranger against the house again and again, following up with elbow strikes to the head. Nothing fazed the stranger. Greater in weight and bulk, Otis used his left forearm to press the suspect against the wall, crushing him, enduring the enemy's efforts to knee him in the groin and stomp on his foot, his right hand over the attacker's hand that held the knife.

The stranger's knee-strikes weakened, then stopped as Otis began driving the tip of the knife into his abdomen. He glanced down at the dark red spot spreading on the predator's shirt. The stranger's eyes locked onto Otis's as he summoned the last of his strength to stop the knife from entering his body further. His grimacing face was inches from Otis. He cursed under his breath as the blade went deeper into his abdomen. When the blade was over halfway in, Otis twisted it twice, then drove it in to the hilt. The stranger went limp. Otis stepped back, letting him slide to the ground.

His back against the house, panting, bloody hands

in his lap, the attacker glanced down at the knife in his belly. His face turned up to Otis. "You've had training, Sergeant."

"Yours, Vold."

He squinted up at Otis. "You look familiar," he said, his voice raspy.

"You trained us. Rangers, Laos, '59. You were a CIA day contractor. OSS before that. Who hired you to kill my little brother and his family, Vold?"

Vold nodded faintly, his mouth open, eyes half-closed. "I remember your face. Not the name."

"The only name that matters is who hired you."

Vold stared at Otis through drooping eyelids. "I have my orders, you know how it is," he said, fading. "I need a doctor."

"Tell me who hired you or I let you bleed out and die right here."

Vold tried to speak, but hadn't the breath. Otis handed him a small spiral notepad and a pen from his shirt pocket. "Write it," he said.

In feeble, hesitating strokes, Vold wrote the letters B, A, and M as his breathing became labored and raspy. In another moment, it stopped. The pen fell from his hand to the ground.

The man from across the street approached the scene cautiously. "I'm the one who called, Sergeant. Are you all right?"

Otis grimaced as he bent down to pick up the revolver with the silencer.

"I am, thanks."

"Is he dead?" The neighbor asked, staring open-mouthed at the stranger lying in his own blood, knife hilt protruding from his abdomen.

Otis made no reply.

HITCHCOCK APPEARED IN the kitchen door wearing his bathrobe, gun in one hand, holding Jamie, growling and straining against his leash in the other. Astonished, he recognized the dead stranger, slumped against the house, lying in a pool of blood.

He looked to Otis, who simply said, "About time, Roger. Call the station."

EPILOGUE

MILDRED MACAULIFFE'S PHONE rang. "I have the most fascinating news, Mrs. MacAuliffe," private investigator Tobias Olson said.

"Do tell, Toby."

"Do you remember the man in an old tan pickup who wears disguises who was stalking Hitchcock and your son's ex-wife?"

"I do."

"Well, as of earlier this morning, he's not a threat anymore. He's dead," Olson said, smirk in his tone.

She gasped. "Dead! What happened?"

He told her the facts. "As the threat is over, I request permission to stand down. We have film of this guy trying to break in, but not of his attacking the police officer who killed him."

Mildred's voice was shaking. "Yes, indeed, Toby. Close it down and send me a bill. I'll pay you right away, with a bonus."

After taking a call from her husband's physician at the hospital, Mildred called their attorney, Oscar Travis, and told him what happened in Bellevue.

"All I can say, Mildred, is wow. What will you do

now?"

"I just got a call from Horace's doctor. He says Horace is going down fast. He may be gone today, tomorrow, a week at most. I want to be with him when he passes. After he's gone, I will get away, travel for a while."

"What about the lawsuit we have going against Allison and her husband?"

"Oh, that," she said, then paused. "You know, Oscar, Horace was a good provider, but he had a lifelong history of affairs and keeping mistresses. I knew about it and learned to live with it. He became obsessed with Allison the second he saw her. Beautiful, a real blonde, innocent, shapely, and very well-endowed. He threatened to disinherit our son and cut off his allowance if he didn't divorce her."

"Which Glendon did," Travis commented.

"Glendon gave in to his father, not knowing what was really going on," Mildred said.

"You mean Horace's motive? Even I don't know about that," Travis said.

"On the one hand, I'm surprised you don't know, but on the other, I'm not. Horace was secretive. I only knew about his affairs from having private detectives follow him. After I confronted him, he didn't try to hide it from me anymore, and I decided to stay with him. You could say we had a mutual understanding."

"I must confess, Mildred, having known Horace for many years, this is a shock."

"Horace kept a journal," Mildred went on, "like

many of his generation. I read it when he wasn't around. The custody lawsuits, hiring a private investigator to drag Allison into court were part of his scheme to corner and pressure her into becoming his personal mistress in return for allowing her to keep her son. She knew nothing about it. When she married that cop, Horace was beside himself. He became determined to get her by breaking that Hitchcock fellow financially."

"I'm out of words," Travis said after a moment of stunned silence. "I didn't know any of this."

Mildred sighed, then went on. "It's true. He readily admitted it when I confronted him and told him I had read his journal.

"You mean Horace told you he wanted to force Allison into being his mistress?"

"I lived with mistresses in the shadows for many years. To me Allison was just one more. When she married, I warned Horace that I sensed this Hitchcock was different, he seemed to have protection over him, an angel or an unseen hand on his shoulder or something like that. But Horace, being an atheist coming from a long line of rich, powerful people, was used to getting whatever he wanted, scoffed at my notions about Hitchcock."

Travis chuckled. "Sounds like the Horace I know."

"Allison is happily married to the man she loves. They're making babies right and left, and Trevor is included in all of it. I don't want to uproot him from a happy home. They've had enough trouble from us. As I have power of attorney, I want you to agree to the

THE MYSTERY OF THE UNSEEN HAND

summary judgment and compensate them for their attorney fees. I also want it, in writing, that if Hitchcock wants to adopt Trevor, I'll agree to it, provided he allows me reasonable visitation for the rest of my life."

"Consider it done, Mildred," Travis said, smile in his voice.

"One thing I've learned in watching all this play out, Oscar."

"What's that?"

"If I ever decided to pursue a life of crime, I'll stay the hell away from Bellevue."

Travis chuckled again. "Yeah, I'd say so."

TWO WEEKS LATER, on a rainy afternoon, Hitchcock and Allie sat on their couch, kicking back, their feet sharing the matching leather ottoman as they enjoyed a crackling fire. Trevor was in elementary school, Jedidiah and baby Benjamin were napping. Jamie laid stretched out on the Karastan rug beside Hitchcock. The phone rang. Allie answered, then brought it to him. "It's our attorney," she said.

Hitchcock said hello, then listened. "Yes, I'll sign the papers and send them right back to you. Thanks for calling," he said.

"More bad news?" Allie asked.

He shook his head. "Not anymore."

She stared at him, waiting.

"Your ex-father-in-law died last week. His widow is in charge now. She's dropping the case and has offered to pay our attorney fees," he said.

Allie stared at her husband. Tears filled her eyes. She began weeping. Hitchcock moved hip-to-hip next to her and held her in his arms as the dam broke, and Allie sobbed, crying "Thank you God!" over and over. He cupped her cheeks in his hands and gently wiped her tears with his thumbs.

As she caught her breath, she took his hands in hers. "I've got good news too."

He gazed at her, lost in her eyes, waiting.

She smiled at him. "I'm pregnant again."

ACKNOWLEDGEMENTS

Inspiration for *The Mystery of the Unseen Hand* has come from Bellevue Police case files of the early 1970s and the recollections of myself, plus conversations with retired officers who served with me during those great swashbuckling years: Robert Littlejohn, Craig Turi, Bob Phelan, James Hassinger and Bill Cooper, as well as newspaper accounts of serial sex offenders and radical political groups that formed during the early 1970s. Hats off to you, boys!

ABOUT THE AUTHOR

JOHN HANSEN draws from personal experience for most of his writing. Between 1966-1970 he served as a Gunners Mate aboard an amphibious assault ship that, while based in Subic Bay, Philippine Islands, ran solo missions in and out of the jungle rivers and waterways of South Vietnam and other places.

While a patrol officer with the Bellevue Police Department during the 70's decade, his fellow officers nicknamed him "Mad Dog" for his tenacity. After ten years in Patrol, he served eleven more years as a detective, investigating homicide, suicide, robbery, assault, arson and rape cases, earning the new nickname of "Bull Dog."

Unraveling complex cases continued to be his forte after his police retirement when as a private investigator for nineteen years his cases took him across the United States and to other countries and continents. He is the winner of several awards for his books, short stories and essays.

Made in the USA
Middletown, DE
24 March 2022

63086860R00250